GHOSTS OF BURMA

SUPERNATURAL CRIME THRILLER

DAVID BYERLEE

SWEETSPIRE LITERATURE
MANAGEMENT

CHAPTER 1

Mon Thaik reached towards her friend Aom, whose protective arms were wrapped tightly around her small son Auk. Plumes of black smoke rose from villages in the distance, a dark beacon of the soldiers' horrific deeds.

On the banks of the Salween River that had been running dry only weeks earlier, they searched for a way across the swollen, rushing white-water. Further upstream, the dead were stacked in rows like kindling; shot by the very soldiers responsible for setting the distant villages alight.

'We should get back on the trail and look for a way over,' Mon said as the sound of the wild water threatened to drown out her words.

They heard a muffled explosion as landmines exploded. Cries for mercy tore at Mon's heart.

'Should we go back? We might be able to save anyone who can walk.'

'There is no going back, we must save ourselves,' Mon said in her Kachin-accented Burmese.

Behind the women, Myint and Yei nodded their agreement. They, like Mon, had left their children with family in villages far to the north. All wanted to leave Burma as the conflict that erupted in Rakhine State with the Rohingya communities continued to spread in all directions towards Kachin, Shan and Karen like a grass fire. The plan was to return for those they had left behind once the troubles eventually faded and blew over like a spent typhoon.

As the group made its way up the embankment and out of sight of the men obsessed with ethnic cleansing, Aom struggled to lift her son. Clawing at the muddy incline, Auk hoisted himself up to the track.

Looking down he said, 'Come, Mother. I will help you.'

Slipping on the wet grass he shifted his footing for a better position but instead a loud explosion rang out and Auk was hurled into the air before splashing into the fast-moving water.

Aom screamed and scrambled to fish her son from the rapids but it was too late. The rush of water pulled Auk from her grasp and he was gone, what waws left of his limp body smashing against the rocks before vanishing around a bend in the river.

'My son, my son, please don't leave me!' Aom screamed.

Frantic she cried, 'I want to go with him. Please let me go with him!'

Seeing the danger of more senseless loss Mon, and then also Myint, held her tightly; jumping in would mean certain death.

'My son, my son!' she called again to Auk. Then by some miracle, his bloodied and pale face reappeared briefly above the surface. With his body still submerged in the boiling river, Auk lifted his hand up as if to wave goodbye to the brave woman who had brought him into this world.

Stricken, Aom collapsed into body-wracking sobs. Then, summoning the last tiny thread of strength remaining, she called out, 'I will come for you. Wherever you go, we shall be together again. Wherever you go.'

Auk's soft face silently succumbed to the raging torrent. Aom fell to the earth only to be promptly pulled back up by Mon. 'We have to keep going or they will find us and kill us all.'

They were interrupted by the overwhelming buzzing and clicking of what could only be described as symphony of a billion cicadas singing, followed by a ball of light ascending from the angry river below. For a moment, the violent waters stilled, then the bright vision drifted upwards before disappearing up into the sky. The buzzing and clicking quieted as the rapids returned, a watery stampede of wild horses.

CHAPTER 2

The Bay of Pattaya sparkled under the moonlight, the waters just metres away from where Tan and Chie Shin sat eating *tom ung gung*, a spicy prawn soup with Chicken Rama at the Siam Star in Pattaya. Tan clasped his new wife's soft hand and they smiled in delight. A haunting Chinese love song added to the magic as the ocean haze that had began to appear at sunset cast a spell over the bay that could go on forever. The honeymooners from Singapore, together for only three months prior to their wedding in Hong Kong, were happy, relaxed and looking forward to a boat cruise in the morning. Now into the second course with a serving of *Kai jiew moo*, a delicious omelette with pork and fish sauce, they smiled and chatted happily together. In no hurry, the couple toasted over a glass of velvety Vietnamese wine and in whispered tones they made secret plans for a thousand tomorrows...

Then, as their crystal glasses clinked together once more, a bulky object sailed over their heads like some stray postal parcel. Within seconds, a detonation caused a massive pressure spike of thermal air and gas, indiscriminately blasting bodies and debris at 600 feet per second; atomising everything in the direct impact of the bomb and reverberating outwards resulting in disastrous and complete devastation of the Siam Star.

After just a microsecond's delay, the roar of the blast was heard as the ear-bursting explosion demolished the restaurant's structure from the roof to the support beams, sending the ceiling crashing down as though swept aside by the hand of a vengeful ghost.

Bodies and debris lay strewn everywhere over what had, an instant before, been the perfect setting for romance. Now, survivors were faced with a life-changing reality. Only after the lingering white fog of plaster particles and the red mist of destroyed blood vessels cleared was the full extent of the carnage clear. The moans and cries for help were appalling to the horrified onlookers just beginning to gather at the fringes of the bomb site. Added to the din was the wail of sirens from approaching ambulances and emergency services amid numerous beeping horns as night traffic started to build and overflow like an uncorked bottle into Beach Road.

Ripped flesh and shredded clothing hung off men and women who staggered in shock through choking asbestos dust and lurched aimlessly around the dead and the dying. Bodies—both dead and alive—had been thrown everywhere. Most had missing arms, legs or both, and open wounds bled out like human fire hydrants.

The dead and maimed lay about in twisted, gruesome poses. One man lay with his leg facing the wrong way, his lifeless eyes staring into nothingness. Another man, still alive, held onto his bleeding stump—the rest of his limb nowhere in sight. A trail of blood marked his progress as he dragged himself across the floor.

With nothing to be done for the dead and with most of the couples, including Tan and Chie Shin, dying together, the walking wounded staggered about in search of help. A stout, matronly woman with mangled arms and no lower body wailed in Thai, '*Phi Tai Hong*' then in English, 'Vengeful ghosts do this. It is a curse. They have power we not have.'

Her high frequency wail dropped an octave then faded to a hoarse whisper as she quickly weakened, her cries coming out once more in Thai, then deteriorating into gibberish as she gently rubbed what had once been a fully intact stomach but was now crudely split open like a bag of squid. Her bleeding innards formed a tributary that flowed south to pool with the blood gushing from legless stumps. Lifeblood was still being pumped out by a heart not yet done. She struggled to keep herself upright in a makeshift seated position, as if fighting the battle against unconsciousness could prevent her inevitable death.

Propped up against part of an upturned table covered in a pile of mangled and charred debris, she mumbled, drifting between Thai, English and other tongues, probably known only to her.

Her now thin tone could still be heard in a strange silence that had descended on the area immediately following the deafening explosion. She said again in English, following sharply inflected Thai words, 'Vengeful ghosts, they come for us. They will kill us all.'

Those who managed to escape from the hellish aftermath of the explosion would likely spend the rest of their lives wondering what happened, replaying the events over, and over again. As one voice faded to its merciful end, so another replaced it. An elderly Thai woman bleeding heavily from the forehead called out in Thai with a loud voice that defied her broken body.

'Where is my son? Where is my son?' The sharp intonation of her words sounded as though she was shouting at demons. But no matter how much or how loudly she shouted, her son failed to materialise and the truth became clear. Her shouts turned to cries of agony. She too was doomed, haunted.

Perhaps realising there wasn't much time she dug into her handbag—the dark leather now white from dust—and pulled out a photo of the son she had just lost. With bloodied, torn fingers she held his picture close to her chest and wailed, 'I am coming to join you, *Phi*. It will not be long.' She kissed the torn photo then a gust of wind tore it from her weakened grasp. Speaking in Thai and then English as the other woman had done, she said, 'My son is *Phi Tai Hong*, a ghost who shall haunt his killers for his monstrous death.' And with the last of her energy depleted from the final cry of a wounded heart, she collapsed as her soul reunited with the son she could not live without.

As the wail of sirens approached, the walking wounded united with outsiders. Anyone who was able attempted to assist victims emerge from the ruins of the building or carry those who couldn't move on their own. One man attempted to help a middle-aged European woman with a twisted posture akin to a broken doll but her painful cry seemed a warning that this could well have been the wrong move: 'My legs, I can't move my legs!'

In the middle the blast zone, a man could be seen lying prone on a bed of jagged glass and debris, staring at what was left of his legs and arms. Silent and in shock, he had no words for the unspeakable. He lay back and folded his arms across his chest as though waiting to die.

Nearby, a young Thai woman sat on the kerb, shards of glass protruding from her gut like translucent daggers. Looking down, her face a mask of horror, one bloodied hand grasped a shard but as she tried to pull it free she screamed in agony. Her head slumped and she let go of the offending protrusion that she now realised couldn't be removed without surgery. The woman raised her bleeding clasped hands in a *wai,* or a show of respect, towards a remarkably intact bronze Buddha, still sitting with a beatific smile over the wreckage as though he was one of the few survivors. The statue's devotee would not be among them. The nameless young lady, alone and broken, knew death was circling like an evil crow about to land on a human perch. She seemed to be praying for mercy, for grace, that final grace. Speaking softly in Thai to herself and to dearly beloved Buddha, she slowly fell over on her side, eyes staring lifelessly at the ruins that had taken her life. A man hurried over and pushed her eyelids down to let her soul rest. This would keep her soul from wandering forever. Her ghost, *Phi Tai Hong,* the ghost of a person that suffered a sudden violent or cruel death, would curse this place until her murder was avenged.

Like radiation after a nuclear event, the toxic blowback promised to bring even more damage than the initial blast. Acrid smells of cordite and dust filled the air evoking violent coughing and choking, possible precursors for lung damage and worse. One young girl, possibly American going by the accent, stood with her hands on her knees coughing up blood between hoarse cries of, 'Help me, somebody help me.' Otherwise unmarked, her prognosis was uncertain as trickles of blood from her mouth segued into a vomitus flow.

Then came sounds of rescue. The eerie silence that had descended after the ear-shattering detonation was replaced by the blaring, urgent sounds of sirens, coming in unrelentingly like a tsunami of sound waves following an earthquake. This aftershock was enough to give aural hallucinations to the many with shattered eardrums. Already they were bombarded with a dull roar endlessly replaying inside their heads like wild surf crashing onto a beach. This noise was now being pierced by a repeated volley of oscillating sirens signalling the arrival of the emergency services. For most of the diners however, it was too late. The Singaporean honeymooners appeared almost unscathed if observed from a certain angle. But they lay silent and unmoving. Forever together in a final, heartbreaking embrace. They would become the night and the stars. Was there a special kind of heaven for doomed lovers like Tan and Chie Shin, or would their souls, too, become vengeful ghosts demanding justice, as told by a prophet now deceased?

—

This micro-world, this small facet of the glittering jewel of a twilight Pattaya, was changed forever.

Po Hmu watched and felt relief at the successful explosion. The relief washed away the tension and replaced it with elation, with joy.

CHAPTER 3

B rodie Jackson poured another drink with all the skill and finesse of the cocktail waiter he'd once been. Around him, guests joked and laughed. The sultry summer air was perfect for a midnight drinking party. He didn't feel especially drunk but knew he was far from sober and he didn't like his chances of passing a roadside breath test. It wouldn't come to that though, he was the host and no one's designated driver.

Filling the glass with Bacardi mix he asked Grace, 'More?' She nodded with a serious look as white rum filled the glass, first one finger then two. He paused and asked with a smile, 'Enough? Or do you want to go the full Monty, sweetheart?'

She smiled. The serious business of liquor strength nearly out of the way. 'Why not? I'm feeling up for it tonight.' Pouring carefully, he stopped at three fingers as the bottle was reduced to mere dregs. He put it on a table alongside another three empties lined up like sentry guards and blew his partner, Grace, a kiss. Tonight she was looking sensational with a plunging split satin dress that showed off her toned and shapely legs. No one could say she didn't have great looking pins, right? No one. One of her best features in fact. It was 1 a.m. and he and his party guests were only getting started. People always said he knew how to have fun and Brodie's aim was to prove them right. It was just after midnight—the night still young—and there was too much fun to be had. There was no need to crash until they saw the morning light. In the background the Eddy Money song, 'Take me home tonight' voiced those very words.

As Brodie fixed a drink for Maggie, his friend Spike's other half, he felt like some mad chemist. One who knew exactly what he was doing, of course. As the triple Bourbon was handed over, he hummed and sang along to the lyrics, 'Take me home tonight, I don't want to let you go until I see the light.'

Taking a look back over his shoulder he called out to his distracted—and possibly flirting—partner, 'Try it now, Grace.' Pulling herself away from a young, smart businessman Damon, she placed the glass to her pursed lips, signalled her approval with a wink, and drained the glass. There were cheers and she turned her back to Brodie once more. Damon, the man who had her full attention, had arrived straight off the tarmac from Heathrow, with his Saville suit and interesting hair style. He was pouring Grace shots of Tequila and, not wanting to appear a spoilsport, Brodie waved his approval. Two could play at that game. Brodie poured himself a drink, also three fingers, and not to be outdone by his hard charging partner, downed it in one gulp. In an instant, there was a rush of Dopamine-boosted blood to the head.

As the warmth of the alcohol flushed through his system, Brodie gravitated towards Spike and Maggie. Close friends, Spike was still nursing the single glass he'd poured himself without any dubious influence from the host. Maggie teetered over the triple shot Brodie had poured her as Spike steadied her with a hand on the small of her back. Someone had to stay sober, right?

Brodie tried to be accommodating; isn't that what good hosts do? 'How's the coffee shop going, Spike? Every time I go there the place is packed.'

'It's been alright, what with the rent and the competition. Sometimes I wish he'd bought that Subway franchise,' Maggie answered for him with a slurred voice.

'Yes, instead of making coffee we'd be making sandwiches all day. As it is we've met some wonderful people.'

'Yeah, like that actor out from Hollywood for a shoot.'

'Who was that?' Grace asked intrigued, her attention drawn back to the conversation.

'I don't remember exactly. But we made a pact not to name drop; it's not what we do.'

'So we won't see it on Facebook, right?' Grace, now back in Brodie's orbit, said with a blank face and in a tone just this side of interested.

Spike smiled as if proud of his ability to keep a confidence. 'Yes, you got it. If we land a really big fish or even a whale, that will make to social media and the rest I'm sure. Have to protect your clients.'

They chatted as other couples joined them. Celebrity media gossip didn't interest Brodie but it was safe, neutral, in that they weren't talking about people they knew or that were even in the same room.

Later in the evening after heavier spirits, including some lethal cocktails, Brodie began to see double. That warm, comforting feeling was being hijacked by unpleasant emotions. Just why was Grace spending so much time with the handsome stranger from Brazil?

It was hot and getting hotter even though it was past 2 a.m. now. A thin film of sweat covered Brodie's forehead but it wasn't just the heat that was making him sweat. Grace, his partner of five years, was making noises about leaving and this get-together was another attempt to patch up their relationship. A relationship on track to implode much like an old Church collapsing after an earthquake. Their relationship was propped up by support beams that could crack and fold at any time.

Brodie didn't want to think about losing his best lover yet and he rubbed his forehead as though to banish the thought. Squeezing his eyes again and again his vision began to swim as if he was looking into those crazy funhouse mirrors. Trying to rise up from the too-deep cushioned armchair, his sense of balance failed him and Brodie crashed into a glass side table. Shards of lethal looking glass, jade daggers able to cut to the bone, splashed onto the floor, one piece nicking him near the elbow. The tiny wound flowed with bright blood that found its way onto the carpet. Too drunk to feel it, he watched the red stream with detached bemusement. His friend, Spike, disappeared into the bathroom and came back with a towel to staunch the bleeding.

Grace looked on with a careless smile as if to say, *I knew you'd make a mess of it.* No sympathy or show of emotion there, she was the dispassionate emergency services worker who acted like she'd seen it all. Being a nurse could do that to a person and even though she wasn't in the industry now, he wondered what she would do if he was really hurt, say with a severed artery, then dismissed this train of thought as something close to selfflagellation. It didn't bear thinking about, but then she put her casual cruelty into words.

'Way to go, Brodie. I spent a few hundred on that and that was down from nearly a thousand,' Grace said in a high-pitched American accent that left out mention of his injury. When angry, her rhotic American intonation became more intense; sharpened, like a blade on a grinding stone.

If they were hit by a category 5 cyclone, would she busy herself with the damaged house and the mundane tasks such as follow up calls to the insurers while he lay down with his head sliced open? How would she play the role of the grieving widow?

'Don't you mean 'we' Grace? Don't you mean 'we' spent hundreds on a piece of furniture? It's only a table for Christ's sake. It reminds me of the old saying about knowing the price of everything and the value of nothing.'

Maggie rushed to his side with a blanket of paper towels to replace the ruined towel and began to apply them to stem the flow. It worked, at least for now.

'Do you want to go to the surgery or the hospital, Brodie?' but Brodie shook his head. He couldn't leave the field without finishing the battle. He was still breathing, wasn't he?

'I'll be fine. It's not the cut I'm worried about.'

He looked at his totally ravishing partner who appeared unconcerned and could even detect a little smile he that could be seen as gloating. 'I guess you're satisfied now you've drawn blood.'

This got the reaction he was hoping for as Grace stared at him with bulging eyes of flaming rage. He could take blows to the head, but being ignored was something Brodie just could not stand. Grace prepared herself like a prosecuting attorney moving in for the kill with a devastating closing argument and with all the hostility she could muster, Grace hurled her drink into his face. With a wide, careless grin Brodie thrust out his tongue as if to take in rain from a cloud burst after a long drought. 'Hmmm tastes great, Grace. You must have an ace bartender. No point in letting it go to waste, this stuff isn't cheap.'

As the ever-caring Maggie rushed to Grace's side, Spike took Brodie by the arm and said, 'Look, we've all had a lot to drink tonight. You two are obviously a bit tired and emotional.'

Looking flustered Brodie said, 'Yeah, maybe it's time to call it a night...'

But as the sob sisters sobbed, Brodie wasn't done yet. 'Hey friend, I'm just getting started.' He pulled away from the unwanted attentions of his friend and staggered towards the makeshift bar. As he did, he crashed into a fulllength mirror that fell to the floor but didn't break. Everyone stared at this lucky escape from seven years' bad luck. There was already enough bad luck to go around without the mirror playing into it.

'See!' he said as if it were a revelation. 'I *do* have good luck,' he paused, 'Even if it is of the rampaging bull variety.'

'Oh, so you want to get smart, smartass,' Grace said in her rhotic, heavy on the *R* sound, American accent that always got sharper as she got angrier.

Picking up an almost empty bottle of Scotch, she threw it against the wall and it exploded into a million slivers.

Brodie saw his own life in the mess that was trickling down the wall. Fortunately, no one was hurt. Not yet.

'Go on, smash them all,' he said as he yanked a tablecloth from one of the tables. Everything, including plates of finger food and bowls of curry and rice, cascaded to the floor in a shrapnel of molten cheese and onion dip. It was a neat trick that never worked, even if it was in keeping with this sudden outbreak of violence. The party itself was in self-destruct mode. Brodie tried to summon up the energy to care but couldn't do it. While only a few people had left after the first shots of this War of the Roses, this latest exchange brought about an exodus as the remaining guests hurriedly made their apologies until only a clearly very worried Maggie and Spike remained.

Then, something unexpected. The large teakwood dining table began to shake and dinnerware and glasses rattled. There was silence as the rocking and shaking continued for a brief time before stopping abruptly.

'What was that?' Spike asked in alarm.

Brodie, thankful for a diversion from the embarrassing fight with his soulmate said, 'Probably an earthquake, we've had them before.'

Spike and Maggie nodded at this plausible explanation while Grace glared at him as though ready to resume battle but before she could there was a knock on the door. Spike walked over and opened it to reveal two police officers.

'We have complaints about a disturbance,' said a burly officer as he eyed a living room transformed into a bloody battlefield.

CHAPTER 4

The man who threw the satchel of plastic explosive into the restaurant killing so many and forever changing the lives of scores more, gloated from across the road on Soi 5. Po Aung Hmu had faith in the *Min Mahagiri,* the Ghost of the Great Forest, and trusted it would guide him home to safety.

The watcher was joined by other watchers as the streets initially cleared by the attack were starting to fill again as onlookers milled about or searched for loved ones. Just outside the perimeter of the bomb site, neon signs flashing *Sexy Girl, Alcatraz Body Shop* and *Sweet Thai Club* in bright moving colours didn't stop. They wouldn't stop while roving bands of men in shorts and jeans cruised for the perfect lover, always just out of reach.

Po, a Burmese national and an angry young man, was satisfied with his tradecraft. In fact, it exceeded all expectations. The authorities could not afford to ignore his, until now, secret organisation. His people, the Ron, would be liberated and the tyranny they lived under would be crushed. This Po knew this for certain.

Still focussed on his mission and energised by a hit of icey shabu that kept fear at bay, Po counted the dead and wounded as they were stretchered off. Using the tricky calculus of battle, of liberation, Po silently planned for an even bigger event during the Thai New Year. The Muay Thai Stadium packed with tens of thousands would be perfect. It would be a whole different scale to this small victory and the whole world would take notice. His forgotten war promised to be remembered, and more.

Po watched on without emotion as an elderly woman with bloody stumps where her legs once were, somehow lurched to the footpath unassisted, only to collapse face-down. It was as if she wanted to be erect, proud in her last moments on Earth. Onlookers were sombre or stricken. Po saw her as collateral damage, one of the costs of the nasty war he had been fighting since birth. At least this woman would get a funeral. Something the men, women and children from his village weren't afforded as they were dumped in unmarked graves after the soldiers were finished with them.

The macabre street scene played out in different ways. Some people cried, and some laughed. But it was the laughter of fear and borderline hysteria. And those crying, were they crying for the victims or were they really crying for themselves? One bargirl in a bikini raced over and leaned in close to the collapsed woman's face. She said something then turned back to shake her head. A sole ambulance officer gave a *wai* of respect as he thought of his own grandmother whom she resembled. He covered the victim's face and placed her on a gurney while fighting back tears. Being the first responder on the scene he felt very alone, except for the morbid onlookers who had no right to point and make disrespectful remarks. That was about to change.

Another ambulance arrived, sirens blaring. The noise was painful and came from all directions as one emergency vehicle after another arrived. Sharp blades of aural pain cut though the incessant throbbing felt by victims already suffering with shattered eardrums and barely coping with something that might linger forever. But that would be only one of many eternal reminders of this day, from the death of a loved one, loss of limb or movement, posttraumatic stress disorder to early death. One young man stumbled sightless and deaf as he called out and blindly stepped around a leg, a torso, a head. Exhausted and bleeding heavily, he fell to his knees and wept.

Po took it all in like a film auteur going over daily takes. Yes, the architect of the mayhem watched on, as though enjoying a movie he had directed, produced and starred in. His own Bollywood movie, but one with real meaning for these interesting times. Smiling, Po was quite pleased with himself. The outcome was even better than expected. He would take his report back to base, certain they would be satisfied.

Paramedics leapt from an ambulance and immediately began mouth-to-mouth on a lady with a chest caved in and oozing thick blood who, minutes before, had been enjoying chestnut noodles and rice. They tried CPR until one of the men, older, presumably more senior, shook his head to signal resuscitation was hopeless. Leaving her lifeless body in keeping with the triage mode, they raced inside the still smoking ruin. With triage, the living came first. The dead could be taken care of later.

Po smiled again in triumph revealing betel nut-stained gums. Far from his home in Burma, today was a loud statement for his cause and for a free Ron state. It was the kind of statement all the world would hear, even if for only a day or what his Bangkok friends called, a 24-hour news cycle. This was the first of many victories to come.

Yes, the devastation, from the burnt and shattered buildings to the high casualties, was everything he expected and more. This was a start and there would be more strikes for freedom. Po wanted a bigger, better target, maybe even the Police Box on Beach Road. Two kilos, he estimated, twice that used today, could wipe out an entire city block. Po's mind raced with possibilities and he felt a deep sense of satisfaction, as if Budda was smiling down on him.

When the rulers faced their mortality, their final reckoning, there would be change. Po was ready to sacrifice his own life for the cause, as always. While he watched ambulances, firetrucks and police arrive he knew there was much to do. One bomb does not make a revolution. That took four, six, many bombs and targeted actions, from individual assassinations to strategic raids. Generals and police would die. Po's time in the Burmese Army served him well. There would be more of course, and in his darting mind he and his brothers had already taken Pattaya and Bangkok and Chiang Mai, up to and across the border with Burma or what the *farungs* called 'Myanmar'.

Ever since joining the army at 17, Po had studied war. From Sun Tzu to Moa to Giap and Machiavelli. He knew how to lull an enemy into a false sense of security. He was skilled in the black art of war, in how to destroy his opponents' morale and make the best use of slim assets. This 'collateral damage', as the Americans called the murder of innocent civilians, was part of the cold trickery of war and Po, a dedicated student of the art of war, was just getting started.

Enthralled, he watched in a trance as victims howled in pain then died. Pain was part of growth, just as it had been when his five-year-old son, crippled and malnourished with dysentery from dirty water, died in his mother's arms. Po recalled the hurt that had been so great that he sat in the forest for an entire night. Drinking whiskey, he spoke with his son's ghost.

'Will you avenge me?' San U had asked, hovering near the treetops.

'Yes, I will avenge you, San. Before I do this, my son, you must put a curse on our enemies.

San swooped down to ground level and a wind blew leaves around like a small tornado.

Po had emerged from the jungle vowing vengeance for his son and for every son and daughter that died. Whether it be because of the sewerage-tainted drinking water or whether they were killed at the hands of government soldiers, such an ordeal was part of the harsh life in the village and somehow necessary for the country, his country, to become all it could be. The parasites that drank themselves stupid and feasted on their young women while they choked in filth, had to know this truth. They would be prodded, lanced with the sharp steel of reality like a boil pricked with a needle to let the pus out. These wreckers of his country, his people, would soon understand when they paid with their lives or their limbs or their face.

Po watched as another woman died on a stretcher, her brains leaking out of her crushed skull. He was sorry for her and for the dead. He grieved for his own even more. He grieved and he raged. The Burmese women that were used like meat in the sewers of Thailand were only slaves, their honour and their bodies soiled. If he couldn't free those whose minds had been infested by the evil of corruption, he would put a stop to more being taken. It might well take a lifetime, or it could take his life. Po knew this from life in battle as a soldier, and from his life as a poor rice farmer in a remote village across the northern border.

As Po watched and indulged in more and more raging fantasy, the watcher was being watched, stalked like a deer in the far country forest.

Chief Detective Timon Kittikachorn, closing in from the bayside end of the street, had some sharp questions for this suspect. The answers to which he would find out one way or another. He walked at a brisk pace but avoided running. No point in drawing attention to yourself while trying to catch a suspect who could easily disappear into a crowded city bursting with tourists. Some of whom still acted as if this disaster were one of the attractions with much finger-pointing and phone picture-taking. Pattaya Police Chief Timon was disgusted. Maybe he could arrest a few later on for drugs or something else. Inevitably tourists, *farung,* brought about their own downfall through bad habits and weak home country laws.

Chief Timon had recognised the young man of about 25 with a sparse beard from the photo that was already being circulated. He was a Maung, a Burmese refugee and still dangerous. As Timon got within a metre or two, the young man, like a mine-clearing rat instinctively sensing danger, swivelled his head sharply to see his hunter was a police officer and ran. The suspect shoved an older man who shouted in a Midlands accent, 'See here, mate!' out of the way as he reeled towards the kerb and knocked over a hot food cart. Fried chicken wings and bottles of masala and chilli sauce splashed into the gutter. A nimble man, Timon, even at 58, was able to jump over this spillage and keep running.

As he ran, Timon knew he had to report to base; he couldn't go on the hunt alone. Following quick response protocol, the detective called for back-up in a heaving, breathless voice, 'Suspect spotted. I'm following in hot pursuit and calling for backup,' he barked sharply into his phone. The response from the female dispatcher, Anwa, was that his men were on the way. Whilst comforting, he wasn't going to wait for reinforcements as required.

Catching or killing the bomber was far more important than sticking to form and letting the suspect get away.

The Chief had been there before when a serial killer of half a dozen local bargirls escaped capture while he helplessly fumed in frustration waiting for reinforcements. Timon knew that each passing minute, each second, gave the suspect precious time to vanish like the ghosts that haunted the city. That monster had never been caught and, for all Timon knew, was still tying up his victims and subjecting them to a slow, humiliating torture ending in unspeakable death.

He could still see the torn faces and lost souls. The ghosts of those women who died a sudden or cruel death, the Phi Ta Hong, visited him every night and he wanted to tell them, *had* to tell them, he got the bad guy. But doing that was impossible so he lived with a storm cloud of guilt that was now an ingrained part of who he was. Timon knew he couldn't exist any other way or be anything else. Only the night before he prayed in the local temple to keep this bad karma at bay. Tonight, he would do the same. There were many sides to his pain. Informing next of kin, usually mothers, was itself a torture. He was determined to do better, much better today. Losing your life on a filthy street was better than dying inside for as long as the ghosts preyed on the wind and lived in his stormy dreams.

Getting closer to his target, Timon picked up speed. The two could hear each other's footfalls and laboured breathing. Crowds of onlookers watched stunned by the chase and while some of English lager lads cheered with raised drinks, most were silent. The suspect turned his head then stopped and took aim with a revolver Timon recognised as a Glock special. As a shot rang out, instinct and training kicked in. Officer Timon dropped to a crouch as bystanders ducked or jumped for cover, the possibility of being killed in the crossfire too real even for the smashed tourists; getting killed wasn't part of the tour. Unholstering his own Police Special .38 revolver,

Timon returned fire as he shouted into his phone on loudspeaker, 'Suspect is still in sight and headed for Soi Buakhao. Suspect is armed and dangerous. I have returned fire.'

As the suspect turned to run down an alleyway he dodged pedestrians and scooters, narrowly missing a packed utility loaded with beer kegs. Timon resumed the chase. Feeling pains in his chest he knew he had to keep going. Taking a breather was not an option with a killer like this at large. He knew his karma would keep him alive, and if not, he was ready for that too. Wait too long and the opportunity for a collar could be lost forever—and there might be worse to come. He would rather die of gunshot wounds than let this murdering devil loose. Better to risk his job and more, than risk further innocent life as the shrill-voiced ghosts reminded him every nightfall.

No, this one was too important to lose and a promotion was not out of the question if he pulled this off. With a base salary barely enough to feed his family of five, he'd always avoided any hint of being bought, of being prostituted with a bribe or favours. He liked to tell family and friends that he had a bulletproof vest when it came to being bought. No, Chief Timon would spare his family shame. He kept running, running on adrenaline as his darting target began to disappear into the distance and into the crowds of bystanders. This young man and prime suspect in this most recent bombing, and possibly more, was again putting physical distance between himself and justice. Feeling frustrated and knowing he couldn't compete in a foot race, Officer Timon drew out his ith and W.38n and fired, just missing the target and several international visitors from China. Kill a Chinese tourist and he might as well put the gun to his own head. Waving his arms in a frantic motion, most of the pedestrians ducked inside bars or fell flat to the floor. He fired again and missed.

The Chief shook his head knowing he had to do better. He knew how to shoot. There were plenty of dead men, and some women, in the local cemetery who could attest to his prowess with a firearm. Many hours on the shooting range honed his gun-fighting ability but would it be enough? Timon fired again with both hands on the gun to overcome a slight tremor creeping in from his weak left side. A stroke he had kept from his superiors was a minor handicap he more than compensated for. The Chief fired three more shots in rapid succession. The sound reverberated up and down the narrow canyon of a street and he felt like a Pilipino cop out on a drug addict eradication mission; shoot them dead then hang a sign around their junkie heads declaring 'drug dealer'.

Bargirls in revealing bikinis and lingerie on a second-floor balcony screamed then crouched to dodge stray bullets and shrapnel. Some ducked inside like many of the pedestrians below yet others waved in excitement as if they weren't about to miss out on the show. Loud 70s rock played from one of the bars as Soi 6 became the OK Corral. Of course, Chief Officer Timon knew there were limits. Pattaya wasn't Angeles City he couldn't execute men, women or children on the street and hang a sign around their necks. So too with bombing suspects, except this suspect had fired first and there had to be a kind of universal law about that along the lines of do unto others…

The roar and smoke of battle, of this far eastern gunfight, drew crowds of people wanting in on the action, wanting a story to tell back in London or New York. The fear of collateral damage was now outweighed with the lemming like behaviour of international guests in search of a little excitement. Yes, for these tourists the excitement of a shooting and the promise of spilt blood outweighed the risk of injury or even death. Young men, many with tattoos and British accents, brayed in merry glee at the moving street gunfight. These descendants of World War One and World War Two warriors shouted out encouragement to Chief Timon. Even here, especially here, the silly foreigners knew better than to disrespect the law. Spending your life surrounded by excrement was the kind of hell many *farung* suffered in shame. It was better to watch someone dragged off to a Thai prison than to end up in one yourself. The price to pay for such a vile offence as higher order disrespect was too great for those foolish enough to try, a price so high it could not be made good, even in a thousand lifetimes.

A crowd gathered near Chief Timon, too close for comfort or safety, and he fired another shot into the air to show he meant business, without killing anyone more than necessary. It worked, the crowd, a grazing herd of beasts so easily drawn to death and disaster, fell into awed silence then cleared off the streets under the direction of backup officers newly arrived. The dispersing crowd resembled street traffic hastily getting out of the way as a firetruck or ambulance sped past with sirens wailing.

Timon caught admiring looks from a bargirl in a micro-dress and cowboy boots. Somehow, despite the commotion he was able to exchange a wink and a smile with her and she gave him a syrupy smile in return. Maybe he could come back some other time when the wife was visiting her mother in Esan. Then again, maybe not. He did not want to cruel his good fortune with such impure thoughts. A little dose of reality never hurt anyone. One lady bent low over the balcony revealing generous breasts and waved an invitation.

'You come and see me,' she called in Esau-accented Thai. *Maybe later* he thought.

Despite this mind mischief, Timon kept a bead and an eye on the bobbing and ducking man who was fast running out of options. As his wily prey scampered in a zig zag pattern, a street level sniffer rat, a move he might have learned in the military or with insurgents, the suspect tripped and fell to the ground and was almost run over by a motorbike taxi. Officer Timon held his gun steady, ready to shoot only to find a mobile street stall blocking his line of sight and way forward. The suspect, a terrorist by definition, looked back in fright, then ran up a flight of stairs crammed between two girlie bars. With the killer almost within reach, Officer Timon ran after him with renewed energy as if he had downed a full packet of Black Ant aphrodisiac pills.

He scrambled after his target losing his footing midway on the rusted metal stairs, then heaved himself up as the rooftop door opened and slammed shut. It was like reaching the summit of Everest. Now there was a small window for justice, a window that would slam shut if he didn't act. Fast. The window was something he learnt at the FBI Academy and Officer Timon had to act while that cracked window was still open.

Now, finally on the melting tar rooftop he was just in time to see the fugitive hurl himself across a ten-foot gap to another building on the far side facing the sea. Knowing that the perp probably counted on him not even attempting such a risky leap, he walked back a couple of paces then ran and jumped, oblivious to the yawning chasm and three storey drop that promised death or disablement. Reaching just the edge of the building and close to falling backwards to his doom, the Chief windmilled his arms in a desperate effort to adjust his centre of gravity. It worked and he fell forward onto the rooftop, sticky from the heat. Heart pounding, forearms scarred by gravel rash, he brushed himself off, feeling no pain thanks to the adrenaline shooting through his arteries like the *shabu* high certain types of tourists liked to destroy themselves with. Only this natural performance enhancer was legal and came from within. Pumped, he could have had his arm cut off and still kept going. There was a job to do, people in danger. As with the lost perp from last year that still preyed on his mind, if this killer got away there was no telling what the perp would do next.

A helicopter clattered overhead. Maybe today was a good day to die. Officer Timon staked his life on the killing or capture of this murderer, a man already convicted and ready for execution in the Chief's mind. The roar of the industrial air conditioners, red with rust, snapped him back from this distraction. Getting to his feet he chased after the suspect who was now just a few feet ahead. Timon got a bead on the bobbing head and jerking arms, then his prey looked back with panic-stricken eyes so wildly dilated they were black cue balls. The man was obviously on something and was making mistakes. He looked as frightened as a chicken about to have its head chopped off.

The chase over, in desperation the fugitive stopped, turned and pulled out the Glock. A lawman gunfighter of long experience, Officer Timon beat him to the draw, an Asian Wyatt Earp, and the suspect was hit in the chest with a thud. Putting his hand to the wound a thick flow of blood ran through his fingers and began to pool on the roof. With a stricken face, Po looked as though he couldn't quite fathom what had happened. The killer crumpled to his knees then fell face down in the puddle of blood.

Timon stood over the body then felt for a pulse. The Maung was dead which was alright with the Chief and saved him the trouble of finishing the perp off with a bullet to the head. Never let a terrorist go to trial, it was bad for business. He wasn't sorry about killing this monster, the only regret was the dead man couldn't talk. Looking through the dead man's pockets, the Chief could find no identity papers. Only the written notes in Burmese gave away his nationality, something Timon already knew.

There would be a lot of investigating to do but, with the suspect deceased, less paperwork. For now. Suddenly a cold, unseasonable wind picked up dust and discarded papers in a vortex-like mini-tornado. Then a faint, keening sound came and went as if the tormented heart of this monster was let loose into the heavens. There was a strange silence until the crashing, gnashing sounds of reality returned.

Officer Timon heard the roar of unseen helicopters which drowned out the noise of the rooftop crowd that had somehow appeared in seconds. It was a mainly local Thai mob attracted to all forms of disaster. This was the kind of dramatic event most wouldn't see in a lifetime. Not even in storied, wild Thailand. A collection of smiling and laughing Thai men and women clapped their appreciation as if watching a staged performance. He smiled back and gave a bow like the local hero he was, then a respectful *wai*. After that he could see the TV news cameras appear, chrome surfaces glinting in the sunlight. Tonight, he would be a TV star. Not that this would impress his superiors in Bangkok who were always jealous or wary of media attention. Not even his wife would show real appreciation and there was a reason for that. But there was someone in his life, someone special, who would be impressed in the way he liked, craved. He would see that special someone later that night. For now, there was more work to do, what the military called mopping up but without the gunfire. The hard war over now came the soft war.

An attractive lady approached him with a microphone and he waved her off. This was no time to chat and flirt with the best-looking reporter in Bangkok. As he turned, some of the officers from his station appeared, including Detective Pranit Nakharin and rookie Dai Punupong and he motioned for them to witness the body and go through the crime scene. This CSI didn't include any tricky DNA analysis and once the perp was chalked and zipped it was all over.

The bombing and chase had to be the biggest story this week, even in a town that was always on the brink of chaos and a mild, for now, form of eternal civil war. The assembled gawkers in various incarnations hung around like concertgoers awaiting an encore. Timon smiled his approval but secretly despised them all. No one wanted to miss out on the fun. Especially reporters that drew sustenance on spilt blood, victims, corrupt officials and ruined reputations. Timon hated them and knew some of their number also deserved a bullet. Again, this was not easy.

He was in Thailand after all, one of the most democratic and equal countries in all Asia.

The Chief turned to see a helicopter with TV1 markings careening dangerously close. Any closer and the rotors could easily strike the tangle of street electrical wiring and the carnage that began with the blast would only grow like secondary explosions in a fireworks warehouse fire. That and the violence were features of Thai streets, his Thai streets. As two young officers made a chalk outline of the deceased killer, Timon waved the reporters back. Then not to be put off, the young Thai lady that looked very much like one of the Thai soap stars came towards him with a microphone. He smiled as if he liked this part of his duty.

Speaking with a northern accent she asked, 'Were you very afraid when you chased after this killer?'

Giving an indulgent smile, as if she were a favourite niece, Timon crafted an alternative version of the truth. He would counter the media's fake news with his own.

'I could not afford the luxury of being afraid. Many people are dead at the restaurant in Soi 6. My job is to preserve and protect the peace. This man—,' he said as he pointed to the crumpled body that appeared much smaller dead, 'threatened the public safety and for that he must brought to justice or die. Me? I prefer he die.'

The admiring crowd which included matriarch *mamasan* Maya, someone he'd known since entering the service, laughed and clapped their approval. It was always popular to kill murderers. It didn't matter that the man that lay lifeless was poor or even that he believed in his cause, whatever that might be. What mattered was that this inert, bleeding waste of humanity was a killer whose luck had run out and his public execution should prove to be a deterrent.

After the show of justice in action was over, the body lay there for three hours, blood congealing to a black paste and the sun bloating the body making it appear demonic, damned by a perverse, very bad karma. Police officers were placed on guard as they waited for the coroner to arrive with a body bag, an item in short supply in recent weeks. With so much trouble lately, today was a good day.

Down in the street the sex tourists and sex workers had already moved on. A row of women in briefs and push-up bras waved and called out from a balcony. 'Hi, how are you?'

A man with a shaved skull and adorned with serpentine tattoos called up to her, 'Aren't you afraid you'll get blown up or shot?'

The girls possibly in their late teens or twenties laughed together. One answered him, as if speaking for her sister bargirls and said, 'No, we not worried. Why worry? Don't worry, be happy.'

Pointing down at him she asked, 'You worried. Why you worried?'

Smiling broadly and seeing the absurdity of it all he shook his head and reached out his arms as if asking for some kind of divine intervention street cred style.

'No, I'm not worried, not worried at all. Mind if I come up?

Thus, the live action was over and the serious business of sex tourism resumed. A Russian man of generous girth spoke with a lady at a bar and business was settled with a discreet cash advance. They crossed the street now alive with the colour and movement of tourist buyers and local sellers, to go to his hotel room. An American businessman with a designer label open-necked shirt fondled a bargirl with bronzed skin as she sat on his lap. The bargirl whispered into his ear and he laughed out loud to show perfect teeth. So, the business of business went on.

A little old thing like a terrorist attack wasn't going to stop or even slow the business model. It would be a hot topic for about a week, maybe more, then something else would take its place. Customers that were scared off came back just as the bargirls knew they would. As an ambulance took away the body like it was a piece of human garbage, bar staff cleaned away the blood with a fire hose. The man was now just a memory and would soon be a memory of a memory of a memory.

CHAPTER 5

Time to pack up. Time to leave. As Grace picked up a prized Venetian vase she said, 'Now, we don't have any problems about who owns this, do we honey?' It was clear she wanted to smash it but now put on a show of turning it to look at the top and bottom like someone appraising an item on Antiques Roadshow.

He shrugged and said, 'Take what you want.'

She gave a dismissive laugh as if to say *what's yours is mine.*

'And the photos?'

'Take them too, I'm good.'

After a warning, the police had left looking relieved to take their leave from a domestic incident. Everyone knew that domestic violence situations were the most dangerous for both cops and players. Who wanted to be a cop killed over a stupid argument?

It wasn't over. As Grace began packing so as to make good on her promise to leave him, he watched in silence. Brodie felt neither sad nor happy. Sloshed, cactus, he was too sedated to care. Events had drained him of emotion, and like his partner he was *almost* past caring.

Leaning back on the leather couch he said, 'Like I said darling, you can take whatever you want. Take it all, I don't mind. They're only things, honey. I never did care about things, you know that.'

She gave him a half sad look and said, 'Are you sure? I remember when we bought it, you even picked it out.'

'Keep it, but before you go through the whole removalist thing I want you to take a look at this.'

Taking a large envelope from a briefcase at his feet he opened it and handed the contents to Grace.

'And what are these, airline tickets?' He nodded as she noted the departure and arrival times with Tiger Airway and the 5-star hotel booking.

She looked through the documents with a sceptical look. 'You've arranged to go to Thailand without asking me?'

He nodded and said, 'Yes. I thought maybe you'd cruel the idea if we just spoke about it considering what you said about leaving here and not wanting to see me again.' He paused then for emphasis said, 'Ever.'

With a frown she said warily, 'You mean 'argued' about it? Is this for real, you thought you'd just go ahead and hope for the best or luck out?'

He shrugged his shoulders trying to be as inoffensive as possible. Never a sure thing with the present hostilities.

Grace was American, she didn't give up and had to have the last word. She couldn't help it.

'You said it darling.' As confusion washed over her face she sat next to him. They hadn't sat that close since before the fragile peace brokered by the hapless police officers. Yes, everyone knew the police hated domestic violence calls.

'Let me see. You want us to go to Thailand, is that it?' she crossed her magnificent legs, the satin dress catching the light and giving her the appearance of a fetching princess. He couldn't lose her, not like this.

He nodded, still unsure how this was going to pan out.

There was a sea change from stormy to placid in her expression and as he stood up she embraced him. He sighed in relief at the breakthrough.

'Why, I think that's wonderful, just what the doctor ordered.'

He smiled. Every American he'd ever met used that expression. The more Australian she tried to become the more American she sounded. He liked her to be natural, to be herself. It was when she struggled against what she was and tried to be what she wasn't that she seemed inauthentic, unreal.

'To Thailand, the Land of Smiles,' they said together, the words echoing on top of each other.

Looking puzzled, but in a positive way now, she asked, 'Is that really what they call it?'

Putting an arm around her he said, 'It's called many things, honey. The Land of Smiles is as good as any.' He scrolled through his phone and pulled up the phrase backgrounded by a picture of a white sand beach flanked by lush foliage.

'Are you in?' he asked already knowing the answer.

'Sure, I'm in honey. We can start out all over again.'

They laughed and made love and he wondered how long it would last. Did it even matter?

One week later they held a small send off. Then a kind of Groundhog Night ensued. They drank, they argued, they made up. The usual. Only this time his prayers were answered and there was no broken furniture or police action.

At around midnight, Maggie spoke about the recent strange event that they'd almost forgotten or halfremembered. 'You know, I searched for any news about the earthquake or whatever it was that other night.' 'Did the Earth move for you too, darling?' Spike said to shared laughter.

'No, you're right, I did the same. There was no tremor, no crashing of tectonic plates. I don't know what it was, do you?'

Maggie piped up. 'Maybe the building is falling down, I've heard of that. An entire apartment block can crack and fold like a Russian doll house.'

Brodie added, 'A perfect reason to move. We all know the landlord isn't going to spend a dime on this dump. Why would he? The place probably is falling down and isn't worth fixing.'

'Yeah, meanwhile a million tonnes of plaster and support beams falls on our heads,' Grace said before finishing with, 'That's it, we're out of here once we get back from Thailand: the Land of Smiles.'

Brodie nodded and said,' Well, I'll second that. It's time to move on.'

'Good luck finding a decent place in this market,' Spike said. A sentiment shared by anyone wanting to buy or rent in the overheated Australian housing bubble.

CHAPTER 6

The sharp, piercing sound of the whistle sliced through the thick forest like a vengeful spirit or accursed *nat*. Gam, the wiry labour procurer with the record number of captures this month, was helped by twelve men with proven skills in finding and keeping the refugees. Escapees constantly streaming through this remote hilly border area between Burma and Thailand. He had orders to round them up before they committed more terrorist acts across the line in northern Thailand. With refugee camps on either side of that border they, the hunted human gold, were out there and would be found. In the distance could be seen great plumes of smoke coming from burning villages. Giving Burma back to the Burmese was in the next phase as the need to remove interlopers in Rakhine moved over to the east and south. Stragglers and terrorists had to be picked up before they disappeared into the forest and became a danger in future.

Catching these human vermin was a service to the borderlands and, more importantly, was profitable. Already wealthy with three houses and several cars, he wanted to be as important as the General with hundreds of men under his command. But this was not the time for dreaming. There was work to do. Important work. Gam and his men were looking for those stragglers who were healthy and young enough to carry out demanding, punishing tasks over long periods of time. The active, healthy, and strong got the best price. This was a law of nature. Gam knew this and lived by this. This survival of the fittest could be seen in the deer and the monkeys and flying foxes they ate down to the insects devoured by the bats. Other considerations like motherhood or being with child didn't matter. All human cargo could be used or killed, Gam didn't care. This wasn't the United Nations and the United Nations didn't care. Even if they did, they couldn't do anything about it. It was the way business was done.

Gam had watched young girls and mothers die when they fell behind or complained. Sometimes through illness and sometimes by his hand—he was happy to relieve them of all Earthly pain. Their ghosts, and there were always ghosts, did not bother him.

The conversation in his head changed direction as he smelt fear. It was a unique aroma like lemongrass and sweat. The refugees, the convicts did not know of his skill as they huddled under plants or trees or hid in caves and tunnels. He would find them. He knew he would find them.

Soon, with his keen eyes, he found three women cowering behind a large, overflowing fig tree. Gam could sense more hiding in a stand of teak trees, he could smell fear. Pulling away a large overhanging branch revealed a group of cowering women. He gave a shout of joy then said in Burmese, 'You know you cannot hide from me, little ones.'

Taking one woman by the arm he motioned with a wave of his machete for the others to follow then led them to yawning mouth of the awaiting truck which shook and rattled like a prehistoric carnivore. A week ago, he cut off the arm of a man who would not give in to the inevitable. That one bled out and died and the latest batch knew better than to resist. He could see on the steely expressions of these villagers that they had courage. Yes, it took guts to flee your home country but it would take much more to do what he had in store for them. Simple courage was not enough. Gam again blew his whistle, his low-tech attention seeking device, then motioned for his assistants to load more human cargo collected from the ravine at the foot of the northern side of the hill onto the trucks.

'You come now,' he shouted waving the long-bladed knife. The knot of women came out from their last refuge looking starved and afraid. Others were less willing to surrender their freedom. Several men ran towards the river and Gam took aim with his automatic rifle and fired. Hit, one of the men froze mid-flight, a bird falling to Earth. Lying face down, his back stitched with heavy calibre bullets, he looked like he had been attacked with a meat axe. Realising escape was hopeless, the other three men, villagers with young families far from here, put up their hands.

It wasn't over. Another man, with the grey hair of an elder, resisted being tied like a farm animal, broke free and ran towards the river. There was screaming in his ears, the screams of children and families herded into sheds that were set alight. He could see those running from the pyre being shot and stabbed rifle bayonets. He was running from the cries for help from the ones beyond help, the screams of horror coming from ghosts. These *nats* would never let him forget how he had left his village, left his wife and daughter to die that unspeakable death.

Zaw was running for the lost, not running for himself or the good karma he no longer deserved.

Just when it looked as if he would make it, Gam, putting down the assault rifle, drew a Walther .38, took aim and shot Zaw in the back. His spinal column severed, this man who was thirty seconds from liberty threw his hands up in the air in a last desperate lunge for freedom, then pitched forward, a felled tree of human sacrifice. There were cries from the newest captives for they had known Zaw since he was a young boy playing in the forest. After such a raw death his ghost, his *nat* would haunt these woods forever.

Terrorised, other men with the crazed look of escapees-in-waiting, bowed their heads in defeat. Freedom would not come today. Without a fair chance of success, making a run for it wasn't worth dying for. Most of the men and women had family safe in villages far from here and each had a duty to survive. Not for themselves, but for those left behind. Self-sacrifice was a luxury few could afford.

Many lost their lives in defiance of these murderers; these slavers and bandits. A setting sun cast a flaming hue to the dying, fading green of the forest. Panthers and deer muted their calls as did all the chirping, buzzing insects in swarms of billions. Gigantic hardwood trees crouched like wooden spirits as twilight faded to black. The forest was closing down for the evening with the exception of night creatures, bats that flapped between trees. With the dark and the quiet came the fear. The forest ghosts came out at night, an oracle or a harbinger of fear, of harm.

As the trucks heaved and bumped over dirt roads, the barely alive human cargo huddled together. The captives were almost all Burmese, with one or two Laotians looking for freedom in another direction. With hands tied and faces showing anguish and defeat, the groups of men and women and some children were huddled together like farm animals. Even the children were too terrified to cry although one young girl who looked in her early teens had her mouth open in a kind of fixed, soundless scream. Whatever had happened to her, that nightmare was burned into her brain.

Gam smiled, the number of captives wasn't that much better compared to other hunts, yet this lot appeared healthy and strong and he knew they could be sold on the open market. They would need to be fit, the demands that would be placed on them were unforgiving of the weak. With high-level members of the military in Burma and Thailand involved, he knew what he was doing was not even illegal. Thirty illegal refugees and possible terrorists would now be indentured into the workforce rather than be a burden on the State, neither the one they abandoned nor the one they were fleeing to. They could help, or hurt, the secret alliance and Gam knew how to please his superiors. Why should the governments of Burma and Thailand pay for uninvited guests on their territory? He and General Saw Ne were doing the State a service that would only be repaid with services in kind. Payments to certain officials in the bordering countries helped his profitable cause and smoothed the way around the authorities. It could have been worse, it could have been much worse. Gam was happy not to go back emptyhanded, something that could have proved awkward, maybe even lethal.

Gam had witnessed the fatal consequences suffered by the last man who had displeased Ne Saw. He could still see his predecessor's head, shrunken and blackened by the sun on a pole pitched against the fortress wall. The execution had taken place in front of his men, the only mercy being shown in the swift execution with a samurai sword.

As the truck rocked and lurched over rutted, red dirt tracks closer to base, Gam thought of more pleasant things. His woman in Chiang Mai was waiting for him and he would not disappoint her. In fact, he had a special present for Fun, a diamond necklace he bought in

Phuket. Gam dreamt of her soft creamy skin, her beautiful breasts and was transported back in her arms. He wanted to spoil her with the best and this latest run promised just that chance. Her joy in receiving a new diamond necklace and bewitching ruby earrings would also please him; she would be thrilled and in turn would please him every way imaginable to Buddha.

Standing at the back of the truck, Gam counted two dozen workers-to-be. The younger women were pretty and the men looked healthy, despite long months in the camps or starving in the village. He clapped his hands then blew the whistle, now more as a celebration than as a dire warning.

With this successful harvest of superior flesh, money-making flesh, Gam was hungry for more. The factories were giant catfish that never stopped inhaling, never stopped sucking up bodies, bodies that were used up then spat out. There were many more fish out there, swimming in eddies, hiding under embankments and between rocks. They were there waiting to be caught and he would find them. He clapped as one of his men, Sri, came over the hill with a dozen men and women. Satisfied he said, 'Alright, we pack up. Time to go. We have had a good day.

Everyone gets a bonus to three thousand baht!'

The men roared their approval and he put his hands over his head in a sign of victory. He smiled, the left side of his face marked by a thick scar from a knife fight back in his youth when he wasn't anybody.

In rapid pidgin Burmese, he said to the group of huddled men women and children, 'Stay in the trucks until we get to Chiang Mai. If you fall out, if you jump or run away, you will die.' To underline this, he pointed a gun into the air and fired. The shot sent a flock of startled birds from trees into sky. 'You came to find a new home and we will take you there. We give you job, we give you home. Do not resist or you put your family and all you have in terrible danger.'

He paused to see he had everyone's attention and satisfied he did, went on.

'You work hard and you can send money back to your family,' he lied. 'You follow orders or you die.'

He paused then added another lie. 'You work hard you eat well you live well you live happy life.' Going by the long faces of the captives there was little trust in his words.

He moved close to one woman and said in rough Burmese, 'What is your name?'

She lifted her bowed head to show powdered cheeks streaked with sweat and tears. This talc remedy for the punishing heat was a distinguishing characteristic of most Burmese women and set them apart from Thai ladies who were broadly similar in appearance.

'My name is Mon.'

'Why are you here, Mon?'

'I have come far to reach Thailand. I did not make it and my friend Aom's son did not survive. He was killed by a land mine.'

'Perhaps he would still be alive if you all had not abandoned your home country.'

Mon gave a grimace and said, 'I did not abandon my country; it abandoned me.'

He stared at her with a sneer on his scarred face. 'Do you want to die?'

At this, he drew a finger across his throat. Mired in the swamp of grief, Mon shook her head without speaking. There was a collective shudder as the group of mainly young women cowered together like penguins on the edge of an ice shelf. As Kachin, Rohingya and Ron runaway villagers from Myanmar/Burma, they were no strangers to dire threats or violent death. Turning back now was unthinkable and even more so in captivity. On the truck, a heavily pregnant woman held her stomach as she retched. He signalled for one of his men to give her a pill that had proved useful in the past. Refugee women with child were rarely taken yet something about this one was different. He decided to keep her so after she took ill he helped her find a place in the front cabin. He had something in mind for her that was best kept secret.

Gam patted the back of the truck like it was a favourite horse as it drove off on the rutted dirt track. There was more to do here before he got back to base. Today his bonus would be high and he would be able to take his wife and his girlfriend out in Bangkok.

The toil wasn't finished. In the forest, his gang boss of bosses, Sao Ne Saw, the *Little General,* ran after three women and a man. He fired three shots and they stopped running. Sao didn't need to be in the field but he confessed to a weakness for the hunt. 'Better than hunting deer,' he said showing betel nut-stained red teeth. General Sao had his choice of women, the main reason he got sweaty and dirty in the tropical heat when he could be smoking cigars in Chiang Mai or Phuket. With dozens of female prisoners in his fortress, the man was insatiable and was not above killing those that displeased him. The General saw himself as an Emperor and did as Emperors do by raping, beating, torturing and killing those who displeased him and even sometimes those that pleased him. It didn't matter much, the real joy was in the killing, the exercise of real power in the most real way. Is that not what Emperors do?

Gam waved to him with a broad red-stained smile. It was an act to humour the strange man who had long ago slipped into madness. Just as Gam cured those who were sick or lazy, he would someday cure the General of his mental illness. Gam hated this man who would not hesitate to kill him at the slightest trace of incompetence or disrespect. One day he would have to act. Today was not that day.

A native of Yangon, or the old Rangoon, Gam could speak several dialects including Shan. Speaking without risk of misunderstanding, a necessary skill when ensnaring unpaid or barely-paid work slaves. The rewards were too good to pass up. In Chiang Mai, he already owned a Jeep, something unheard of in his village. Wanted for war crimes, he too could never go back unless it was under the cover of darkness and then only briefly like a panther hiding in the forest.

With a hand cupped over his ear, Gam listened to the voices of the forest, the screeches, the roars, and the birdsong. Then movement. Near a large umbrella tree, he could see a group of men and women scatter off into the woods with the frantic look of hysteria, of galloping panic. He blew his whistle again and helpers emerged from the bush. They went through the thick undergrowth, beating the tall grass with long sticks as if hunting treehugging monkeys.

A group of women stood up and raised their hands as if surrendering to the military or police. Sao Ne Saw smiled this was easier than he dared hope. He knew his secret managers in Yangon, Bangkok and Macau would reward him well when he got back to the factory. It had been a good day, a very profitable day if his guess was right. As the Commander and overseer, he did not *have* to chase prey in the forest yet he knew that to keep the quotas up his presence was vital. There was no substitute for being on the ground. He had to know what his men were up to otherwise they might be tempted to malinger, an offence punishable by execution and witnessed by all. Only the week before, an informer was caught relaying messages by phone. The culprit, a villager named Ko was beheaded on the spot with a clean slice of a long-bladed knife wielded by Sao Ne Saw himself. Ko's co-workers were made to watch as a reminder of their fate should they go down the same treacherous path. Sao hated disloyalty and was always eager to punish this most terrible sin. The night held much promise as Sao Ne Saw and his human cargo were driven back to the fortified compound.

CHAPTER 7

The lumbering A380 made its final approach to Bangkok International just as Brodie put on the Thai news and listened through headphones. His ears began to pop while the plane moved into a slow holding pattern, a massive bird circling for a perch. Surely, the plane was too big to crash, too big to fail. As Brodie pondered that absurd thought, the sights and sounds coming from the TV were disturbing. Blood and what looked like blurred body parts were spread around a bombed-out restaurant as a shaken Thai reporter described the scene in dodgy English. The plane wings dipped and the vast expanse of Bangkok spread out towards emerald mountains. As they banked, Brodie wondered what would happen if the wing or tail section fell off. Or if the massive jet ploughed into buildings. What would it feel like when it exploded into flames?

There was a reason for his catastrophising. On screen, shredded bodies were being carried from a bomb site. A local reporter hyperventilated in serviceable English, 'There are many casualties. Early estimates are of eleven dead and many more severely injured.' Barely registering the Captain's announcement, 'I hope you've enjoyed your flight. We will touch down at Bangkok in about ten minutes,' Brodie was glued to the screen showing ultrahigh definition images of torn, broken bodies being dragged from a pulverised Thai restaurant.

Alarmed, he immediately surfaced from the fug of jetlag. The IED explosion had happened only the day before in Pattaya, their ultimate destination, so Brodie switched the news off before Grace noticed. It was already going to be a hard sell without dealing in hypotheticals of the deadly kind. Although anxious, he pasted on a smile and squeezed

Grace's hand. She gently put her head on his shoulder like she always did when she was feeling affectionate, when she was feeling happy.

Holding hands as the huge Thai Airways Airbus 380 landed, he tried to think ahead. He developed a plan. The charming Grace would have to be charmed. After a longish wait in queues of milling world travellers, they eventually made their way through customs at the massive International airport despite sniffer dogs and armed police reminding everyone there was a mid-level terrorist alert as advertised on the in-flight news. If they didn't find any terrorists they might catch drug smugglers as a consolation prize.

'That didn't take too long now did it, honey?'

Grace shrugged her shoulders and said in a tone this side of jaded, 'Not if you consider an hour and a half reasonable.'

Not wanting to ask any more leading questions he pulled her closer to him and said in a whisper close to her ear,

'Don't worry, sweetheart, this is where the fun begins. You'll see. This will be the best vacation ever.'

'Wherever we're going, I'll follow.' She paused then added a qualifier. 'Of course, I want to be taken to interesting places.'

He squeezed her shoulders and said, 'I can do that. This will be more fun than ever you'll see.'

She gave him a playful punch on the shoulder. 'Of course you can, darling, I'd expect nothing less.'

Still holding hands, they snaked through long lines for passport checking and stamping. Sniffer dogs shadowed bags and tourists in the baggage area. As they waded through crowds of travellers he said, 'God, you could get lost here for years.'

'Well, as long as we don't.'

'Remember that guy who was stuck in an American airport without papers or a passport?'

She stuck a finger to her chin as though trying hard to recall then said, 'I remember it became a movie with, let's see, Tom Hanks, right?'

He nodded. 'Yeah. Well this reminds me of that. I could imagine being stuck in here forever.'

'Not my idea of fun, honey. Let's move on.'

He shook his head he couldn't help catastrophising even when things were fine. He saw a man, a white man from wherever, staring at Grace's ample bosom and wonderful legs. Brodie caught his gaze and glared. The man turned in an abrupt head motion that must have left him spinning.

Finally, outside the teeming airport terminal he tried to hail a cab. With no takers, he pressed on. Then he could see people taking tickets before hailing and hopping into taxis. He saw a man in sunglasses and casual attire staring at him. Brodie returned the eyeballing and the stranger blinked first before walking away at a brisk pace. It occurred to him it might be a case of mistaken identity then cleared the thought from his mind. As hot winds rushed outside the futuristic terminal they searched for a taxi after taking the mandatory ticket. That changed everything. An eager flock of cabbies surrounded the couple vying for business. Brodie chose one young man at random and the cabbie gave a wide smile with red-stained gums and teeth to show his appreciation.

As the thin man with the smooth face of a twenty-something loaded their luggage into the vehicle, Brodie and Grace got into the back seat and kissed. It was a slow, languid kiss that made all the transit blues and agenda angst disappear.

'Take us to the Silverton Cay Shores in Soi Seven Pattaya, please,' said Brodie as he handed over 3000 baht or $15.

'Yes, very good. You enjoy Pattaya. Many places to go, many things to do. I recommend the *Temple of Truth.*'

Brodie nodded. Yes, the *Temple of Truth* was a place he knew well but that was another lifetime. He didn't want to explore that ghost of the past just yet.

Frowning slightly, Grace asked, 'I thought we were going to Phuket? Isn't that where everyone goes, darling?'

Brodie kept quiet. He was waiting. He scrolled through some pictures of Pattaya, pointing out the beaches and islands. She watched with a tight smile. He knew the precursors of outrage.

'Doesn't Phuket look nice, darling?'

She smiled as the cab streamed past billboards displaying fantastic islands shooting straight up from azure waters ringed with perfect sugary beaches. He knew Phuket was her first choice. It was up to him to convince her they, or rather he, had made the right choice. There was some explaining to do. Brodie could do that.

Brodie put his hand on hers like a doctor preparing a patient for a difficult prognosis. Something along the lines of you're not losing a leg, you're gaining a healthy body. He struggled to find the right tone. 'We are going to have the time of our lives, honey. You'll see.' Buy on the rumour, and sell on the facts. That's the way he played it.

Scrolling through Facebook photos on her own iPhone, Grace looked at doctored pictures of Pattaya beaches.

Seeming satisfied or at least convincing herself she was, Grace leaned back in her seat; the storm passed for now.

They rode on in silence. Brodie couldn't dare hope Grace would drop it. He knew her. It wasn't in her nature.

They slowed to go through a toll booth as lights flashed by, a relief from the monotony of a black, moonless night.

'Depends on how you look at it dear. With the money we save here, we can go more places and buy more stuff.

Nothing but the best, honey, you know what I said.'

Her blank face radiated scepticism but then she burst out laughing. 'It's alright, I forgive you. We'll make the best of it.'

Putting his arms around her waist, 'Oh, we'll do more that, hon. We'll do great,' he said as the black, featureless landscape of night rolled on. This was wild Asia when the sun went down. Perhaps there were dragons out there, invisible ghosts come to haunt, to exact their revenge. Finally, out of the darkness they were clearly in the city as scooters buzzed around and past them. The city was bigger than expected even though he had been there just seven years ago, back when Grace wasn't even on the radar. He kissed her on the cheek again and just as he did they arrived at the circular drive of the Pattaya Copacabana. They stepped out to be greeted by a concierge. As bellhops took their luggage to reception, the couple kissed like newlyweds.

'You're right, at least it's five stars. You mean we're going to a poor man's Phuket, is that right?'

'No, it's more than that, much more,' he lied. With everything cheaper here compared to Phuket, she wasn't wrong. Reputation saved, they kissed again. It was slow and languid and felt like it took up the universe with the two of them the brightest stars. The black hole that threatened to suck his energy and destroy his soul was gone. For now.

In a touching show of affection, Grace brushed the hair from Brodie's eyes. They hadn't been this close for a long time and this touchy-feely phase was becoming a habit he could get used to. Maybe in some way they never really were separated and those six weeks in the wilderness were something dreamed, not lived. Then, like a dark storm chaser when that dark storm passed he woke up and it was fine. It didn't matter. He knew they were going to make it. Somehow their stormy relationship had righted itself.

Feeling great he let out a yell to show the world his delight. Not to be outdone, Grace did the same.

With arms, wide in a gesture of release or salvation he said, 'We made it, honey. Tonight is the first night of the rest of our lives!'

They kissed. They made love. Sleep came easily.

CHAPTER 8

The overfilled Toyota truck moved slowly over rutted dirt roads until it came to a gate manned by uniformed men holding rifles. On the road for hours, the time had come for rest. An expectant Sao Ne Saw waved and they were let through. As they drove over a rise the Great House of evil spirits could be seen. Only a year old, it was massive by local Myanmar standards and had taken hundreds of men working day and night to build in the space of a week. Rising five stories and surrounded by trees for cover from the air, he was proud of his bamboo and teak creation. Getting out, Gam pulled back the cloth flap to reveal a mass of people standing huddled together but restrained with leather, rope and plastic ties.

As slave consignment workers and armed guards poured out of the Great House to give ominous welcome, the miserable looking men and women were helped down from the trucks and lined up in rows. The more or less healthy and young were separated from the old and frail and there were pitiful cries as loved ones were separated. Would they ever see each other again? As they were led to bamboo holding pens, Sao Ne Saw got out of the second truck, called Gam over and said, 'We have had a fine day, my brother. The quality of these prospects is better than the last run. The returns should be excellent.'

Gam smiled, it was not often he was paid a compliment by this, the most feared man in southern Burma.

'Yes, we can do better soon. The Burmese army is doing another sweep for drug and cultivation offences. We can use that as a cover to wreak our own havoc.'

The two embraced then watched as more captives were separated by age, sex and physical fitness. Gam eyed one woman who was uncommonly tall and beautiful. She had the powdered cheeks that was the Burmese custom.]

Inside the Great House, beef and pork on a spit was being roasted, the smoke wafting out through a chimney made of blackened river stones. Two women danced to an ancient tune, moving arms and legs in unison. Above them hung a *nat sin*, a shrine to the village spirit or *ywa saung nat*. It was a supernatural presence with a headdress and offerings of fruit and gold. Gam gave a *wai* of respect. This ghost, this spirit of the mountains and the forests, watched over and guarded their stronghold. It could also ward off the ghosts of those he and his men killed or who had died in the work camps. Some refused to believe, yet dared not dishonour karma with any show of disrespect.

Sao Ne Saw motioned for one of the women to join him and he offered her a generous piece of pork thrown together with fried vegetables on a tin plate. Not responding at first, she seemed to be telegraphing her reluctance to accept his gift. As Ne Saw frowned with more than a touch of menace she gave a forced smile then hungrily devoured the succulent meat. Better to eat than perish.

As the new couple feasted, Gam aped his superior and beckoned another pretty concubine-in-waiting to join him. This time there was no avoidance strategy and she playacted the role of a grateful supplicant, a possession he could tame to his will. During the meal first Sao Ne Saw, leaning across from his own conquest, then Gam, kissed the woman deeply before fondling her breasts and more.

Gam laughed and said to the borderlands master of men and women as far as the eagle flies, 'This one has spirit.

Like a wild horse that has to be broken in.'

He again kissed her fully on the lips then pawed her breasts and thighs. Trying to pull away by wriggling her body, he picked her up and threw her over his shoulders, another find from the forest to be plundered.

He laughed hard and his master did the same. She was his and he could do what he wanted with her. Not all women, willing or not, survived his attentions. He had ensnared many souls and did not fear their ghosts. Taking her upstairs by way of a wooden ladder the couple disappeared into the loft. Sao Ne Saw took his woman by the hand and went into the large bedroom that was behind the Great Room.

Back in the human holding pen, Aom and Mon managed to find each other through the bamboo slats that separated each cell. There was a thin reed of hope and this connection could mean nothing or everything. Aom, still grieving over the landmine death of her young son Auk San, was mute. The memory of his murder would stay with her as long as the sun set on these hills. The explosion was so big she could find only a hand when the smoke and dust cleared after his small body was swept asway. In shock, she had buried the hand and watched Auk's spirit lift to heaven. A Kachin Christian, she also believed in the spirit world. Now her lost son would guide and watch over her just as she had failed to do for him. He spoke to her through the night. 'I will look after you mother. Please do not break your heart,' he said as he cupped her hand with both of his and finished with, 'Don't worry, I am here.'

Moving her hand through his wispy form she saw him smile which made her smile. He was gone, yet Aom knew Auk San would watch over her always.

Back in the real world, she saw two men from her village in Karen in another bamboo cell facing hers. Myint and Yei acknowledged her with very slight body movements; one moved his shoulders, the other his hands. It didn't pay to stand out. They had all seen what happened to anyone who came to the attention of the guards. An older man, a grandfather named Wai, kept begging for water. His voice croaking and his frail body going into convulsion, he was shot.

Gloating over the corpse and waving around his Glock pistol, the soldier some now called the Demon, said in an angry tone, 'This is what we do to wounded animals who aren't of use. If you complain, if you are trouble, if you try to escape, you will be shot.'

Mon said in a soothing voice, 'Aom, your son is not real anymore. His body is gone and we shall live for him.' Aom lifted her eyelids and returned to the natural world again. She would join her son when the time came. Until then, she would fight on for his lost life. His ephemeral presence made it seem as if he had never died.

As they touched fingers, the edge of their nightmare tore just enough to allow a tiny point of light to spark. It was just enough lift her spirit. A surge that began deep in Aom's spine shot through to her brain like a shower of fireworks. Elated, energised with natural chemicals she said, 'Do not lose hope, Mon. We will find freedom.'

As Aom spoke in heavy tones weighed by trauma, tears welled in Mon's eyes. The words were comforting even if they could hardly be true.

'We will find a way out of here, Aom.'

Nodding her understanding she said, 'Yes, I know. Auk San promised.'

Through the opening they held hands, as if doing so would save them from all harm. This was something the Kachin Liberation Army could not do.

A guard barked orders in the Myanmar language, 'No talking. No touching. You will be given instructions tomorrow. We have hot food here. Eat it if you want to survive.' As he spoke, shirtless men moved food carts laden with huge pots of steaming rice and stew and each prisoner was handed a wooden bowl filled with the maggot-infested gruel and ordered to eat.

As Mon clutched her bowl with shaking, terrified hands she turned her back to Aom. It was a protective move, not one of rejection. No one need know their connection.

Mon ate slowly and was surprised by how delicious it tasted. It wasn't the usual rat or dog. Rice and chicken with sauce. She understood this was not to please inmates, only to keep them alive and fit for other duties. Money mattered in this place, only money.

A man close to her, a stranger with hollow cheeks, asked, 'What will they do with us? Will we be killed?' Shaking and sweating from a low-grade fever she wondered about his survival. She knew from other camps that sickness brought death. When the guards thought you were near death even the simple luxury of food was taken away.

Death came slowly or quickly. Some took their own lives to escape the pain, the shame of captivity.

Mon shook her head and said, 'They would not be feeding us meat if they were going to kill us.' 'What then?' he asked with panic-stricken eyes.

'We will be used as workers with little or no pay.'

'You mean like slaves?'

She nodded with a grave expression then knelt to the straw-covered floor. The talk drained her energy, she had family to live for and could not afford the luxury of wallowing in self-pity. Within minutes she was asleep.

Through a metal grate she could see men in uniforms that must have been officers judging by the visor caps and braid. She recognised one officer as a general in the Burmese Army. The other had a different uniform and Mon guessed he was Thai. What was a Thai general doing in a slave camp disguised as a refugee camp?

Before she could think any more about that she was pushed along with the others in single file back to the factory floor. As the constant stream of smartphones resumed, she bent her head in concentration to insert batteries and phone covers, while simultaneously using another part of her brain to plan her getaway. It would not be easy. In fact it would be virtually impossible. But Mon would choose life. Staying, doing nothing, was the way of madness and the end of life.

CHAPTER 9

Water thrust upwards as Grace kicked her shapely alabaster legs at the far end of the hotel infinity pool. The toilet of Thailand didn't look half bad from up here. Brodie cheered and splashed his appreciation, happy that she was happy. Grace shrieked in delight as she slapped water back at him in the kind of play they hadn't done since forever. On the 14th floor pool deck, you could see the coast and the islands and with your face so close to the surface, it felt like being in a sky-high ocean floating above paradise, albeit a paradise with dodgy plumbing and street smells you didn't want to know about outside the confines of 5-star venues like this.

No, up here in the Imperial Hotel they could remain innocent of the awful reek of the city's imperfect sewage system and roaming platoons of street hustlers, male and female. Would Brodie ever understand that soiled toilet paper was supposed to be thrown in a bin instead of the toilet? More modest hotels had more earthy digs and customs. Putting human waste in a wastepaper bin was something he still remembered from his first introduction to Thailand all those years ago. Thank god they had modern flush plumbing at the Imperial.

As the mock water fight ended, and not wanting to miss more fun to be had, he dived in at the deep end and swam underwater until he was close enough to grab her by the legs. His left hand moved down and covered her tiny ankle tattoo of the stars and stripes as she tried to pull away. His lady rarely spoke of America yet he knew, like most Americans he'd met, that she was, somewhere deep in the fissures of her soul, patriotic, maybe even a super patriot along the lines of the bombastic American Head of State.

Brodie surfaced to screams of delight. She always described the tramp stamp inking as a youthful folly and it was like she was that carefree kid again. A wild, yet good girl, teenager with attitude. Somehow, it proved the wisdom of being there and brought a feeling of vindication. In forgetting herself, getting out of her head, she was back and he was glad about that. Very glad.

'Come on, race you to the end.' With a doubtful look, he couldn't be sure was real or fake, she began to shake her head. Then, getting a cheeky head start, she began swimming at a fast clip to the far side of the pool. He took off after her. They even drew a crowd with a couple of bikini clad ladies from Manchester cheering them on in Geordie accents.

Swimming freestyle he almost caught up. Did he want her to win? Of course he did. Streaming past him like a cruiser, it was too late, she pipped him like a champ.

'I won, so what did I win?'

Putting a finger to his chin in mock indecision he said, 'Now let's see. What should I give you for that magnificent feat? It's a wonder you didn't get to the Olympics. You're a regular Shane Gould.' 'Who?' she asked with a blank look of incomprehension.

'She was one of the best, an Aussie of course.' Seeing she still didn't understand what he was talking about he said, 'I forgot, you're American. Think of Olympic champion Mark Phelps.'

'A man? You want me to compare the two?'

'Sorry, I can't think of any female American swimmers. Think Chris Evert. No. Who to compare to? Surfers maybe, like Mary Ho? But not swimmers. I know, how about a Venus Williams of the pool?'

Making a face at the comparison, Grace leaned forward to peck him on the cheek then said like a brassy, American reality-TV housewife that could well be her destiny, 'That's alright. Having you is prize enough, even if you are a lousy swimmer.' She paused before finishing with, 'And an ordinary cook.'

'I know, I just thought it might break up the day. But no, honey, I insist. Don't worry, I'll come up with a surprise that will blow your mind.' To illustrate the point, he put his hands to his head then threw them outwards to mimic a brain explosion.

Grace gave crooked smile. It was the kind she put on when she was truly enjoying herself. He hadn't seen it for a while and liked what he saw.

'You can have that. My mind's been blown enough. Remember, I'm from California.'

'Sorry, how could I forget? You guys invented wild times, am I right?'

She gave a smirk and said, 'Something like that. It's all fuzzy. You had to be there.'

'I'm sure. And tomorrow we go out to the island.'

'And tomorrow, and tomorrow, and tomorrow. You make it sound like a bucket list.'

'You never know what might happen. We want to get there before the next tsunami does or the end of the world as we know it comes. We have sharks, tsunamis, volcanoes, and earthquakes.'

She gave him a look. Images of that tsunami crashing into Thai hotels, broken and dead bodies everywhere, were part of the collective consciousness. It had an instant sobering effect. She frowned.

'Just kidding, it's going to be perfect,' he added, wanting to put her at ease.

At the far end of the pool standing near a glass top table, he could see a man looking at them. He had on Ray Bans and an open-necked shirt. Unlike the stranger at Suvarnabhumi Airport. The first was a foreigner whereas this man was Thai or close, maybe Lao.

'What are you looking at, darling?' Grace asked.

Brodie turned to reply, 'Oh nothing. I was just admiring the sea view. I don't know where that freezing wind came from. Maybe it got lost on its way down from the North Pole.'

Looking back again, the man was gone. In his place, a whirling wind like a dwarf tornado blew in cold air. Then it left as soon as it materialised.

She smiled and said, 'I didn't feel a thing. Are you sure you're not imagining things, sweetheart?' 'Being with you is always a dream. I can't believe my good luck having you by my side.'

He smiled then kissed her again.

CHAPTER 10

The assembly line passed an almost catatonic Mon. The conveyer a relentless, demanding train of machine parts that never stopping consuming her strength and her spirit. Mon knew she would likely die making these rich man's toys. Back in the village, she could never dream of being able to pay for a high-end branded smartphone.

No matter the devil machinery. No matter the soldiers guarding and threatening with rifles and bayonets, the men that owned this hell and everyone ruled by them. None could defeat her, none would defeat her. Even if she died, her spirit would avenge her, just as her friend's murdered son's spirit lived in the forest and came to them at night. There was her family to live for and a daughter, Lun, she wanted to believe was safe.

She kept going, Mon had to keep going, as she was told again and again. It was the same thing over and over again, plugging in circuit boards and snap fitting the housing for the endless stream of brand name cell phones that spewed out the other end. This monster never stopped eating so she couldn't stop either. It didn't pay to stop. For anything. Stopping could lead to a beating, something her friend, Aom, learned through painful experience. Stopping for anything, including peeing, could be fatal. After days of toil with breaks few and far between, Aom fainted from exhaustion and was subjected to physical violence with rifle butts to the head resulting in a swollen face pummelled so hard it looked like an overripe, split eggplant. Mon watched in horror as the beating went on, not daring to interfere, knowing she could be next.

Then days later another factory slave named Zhang, also from Shan, folded like a brick chimneystack in an earthquake. Zhang had been riding for a fall after 14-hour days and any number of weeks became too much and she crashed to the floor as if felled by a massive seizure. Later they found she was pregnant. She wanted to cry but couldn't. Crying sapped her energy and will to live. There were others to think of she could not afford to lay down and die.

Since a battle with Thai troops on the borders, rations had been cut with dire consequences. Food, once clean and even tasty, was now dirty and dangerous. The watery rice and rotting meat was toxic enough to sap energy rather than give it. They were all dying but Zhang was weaker than most and so the first to crumble. Barely breathing and as white as the river spirits that haunted the Irrawaddy and Mekong, even when given water and a little untainted rice she couldn't rise. As if in protest against outrages against it, her body gave up so she lay still, barely breathing. Guards clustered around less worried about her likely death than the delay it would cause.

'Get up, you must get up,' a stout guard shouted before slapping her across the face.

Mon called to her in a desperate tone, 'Zhang, it is not your destiny to die here. Save yourself.'

Another guard this one tall and slender hit her in the back with a rifle butt. She gasped in pain while the guards carried her away to an unknown fate. They stopped when she began to retch blood.

If she did slip off into the Delta to join the damned it would be the third death in a week. Mon didn't know what they did with the bodies although her bad dreams told her the destroyed souls became food for the monstrous catfish that trawled the waterways. The souls of the bottom-feeding creature and the dead would merge to wreak vengeance, the outrage of their murder would not go unavenged. All would become ghosts, *nats*, on an eternal quest for justice, for peace and a resting place free of torment and involuntary servitude. Mon watched her new friend go limp like stiff noodles in a boiling pot and she knew her friend would soon join the spirit of her lost husband, shot in the back while shielding her.

While her co-workers looked away in fear of bringing unwanted attention, Mon saw what was happening and tried to help but armed guards with sneering grins and heavy hands held her back. She recognised one as the man who had beaten and raped Aom. That meant he killed two, including the unborn child. Mon hoped he would be tormented by the ghosts of the dead, his flesh stripped and eaten by the forest bats that came out only at night. She hated him the most and vowed to kill him some day. With the shaved head many of the guards went for and a thick scar across his forehead that could have been slashed by a sword in battle, he looked somehow less than human. With a powerful build and thick veins, he would bleed well when she cut his throat and watched him die.

As the killer guard seized Zhang by the throat, Mon begged for mercy only to be kicked hard in the chest by another guard, the heel of his boot leaving her gasping for breath. Wanting their fun on an otherwise tedious detail, the guards took Zhang into a back room where she was slapped and kicked amid howls of pain. Her face soon turned puffy and black like a rotting corpse left in the sun. The attack was not without limits. Rapes had eased off after a General executed two guards in front of the force.

Zhang's cries of hurt, her pleas for mercy were knives stabbing Mon's heart so she put her hands up to her ears as if to drive the horror from her mind. Going mad was an indulgence she could not afford. Too many depended on her, she had to survive. The roar, the rushing sound and ghostly voices didn't stop, would it ever stop? Then in an act of courage Mon uncovered her ears. She wanted to hear this, remember this.

Zhang disappeared, dragged from the room unconscious. No one dared to ask what became of her. Mon hoped Zhang would find peace with her husband in the spirit world.

Still alive, saved by kind ghosts or Gods, Mon went back to work yet she was changed, somehow different. She could not trust another man and would kill whomever tried to violate her or anyone close to her. Preparations for escape were now well-advanced. With a blade fashioned from broken machine parts, she was ready. Hardened from her experiences like a panda poked and prodded in a zoo, she would use that power to survive.

She would channel this well of strength just as she would seek out the ghosts that might aid her cause. She would not lie down and die as some poor souls did. Mon could see all her new friends had changed, their souls destroyed. And Mon had not escaped this insult to her soul. It was frightening, as if vengeful ghosts were tormenting her for past sins, dooming her afterlife but Mon would not let this defeat her. That way laid madness, death. Most inside were so broken in spirit they lost the power of speech and had become catatonic inmates in an asylum. Her friend was worse off than that. Aom wasn't Aom. She was broken. Bent like a piece of iron hammered into an entirely different shape. She had been beaten down so hard she yearned for the release of death. Something was broken in her, something that couldn't be fixed in this slaughterhouse. Mon tried to bring her back to the surface, back to the calm water's edge and away from the river monsters that devoured lost souls.

It wasn't much use. Mon sat by her friend on breaks, trying to get her back.

Aom no longer smiled and didn't talk about happier times in the village or about her daughter, Mee, now six. Perhaps she had herself become a lost spirit in the underworld like her lost son. Mon felt terrible sorrow for her friend just as she felt sorry for herself. *'This life is no life'* Mon said to herself. It was the life of a cockroach after a Hindu reincarnation, a cockroach that could be squashed under the booted heel of their cruel watchers and masters. Inside this place they all were insects, vermin to be exterminated without thought.

As Mon tried to keep up with the wicked dance of machine parts demanding to be made whole, her mind raced through the tunnels and crevices of this hell. A plan, a fantastic plan, slipped into a mind that could do two things at once in perfect harmony. Twin fighter jets flying in formation ready to strike at separate targets. The snaky path to freedom, like the great Irrawaddy River, came to her like a dream as she sorted the tiny parts for the cell phone. Each shiny precious metal component a glittering, tiny ornament that gleaned and winked encouragement.

As she attached the shiny pieces of smartphone designed by clever men far away, she developed a plan of escape. She could feel it, taste it. Freedom was succulent duck soup, each spoonful to be savoured and drawing strength from each morsel. Freedom was a wonderful place with sunny fields and serene elephants ready to protect, ready for battle. This place in her head, this refuge from evil and death, was her haven in a warring world. Her tormentors owned her body yet tried to get in her head and failed. It was the one place she could go and rest, like her village near a field of poppies, the only place where she could be free in tiny slivers of time. The dream kept her alive, kept her from surrendering to the rushing tide of fatigue dragging her down with fingers that beckoned and pulled her gently to that final sleep and final resting place innocent of the pain of torment. It would be so easy to give in to that temptation but she could not afford that luxury. Mon knew she would, she had to, survive and be free of this misery, this swamp that consumed. Mon knew she would be gone one way or another, even if she died in the attempt. She knew Po was dead, one of the girls, she couldn't remember who, told her in stolen whispers how he died killing innocent people in the name of the Kachin, Rohingya, Shan, and Ron people. His act of murder in Thailand was a crime against his Kachin people and would not be repeated following his muchdeserved death. He had to die. She felt no pity for this man she had known since childhood, he had set back their cause and deserved to perish. When she re-joined her sisters and brothers of the movement for emancipation for the Kachin, Shan, and Ron, she would put this right.

At the afternoon 10-minute break signalled by a blaring fog horn the robot slave side of her brain switched off and Zhang went outside as if to join the army of smokers, then ducked back towards the garbage bins and climbed around the wooden staircase behind the flimsy barrier. Partly hidden by bamboo and thick palms, she watched the closest guard then moved when he moved to the other side of a tree. Once up on the third floor, she hoisted herself onto the roof. Although weakened by the punishing slave labour, she still had the nimble skills of an acrobat. On the roof, she had a clear view of the busy factory and the insect-sized people below. Swaying she closed her eyes tight, then fell forward into the void. Sailing towards earth, Zhang imagined being with her family, the family she'd come to Thailand to provide for, only to see her life pulled apart like tiny wings from a butterfly. As she fell she opened her eyes and saw a whirl of trees and huts, green and brown, then nothing. Just before she smashed into the ground and broke her neck, Zhang knew she would become a ghost, one of the ghosts all the inmates spoke of in this hell. Then, in the terminal blackness of death her spirit rose from the twisted body on bloodied ground. Alive in spirit, Zhang rose up to her destiny as a river ghost. She would watch over those spirits to come from the torment of the living. A keening wind started and blew through the camp making it so cold those without coats, and all the prisoners, began to shiver.

In a truck just leaving the compound Myint and Yei crouched with their hands tied behind their backs. Along with them were another thirty men crammed tight in rows. With no stops in a ten-hour journey it would be yet another survival test. Already one man was slack jawed and slumped in a dead faint, his future uncertain. He knew they were headed not inland but towards the coast. Just what coast was a mystery.

CHAPTER 11

Grace, looking relaxed, said, 'I think this place is starting to grow on me, honey.'

Brodie reached for her hand and squeezed it. 'I knew you'd come around. We can go over to the Island or take a jungle trek somewhere?'

Putting her hand to her mouth, 'Oh my God, you don't mean on an elephant?'

With a wide smile, Brodie held up some tickets and said, 'As a matter of fact, we're booked in for tomorrow.'

'Well, as least we'll have a few interesting photos and footage illustrating our very own adventure into the rainforest.'

Off in the distance, Brodie could hear loud smacking and kicking. Turning in the direction of the sounds he could see a boxing ring. Not just a boxing ring but a Thai Kick Boxing ring.

Downing his beer in one gulp Brodie got up and in an excited voice said, 'Come on, let's take a look at that. I used to watch the Kung Fu flicks when I was a kid now we can see the real thing. Look, it's right next to a bar so we can have a drink while we watch.'

Grace gave a puzzled look then grudgingly tagged along as he led her by the hand to the Kung Fu fighting or rather *Muay Thai* fighting.

At the Hacienda Bar, a medium-sized boxing ring was set up and two *farung* were inside fighting with gloved punches to the head and kicks to the thigh and gut. The couple could hear loud smacking sounds as the gloves came into contact with head and stomach and each of the men grunted or swore. One *farung*, red haired and English going by his northern accent, gave his blond-haired opponent with a Dutch accent a crippling blow with a head-high kick. The man collapsed like a pricked balloon.

The northern man raised his gloves high triumphant in victory.

A Thai man with a beautiful smile called out, 'Anyone want to challenge Hacienda champ?'

In the crowd Brodie could see some lager lads shaping up as though on the verge of climbing into the ring.

To head them off he called out, 'I'll take on the champ. What's the prize?'

The Thai man smiled and said, 'All you can drink until you drop or go home.'

Grace tugged at his shirt hissed, 'You're not really going to do this Brodie? It's barbaric, I can't watch.' Giving a reassuring smile, he said with more bluff than genuine confidence, 'Look, it'll be fun, you'll see.' She closed her eyes as if blotting out a premonition of him being beaten to a pulp.

Brodie climbed the ladder into the ring, stripped off his shirt and threw it to Grace then donned the gloves.

Fortunately, he had runners on and so began pumping his legs up and down while shadow boxing.

'You going to need more than that, son. I think you might be out of your depth, laddie.' The red haired Northern man was cocky alright.

They touched gloves, 'I'm Brodie,' he said as his opponent said, 'and I'm Seamus. Fraternisation with the enemy over, the two danced around each other.

Brodie tried a smile and came out with a sneer. Not wanting to get drawn into any psyche-out fight talk he moved in close, his gloves up near his head in a defensive pose. He threw a left then a right. The first missing, but the second hitting the fat face of the enemy. The red-haired Irishman's nose and lips squashed into a clown's face. The man called Seamus shook his head as though to clear his senses then came at Brodie with quick action punches that left Brodie winded.

'Come on, Brodie, you can do it,' Grace called out. At first jaded over the very idea of a boxing match, now she had some skin in the game there was a complete sea change in attitude. In a show of support, she slammed her hands on the ring base building up a beat and a momentum. The red man's friends shouted their support urging him on with the words, 'No surrender. No surrender to the Australian.'

As he turned to give a bow and pat his gloves together to show his appreciation, Brodie punched, then kicked him in the rib cage and stomach. The red haired man doubled over and the Thai ref raised Brodie's gloves declaring, 'We have new champion!'

CHAPTER 12

Near Beach Road, fronting the smooth waters of the Bay of Pattaya, Sirawit Puna and Khin Maung lugged a heavy duffle bag into the back of the Hustler Go-Go Bar, just around the corner in Soi 6. Not yet noon, the bar was almost barren except for a pot-bellied man from York with a sunburned face, still on his third drink. It was early for Jimmy and he was just getting started.

Looking maudlin as if over some regret left behind in the dumpster of his life back home, he sat in a stupor too wrapped up in his sorry, star-crossed karma to spot the delivery. The man who called himself Jimmy was oblivious to the slender bargirl powdering her nose and applying lippy beside a pool table. This was early for her too, only a *farung* had already paid a bar fine with the promise of more to come when they met up in the hotel in Soi 7. He told her he had to wait until his wife went shopping before she got the call. Even though Chailai already had the cash, there was no thought of cheating this client. Irish Carl had a wallet stuffed with thousands of baht and she was not about to blow off someone who could become a regular customer in the uncertain days ahead. He might even turn out to be a *boomerang* and make regular visits. If so, he would be her third man on a string.

Chailai had no interest outside her world and ignored the suspicious man and his mystery luggage. It didn't pay to meddle. Interfering could get you killed, like young Sik. Shot by a jealous wife and left to stagger onto the street clutching her stomach, she died before the ambulance arrived and Chailai vowed not to end up like that.

The bargirls, like most Thai bargirls, took no notice of such things, something expected of them in these troubled times. This was serious business generating serious money, with the sex tourism and more, so they knew not to interfere. Interfering with men of importance, whether they were gangsters or police, risked very bad karma including death or a life sentence of penury and heat inside or outside prison. That was no ghost story, it was a real threat that hung over her like a poisonous cloud.

One girl in Soi 5 had acid thrown in her face when she informed police some bars were using illegal aliens from Laos and Burma. Plastic surgeons performed miracles in Bangkok and in the right light her melted, crinkled skin still looked almost beautiful. It was true, she *was* beautiful, but the *farung* wouldn't look at her now so she worked out of sight of customers. No, it didn't pay to see, to tell. Here, a woman without a face was cursed with a life hardly worth living. Yet Ning lived and her life with her family was not worthless. No woman in Pattaya, no bargirl in Thailand wanted to end up like that. Naturally there was a thin veil of security given by the police, yet this could easily disappear like paper swept away in the wind.

The police knew everything, or pretended they did, but didn't always help. They were paid too little to help everyone and a few thousand baht was usually enough to get them to look the other way. Some paid that every month for what amounted to immunity, at least until something better came along. Once, the Russians tried to take over, until one Russian bargirl was shot in the face and all the concubines were airlifted out the next morning.

There were many players in this city of booze and women and bad men from across the world. They were all actors in her favourite Thai soap opera. Everyone had a role to play and everyone from the lead to the understudy was expected to stick to the script. To survive, everyone needed their excuse, their alibi, or 'plausible deniability' as they called it in the movies, when something happened. This was Thailand, the Land of Smiles, something always happened and being indiscreet or having a big mouth was not an option for workers on a few dollars a day.

Around the back of the Cowgirl Bar in a locked room, 26-year-old Sirawit wiped pools of sweat from his forehead with the back of his hand then opened the bag to reveal gleaming rows of rifles, semi-automatic or automatic, and pistols. Khin Maung, a Burmese man new in town gave a soft cry of joy and said in Burmese, 'Yes, exactly what we need.'

An older Thai man of 60, Teerasak Krit, looked at the pocket armoury, whistled his appreciation, and began placing the guns on a large table. After half a dozen such deliveries in as many months he had his routine down, even if dealing in weapons like this was anything but routine. Handling the new firearms with care, he examined each one, sometimes placing the stock on his shoulder to check the sighting then placing it on the table before moving to the next. Satisfied after 40 minutes of this he placed the last guns into two wooden boxes then fastened locks to each before moving them beneath a trap door.

Speaking in a northern dialect of Thai he asked, 'When will the next shipment come?'

Sirawit mulled over the question as he stroked his chin with his thumb and forefinger. His life depended on a successful outcome and giving the correct response to words or actions was more vital than ever. Supplying Myanmar rebels as they battled slavers was a risky occupation to say the least. Yes, Po was dead, but never again would an attack be launched in Thailand. If he hadn't died, Sirawit would have killed Po himself. They had to be more careful. All arms of the government would be after them now.

As with so much wrongdoing in Asia, getting caught was the worst crime. It didn't bear thinking about and in the lead-up to the inevitable execution there would be days of unspeakable torture as his enemies, including the police, tried to get him to inform. If there was time, and there was so little time, a bullet to the head would save Sirawit from this ordeal. Helping to free those enslaved by Crime Lord Subcontractors was an even riskier proposition but doing nothing was unthinkable.

'Soon, maybe tonight. More likely tomorrow. The whole consignment will be at the border by next week.'

'Good, we need to take precautions,' Teerasak said, alternating between Thai and Burmese. Once a student at the University of Yangon, he wanted to be of use every way he could. English words like 'Okay' and 'Stop' even 'Fuck you' were sprinkled like turmeric on stewed duck.

Sirawit tapped his fingers on the table adding to the tension already thrumming like power lines.

'Are you sure this is the best place to bring the guns?' he asked looking around at the room directly behind a public drinking house.

'We are, what they call, hiding in plain sight. Every warehouse around the city is checked for drugs, for guns. We deliver here and hold before sending the weapons where they are needed in Burma. This will all be gone by tonight,' he said in accented Thai.

Sirawit nodded his understanding. He knew someday they would be raided but not anytime soon and not when he was here if he could help it.

Teerasak, satisfied there was an understanding moved to the next phase of the process.

He peeled off 400,000 baht in soiled, low denomination, non-consecutive notes that were almost impossible to trace and when spent wouldn't attract notice. The men had been through this before and would do it again for as long as the struggle went on. In some ways, it was a war that hadn't stopped since World War 2. Friction between the northern neighbours of Myanmar, Cambodia and Thailand, although downplayed for political reasons on the world stage, would not end any time soon. In fact, the Golden Triangle was forever in turmoil. Going by the fire fights of just the last few weeks, he knew for certain the war over human trafficking, drugs, and territory would go on and on. It was a hydra-headed war with State and criminal forces battling over drugs, human trafficking, and body parts to name just a few. Armies, States and crime gangs in the tri-nations areas fought on both sides of the law. Parties would switch sides to gain advantage or to stay in the game.

'I will see you at this time next week at exactly 11 in the morning.'

Teerasak waited for a response, and satisfied with a nod and a word, he went on.

'We know where the concentration camp for the hostages and slaves is and we know when the overseer Sao Ne Saw is there. He is cruel and a murderer. He calls himself a General, but he is not. There are real Generals involved from both Burma and Thailand and there is danger there. Clearly, with exposure even the once-mighty Generals will melt into the night. This I promise,' he said with a raised finger to underline his commitment.

'This man, Sao Ne Saw, shall pay for his crimes. Timing is important. He comes and goes, sometimes vanishes for months on end. We are not yet ready to take him on. But ready or not we will take him on soon. People are dying and we cannot afford to allow this to go on. The daughter of one villager in Kachin, a woman named Zhang, was captured and killed after trying to cross the border a few days ago. If they know we are coming they could kill everyone there, and in the factories just over the border.'

He paused as they exchanged grim smiles. Death dogged this garrison world like a black crow on the shoulder, it was never far away and could take you without warning.

'You know what to do. No large purchases, no bargirls, no talk. Forget friends and family, this will keep them saf*er*, even if they will never be completely safe. Not until we make a free State. Stay indoors and keep to yourself.' Teerasak spoke with a blank face as if masking his expressions, hiding feelings made him less visible when they disappeared into the night when darkness came. Too many people were gone for either one of them to make mistakes they couldn't afford. There was no alternative and of course doing nothing was worse than the death that came soon enough.

'Yes, I value my freedom as much as anyone. I will not be diverted from our task. My life, and the life of many people, depends on it,' said Sirawit

The elder said, 'You need to value it even more than your own life. You have much more to lose, including your family.'

Sirawit smiled. No one knew more than he how high the stakes were. No doubt it was true they could take away his family, put them through unspeakable pain and nameless horror. But he would not let this happen. Sirawit would make this evil this terror work for him and he would stay alert, alive to any danger. A hidden tiger in the jungle watching with keen eyes, ready to spring into the offensive with tooth and claw. The pressure was something he made to work from him to boost his awareness. With weakness comes strength, when you believe.

CHAPTER 13

After breakfast, Brodie and Grace went shopping at the markets along Beach Road and then the unthinkable happened. After buying a fetching silk blouse, Grace caught Brodie eyeing an attractive Thai woman. She was almost the tallest Thai lady he'd seen outside of the she-male *katoeys* that were everywhere. The long-limbed lady had one leg stretched up on some concrete steps and it was perfect. Smooth, toned and ready for anything Brodie thought, and today his thoughts were transparent. It was hard not to look at the beauty of clearly available bodies. Young women could be seen in every direction. Beautiful bodies were part of the scenery. They were on vacation, right? Trying to avert his gaze he couldn't help eyeballing her. She was tall and all legs, yet those legs were the kind men wanted to climb. Brodie saw that she stood out from the crowds of bargirls and a short dress teamed with impossibly high heels added to the effect.

Grace frowned as he tried not to notice with an abrupt turn of the head that was fooling no one. The gawking too obvious for Grace's liking, her frown lines expanded into deep furrows of sheer unhappiness. Caught, he held out his palms in a mute, disarming plea for forgiveness. His partner gave him a scowl in return. The mystery woman was a stunner and hard not to notice in a place like this with delectable ladies everywhere. Now with his back to the eye candy, Grace tilted her head with a knowing look towards an ancient man being pushed in a wheelchair by a lady young enough to be his granddaughter.

'Keep perving on girls like her and you'll end up like him, Brodie. Look at her, she's young enough to be his granddaughter.'

Trying to deflect the coming attack he said in an innocent tone that was fooling no one, 'Now why would I want to look at anyone but you, Grace?'

In a calculated if calmer tone she said, 'Well at least you're making the right noises.' She paused then finished with, 'Even if I don't believe you.'

In an effort to move past this he steered her towards a string of bars. They kept up the drinking in a kind of pub crawl that was new to Grace then ended up going to the famed *Temple of Truth*. The large building was in pagoda traditional Asian style and was a multi-faith place of worship of the tourist kind. An elephant nudged her with his trunk and Grace hopped on for a fee as Brodie snapped stills and footage. A quick look showed winning images that would shore up happy memories. The place had bad memories for Brodie from another lifetime as if the place was full of ghosts. As they walked hand in hand through elaborate stone carvings of mythic Hindu and Sikh, he made a running commentary.

Pointing to a figure striking an impossible pose with one leg over the shoulder, the other circled by a serpent he said, 'Now this one defied all medical wisdom of the day. It's all here in the Temple of Truth.'

'Alright, you know so much, so what is the truth, Brodie, I'd really like to know.'

'Well, seeing how we're playing truth or lies, here goes.'

'I didn't really want to come here, you know. I know this place, I've been here before.'

She blinked and he knew she was thinking hard on a witty rejoinder. He knew her. She couldn't help herself. It was what she did. It didn't take long.

'Alright let me get this straight, it was my idea. I suppose it was also my idea to want to patch things up.'

He hesitated this was getting into dangerous territory. Thinking of what to say there was a long silence. She broke first.

'If you didn't want to come here Brodie you're free to leave at any time.' She turned her back slightly to him and he wondered what would come next. She was as volatile as a sea squall. Enough for small craft warnings with him as the little boat bobbing on a raging sea.

She turned to leave and he said, 'Come on, honey. You have to learn how to take a joke.'

Standing with her hands on her hips she said, 'Well, I'm not laughing.' Somehow, the shaky couple made it back to a bar.

Further down the coast at Jomtien Beach, men in casual gear unloaded human cargo from two trucks. Myint and the other captives were quickly toileted and showered fully clothed in public conveniences on the beach front.

The guards had on Thai military uniforms which were credible considering some of the men were enlisted in that army or the one north of the border.

Without the circulation restraints, Myint felt a sense of release, however fleeting that would be. Within the hour the men were put on inflatable power boats and headed out to sea. Forty minutes later they were in deep waters in the Gulf of Thailand. Through the darkness of cover all seven-rubber craft met in a calm sea where three large fishing trawlers were clustered together. One man, crazed by fear and fatigue diving into the water where he began to flail about. He was shot from two directions first through the temple and exiting through an eye that exploded then in the face. Sinking into the inky sea and onto eternity. A muffled voice somehow disconnected at least in body, called out as though already faraway, 'I will come back, I will come back.'

Unable to cry, the deprivations had soaked that up even if he knew his soul was intact, Myint prayed for the stranger's soul and in so doing paid respect to all the lost souls whose journey he witnessed. Such raw death promised afterlife as if they never died.

CHAPTER 14

The rice tasted meatier today and Mon wondered what was in it. When the meat was too rotten she only ate the rice. Getting dysentery could be fatal, as the small graves near the forests showed anyone foolish enough to forget. She wiped her mouth with the back of her hand then began to separate the clumps of rice. Two tiny rods poked though the cluster and she made a face as she realised it was the head of a cockroach. She spat some gruel on the floor and saw a guard make a move towards her. Instinctively, she put a handful of tainted rice in her mouth and playacted someone enjoying their meal. She made satisfied noises while rubbing her belly and it worked. As if convinced, the armed guard with a rifle slung across his shoulders stopped and turned around. Another truck arrived that night and she didn't want to be on it. It was a mystery where the trucks took the prisoners and she wondered about the high-ranking officers that came and went. She knew her people were being sold and knew she would do something about this when she broke free from these cages. Dying was better than being treated like animals and sold like cattle.

Mon kept eating and she gave a wink to Aom. The rice was rotten, barely enough to feed to the pigs but just enough to keep her alive, or so she hoped.

Every day brought new challenges and threats, like the tiger that rampaged into the camp before being shot by the guards. The beast lay on its back, fangs bared, claws extended, as it gave one last growl. Mon cried for the tiger and she cried for herself. She would not go the way of this brave and magnificent animal. The tiger, too, would come back as a green forest ghost. No unjust killed would be forgotten by the spirits of rivers and trees and mountains, and not least by the *nats* of wasted Maung. Mon ate the rice one piece at a time. Sometimes she threw in cockroaches and ants to build up the protein in the mess they called food. Some were disgusted by this but some of the doubters were no longer with them. Anything that helped her survive, even the rat's head that poked out of a gangrenous broth, was thrown down her throat before the vile taste shot through her senses.

She had no intention of finding out the long-term nutrition value of tainted meat and doctored rice. She wouldn't be here long enough to find out.

That night she and Aom crept out of their hammocks as the barracks guard dozed. These men were brutal but lazy and when the overseer wasn't looking would steal minutes of sleep here and there. On starvation wages themselves, the men took what they could get including sexual favours for leniency. They too were prisoners, although she could never show pity for the men who had killed her friends and girls she worked close with. Even the devil and his ghosts could not forgive that and they would all surely die a horrible death.

Higher up, including all the officers and one man whom she guessed was a Thai General on his rare visits, were fat like pigs. The General didn't have the uniform of People's Revolutionary Army and he didn't look Burmese he looked Thai. Thai or Burmese, these men were pigs. They were drunk with arrogance to think they could cage her and Aom and all the other Mons and Aoms. Any chance the guards got to sleep was taken up on or off duty. Like the inmates, they too were dying. Unlike the inmates, they couldn't be punished in the physical sense. Being terminated, sacked, was rare too. The bosses couldn't risk letting them go because they knew too much. Of course, she expected some of the men were killed, or disappeared, from sight. It could be they were all prisoners, even if their guards were prisoners that ruled and killed those under them; in turn deserving death themselves.

In this hell, everyone was guilty. The only question was one of degree.

Mon was ready to pay for her sins, in fact they were paid in full. She was ready, these bandits and devils were not. All this would matter when they joined the spirit world to become ghosts. Evils spirits and those with good karma would clash and she knew the good would win. Even an evil man could have goodness inside, yet this would not change his fate. Occasionally, some of the men like the kind-hearted Mung who would give extra rations to the women he liked, disappeared, presumed murdered. Feeling sorry for any of the keepers, tormenters was out of the question, of course.

As they crept through the underside of the long house, they looked for an opening in the teak floorboards and finally saw it. One of the sentry boxes was unattended and she guessed it was because one of the guards wanted to pass water. It was an open secret the guards drank while on duty and frequent trips to the woods or the urinal was almost unavoidable.

She heard a guard call out to another in Burmese, 'What time is it?'

Then hearing the answer, 'It's three thirty-five,' they continued the slow crawling under creaking floorboards. At the end of the bunkhouse they moved out into the open but stayed concealed by trees and palms. Black shadows disappeared under the glare of search lights as they huddled together in the vegetation. Insects made clicking sounds and the plants vibrated with life as though struggling to tell her something. With another hour or two before dawn there was time to make their way at this pace. Dun-coloured clothes were a perfect camouflage in the thick brush that edged the forest. Then, a shaft of intense illumination from a search light had the two woman ducking their heads beneath a stand of wide-leafed plants. They were almost at the edge of the thick forest. A large Ironwood tree loomed overhead giving more cover. Beyond that was a thick stand of bamboo she knew they could hide in. Then, the sound of a whistle, the same sound that signalled their capture so long ago. She knew it was time to act. Mon stood and took Aom's hand.

'We must run. Run as fast as you can,' she said in Thai, then Burmese.

As shots rang out they ran towards the woods. Aom stumbled and fell before Mon pulled her up and the two limped into the cover of trees and brush. Then a bright light, a white ball of fire hovered in the air.

'What is that?' asked Aom her voice hoarse with fear.

Mon looked at the apparition as it gave a soft, buzzing sound. Then it spun in circles and disappeared through a stand of trees. She could see a small figure walking. It seemed familiar until she realised it was the same limping walk of her friend's ten-year-old son Auk San.

She called out in desperation, in hope, 'Is that you, Auk? Where have you been? What have you been doing?'

The figure turned towards them and smiled. His face was powdered and he had the milky ephemeral look of a ghost, a *nat*.

Accepting him for the spirit he was and knowing she must keep her composure she shouted in a voice cracking with emotion, 'Can you help us, son. Can you show us the way?'

The spirit of the murdered child gave a slow, eerie smile and pointed towards a stand of Ironwood trees.

'Go this way, Aom. Go with her, Mon. This is the path to safety, the key to your freedom.'

His pale face, buzzing and flickering like an image on a TV with reception fading in and out gave a crooked smile. Then the ghost of Aom's son lost definition and turned to smoke, to fog, like a dawn mist on the Irrawaddy thick enough to vanish a long boat in an instant. Auk disappeared.

Walking at a quick pace that soon became a trot as they heard gunfire Aom called to her lost son, 'I will never forget you Auk. I am proud of you and will do all I can to bring you peace and free your tired soul from wandering.'

Mon, with tears in her eyes added, 'The beauty of your soul shall live forever.'

Moving quickly Aom and Mon found the hidden trail her *nat* son had directed the escapees to. These men, this army of killers and rapists, didn't know this country like these two villagers. The men swimming in bad karma misled to their doomed fate were clumsy bears in the woods clawing at air while Mon and Aom made a stealthy escape like a fox in the woods.

CHAPTER 15

The reconciled lovers had moved on to the lush *Ko Lan* island, just offshore in Pattaya Bay, where they lazed in the sun, in an effort, to forget about recent disturbing events. He stood before a Buddhist temple and moving his clasped hands upwards and bowed in a *wai*. Looking puzzled, Grace asked, 'What was that for? Good karma?'

Brodie gave a smile and said, 'Sure, why not? We could all do with a bit of good karma, right?' She smiled in understanding and did the same as if it were an Asian version of knocking on wood or throwing salt over your shoulder.

They drank. They argued. They made love. Only to fight all over again. Outside of an actual Muay Thai boxing ring, it was Brodie's lover who was the reigning champ. After a long day, there was a stony silence that lasted all the way back to the mainland and the hotel. Karma wasn't coming their way yet.

Later, in the early evening, near the nightclub district called Walking Street they were sprayed with blue coloured water by laughing men on a slow-moving tankard. Drenched, Grace said, 'So, what is this? Some kind of fertility God ritual or something to piss off the tourists?'

Smiling Brodie said, 'Close. It's a celebration of the Thai New Year called *Songkran*. It lasts for days and it's bigger here than anywhere else in the country.'

He watched as a bunch of pissed British lager lads sprayed and squirted each other and anyone close by. Although laughing, the obviously steroid-taking weightlifter's buffed abs signalled they were ready to argue the point with anyone on the receiving end.

'Water fights, we've had a few of our own.'

As he spoke, a boy of about ten blasted Brodie with green liquid from a wild looking orange toy laser gun. As he laughed with the playacting assassin, Brodie was left wondering if the kid would have used the real thing in another time and place, like the kind of child mercenaries that used to terrorise villagers including their parents from here to Africa. Nearby Kampuchea came to mind, but he thought better of sharing that with an already anxious, if not hopelessly strung out, Grace.

'All this water… isn't there a drought?'

He nodded agreement then said, 'Yes, but the Thais and tourists love it. Lots of it's polluted according to Google, so don't get it in your eyes. It's a holiday, everybody loves a holiday, right?'

Without answering directly, she made a show of examining some dresses hanging on a rack just out of the line of fire. Then, satisfied the loud patterned frocks weren't for her, Grace turned back to the spectacle on the street. An army personnel carrier, its surface covered with laughing, spraying children, rolled past. Even the military got into the act.

While they watched an elderly man scowl at the unwanted drenching she said, 'Maybe the rich travellers pretend to like it to keep their girls on side.'

'Sure, what happens in Pattaya stays in Pattaya.'

At once he realised it was the wrong thing to say and followed it up with, 'We're on a different journey. We are making memories, beautiful memories.'

'Just like the brochures say, right?'

'Yeah, something like that. No everything like that,' he said in echo of her earlier sound bite.

As they walked past the girlie bars with bikini-clad women or men dressed as women she stopped and confronted Brodie. 'Tell me, lover. Is this town one big brothel or what, Brodie?'

Dodging the question he said, 'It is what it is. I wouldn't call it that and I never came here for that,' he lied. 'Almost all these ladies send back money to their families in remote villages. It's been going on since World War 2, certainly since Vietnam imploded back in the day.'

'I can't believe it. You took me on vacation to a city-wide whorehouse?' she persisted.

'I didn't say that. Those are your words, Grace. To me, the place is fascinating; a micro-world unto itself. It's unique, a unicorn.'

She gave him a baffled look then said, 'Why are we here, Brodie?'

He left the question hanging in the air while pretending to be interested in carved elephants laid out on the sidewalk.

Later, after tacos in a passable Mexican restaurant off Soi 7, there was room for last drinks before the witching hour.

'One more?' he asked, raising a stubbie of Tiger beer.

Shaking her head, she said, 'I don't want to get drunk darling.' She paused then stood up, her body slightly swaying in the breeze like a ship's masthead in a gale.

They both laughed. The words didn't match the picture.

'Well, at least not too drunk.'

With a smile he said, 'No, we wouldn't want that, would we?'

They laughed and had two more beers. They could do what they wanted. After all, what happens in Thailand…

They called it a night and while not exiled to the couch, they slept on opposite sides of the bed. In the morning, they decided to go their separate ways *to give her a chance to go shopping*—or something like that.

'I thought you'd changed, Brodie. Truth is, you haven't changed at all. We need a bit of space you know?'

'Sure. I know, take the day off. Do some shopping. Splurge. Have some alone time. Whatever, I'm easy. We're here for a good time—no, we're here for a *fantastic* time, remember?'

'Yes, I remember and yes we can.'

While she went off on a spending spree or whatever it was she wanted to do, Brodie repaired to a bar near Soi 7, although not that particular notorious street of hookers and dipsomaniacs.

Brodie chatted with a lady from Esan, north of Bangkok, a rural, struggling area that provided many of the women in this huge brothel of a city. Her skin had a darker hue than most and she was achingly beautiful. Shinawatra, the glamourous former Prime Minister, now a fugitive from rough justice, came from there and he had always had a crush on her.

Brodie saw the lady who caught his eye the day before. She represented danger to his relationship, something he was up for.

Moving close to her he said, 'Excuse me, I couldn't help noticing your beautiful hair.'

Looking shy, she smiled. She didn't say *thank you*, or *get lost* for that matter. It could be she'd heard that come on, or much worse, a million times over, but she wasn't saying. With her lustrous black hair and attractive rail-thin body she was perfection. She smiled and flounced her hair.

Yes, this lady was young and beautiful like so many in these teeming streets. Still there was something about her above and beyond the rest.

Not knowing what to say or even if she could speak English, he quickly opened his hands to show there was nothing there then reached behind her ear to retrieve a 50 baht coin. She laughed in appreciation, putting her hand to her mouth in a show of modesty like a Harajuku Geisha.

She giggled and laughed at his jokes. Brodie did most of the talking and almost forgot she was only humouring him. It was all playacting, just part of the show. Somehow, this woman helped him forget that. Just as she kissed him on the cheek, Grace walked by. Brodie didn't notice her at first but his new friend did and motioned with her head.

Brodie turned to see a clearly unhappy girlfriend. The shock made his face red hot, hot enough in tropical Thailand to make him sweat in nanoseconds. The thought *nothing good will come of this* gave him a shot of adrenaline, the natural neurochemical for flight or fight. With a lot of explaining to do he had to scramble, think fast before it all blew up.

Shaking her head Grace said, 'Oh my God. She's young enough to be your daughter. If this was Sydney you'd be arrested.'

Speechless, his head felt like a furnace. Not content she went on, now directing her barbs to the Thai lady.

'Playing grown-ups are we, sweetheart? You almost had me fooled with all that makeup and the high heels.'

The bargirl who had introduced herself as Chailai frowned and said, 'Sorry, no English. I no understand.'

'Oh, you understand, sweetie. Stay the fuck away from him.'

Brodie frowned. This wasn't in the script. His new friend didn't deserve this, no one did.

'No need to be unkind, Grace. I was only talking and having a drink until you got back.'

'Really? You had no idea when I was going to get back. I figure you two were waiting for an opportunity. What have you two been up to while I've been gone? Steal an hour away in a hot sheet hotel room?'

'Come on, Grace, that's not fair. She doesn't deserve this.'

He blinked hard. Grace could be moody, even bitter but this was new.

'And what about me, Brodie. What do I deserve?'

With her beautiful long, black hair and legs to match, Chailai was unfazed. She didn't smile or frown. Perhaps she'd been through this movie before. It was easy to see how she could steal husbands, boyfriends, whole lives. Grace stared down her enemy. This charming lady of the night strolled through life picking up human collectibles along the way. She seemed enigmatic, as though all the secrets in the world could be found for the asking. She gave him a wink and it was all he could do to not go over to her and make a pass.

He didn't and knew he would regret it. Such is life, he was here on a mission. This wasn't the time to deviate from the plan. Not when he was so close to success. It was complicated. Chailai responded by stepping away.

'Grace, I'm sorry. Really I am.'

'Yes, well you will be, lover boy, if you keep this up.'

As if retrieving an item from lost and found, Grace took him by the hand and jerked him away from the young and the beautiful bar hostess.

"Grace, let me—' he began before Grace cut him off. 'I don't want to know, Brodie. You knew what you were doing so don't try and bullshit me, alright.'

CHAPTER 16

Somehow, the next few days were tolerable, if not without tension. Quite a bit of tension in fact, as he watched her pack and unpack bags then make up with kisses, only to break up with tears. He found it hard to take and after a short while, neither of them could take it. There was another trial separation of sorts then another hit at making up. Brodie was willing to try anything to avoid a humiliating break up thousands of miles from home.

Anything.

The two took a break to, 'Do their own thing,' as Grace put it. Brodie didn't like the sound of that but, with no choice, pocketed his doubts and settled into an old-style English pub, complete with half timbers and a Scouse barkeep. The room was cheap enough to take without blowing the budget.

Out shopping alone, Grace strolled down narrow Soi 3 past hotels and a 7/11—which even here could be found everywhere. Anyone really homesick could camp out in any number of McDonalds or KFCs or Burger Kings that littered the city. What was once a lazy fishing village pre-century, now a crowd-pulling consumer sex tourist mecca in a country swarming in them. Scooters buzzed past dangerously close like killer hornets on the prowl, some with three or more passengers. Grace pulled a newly purchased genuine leather Vuitton handbag close to her chest. She recalled the posters warning of theft at the airport. Feeling a sudden sense of alarm, she watched for bag snatchers and kidnappers.

'Grace, is that you?' She turned in surprise to a familiar voice and was hugged by a youngish woman with oversized earrings and bracelets that glittered under the hot July sun.

'Lisa, what are you doing here?' It had been years. Once old college best friends, it felt reassuring to run into her in this strange place and strange time.

She smiled and said, 'Same thing you are, to have the time of my life. See any suitable men?'

'It's wonderful to catch up with you.' Lisa smiled as Grace looked on with interest. They were once besties but someone got between them once and it wasn't a man. There was a pause in the conversation before the long-lost friend asked, 'So, how is the new boyfriend? Spoiling you I hope.'

Grace winced and replied, 'I'm too old to have a boyfriend but my partner Brodie is fine. I don't know if he's the one but more about that later.' They laughed together in the easy way friends do. Grace let out a sigh of relief.

She was feeling better already. Their re-acquaintance felt like an omen.

Lisa kept a level gaze as if this wouldn't do. *It's me you're talking to, was* the implication then she actually said it like Grace knew she would.

'Come on, Grace. It's me you're talking to. I see pain, I feel pain.'

Grace gave a rueful smile, proud of her mindreading skills. 'Well, that means you're either a faith healer or a doctor and I know you're neither.'

They stopped at a restaurant that opened out to the sidewalk. After ordering they chatted until the light seafood meal arrived.

There was another long pause as Lisa moved her salad across the plate for want of anything better to do. Like many dieters she often played with her food without eating it.

'Alright, alright I give up. He's alright, just alright, and he's all I have. I'm happy.'

Another long silence then Grace said to a silent and still sceptical Lisa, 'Really, I am, Lisa. There is life after breaking up.'

'You mean you're breaking up?' she asked with a little too much eagerness for Grace's liking.

Shaking her head and smiling Grace responded with, 'Look I'm alright, I'm fine.'

Sounding unconvinced her friend said, 'Alright, I believe you… thousands wouldn't.'

Her faux happiness now established, the friends fell into each other's company. It was what they used to do before the world changed. Moving on, they shopped together until the consumer urge was slaked with bundles of dresses, blouses and jewellery.

Looking at each other Lisa said, 'You know, we're never even going to wear half of this stuff.'

Grace gave a smile and said, 'I know, it's the retail therapy I need.'

'Don't we all?' her long lost but newly found friend said. Spent, they gravitated to a western hotel like horses resting after a long journey with food and drink. For an hour, they moved from one bar to the next as the sight of decrepit old men with women who looked like they could pass for underage charges proved more disgusting than expected. As they stepped back onto Beach Road they could see the narrow beach curve around towards Walking Street and the Pattaya sign on the hillside. As tourists, some speaking Russian, dipped in and out of the impure waters of the gulf of Thailand, the two Americans chatted. To Grace, meeting Lisa here was so miraculous as to be a revelation. She too confessed being lured there with a cut-price offer over fares and accommodation. Even the rich, or nearly rich, had to economise.

'When I got off the plane a Dow Mueang Airport I wondered, *what the hell am I doing here*?' 'You too, Lisa?' Grace said to shared laughter.

There was a pause before she finished the thought with, 'Seeing you here has made the whole trip worthwhile.' 'Me too,' Grace said as she kissed her fellow American on the cheek.

As they browsed some of the shops and stalls where Lisa bought a pair of Jimmy Choo shoes, the new best friends kicked along conversation that touched on more intimate matters. This was the breathless, staunch girlfriend she remembered from the days just out of bubble gum and braces through to their first marriages.

'Brodie got me here on false pretences really. I thought I was going to Phuket and here I am in this swamp.'

"I know, I'm only here for a boob job. It's cheaper than Bangkok or Phuket,' Lisa confessed as Grace paid closer attention to her friend's chest than usual.

'You're kidding,' she said before looking down at her own modest breasts to say, 'Maybe I'm due for one myself.

A girl could always do with a bit of upkeep.'

Shaking her head Lisa said, 'You're fine. And as far as the upkeep goes, I always say marry well and the rest will fall into place.'

They laughed and the quasi-depression lifted away lifted like fog under the noon sun.

The friends drank and talked, their day had been enjoyable and filled with laughter. Then, a terrific explosion. Chaos. The vast room was instantly filled with the smell of cordite and obscured by gas and atomised plasterboard. Grace found herself on the floor, her ears roaring and deaf to intelligible speech. She felt underwater or in some kind of suspended animation.

Within seconds, the room was crowded with soldiers and police. Shouting in Thai and broken English, Grace and her friend were shepherded out by officious uniformed men. Then, a burst of machine gunfire and several soldiers were wounded, some fatally. Blood and tissue spattered over tables and walls. Grace wanted to scream but couldn't, or at least she couldn't hear herself scream. Both ladies staggered around, their clothes whitened with dust and debris and wet with blood. The dead lay in heaps like piles of bloody rags.

'Go, go, go! This is not safe!' shouted a military man with the insignia and commanding presence of a high-ranking officer. In no need of convincing, they followed directions and the couple run outside to a street choked with firetrucks, ambulances and army and police vans and vehicles. In a state of shock, and for want of an alternative, the shocked women drifted towards another bar.

'God, we could have been killed in there.'

Lisa waited for a response and when none came from a shell-shocked Grace, she went on.

'I'm sure they'll all see this back home.'

Grace put her drink down on the table hard enough to make a sharp sound. 'I don't want to discuss it. People died in there today.'

With brimming eyes and ashamed, Lisa said in a croaky voice, 'I know, I'm sorry. Really I am.'

CHAPTER 17

To collect her thoughts and perhaps her damaged sense of identity, Grace took refuge in the familiar surroundings of a Starbucks on Beach Road. She wasn't ready to face Brodie. Not yet. Sensing her sorrow, the young Thai Man making her latte tried to cheer her up.

'Mai pen rai', it'll be alright. We say this in Thailand. We want to relax, it will be alright.' The Starbucks employee explained after her question about why Thai seemed so happy without the material safety net Australians, if not most Americans, enjoyed.

'Thank you. I guess it's true that money can't buy happiness.'

Not even sure if that was quite right she closed her eyes, wanting to concentrate on that thought and make it happen in this town running on cash flow. Thinking hard she frowned. Then an idea blew through her head like a white squall hitting a calm sea. A bit of mindfulness was overdue. She visualised a perfect white beach, the kind she'd thought she was coming to. Only it wasn't. The kind of high octane beach that featured in every big production movie ever located in this *Land of Smiles*. Pattaya wasn't it. It never made it. Not yet. Maybe never after the last catastrophe.

She stirred her coffee. The fifth one. Alone after Lisa flew home in panic yesterday, Grace was lost in Starbucks limbo, the coffee shop crowded with other psychic drifters from the Anglosphere and more. She contemplated her future. There didn't seem much to look forward to, not much to hold onto.

A man approached the table. Looking to be late middle age, he was the wrong side of 45 but it didn't matter. She looked up and smiled her best.

'It's a beautiful day, isn't it?' he asked in a baritone North American accent.

She smiled. It sounded like a pick-up line, a version of, 'Hello, is it me you're looking for?' Maybe Lionel Richie was about to pop up with his grand piano.

In a faraway tone she said, 'Yes, it is. Although nothing I can't get back home.'

'Home, that wouldn't be California, would it?' he asked in a distinct Californian drawl.

'No, Sydney, Australia. Lately, the Gold Coast if you really want to know. But yes, I used to live there in another lifetime.' Grace paused then said, 'San Francisco back when it was still San Francisco.'

Giving a winning smile that got her smiling he said, 'Sure, I know what you mean.'

She squinted at him and said, 'Don't tell me, L.A., right? Maybe Silicon Valley?'

'Ah, the mythical Silicon Valley. No you were right the first time. L.A. it is. I have a place in Brentwood.'

Digesting that she tried hard not to look awed. 'Brentwood, isn't that next to Hollywood?' Grace asked in a tone betraying how much she was impressed.

He chuckled and said, 'No, not exactly. And Hollywood has seen better days. At least when you're talking about a place to live.'

Looking slightly puzzled she said, 'Yes, well the studios are still pumping out tent-pole flicks.'

'Yeah that's about all we get nowadays. Bigger isn't always better.' He paused then said, 'Anyway, enough about that. I'm sure the place will do fine without us.'

'Us?' she asked in a tone as if considering the personal pronoun in a different way for the first time.

With a wide smile he said, 'I mean you, and me, and everyone here on holiday or settled here,' then gestured with his hand going back and forth. 'I'm sorry, I haven't yet introduced myself. My name is Dane Van Dyke.'

She gave a warm smile. 'Pleased to meet you, Dane. My name is Grace Winters.' The two looked at each other in a kind of mutual appraisal. The attraction was unmistakeable.

'Look, I have a visit to the mountain top Buddha on my agenda. It's a beautiful sight. Would you like to come?'

'Well, my partner is getting some dental work done', she lied then embellished the lie with, 'actually extensive dental work. He'll be there for hours, so I can't see why not.'

The ride to the top was in a late model cab not a *Tuk or a sentego*, a luxury by local standards.

He kissed her on the cheek as they parted and pressed a business card in her hand. She looked at the embossed card with a hologram. Dane Van Dyke, Trader in Commodities and Services.

Looking up from the card she asked, 'Bangkok? I thought you said your offices were in Rodeo Drive?'

Nodding he said, 'They are. This is my Thai card, I could give you my Stateside card.'

'To add to my collection? Yeah it might be fun to show my friends back home.' There was a long pause before both said almost in unison, 'Back home in Sydney.'

'I don't actually live in Sydney anymore, I live on the Gold Coast. Know where that is?'

With a stereotypical high wattage, sunny California smile, he said, 'A beautiful place, a very desirable place to live.

As a matter of fact, I've done business there.'

The fellow American moved his chair closer to hers. She encouraged him with a smile, happy to let him do all the talking. Too soon, they parted with promises to meet up again and she left wondering if they ever would.

'You know I don't usually seek out Americans—' Grace began.

'And so…' He stared at her for a long moment. She finished the thought with, 'But with you I'll make an exception.'

Dane got up and pulled Grace in close to give her a kiss on the forehead.

'I like the sound of that, Grace.'

She gave him an approving look. This new man in her life certainly had excellent timing.

CHAPTER 18

'When did you come here?' he asked the reed-thin woman before it was translated into Burmese. The lady introduced to him as Mon sat beside Chailai, her translator, and was wide-eyed in hypervigilance as if expecting to be handed over to the authorities at any moment. Nervy body language showed a person who knew it didn't pay to be caught unaware, to be caught sleeping while your world was on fire. Villages were destroyed, families lost if you were caught out. Rest was not a luxury she could afford.

'I came here a week ago. It is a place where I have friends,' she said in halting Burmese as she looked to Chailai for reassurance. Tears welled up in her eyes and she screwed them tight as if to ward off a flood of emotional baggage.

Brodie stayed quiet not wanting to be the cause of any more pain.

Mon's sister in escape and quest for freedom, Aom, sat with downcast eyes. It was clear she had no wish to speak and would let her sister do all the speaking for her. Barely trusting of the other Maung or Burmese in town, she didn't know what to make of these strangers.

'When the army began to torch the villages, we thought there must be some mistake. Sometimes we saw tanks and planes in the area like when the army wanted to show its strength. But now the army was attacking us and we didn't know why.' Mon wept as she continued, 'I will never know why they do this. My father fought with Burma Army.'

Between choking sobs, Aom said, 'This is unforgiveable outrage. The army is murdering its own people.'

Mon put her hand on Aom's as if to reassure her stricken friend then went on. The lady from Myanmar spoke her piece in Burmese as Brodie listened for the translation.

Chailai's translation skills seemed to be improving by the minute, something that made English-only Brodie feel wanting. Wasn't it true that native, if you like, first-language English speakers, were lousy foreign language speakers? Everyone spoke English, didn't they?

Putting his hands on his chin, a mannerism that for Brodie came with intense thinking, he listened carefully.

'The Maung,' Chailai said, using the Thai term for Burmese, 'were cruel to their own people, not just the Muslims or Rohingya or Kachin, my people. Villages in Rakhine were destroyed by the army so the Rohingya were forced to leave, but the Ron were part of Burma. In history there were revolts, but ethnic cleansing never in the east in Shan, Kayah, or Kachin states.'

Aom, quiet and almost invisible squatting on the floor, pulled on Mon's sleeve and spoke in Burmese.

Chailai waited until she was finished then said, 'The military men give excuse that they are looking for Rohingya or Mon or Kachin terrorists fleeing through Shan and the other Border States. They blamed the Kachin Liberation Army but that was a lie. The army is not a real army it is the ghost of an army. Those not caught on the Myanmar side are rounded up into slave camps in Burma or Thailand—whoever wants to claim them. The Generals share, but this peace shall not last either.'

As she listened to the English version of her nightmare, tears began to well in Mon's eyes. The two freed Burmese slaves looked stricken by the bleak vision they had outlined. It was too much for the more vulnerable Aom.

As Aom began to weep she said in word bites translated along the way, 'We never thought we would be hunted, burnt out, enslaved. Never.'

Her interpreting job over, Chailai said, 'Ma twe tah kya bi,' then in English, 'Long time, no see.' 'Min-ga-la-ba'

The two survivors said as one, 'Min-ga-la-ba.'

Chailai gave a brave smile that reflected the sad smiles of her Burmese sisters and said, '*Min-ga-la-ba* means they wish us good night.'

Brodie *waied* them with clasped hands. 'And I hope to see you again soon,' Brodie said he shook the limp hands of both women. He made his exit into the hectic night life of the Beach City or Bangkok

Lite as some called it. They would meet again, he was sure of that. Walking alone along Pattayasaisong, or Second Road, he could hear live music. Going inside he saw a Thai lady with heavy makeup singing a tune, 'Walking in Memphis' that spoke to him.

'Saw da Ghos a Elvis, on Union avanoo, follow him up to Gates a Graceland then I watch he walk right through, now secure not see him, they just hover round his tomb….walkin wid Elvis with my fee ten fee oh da Beach rd.'

He clapped his approval and smiled to himself before ordering another beer. The lyrics were out both by accident and design, yet it was a touching take on a soulful tune. It was as if she knew the words phonetically but didn't quite get the meaning. This torch singer was creative, filling in the gaps as she went along. He smiled to himself. You didn't have to be a second-language English speaker to make the right noises and not know what you were talking about. He thought of the Ghost of Elvis and the ghosts Chailai and her friends paid homage to. Around midnight he walked back to the hotel, the altered song ear worm looping over and over in his head. The Ghost of Elvis.

CHAPTER 19

Later, after several Facetime phone calls, the first of which she ignored, Grace and her fellow American met up to have secret drinks at the Sofitel Penthouse Bar.

As the coast stretched in an easy arc along Pattaya Bay, the ocean water seemed cleaner, more sparkling from the

15th floor. Jet skis and pleasure craft giving the view a dynamic quality. The sleepy fishing village that once was Pattaya was something else again and seemed ready for take-off.

Taking in the view, Grace started with, 'I hear you should never rent one of those,' as she pointed to a jet ski doing rooster tails and coming wildly close to swimmers and small craft.

Dane nodded and said, 'Yes, that's true. It's a scam run by local hoods with the help of some of the police.' She nodded not quite wanting to explore that issue further.

'It's great to see you looking so well after that horrific explosion.'

Looking up from her double latte she said, 'Right now, it's all an act. I'm just getting by.'

'Well, I think you're very brave.' Dressed in designer label smart casual attire, Dane oozed success and mindfulness.

'Brodie and I really had to save for this. You look pretty well-heeled, a budget wouldn't be much of a problem for you.'

Dane gave a self-conscious shrug and a wave of the hand to reinforce the notion money was no object yet it didn't mean much to him.

'I don't like to talk money, I'd rather make it.'

'You mean along the lines that if you're talking about it you're not doing it.' She paused then finished with a phrase she was becoming addicted to, 'Or something like that.'

They smiled at the sexual connotations. 'Yes, or something like that.' He gave an engaging laugh and wasn't disappointed as Grace crossed and uncrossed her legs to show them off. It worked, if the high colour on his cheeks was anything to go by.

'People say that about sex, you know.'

'OK, let's go.'

Surprised, Grace said, 'Are you serious? We hardly know each other.'

Dane reached out, cupped her hand with both of his and said, 'I have never been more serious in all my life.

CHAPTER 20

The blood poured down the man's cheeks then he collapsed. A woman knelt by his prone body and began to cry. A ghost appeared with bloody fangs and a disembodied head trailing innards. She began to scream as it spiralled around shooting bolts of light, fireworks from the undead. Over on the bed, Brodie switched channels and the Japanese horror movie *Doomed to Live* was replaced by idyllic scenes of the Phuket Islands. He lay back on the bed exhausted. Being alone in a hotel room was not his idea of a vacation. He had no idea where his partner was.

He tried to call Grace and it rang out. Fear mounted as he tore through his mind to find a solution. Frantic, he raced to the reception and asked if she'd checked out.

The young Thai lady with a white blossom in her hair shook her head and said, 'No, she has not. Is there a problem?'

'No, that's alright. Maybe her cell phone went dead. You know, those new batteries can explode like Vesuvius.'

Looking confused he explained, 'You know, like a volcano.' She nodded politely. Foreigners could be so strange.

Darting from the reception counter and out the lobby into the crowded street his mind raced. Was she in some kind of trouble? Was she lying comatose in some reeking hospital after being hit by one of those motorcycle maniacs? After all, Thailand has the highest number of road deaths in the world, hard as that was to believe when he considered the armies of crazy drivers back home.

Frantic, Brodie dialled her number again and was told in dulcet tones, 'This phone has been switched off.' He raced from bar to bar and all the restaurants in between, holding up her photo barely able to control his voice as he asked over and over, 'Have you seen this woman?'

A man of about 70 with a woman who could be no more than 20 at best gazed at him with hooded eyes and said in a reedy voice, 'I'm sorry. Never seen her before,' before turning back to his young lady. The tone in his voice said *I'll be dead soon so I have zero interest in the recently departed.* The girlfriend said something close to the old man's ear then giggled. He patted her bottom in appreciation and gave a wheezy laugh.

They weren't the only ones with such a vast age difference. One elder, at least in his seventh decade, probably his eighth, sat in a wheelchair and shared drinks with a lady no more than 30. Love couldn't be bought he figured, but it could certainly be rented and faked. These geezers knew the score and played along like it was real. Unhappy? Get yourself a drink, buy yourself a nice girl.

Sensing he was in hell, Brodie stood on shaky legs. Credence Clearwater Revival blared in the background as if the playlist was designed to bring back youthful memories to randy pensioners on their last legs of the bucket list. As the May/December couple canoodled Brodie wanted to yell, 'She doesn't love you. How could she love you?' only to realise they both already knew that. Everybody knew that. The old preyed on the young and got cleaned out in the process.

As he stood there, more dinosaur rock filled his ears – first the Doors, then the Beatles. Bargirls danced on the bar, fluoro lights colouring their bodies with shifting twirls of orange, blue and pink.

With no sign of Grace, Brodie ran down Soi 7 and rushed into the bar where Chailai worked. She emerged from the back looking surprised to see him. Her surprise soon turned to worry and a frown crossed her face. Chailai's English was still improving but her grasp of body language allowed her to easily read moods, including his. Brodie pasted on his best high-wattage smile only to be rewarded with a blank expression that seemed to say, *I know you're unhappy and afraid. You cannot fool me so putting on a show is useless.*

'Is something wrong, Brodie?' Chailai looked anxious and perhaps a little concerned for his sanity.

Was this *farung* crazy? Brodie couldn't blame her for he was beginning to wonder, himself.

'I can't find Grace. And then I heard the explosion and I saw the siege from the TV News.'

Shaking her head Chailai looked confused. 'This siege. What does...'

Her voice trailed off as she made the logical conclusion. Suddenly, there was a loud explosion and they both instinctively ducked. The war had arrived. Then they noticed deranged laughter; it was only firecrackers and a motorcycle backfiring. Brodie could see a half moon silhouetted against a Buddhist temple. Something was happening tonight; something elemental, like crashing tectonic plates making mountains that touched the sky.

On the street, the lunatics were running loose as if the end was nigh. Brodie felt a sense of chaos and, 'anything goes' had descended on the city. Above them a full moon shone pale white. Some people, Mon included, saw faces of the dead on its faraway face. It was perfect conditions for the ghosts to come out to play, come out to terrorise.

Brodie could see people possessed by these ghosts, rocking cars until they turned over while fellow rioters ransacked shops. The local McDonald's had its window kicked in and food including hamburgers and buckets of fries were thrown out onto the street. Careless of the consequences, there was a collective madness about. On the plaza at Beach Road a tank was parked; its turret swivelling to show it meant business. A group of drunken, English louts were carrying on as if to say

'Don't start the war without me!' Brodie wanted to warn them they were flirting with twenty-to-life. Then he saw a group of heavily tattooed lager lads sporting singlets letting off firecrackers and colourful smoke bombs all to the amusement of local ladies of the night and assorted rubber-necks; letting the shock and awe wash over them. Up and down the streets, bright neon signs looked like boiled sweets, as Kandy Kane Tangerine-Flake fluoro images of near-naked women bumping and grinding duelled with flashing words and letters. You could almost hear the excited molecules tear and buzz a dance of invisible particles.

A loud American, maybe a military man, hollered, 'Yeah, keep it coming. Just like the 4th of July.' Brodie turned to see a man in shorts and sandals swaying in the turbulence, a twisting tree in a hurricane force societal breakdown. 'The end is nigh, folks. Might as well sit back and let it wash over you.'

But no one paid him any attention; they were here to play, not be lectured about the end of the world. An ending always promised, never delivered. The man was a lone voice from the 'greatest country in the world'. A nearly-extinct breed here, his tribe of United Statesmen. Since the Nam heyday they had faded away, like old photos left in the sun now all bent and distorted. Weird. Brodie figured Aussies and pommies outnumbered Yanks by at least ten to one. All reports were that the average American working Joe didn't get paid enough to make it over here unless they were in the armed forces. Too bad. Brodie couldn't feel sorry for them, not after hearing so often about American exceptionalism. Anyone in the lower ranks missed out on the American dream. Maybe they could jump the Wall-in-progress and hang out in Mexico. Whatever—it wasn't his problem. Like Brando used to say, he couldn't give a flying fuck in a rolling doughnut.

Another explosion brought Brodie right back to earth. But there was no wrecked building with masonry heaped over smashed bodies to be seen. Then a string of firecrackers detonated, and he resisted the urge to dive for the pavement. He saw Chailai give a wide smile that was clownish in the nightmare sense like she was a character in some absurd black comedy. Shell-shocked, Brodie put his hand over his face in an act of self-protection that did absolutely nothing.

Now was not the time to get distracted or 'wig out' as Grace liked to say. The idea he might have to take Grace home in a body bag was more than terrifying. Amid the sounds and flashes that shook and tore straight through his body, Brodie felt as if everything was in slow motion. A man in his twenties with a broad Yorkshire accent yelled, 'Here's a present for you,' as he tossed a cherry bomb that exploded like a hand grenade. Brodie saw a beautiful woman glide past and *almost* wanted to follow her. This time it wouldn't be to make a pass at her, but because she might know where his now ex-partner was or maybe even just lead him to safety. It didn't make any sense. Only the sense of a desperate man with a racing mind. In the distance, down near

Walking Street, he could see thick plumes of black smoke. Sirens of emergency services vehicles blared as they raced towards ground zero.

Frantic, Brodie lurched from one stranger to another, showing her picture on his iPhone, a madman on a lost cause. Stricken, he almost welcomed death. Surely the end would come soon, what with the town blowing up all around him. Pushing his iPhone screen into a young woman's face he asked, 'Excuse me, have you seen this woman?' But the young woman just shook her head and hurried on.

CHAPTER 21

Brodie and Chailai sat quietly eating dinner at the Coco Cabaña Bistro Bar. At the beach end of Soi 2 it was well away from her place of work and the prying eyes of the *mamasan Choi*. A young woman dressed in an elegant traditipnal dress with a gold tiara danced with fluid movements of hands and arms. The music was atonal with percussion cymbals and strings in the Asian style. He replied when she asked him how he liked it, 'very much there's something about it I could get used to.'

'We should come here more often,' she said as she clasped his hand.'

'Yes, I'd like that very much.'

It was more complicated than this of course. Much more complicated. Grace was still missing and he'd had to field several frantic phone calls, some from her mother in Denver visiting family.

'What do you mean they can't find her have you alerted the police?' After patiently telling her that he had indeed told the police as well as the Australian embassy there was stunned silence on the other end. He could feel the tension on the other end, a tone of *what did you do to my daughter?* Mother Miriam was not happy, and that unhappiness was travelling at the speed of light direct from another continent.

Looking up from his seafood meal he said, 'it's a beautiful night, isn't it?'

Chailai gave a sad smile. Even a lost, missing Grace made her presence felt. She was a ghost that wouldn't go away. 'Yes, it is. Your wife, you find her?'

He shook her head. 'Is it true that the murdered become ghosts?'

Averting her eyes, she replied in a nervy voice, 'if you believe it becomes true.'

They held hands and he wanted to tell her something before it was too late.

Before he lost her too.

'Sorry I'm not much company.'

She brushed his cheek in a tender gesture that melted something in his icelocked heart. He smiled in recognition, it was something she did to soothe. It worked. Brodie needed it more than he could say. His mind was racing with the idea Grace wasn't just missing, she was dead. Shot. Blown to pieces in a useless act of terrorism. He could visualise her fragged body lying in a city killing field. If she really had bought it the guilt would never go away. Never.

After the waitress cleared away the table they went back inside his alternative hotel room where he gravitated to the big screen. It didn't happen if it wasn't on TV, right?

In an act of escapism, they sat in silence and watched a Thai soapie called *Forever Yours*. A handsome man with jet black hair stood on the edge of a cliff as if contemplating suicide by leaping off. An impossibly beautiful lady with pale skin rushed to his side weeping. Chailai held his hand and they kissed like their counterparts on TV.

'You want to go to bed?' She pressed his hand with hers. He nodded knowing it was the wrong thing to do. Never mind the sex he needed the companionship.

The next morning at 3 AM he got a call from the *late*, the very late Grace.

'I'm sorry I didn't get back to you. I had problems with my phone. You know I have the kind that blows up catches on fire.'

'Let me guess, did it blow up or catch on fire?'

Silence. He could recognise an avoidance strategy.

'I sorry,' she said in a tone the opposite of that.

There was a long pause as he wondered what to say. 'I'll be home soon. Don't worry I have to call some people back home.'

Another long pause. There was something wrong. He knew it. 'And you if you want to know this will be calls back home to Colorado and the Gold Coast.'

'I thought you were from California?'

'I was my parents live there now. I told you that silly.'

She hadn't told him that, only this was no time to argue. As she turned back to her phone to scroll through endless texts and emails piled up during her absence he said, 'give them my love.'

'I will honey I'll be home soon.'

Over on the Dark Side Challai rode her motor bike up a hill and then down into a little dead-end street. Stopping to get off she could hear children speaking in Burmese as they played with sticks and balls. She called out 'kan-kaung-ba-zay' or good luck.'

The small group of girls and boys under ten replied, 'min ga la ba.' She handed some baht notes to each child without wondering what their parents, if they had parents would think of this.

Waving good bye, she walked to a ground floor apartment and knocked on the green door. Ushered inside by Sirawit they kissed with passion and made promises to each other. 'I want you to stay a night with me again,' Sirawit said with sad eyes. The sadness catching like a virus she brushed away a tear and said in Thai, 'we shall have out time.'

He nodded and said, 'Yes you are right I will be patient, we will both be patient.'

That said they moved into the cramped living room. Above them looming like an angel of death was a Nat Oun, a shrine to the spirits of the martyred, to the countless murdered across the border in Burma. She wai'd and silently murmured words of respect. Your death Zhang shall not be in vain your spirit shall find peace.'

She turned to see Krin Maung sitting in a chair texting on his Smart Phone. He looked up to smile showing red stained gums and gaps between bad teeth. Beside him sitting on his haunches was Teerasat and a woman she hadn't met.

'My name is Mon,' she said in cultivated Burmese. 'And my name is Challai,' she said in Burmese that was fluent if not as perfect as she would have wished.

'I have something to show you,' she said as she retrieved an iPhone from a small leather bag.

Around a large plastic table Burmese and Thai looked at video images of burning villages and slave factories.

Staying in Burmese Challai asked, 'did you take these?' Shaking her head Mon replied, 'no they were smuggled out by a journalist who paid some of the factory guards to take pictures.'

'They must have paid a lot I'm sure those workers would be killed if caught.'

Looking at her with sad eyes Mon said, 'not really the workers too are slaves. Like the factory slaves the staff know too much. It's much easier to kill them than take the chance of being informed on.'

'I see, what village is this?' She asked as the wide screen phone spewed forth images of Burmese Army soldiers lighting the thatched roofing of village long huts.

A soldier smiled, pleased with the carnage, and spoke to the cameras.

'Pakyiko is a hiding place for criminal gangs and enemies of Democracy. Village people have killed innocent Burmese and brave soldiers. This could not go on.'

At this he reached down towards the ground and out of camera then stood up holding a severed head like a modern Genghis Khan. Giving a Burmese red mouthed smile he said, 'this is the fate of enemies of Burma. We shall hunt you and kill you. The forest is not deep enough or wide enough to hide you.'

Off into the distance other villages burned like pyres, flames reflected in the clouds.

Mon tapped her Oracle cell phone and the images morphed into another setting this one indoors.

The shaky, blurred footage was just good enough to clearly show the factory setting Chalia and the rest aimed to liberate.

'This was taken before I arrived. But the hell hole hasn't changed.'

The footage showed cramped working spaces with unpaid workers labouring over assembly lines that inhaled machine parts on one end and spewed out finished phones on the other. A soldier stood guard over workers, mainly women as they slaved over phones they could never afford and would never own.

Most of the women appeared energetic enough to do the job with one exception. A slight, stooped woman stopped moving then slumped before crashing to the floor. The guard barked orders at her and hearing no response hit her in the head with a rifle butt. As blood poured from the gash she was dragged away. With a broken hise of an artery gushes blood it was clear she woud die without the ministrations of a modern hospital emergency ward.

Brodie could almost see her soul, her spirit fly off to heaven.

Chailai gasped then put her hand to her face in shock. Mon put a reassuring hand on her shoulder.

'Yes, it is hard to watch. It is much harder to put up with this outrage when you are there.' 'What happened to her?' asked Teerasak.

'I do not believe she survived her injuries.'

'She died?'

'Yes, she died.'

Kring turned away and bit his fist in an agonized gesture of frustration and impotence. He began to sh0ut in his rage.

'We must do something. We must do something!'

Mon turned off the horror show and said, 'yes we must do something.' 'What about the United Nations?' Chailai asked.

'They know, the UN have made objections just as they did with the Rohingya in Rakhine. There is no appetite in Geneva or Brussels or New York for a Blue Helmet army to fight an Asian land war.

'Then we shall have to have our own war,' Teerasat said in an even tone.

CHAPTER 22

'The time has come to ask you to come with me.' The Quiet American Dane was dressed in a light suit, more formal than usual as if about to go to one of the high-level meetings he spoke so much about. Was he for real?

She averted her gaze, so she didn't have to take in his soul. There was something needy, something incomplete, about Dane she couldn't quite define.

'Ask me what?'

Without another word, he pulled out a jewellery case and made a show of opening it.

In the display box was a gleaming diamond. Dane beamed his high bandwidth all American smile. This proposal was going to be a Hollywood production. Just like in the movies.

'I got it from Tiffany's.'

'Park Avenue?'

He smiled again and said, 'no Bangkok.'

Reverting to on task mode he said in a tone lower, more serious, than she was used to from light-hearted Brad.

'I want to spend the rest of my life with you.'

'You've done this before haven't you Dane?' She looked at him with a knowing smile. The man had a past. Some of it was on the internet not that she was letting on.

Nodding he replied, 'once or twice but I've never felt this way before. I really mean that.'

'You shouldn't have to say you really mean if you really do.'

'Well I really do I can't say it any more clearly than that', he said in danger of sounding lame.

'No, you can't. It's just that it's all so sudden. You're a wonderful person Brad I just don't know.'

Moving nearer, his face close to hers, he placed and enveloping arm around her shoulders. Grace said internally, *anyone for possessiveness?*

'Come home Grace. Come back to your family, our family if we go ahead with my proposal.

'You make it sound like a merger.'

Dane frowned with a, *this isn't what I want to hear* expression. The man had a script and was staying with it.

She touched his cheek and softened her tone. 'I'm a gypsy Dane, anywhere I hang my hat is my home.'

He began to hum a familiar tune and sang the words, *everywhere I hang my hat is my home.*

'I want to know Brodie, are we going to the snow?' Grace had a raised eyebrow that he found irritating. Trying not to show it he said,' yes the snow would be nice I was thinking of something a bit more tropical.

She looked at the sparkling ring and fell silent. Was this really an offer she couldn't refuse?

CHAPTER 23

Later, sitting alone in the hotel lobby Grace recalled, as if from the distant past, some of the times she'd had with Brodie. On the beach on that island they pretended was deserted they had whiled away the hours. It was like a memory of a memory and seemed so long ago. Half remembered vignettes covered in aspic.

'Look at those clouds they just seem to be drifting away like we're on a stroll.'

'We are on stroll,' he said as he squeezed her arm. 'We're on a stroll on the first day of our eternal lives.'

'Eternal? You never told me you were a Scientologist. You plan on being round forever?'

'Forever with you maybe?'

'Maybe? You mean like as long as we're having fun, who cares if it lasts?' He stopped to consider this as though not knowing how to reply.

'Put it this way as long as we're having fun we might as well be together forever.'

She nodded and said, 'forever is a long time no point in getting ahead of ourselves lover.'

'Yeah ok let's be in the moment like.'

'Like there won't be another moment like this again and we will just savour it and enjoy it. How's that sound?' she asked with the kind of irrefutable logic Americans excelled in, whether it was true or not. It was one of the things he loved and hated her for. Love of course had no logic and there was little reason for their coupling, maybe any coupling when you thought about it. Which he did. A lot.

He recalled a previous conversation just days before when they were thin slicing where to go. The snow in Perisher, Las Vegas, Oahu and Waikiki beach. Endless possibilities. "We can go anywhere, do anything,' Grace said as Brodie joined in repeating the mantra. It was true in principal of course some choices, including the gambling Capital of the world Las Vegas, were deleted when they couldn't fit the budget. She pouted her disappointment. Somehow, he was able to steer her towards the more familiar and less expensive Thailand. He would leave the fact they were headed to a less expensive part of Thailand.

Brodie grinned. He was talking like a cancer patient ticking off the bucket list.

She turned to him and they kissed. Across the aisle she could see an older woman wiggle her nose that was some cross between envy and resentment.

He couldn't decide which.

'This is beautiful isn't it babe?'

Grace lifted her sunglasses and gave him a look.

'What did I say about calling me babe?'

Brodie's smile faded like a shirt after too many washes.

She leaned forward and kissed him fully on the lips before saying, 'but in this case lover I'll make an exception.

They drifted off, lost in a languid kiss. This taste of bliss made him feel like they were headed for heaven. Then came images of the terrorist attack that blew her world apart.

CHAPTER 24

The cocktail was a green lagoon that he swam through one languid sip at a time. Brodie was falling into his drink as if he'd become the Incredible Shrinking Man. Clearly cuckolded he moved closer to oblivion one nip at a time. The booze slowly built up his feelings of resentment like a capsized ship refloated to reveal the breached hull. Grace was dancing with her new American fast friend, a guy he hated more by the minute even if Brodie owed his freedom to the bastard. This guy Dane, her not do young American friend, (bring on the background music of Bowie's Young Americans) was good looking enough if not quite young anymore. He might not have much change out of 50 but he was loaded, something very important to the average yankee with a basic wage still below $10. Not that the stylish Grace was exactly poor, only that marrying up was a mantra drilled into her by a mother who lived by it.

Brodie knew the handsome stranger wouldn't last even if there was every chance he would lose her. Dane did a fancy two step then twirled Grace around like Fred Astaire. Some in the audience clapped appreciation as Brodie glowered. This chancer Dane was a piece of work. Of course, he was showing off. Brodie had seen this kind of work before. Didn't American excel in that, didn't they have a leader who was most likely the world's greatest show-off? Of course, they did and anybody who didn't approve of that, appreciate that, was a loser.

The bastard hadn't even asked. Hadn't said, 'do you mind if I have this dance with your wife', or some such pleasantry meant to disguise the fact he was on the make. No, the Ugly American took her by the hand as the band played and the lead Thai singer sang 'Rhinestone Cowboy' in broken English. The singing was comical and drew laughter. Brodie didn't see anything funny about that or being cheated on.

Grace waved over to him with a wide smile and he ignored her. Not the way to go but he couldn't cheer on while another man played patsy with up-close and personal dancing. The temptation to sock him one was just that, a temptation.

It wouldn't do to get an assault charge in Thailand, wouldn't do at all.

Making an excuse to leave, 'I have to call my boss and the family', Brodie found himself in the arms of Chailai as Grace made time with Brad.

In the Hilton room service came and went. Oysters and Champagne, what more could you want? Grace rolled off the bed and got up to fetch her phone from the dresser.

'Everything alright darling?' she turned back to frown and say that's what Brodie used to ask. Is everything alright.'

'Well, is it?'

'In answer to your question is no. Everything is not alright.'

Music blared as he strolled through walking Street. Grace was gone again. She wasn't saying much. He'd see her soon was the text message.

'You like some spicy Thai chicken?' a street vendor asked a steam wafted from his cooker.

'Sure, why not,' he said as he peeled off some note.

'You here on holiday?' the gap- toothed vendor said in passable English and a wide mile.

'Yes, something like that.'

CHAPTER 25

Brodie sat in the cell staring at the greasy tiles one with scratch marks screaming *let me out of here*. An Englishman with a pot belly and a bleeding black eye was moving back and forth as if constant movement would beam him up. 'Feeling a bit restless?'

'How I'm feeling is none of your bloody business,' his fellow inmate said with tattooed arms waving about as if wanting to fight.

Brodie lowered his head. 'But if you really want to know I feel like crap.'

He looked Brodie up and down and pronounced, 'whereas you are a picture of health.'

Then laughter erupted. 'Sorry mate if anything you look like I feel. Death becomes me.'

Brodie shook his head he didn't have the energy for this. He only barely remembered the fight that got him locked up. At Chailai's bar the night before he had been drinking white spirits, gin, vodka, you name it, with chasers. He and his new old friend Jimmy drank like pirates.

'A couple of years of this and you'll be just like me,' Jimmy said as he threw an arm around his shoulder.

'That's a comforting thought,' he said as they both broke into laughter.

One especially obnoxious man from Liverpool who introduced himself without invitation as Jock, made the unfortunate comment about Chailai,' oh I'd love to get her in the sack.' Brodie, in defence of her honour, and also because he was feeling sour, punched the man square in the jaw. The Brit with the crazy tattoos blinked as blood dripped from his nose.

'Don't take that, smash him one,' one of his lager lad mates said in a menacing Geordie accent. Egged on and not to be outdone the thug head-butted Brodie and the fight spread across tables and into the street. Now at the end of a trail of smashed glass and broken furniture the men staggered to their feet in a concussed daze of swirling stars. The Brit, his nose gushing blood and swinging like an outhouse door looked ready for the emergency ward. The police came with whistles and sirens. It wasn't over. More men, one with evil looking face tattoos that snaked around eyes, nose and lips, joined in. As the bar girls shouted encouragement and abuse the brawlers were taken away, one on a gurney to an awaiting ambulance. Blood smeared the floor turning the bar into a slaughter house.

Flash-back over he saw a guard walk to the bars and take out a jangling bunch of keys from his pocket. Through the window he could see the high, razor wire topped walls of Pattaya prison. He had 13 fellow room-mates in the cell with one hole in the floor toilet.

'You have visitor Mr Brodie.'

'And who is that the Australian counsel I asked for?'

Poker faced the guard said, 'no counsel, just man want to see you. You want or not? A lawyer you not have.'

'Take it mate or you might never get out of this alive. Fancy a stay in the Pattaya Hilton?', the northern man he'd fought the night before snarled. Sizing up the alternative he said in a defeated tone, 'Ok I'm in.'

Shuffling past the lines of cells in the humiliating leg irons, the loud abuse from antsy inmates started up just like it had when he was put in lockup the previous night.

'Your boyfriend come to visit you?'

'No maybe yours has', he called out over his shoulder.

The visiting room was crowded as usual. Families and friends, Thai, English, Australian American, German or whatever sat across tables or sprawling on the floor to secure some space. One blond haired man with a deep gash across his forehead held hands silently with his Thai companion. He didn't look like he was getting out any time soon. Except maybe feet first.

He was led to a man whose back was facing him. Speaking in halting English the guard said as if making a delivery, 'Mr Dane Van Dyke, Mr Brodie Jamieson here to see you.'

Walking slowly, painfully, into the visitor's room in chains Brodie could see who was there to greet him. A feeling of disappointment washed over him. The chances of Grace being there weren't especially good but having his rival instead was hard to take.

They shook hands before Brodie sat down.

Dane said, 'it's good to see you Brodie these places can be hell.'

'How would you know?' he said before remorse set in and he followed up with, 'sorry this place can get to you. Truth is I'm glad to see you the company around here isn't the best.'

Giving a reassuring smile Dane said, 'I understand.'

Sounding vulnerable Brodie said, 'I was hoping,' before his voice trailed off.

'I know you were hoping Grace would come. She wants you to know that she hopes you're alright and can get out of here soon.'

'I wanted to hear that from her.'

'Yes, I know you did. She's in a bad place right now. It's too painful for her to come here. I do want to do all I can do to get you out of here.'

'How long do you think that will be?'

'I don't know how long is a piece of string? It might take some cash.'

'I don't have much cash. Maybe I'll be here forever.'

'Don't worry about that. I've already helped the local police chief pay for his daughter's education. I think he might be willing to make an exception.'

'You mean I can get out tonight?'

With a sad smile his rival said, 'I'm afraid not, not tonight anyway but soon. This man Officer Detective Timon Kittikachorn wants to interrogate you about a few things.'

'What things, how do you know this?'

Sounding evasive and giving a furtive look around the room he said in a muted tone, 'for this to work you have to trust me. Remember Brodie we're in the Land of Smiles but beneath that there is corruption, there is an autocracy. I can't say any more believe me you will get out you just have to show a bit of faith alright?'

He nodded and said, 'alright I get it. To get along I have to play along.'

He was led back to his cell hands and legs burdened by the chains that threatened to be the story of his life. He waved off his dinner at supper time. He wasn't feeling very hungry and it was really a sign of protest. Better to starve to death than endure a living hell for too long. Staying in a cell shared with dozens of convicts, some on death row didn't appeal. At half eight he got the call to appear for interview. Refusing didn't bear thinking about. He was shown to a room with air conditioning and a long table. The officer was an older man who looked as if he had survived many battles.

CHAPTER 26

They shook hands and his overlord got down to business straight away.

'My name is Timon Kittikachorn.'

'I know,' he said without explaining exactly how he knew.

'My street name is the enforcer.' There was a long pause as if to let this to permeate his consciousness. It worked. It was anybody's guess as to what this enforcer would do to him.

'Mr Jamieson, we have drugs all through Asia. If you look at Philippines, if you go to Bali you will see strict enforcement of law.'

'What do you mean by strict enforcement?'

The Chief remained silent as if the answer was so obvious, so clear there was no point in him spelling it out. His very detention in a fetid cellblock made this clear with each passing minute and hour.

'We have many *farung* that get caught this way. You have been to the prison you know what this is like.'

'Hell, you mean. An eight by ten metre cell with thirty people. What has this got to do with me I was locked up because of a fight nothing more.'

'And that remains to be seen. At the moment, we are keeping you for your own protection.'

'In this place?' he asked holding up his hands as if it was all he could do to prevent a meltdown.

'And did you expect what you call holiday camp.'

Brodie, suffering from racing mind, thought of grieving family back home. They didn't know where he was yet. It was only a matter of time before they found out. He cringed at the idea of making some grovelling confession like some desperate stooley willing to say or do anything to get sprung.

'What is it you want to know? I'm not into drugs and there is no evidence of that so why am I being held against my will?'

The Chief took a deep drag from his cigarette and blew the blue smoke slowly so it wafted in the air.

'There is no against your will. We have strict terrorist laws in Thailand. You can be kept here as a suspect for as long as we like. I am not here to play games. You are not here to play games understand?' he asked as he flicked the lit cigarette against his prisoner's forehead.

Shaking from searing burn, the humiliation, Brodie felt like indulging in an act of physical violence himself, which in this case would be an act of suicide. The man had the eyes of a killer and could easily eliminate this Australian at will.

Now the importance of Brad's support became perfectly clear.

'I'm not a terrorist. I am not a criminal can you get this through your head Mr Policeman?', he said in half Thai then English. He meant to do this to remind his tormentor that his disappearance would not go unnoticed.

Tapping his skull as if the answer to all these riddles was somehow contained within an ocean of experience the chief parried the question.

'There are many things that go through my head Mr Brodie. I have spoken to many men and women too in my career. Everyone say they are innocent but I always find the truth.'

'I still don't know why I'm here.'

Officer Tim leaned back in his chair then said I want to show you some photos.

Holding up his smart phone he showed a photo of Brodie at the bar where Chailai worked.'

'This is you yes?'

He nodded and replied,' yes that's me but I don't see.'

Scrolling through the pics he showed a picture of Chailai and asked,' do you know this woman?'

'Yes of course she is a friend of mine.'

'You mean you are a client of hers correct?'

Feeling more trapped by the minute he answered, 'yes alright I accept that.

Don't tell me that's a federal crime. If it is you'd have to lock up half of Thailand.'

'I do not care about your extra-marital activities.'

'I'm not married. Ok you got me I'm involved with Chailai and my partner isn't aware of that.'

He gave a snaky smile and said, 'even if your partner is herself having an affair.'

'No, I didn't know that,' he lied. This man knew too much even if he thought this was his job. It wasn't. This guy might know more about him than he knew about himself like the enforcers in 1984. His inner voice told him *best to play along tell him what he wants to know.*

Clasping his hands together in an attempt to curb shaking that came from nowhere, Brodie gave his interrogator, his inquisitor, a hard look. The captain stared back until Brodie looked away. He bent his head knowing there was no way he was going to win a contest of wills with a state sanctioned killer like Chief Timon Kittikachorn.

The man got up from his swivel chair and moved close to his informer. Personal space invaded, Brodie began to breathe heavily as his metabolism shot up like mercury in a storm.

'I know that you know these men. I know that you know what they are doing smuggling arms.'

There was a pause which Brodie filled.

'I don't know what you're talking about officer. This has nothing to do with me I'm being fitted up by somebody.'

Chief Timon moved close, his head only inches from Brodie's face. The Chief of Police smelled heavily of after shave.

'And these men you can see them yes?'

He nodded, clear that the line of questioning was veering into dangerous territory.

The Chief shoved the iPhone close to Brodie's face. Forced to look a picture he saw a group of men were clustered around a picnic table round the back of Chailai's bar. He recognised Sirawit Puna and in the middle of the huddle the older man Teerasak Krit.

'Yes, as I've said I know these men from the Go- Go bar my friend Chailai works at.'

'I see so your mistress introduced them to you?'

'Not as any formal introduction. You'd see them around.' The Chief gave him a sceptical look as he went on. 'These guys were part of the furniture they were always around. People are going in and out of there all the time. You could question any number of tourists and they will tell you the same thing.'

The Chief stepped backwards then did a slow 180 degrees turn before getting in Brodie's face again. Scrolling through pics he stopped at one that showed Sirawit and Teerasak carrying what looked like rolled up carpet.

With more dark energy in his voice the Chief asked, 'do you know what's in that bundle?'

Shaking his head in denial he said, 'how should I know do I look like a fortune teller to you?'

The Chief took a step back then hurled himself at Brodie with a hard slap.

'This is not games Mr Jamieson this is not joke. Many people die so you must tell me the truth. No tell me lies, tell truth you have. Thai people demand this.'

Wiping blood from his mouth Brodie said in a voice choked with it, 'I am telling you the truth. Please dear God you must believe me as God is my witness.'

The Chief sneered. All the farung men, these weak men that preyed upon and insulted the honour of Thai femininity were all weak. All had a breaking point.

He could always find the breaking point, this was only a matter of time. 'Yes, God is my witness too and my God is named Allah.'

'Same thing I guess.'

Shaking his head, he said, 'no not same thing, this is where you make mistake my friend.'

Grinding out the fag end of a cigarette, his face twisted into a snarl.

'You give names, or you stay. You stay here and maybe you not get out for long time I afraid.'

Brodie felt a tooth loosen in his mouth. It was if this part of him was preparing to abandon ship.

'I have no names to give. You saw me in a bar which happened to be a meeting place for the guys you are looking for.'

CHAPTER 27

The Gulf of Thailand was barely visible under a moonless night. Black waters threw up low chop that smacked against the hull of the *Sea Pearl*, just enough to give a gentle rocking. Ropes and cables rattled and clinked with the masting. Enough sound to hide behind. Sirawit and Teerasat drifted close 70 ft. pleasure craft until his hand reached the starboard side. He knew the luxury vessel could carry several dozen safely but really held about 75 women with a sprinkling of men. This playboy's toy decked out with a helipad was their watery prison and for some, the last place they would ever be. Away from prying eyes and well under the noses of the authorities it was a 5 Star holding pen and light years ahead of what they were used to in Burma. Here they would learn *hospitality* and how to *entertain* a man. It was a secret without a secret. Of course, the police knew all about this floating cell from hell and only hefty kept a raid at bay. Sirawit knew this place too having scouted it only a few nights before. His informers within the people smuggling cartel gave him enough intelligence to get where he was now. The easy part over now came the hard part.

Putting his finger to his lips to signal continued silence Sirawit hauled himself up onto the deck. Barefoot he ran along the starboard side until he was almost at the stern. A security guard noticed him and ran to meet him only to be knocked to the deck with a Muay Thai kick to the head that left him gasping. Sirawit pulled out a cloth soaked on chloroform and pressed it on the guard's face until the struggling stopped and he was comatose, out. For a second, he looked at the dreamy expression and the man whose night was over. He did not envy him at all, failure on his watch was terminal. Swinging around he kick boxed another guard preparing to fire. He fell backwards into the black waters.

Khin Maung gave a roundhouse kick to a man emerging from below deck. The heel of his foot drove the slaver's jaw into the roof of his mouth instantly killing him. Khin pushed him backwards into the water with a splash louder than he would have liked.

Alerted to the sound another guard rushed above deck and was hit by a taser then dropped in the water. At first, he floated face down in the sea and Sirawit wondered what to do until the floating corpse revived and began to thrash in the water. He threw him a life buoy. It was what his leader in northern Thailand called damage mitigation, a term he had in turn learned from American Special forces that had been coming and going for generations.

Above the hold he ripped off the covered and scurried down the stairs with his automatic Glock primed and ready.

The ladies began to scream. He spied Raun, the woman he had come to rescue.

Of course, there were almost a hundred more like her on board. With luck and Budda, he would get them all out. As the gagged captives muffled sounds of joy and relief he undid the hand and ankle ties of grip-lock, cutting or undoing each one. As he freed one she went to work freeing her sisters in captivity and within minutes all were released as if in a dream. Raun came to him after her own rescues and kissed him on the lips.

'It has been years', she said in accented Thai.

'I don't know, we will talk later Raun. Help me get the women out of here and onto the boats. We will make plans later. I can assure you of this,' he said in basic Myanmar.

Sirawit placed his hand on her bruised cheek as if to make sure she was truly free then turned and went to work calling out directions. The exit had to be as perfect as the entry if he wanted to avoid unacceptable casualties.

'Put these grip locks on the guards.'

As she did one of the guards with a wild-eyed look as if waiting for the main chance to overpower her made a lunge. As the two struggled Raun rushed to her side and placed a long-serrated fish knife up to his jugular vein.

'If you want to live you will listen carefully and closely follow what we say.'

Bending his head in defeat he ended resistance as an alternative survival strategy. At the other end of the luxury boat came a scream. Sirawit had his foot on a long-haired employee of the slave ship. He gave the well- muscled slaver a steel hard back hand and he dropped to the deck like a dead weight of bagged coins. Sirawit wrapped some rope around the perp's neck. As he pulled it tight the man's eyes began to bulge, a puffer fish gasping for air. He could kill the killer in seconds and knew this man would do just that to him if given the chance.

Leaning close he said, 'now if you try something like this gain I will kill you. That is a promise my friend.

He shoved him away then kicked him in the ass. Would he make good on his promise? Yes, and it would be right. At 2:23 Am all the ladies were taken in outboard motor boats the English called runabouts.

CHAPTER 28

Chief Timon nestled Angel's face in the nook of his shoulders. Her naked pale breasts seemed to quiver at his touch. She had been his for two years.

She turned to look at him and said, 'I'm going for my facial and my hairdo tomorrow.'

'Yes, I know what that means,' he said in Bangkok accented Thai as he threw thousand baht notes one after the other onto the bed. She was an angel and angels had to be kept happy. Yes, sexy women cost much even for Thai, and especially if Thai is old man like him. She knew he would give her whatever she wanted. He told her this many time. And both knew it to be true.

Looking worried he said in a confessional voice, 'I was always honest and never took money. Now here I am past sixty and I nothing to show for this.'

Pulling him back to her she said in Laotian accented Thai, 'Yes I know you have been honest. But you must be ready for life after the police. 'I have children about to go to college. I have many bills.'

Touching her hand, he said, 'I don't want to lose you either Angel. I will give you whatever you want when the time comes. Have patience.'

As though to finish the thought on a high, and not the kind that wrecked *farung* lives, he handed over another 5000 baht. She belonged to him yet that could never come free.

'Go to Bangkok if you want to. Get your teeth done get your tits done whatever you want but go to my doctor he do best job.'

'And is the cheapest because he went to Bangkok University with you brother.'

'Yes, cheapest and best. I know this man and he is the best. Please go to him I want.'

'Are you sure?'

'Yes, I'm sure.'

The phone rang. 'Don't answer you only have to be back on duty in a couple of hours.'

Shaking his head and laughing he said, 'not if you're the chief darling. We never sleep.'

He picked up the iPhone and saw it was an unknown number.

'How did you get this number? This is a priority police box number and no one outside personnel is authorised.'

A smooth sounding Thai voice informed him, 'I am with the Bangkok Times my name is Amrat Saurez and I wanted to get your reaction to the rescue of 76 socalled ship slaves anchored just offshore.'

'I don't know anything about this.'

'But this was part of an inquiry that came out with a report last year. Indentured workers, real modern-day slaves, are being captured or coerced into coming to Thailand only to find that they are labouring under a large debt for food and lodging. Of course, the food is terrible, barely edible and the lodging is being chained up on a reeking leaking vessel after working 12, 14 or sixteen-hour days. It is criminal.'

'Yes, I heard this, but it is only speculation.'

'Could we meet before going to press. At the moment, I am the only one with the story.

Cupping the phone, he said to Angel, 'get ready to go honey I have to get out of here.'

'Where can we meet? We have much to talk about.'

CHAPTER 29

rinking in his first taste of freedom with a daiquiri Brodie floated in the infinity pool. Alone.

The last conversation with Grace went through his mind and back again like white noise, wallpaper music.

'Are you alright?' he asked, relieved to finally get through.

'I didn't want to leave you. My father can be a pretty persuasive man.'

'I thought he was dead.'

'You know he's not.'

'I know I just wanted to hear it from you.'

'Why all the,'

'The intrigue? The secrecy?'

'I guess having a father in the CIA can attract that. That's all stock and trade for spy craft.'

'We lived, we're still living it.'

'Only if you let it.'

CHAPTER 30

Brodie counted the cracks in the tiles. He couldn't believe he was back in jail but that was the new normal. Within about a 2-metre radius he could count 657 cracks if you count branching blood- stained fractures brought on by violent blows to the head as separate. He hadn't gone through that yet but sometimes late at night the cries of the tortured wafted in from the pipes. In the exercise yard, he had already walked to Bangkok and back again which amounted to a grand total of 89 kilometres. In fact, he hadn't really got that far at this point in time after 8 days it was more like 5 kilometres. The 89 klicks would happen if he did real time here say an American big house nickel or dime.

'Today your lucky day Mr Jamieson.'

Eyeing him suspiciously Brodie asked, 'what do you mean, another visit from the Chief?'

His guard wiped his brow and said, 'No I mean you're getting out.'

'What no trial, no deportation? Hey that's great really that's great.'

He was taken into the visitor's room where his guardian angel Dane was waiting. Somehow, he didn't feel lucky that the man who'd taken his lover was here to help him. He didn't want help he wanted out.

'I didn't think I'd say I'm glad to see you but hey I'm glad to see you.'

'Well I'll take that as a compliment back handed or not. Come on let's get out of here before they change their minds.'

'Didn't you say that last time?'

Giving a wry smile, he said, 'yeah something like that. Now do you want to stay here or get out of here?'

'I hear you talking man,' he said sounding vaguely hipster. His patron, and allaround carer, was sounding more Australian with his use of mate and g'day and the rest. It was an angle didn't all Americans have an angle? Even so it was a two-way street of cross contamination. Brodie for his part was saying awesome and lousy, words he'd never used before. Or almost never.

The rode in a chauffeured limo back to the city and then to Beach road and the Hilton. The size of the Lincoln Continental was presidential in scale. When they got to a large gated house the doors opened to swallow them as the mouth closed shut.

Moving past mirrored walls and a sumptuous atrium Dane led the way into the elevator and up to the Penthouse.

'You need to stay here until you head back home.'

Sounding ungrateful but determined to say it as a kind of declaration of independence he said,' Is that really necessary? I mean it's a bit awkward aren't you going with my girl Grace?'

'In answer to your first question yes, it is absolutely necessary for your own security.'

'I wish everybody including the Chief of Police stopped being so nice to me. Brad what you did was tremendous I'll always be in your debt. I know that but I am not about to be kept by someone who stole the heart of someone who stole my heart.'

'Well aren't you being a bit melodramatic. You have completely misread my intentions as to the young lady in question.'

'How about we call her Grace Braddock?'

Conceding with a nod he gave the kind of smile that was almost genuine but didn't quite make it.

'I mean you asked her to marry you and go take her back to the greatest country on Earth. Isn't that right Brad?'

'Well yes but I wouldn't quite put it that way. Granted I did ask for her hand in marriage and it was one of the greatest disappointments in my life that she declined my offer.'

Waving an admonishing finger Brodie said, 'I know you Dane you won't give up. You Americans never give up you go for the long game. Sooner or later the Macdonald's is going to eat the local takeaway. The law of the jungle like the top of the food chain takes what it wants right?' He stopped to see if Dane was paying attention.

'And?' Brad asked as if not knowing where this was going.

'What you can't win in battle you persuade with inducements. What did you offer her this time, the Hope Diamond or half of Oahu?'

Making a line for the open drinks cabinet (had Dane been hitting the sauce?) his host asked, 'like a drink? I think we both need one if you ask me mate.'

Shaking his head and picking up the back pack that held his worldly possessions, 'no thanks this is where I get off. And mate that's a nice touch, a couple of more weeks and you'll sound like Paul Hogan. Thanks for your help but do me a favour don't do me any favours.' He paused then said to underline the point, 'Don't help me mate. And don't call me mate, mate. OK got that? I can make it on my own.'

As he headed out the door without saying goodbye, he could hear Dane calling out, 'can you? Can you really Brodie. Jesus, I hope so I really hope so because from here it doesn't look like you can do shit. Maybe next time you can stay and rot inside.'

'Fuck you,' he called back.

He took a cheap room on the Dark Side. Most tourists were warned off staying there but he had a hunch it would be safer than one of the upmarket haunts on Beach road or near it.

CHAPTER 31

Chailai gently removed herself from the bed. She didn't want to wake him, and he play-acted along with a convincing snore.

Later he joined her at the bar, something Dane warned against for security reasons. Brodie was in no mood to follow the bastard's advice.

He went to the rest room and then he saw something he knew he wasn't supposed to see. It was Sirawit and his offsider.

Risking everything, he approached the man whom had indirectly led to his arrest. Sure, Brad saved him but even that was bitter. Would it be better to be dead than be saved by a bastard like that? Probably not. As for Grace, she'd been duped by someone with deep pockets and not much else going for him beyond the trust fund. Whether or not she could be lured into a gold-plated cage with open doors remained to be seen. The fact this Yank put her on a guilt trip for not living in the United States was the worst thing he had against this hustler. No matter with any luck he wouldn't see either of them again.

'Sirawit, thank God you're alive. I saw the news report.'

Sirawit took hold of his arm cutting him off and with the clear understanding these were interesting times.

'You saw nothing Brodie nothing. You just got out of jail do you want to go back with no possibility of release?

Shaking his head, he tried to respond only to be cut off again.

'You must leave here. I will not talk about what happen. This for world to judge not me,' he said placing his forefinger against his chest for emphasis.

'Sirawit no wait,' he said with desperation showing in his voice. He didn't know why exactly he wanted to embrace danger, quite possibly mortal danger but he did. There was something about Sirawit, something very special. He was a charismatic leader and dangerous. Bodie envied him in a way. Loyalty to a cause was just the thing missing in Brodie's life. Perhaps that's what this superannuated boy scout had going for him. Outside the truck loads of money of course. Maybe it was like those Oxbridge undergraduates who took up a cause bigger than themselves only to betray everything they had been raised and taught to believe in when they made it to CEO. Maybe the thrill of the chase got the better of them and the cause whatever that was faded, anyone for world peace? It was a board game, a game of chess, once you cornered the king it was game over. Cowboys and Indians and cops and robbers. The danger, the mortal danger made it just that much more exciting and real. Playing for keeps as his American former friend might have said was where the action was. The hell with the risk like the marines going over the top he *didn't want to live forever.*

'Please let me help. I want to help. I believe.'

At this Sirawit gave him a disbelieving look then shrugged as if giving up the effort to keep him away.

'Alright you do as I say. Do that or I kill you myself.'

Chapter 32 *Bring me the Shoes of Imelda Marcos*

'How about this honey they really suit you?'

Holding the Marino Blanko shoes, Grace was a picture of indecision.

Putting on the impossibly high heels she said playfully, 'do I look fat in these?' 'You don't look fat in anything.'

Above them on the wall was a flat screen HDTV. It was showing groups of women being cared in some public health facility. The English-speaking newscaster could be heard speaking breathlessly as he followed the women and uniformed men walking up steps carved into rock leading to the respite home.

In Cambodian accented English, the reporter with the captioned name of Angelina Suarez said, 'after the terrible conditions of their captivity in Myanmar these virtual slaves are getting some much-needed peace and quiet.'

Behind her could be seen vision of burning villages then lines of fleeing refugees. It looked as if the whole country was a war zone.

'Dane how do you,' she said her voice trailing off as she saw he was engrossed in the news report.

She stopped to watch as well. The urge to see and hear what someone was so taken with that everything else was blotted out proved irresistible.

Thirty streets away coming in from the Dark Side Chailai rode her scooter over low lying hills. Overhead thunder rumbled, and lightning lit up the sky.

She stopped and looked up. Thick black clouds swirled overhead like gravitational waves radiating from a cosmic event. Getting off her bike she wai'd a Nat shrine that overhung the Mandalay Restaurant owned by her new friends Sung.

The wind made a whistling sound, a keening sound like that of an apparition, a ghost. She saw Zhang, the murdered factory woman hovering above her speaking unintelligible words, a spiritual autistic with a coded message.

'What are you saying I can't hear you?'

The keening, howling noise went on. They were trying to communicate.

'You must leave the place where you meet.'

'Why, why must we leave?'

The howling went up a notch and a table blew over, the covering ripped into the air and out of sight as if devoured by the disturbed nat, the vengeful ghost of Zhang and anyone who lost their lives in the prison factories. Chalai raced outside and stared up at the sky in horror. Angry black clouds swirled clockwise as if by some supernatural force. On the Bay a strange mist crept in from the Gulf like a magician's trick. This fog, never before seen in Pattaya, closed in on the beach swallowed boats and bathers like an invisibility cloak. As it moved from sea to land the mist made its way through the streets.

'Stay away from me, I have done no wrong,' screamed a woman who tried in vain to outrun the blinding vapour. A loud crash of metal and glass couold be heard somewhere in the mist as blind drivers crashed into one another.

Then before the town got paralysed by fear and unnatural blindness the haze left as soon as it had come. The unseasonable and unheard-of fog burned up under the hard Thailand sun and a degree of normalcy was restored to a shaken Pattaya City. The sun now shone on a changed city, one more superstitipus than ever.

That night she made a few calls and the flat was vacated. When the last of the furniture and belongings were taken away and the place was emptied a commando style raid by Special Ops soldiers descended with armoured vehicles and machine guns. Two of their neighbours were killed as they came out of their homes with their hands up.

Regrouped in another apartment this time near Maung that were strangers to them they watched what would have been their fate.

'The warning was real. The nat knew we were marked for death and she warned us.'

Teerasat no lover of Nat lore sat and stared. His face had an expression of *is the world going crazy?*

In serviceable Burmese 'I heard her too.'

'Who, the nat?' Chailai asked hardly believing her ears.

He nodded. 'She told me same warning but I did not want to believe it. I am a Bangkok man, a city man, I am not opposed to believe in ghosts and did not want to believe.'

He fell silent. Then he spoke slowly as though wanting to get it right.

'She gave me a sign. Now I believe. The *nats*, the ghosts shall watch over us.

Now and forever.'

CHAPTER 32

'I have a mission for you. You may decide to take it or you may not.' Smiling Brodie responded with, 'yeah I know *Mission Impossible* and all that.

The men, the team, as Dane called the chosen ones, stood staring at him with uncomprehending eyes, the joke falling flat. Only English speaking *farung* were familiar with American television or at least half century old fare. Didn't they play that on cable anymore or was he getting out of time?

'I want you to take some ladies to the airport where they will take a flight to Singapore and then onto London and Toronto.'

'Take them to the airport. Sounds like there might be a good chance of getting picked up.'

With a frown Sirawit said in an agitated voice, 'you are a free man and these women are free too. There is nothing to worry about.'

'It's sounds interesting.'

'I don't want to know about interest, will you do it?'

Brodie nodded with stiff body language, afraid of what he might be getting into. Afraid to ask more questions or get even more paranoid than he already was he fell silent.

CHAPTER 33

They took the taxi into Suvarnabhumi International Airport, Bangkok. A private car just wouldn't do on a *mission* like this.

The ladies were introduced to Brodie even though he guessed they were assumed names. Even so he couldn't remember the names and thought that might be self-defence mechanism to deal with possible loss, like imprisonment or untimely death. Somehow, he felt up to it in these interesting times, in this hectic year of living dangerously.

The women, all in their twenties he guessed, talked excitedly among themselves. Only in contact for less than 48 hours he already felt protective towards them. He rode in silence in the maxi-cab while he imagined all the things that could happen to him. Getting arrested was the first that came to mind. For what? Immigration violations and worse charges like sedition or even terrorism. Handcuffed and manacled deep in the bowels of the Bangkok Hilton possibly with waterboarding torture. How about the bamboo shoots though the ass and bamboo slivers shoved under the fingernails? Like Winston in 1984 he would rot and go into decline with each passing day.

Inside the vast Airport the place felt different somehow. He watched a security guard staring at him until the man looked away. The uniformed man disappeared around a column which left Brodie's heart racing. He motioned for the five ladies to move faster. All he had to do was deliver them to the check out and then take off. It was both simple and complicated. Ahead were lines of travellers and in the far distance the massive windows that faced the tarmac. It was hot out there, yet *out there,* is where he wanted to be. Then a sudden rush of chilled air as if the aircon had malfunctioned. The ladies shivered and looked frightened. It was if something had snaked through the ducting and blew out to make its presence felt.

He kissed each of the ladies. Then had a quality moment with the one with the best English, Baby Choy. She was the chief interpreter and a kind of den mother.

'You've been through a lot girl. I wish you the best of luck.'

She nodded, and he could see tears. Brushing them away he said, 'you know we never did get to know each other very well but I'll miss you Baby.' She managed a laugh. The first for days.

'I will write.'

He shook his head and she nodded her understanding. They left crying but happy. Brodie knew he would never see them again. The flight was to Singapore and from there anyplace from London to New York.

Later back in Pattaya he collected his thoughts. With a head crammed with so many events and people his mind raced from jail to the jungle, from Chailai to the Chief. Like a bundle of whirring buzzing atomic particles they threatened to collide and explode.

Walking along Soi six Brodie had a sense he had lived here his whole life. Maybe less, maybe more like five years. He had been bloodied and detained and more as if five years of living were compressed into three weeks. Of course, it was an illusion like a desert heat wave that came up as an oasis or cresting sea. At least memories of home were far distant, almost inaccessible, like a lost weekend somewhere in the recesses of his mind. In the narrow street, he looked up to apartments, one with an older western man taking in the breeze from his balcony.

He waved, and the cigar smoking foreigner waved back as if they knew each other or would soon meet. He wondered about his new acquaintance. How long had he been here, and did he ever want to go home? Was he one of the chief's spies on a payroll? Overhead he saw a neon cowgirl shoot off her six guns then blow the smoke away with a fetching wink. Brodie could use a girl like that. He moved on past bar girls in skimpy dresses and looked the other way when they smiled perfect smiles pasted on silky smooth skin.

Back at the hotel counter he checked out with a smile and left the kind of 500baht tip Australians almost never handed over. Nutcha, the lady assistant manager, gave him a smile showing perfect capped teeth, a walking, talking advertisement for the local dentistry industry. She asked, 'you don't like here? You go someplace else maybe 5 Star?' She looked disappointed like she really was sad to see him go.

He shook his head no and gave her a sad smile in return. 'No, it's not that, I've really enjoyed staying here especially with you around,' he said as he touched her hand. Any idea of making a pass at her was out of the question. The walls, the floors had ears and eyes, just some of the million million eyes and ears cameras and microphones in this city and all the other cities. Her expression darkened. She knew.

As a kind of consolation he said, 'I'll come around sometime and drop in to say hello.'

She bowed liked the princess she was and said, 'yes I would like that Mr Brodie.'

This time he didn't correct her with the fact was he'd grown kind of used to it. He parted with a wave and walked into the breaking dawn. Like a sea creature he was drawn back to Beach road and the ocean. It was as kind of homing instinct, waves and beaches reminded him of home assuming you could have a home outside where you lived. He was a turtle, a Tasmanian penguin that had travelled many thousands of miles on instinct. Tiny waves broke against the tiny beach as he sat on concrete steps surrounded by sun worshippers and the homeless.

'Hey, you got a light?' asked a bearded and dreadlocked European he took to be German maybe Swiss. Brodie pulled out a lighter and was rewarded with a beautiful grin. This beach bum was John the Baptist on a journey through the concrete wilderness. Something like that.

They spoke about everything, about nothing. The man who introduced himself as Hans seemed every bit the outlier Brodie was. If nothing else that made him feel at ease which was why he was drawn to the stranger. In a treacherous world, the underground always beckons.

"I'm an insurance salesman just out here for a bit of R&R on my own,' he lied. Lying was second nature now going on the principle that telling anyone the whole truth would put them all in danger.

'I just checked out at the Castaway.'

'Didn't like it?' Hans asked in a tone that suggested more.

'Sure, I like just like to move around that's all.' Hans drew in a puff of smoke and blew out smoke rings.

'I do the same. I don't like to get tied down. I used to be a wage slave and pay off a huge mortgage with a wife and kids.'

'They're not with you now?'

Looking suddenly wistful his new friend said, 'she found someone else when it became clear I wasn't going to be a corporate slave or confine myself to an open cage. I wasn't the guy she thought I was, so we parted.'

On impulse, he put his arm around the lost German's shoulder and said, 'hey you're my kind of people as my American girlfriend says.'

'I thought you said you were single and came out on my own.'

There was long pause until Hans said, 'never mind about that we're in Asia, whatever happens here,' he said as Brodie joined in, 'stays here.'

'I'm looking for a place to stay. A place where I can go under the radar.'

'I know a place,' Hans said as he got up and began walking towards the street.

'Where?'

Without turning back to face him his new fast friend said, 'follow me come with me.'

Hans stopped in front of a scooter standing in a rack and said, 'alright hop on.'

'Where are we going Hans?'

Hans frowned as if he were asking too many questions. He put his helmet on then handed one to Brodie.

'You'll see when we get there. All your questions will be answered. Questions that can't be answered won't be. Remember where we are.

'Why don't you just go home? You've been in trouble with the law and it's not the same as getting in trouble at home. I know men and it's almost always men, I know men who are still in prison with no hope of ever getting out. It's a hell of an existence. A life hardly worth living.'

Stretching back on an ancient battered bean bag he said to his brother alien, 'sure I know is the fact I the law is making me stay here. I have to appear in court on a consorting charge.'

'A what? What is this consorting?'

'Yes, that the term they use in the states and Australia. It's about associating with known criminals.'

'God how did you get into that?'

He gave a smirk and said, 'it's complicated. I met this girl in a bar and she is friends with some guys that are not exactly flavour of the month. Not in a military state like this.'

'Drugs dealers, people smugglers? What?'

'Well these guys aren't people smugglers. They're trying to stop the people smugglers and they recently rescued about 80 women from one of the slave ships just offshore.'

Open mouthed Hans was speechless.

'Oh my God are you kidding?'

He shook his head and said, 'no, I'm afraid not. I got into some very deep shit it's a wonder I got out of it. I probably shouldn't tell you but I'm tired of being afraid.'

'So how did you get out of it?'

'Well I didn't give anyone up if that's what you want to know.'

His fast friend gave a look of relief. Brodie had already said too much and wondered where all of this was going to end.

CHAPTER 34

They rode the jet sky out to the boat and cut out the engine about 100 metres from the target.

Brodie got out a pair of infra-red night vision goggles. He could see men patrolling the top deck. It was the same arrangement Sirawit found when he sprang his aquatic prison break. Brodie was pleased with himself having finally made it to tram member status.

'They're in there I can tell. Why else would you have ten guards top deck unless something very dodgy was going on?'

'Do the police know about this?'

He gave him a look in the moonlight then said, 'of course the Thai police are in on everything one way or another. They always get their cut. You know the saying it's not personal it's business.'

'Sure, I understand now can we get out of here before the water police show up.'

Brodie nodded, and they jetted off. As they did a water rat power boat cruised past in the dark waters like some enemy vessel in wartime. This was no PT 109.

At the Westin in Pattaya City there was a knock on the door and Grace said, 'who is it?'

'It's me Dane.'

She sighed and said as she opened the door, 'Look Dane, sorry we've been through all this I need time to think. I'm not ready for this right now.'

'You don't understand I have someone here to see you.'

With irritation in her voice she said, 'not the police or the embassy people please Brad I'm not in the mood for this now.'

'No this is not something to talk about on the other side of the door.'

Then the man standing next to Dane spoke. 'Grace it's your father. I know it's been a long time, but I'm here to see you in spite of everything.'

She opened the door to reveal the two men, one of whom she hadn't seen for 15 years.

She saw that the man also known as her father looked remarkably youthful as though the intervening years were a pause in the riptide of time. Plastic surgery anyone? No, she forgot. He was ageless like the Sphinx.

She held out her hand as though to shake and he kissed her on the cheek.

After exchanging pleasantries, they decided to take off for a local restaurant that Brad liked. They walked to the back of the room with many tables and sat down.

As they did Dane said, 'I know you two have some catching up to do. I'll just be outside making some phone calls.

'So here we are dad. What can I do for you?'

Knitting his eyebrows, he said, 'look Grace I know it's been hard for you all these years. I really do.'

Unsmiling she said, 'you don't know the half of it father. You know we've thought you were dead all these years what am I supposed to think now?'

He reached for her hand and she pulled away. 'It's great to see you but I don't know what we're going to talk about if you don't tell me what happened.'

He called a waitress over and he said, 'what would you like honey?'

'I'm not feeling very hungry.'

'How about a drink? '

Feeling as though she wanted to call an end to this momentous and unwelcome meeting she said in a tired voice, 'yes alright make mine a scotch on the rocks. Double. What are you having? Don't tell me, gin and ice shaken not stirred.'

He nodded and gave the waiter a tip. Unlike the chintzy British and Australians, he knew all about the power and importance of tips. It could even save your life and had on more than one occasion.

'I think you might have me mixed up with James Bond.'

'Come on pop a lot of people had you mixed up with James Bond.'

'Yes, I forgot I need you to remind me.'

She folded her arms and said, 'it's me you're talking to. You never forget about anything.'

He raised his drink and, 'touché.'

They drank through the night. Brad tried to join them again but he was politely waved away. Father and daughter needed to have a word.

CHAPTER 35

Brodie played Extreme destruction on his iPhone. His army finished demolishing the castle of his enemy before sacking a surrounding village. No one was spared. The score was not what he wanted but the distraction was. When the call came he saw it was Grace. For a split second, he thought of letting it ring out to voice mail then decided against it.

He picked it up and said, 'Grace what a pleasant surprise it's great to hear from you.'

'Yes likewise', she said in a tone suggesting she didn't know why she was calling.

Then silence. Not knowing quite what to say he stuck with the banal.

'Are you alright Grace are you feeling OK?'

'Sure, about as well as can be expected. You know I'm coping, just coping.'

'I'm worried about you.' There was a laugh on the other end before she said,

'you're worried about me? You have to take care of yourself first.'

'Well I do you know I do.'

'Do you do you really? Sometimes I wonder.'

'I don't think I follow you Grace are you sure everything's alright?'

He could hear sobbing over the lines. Concerned he asked, 'what is it Grace?

Why are you so upset?'

He waited as the crying subsided. 'It's going to be alright you'll see.'

There was another wave of sobbing this one even more heart rending than the last.

'No, it's not going to be alright Brodie. Did I tell you my father washed up after 15 years on a deserted Island or someplace? Just came out of nowhere.'

'I don't understand I thought you said he was dead.'

'Yeah me too. He really had us fooled, didn't he?'

'I still don't get it.'

'He found me through Brad. I might have told me my father was in the CIA well it turns out Dane is an operative. Got to hand it to him he has a great cover.'

'Sure, a great cover. Well else don't you know about him? Looks like he was on a covert mission himself.'

'Yes, I've been thinking the same thing although you'd probably be rotting in a Thai prison without him.'

'At least he's come into some good use. He was there when I was growing up.'

CHAPTER 36

Brodie sat in the room fidgeting. The self-described *Good Samaritan* called him in off the street for reasons he could guess but wasn't about to own up to. Just yet.

After five minutes, every second of which he assumed was being recorded for the good folks in Bangkok and Washington DC for all he knew. Chief Timon entered the room and they shook hands.

Electing to stay silent on the advice of Grace and her rebirthed father he waited.

'So, you know why you are here yes?'

Shaking his head slowly he said, 'no I don't know perhaps you could enlighten me Chief.'

His inquisitor gave a smile that was less than pleasant and said, 'well if you want to play games we can play games. You will not leave my building until you confess.'

Feeling a shaking in his hands he put them below the table. The Chief's eyes followed this coping strategy and the off-putting smile reappeared.

'There has been an invasion, an act of piracy on a yacht anchored just offshore.

I wanted to know if you knew anything about it.'

Trying to fake honesty and innocence he said, 'I don't know what you're talking about Chief. I wish I did or I'd tell you straight away.'

Losing his counterfeit smile, the Chief threw a large yellow envelope onto the table. He emptied it and a stack of glossy photos fell out.

Picking one up showing Hans and he on the Jet Ski. 'Here are some photos you may find interesting. They were taken recently I'm sure you'll recognise yourself and your new friend.'

He thumbed through the photos it showed him with everyone except Grace,

Dane and her father. That was a clue he wasn't about to explore now.

'Yes, we went out for a moonlight cruise. It sounds crazy and it seemed like a good idea at the time.'

'And this moonlight cruise does you know this is illegal in Thailand? People are killed on jet skis in daylight. Going out in darkness is both crazy and a crime.

'You have the right to remain silent, anything you say,' the Chief said before being cut off with the words, 'save it I know the rest, just tell me what I'm being arrested for.'

He spent a fitful night trying to sleep in a cell shared with 20 inmates. He was shaken awake by a scar faced man who seemed capable of killing him in a heartbeat.

'You have a visitor.' He looked up from the huddled mob in the cell and saw the guard named Thur smiling and nodding up and down as if to disprove the Chief's line this wasn't a game. Thur loved games like dropping Brodie's hot meal on the floor before making an effusive apology. There had to be some way to pass the time on death row.

Brodie stirred from his bunk. The only thing to do here was sleep and sleep was impossible when you shared a cell with ten men. He moved past the Scottish ice dealer and the Englishman charged with the manslaughter of his young wife. Jack's excuse was he woke up to find his bloodied and very dead partner lying next to him. Like everyone there including Brodie he was of course innocent. Nice enough, all of them, not that he trusted a single one. It was that kind of place. Only a few days before he witnessed a knifing in the showers. Everyone played dumb, after all the guy was still alive. No percentage in getting knifed yourself for snitching.

In the visiting room, he saw Grace's father. Ex-military man Major Dane Van Dyke was nowhere to be seen which was fine by him. Something about the father with his white moustache reminded him of Stan Lee.

'Thank you for coming Mr Winters. Really you didn't have to.'

'Yes, I know that and please call me Ralph.'

'Sure, OK Ralph.' He coughed into his fist not sure how to play this. 'Is Grace alright?'

The man who looked like he was used to exercising high level authority frowned and said in a controlled voice, 'this is a difficult time for her. She hadn't seen me for the better part of twenty years and she doesn't quite understand.'

Brodie thought to himself that he didn't quite understand either but let that slide. The man was here to help obviously so this was not the time to discuss family issues or anything else outside his own dire situation.

'You're in some deep shit son, some very deep shit.'

Brodie nodded. The logic of his statement was irrefutable. It was like saying there are sixty seconds in a minute or Trump is American.

'I can help you. I can help you get out of here.'

Brodie smiled at the good news. 'Great I'll get my things and we'll make tracks.'

Another smile creased Ralph Winters' face as he held up a restraining hand like a traffic cop. 'Not so fast. I'm afraid it's not quite that simple. There's more to it, much more to it.'

'Yeah how did I know here was going to be a catch?'

'We're in a third world country. There's always a catch **Brodie** it just isn't always very obvious.'

'What do I have to do exactly to get out of this? Do they want money?'

'If it was money it would be far more than you can afford. This has become a big story. Information is what the authorities want. Names, dates, places, contact numbers. If you know something my advice is to inform it might be your only chance.'

'You mean I have to give up the people who are trying to free these slaves?' Ralph looked down at his liver spotted hands.

'I'm afraid so. It's the only way Brodie. If I could pull strings I would.'

Feeling resentment rise he said in a cutting voice, 'hey aren't you in the CIA? You guys can walk on water.'

'Tell that to the men lost in the Bay of Pigs.'

Confused and not knowing what the man was talking about he shouted, 'what? Is that a joke?'

With a grim face, the man who could have been his father-in law in another lifetime said in a grave voice, 'I'm afraid not Brodie. These people are deadly serious. They are playing for keeps. I know these guys when they have you they don't let go. They sometimes need a bit of persuasion if you will. It was once said by a very wise man, Nelson Mandela in fact, that you only get to know a country when you have been inside its jails.'

He paused then said, 'this is serious stuff son. You're in over your head.'

His blood rising, Brodie replied, 'well I play for keeps and I'm deadly serious old man. I would rather die than give up these good people.'

'They're not angels do you know the atrocities these terrorists you call good are responsible for?'

'That's bullshit. You'll say anything, do anything to prove a point even when it's a lie. Isn't that what you do?'

With a frowning look of indignation, the old Company man began to scroll through photos on his iPhone of bomb blast victims on the streets of Phuket, Bangkok and Pattaya. There were gruesome shots of women and children with shredded limbs and heads half shot or blown off. Brodie turned away in disgust. It was the kind of stuff anti-abortionists showed those who believed in a woman's right to choose. To Brodie they were alternate facts and fake news in the most real sense. A form of counterintelligence from a Master of this black art. It was the Chief's old trick and he felt shot through with paranoia. Deconstruct the detainee's business model and leave him with nothing. Stalin and Pol Pot would be proud, maybe even the smiling assassin JFK would applaud from Mon's spirit world. Maybe he would in them soon to become one of the ghosts she speaks of. Could he still get a massage up there, or room service?

Alarmed and now convinced this White Knight rescuer was in cahoots with his bent Black Hat jailer he shouted, 'I'm ready to go back to my cell now. Guard, guard!' he shouted as he held up his manacled hands. Ralph stood with a pained smile that said *maybe you'll come around to my way of thinking when you get back to reality.*

In an act of defiance Brodie spat on the floor. 'Get me out of here please.' It was an excellent performance and he hoped the guards were taken in.

CHAPTER 37

Chailai sat on the concrete seat with her client. This one was older but kind, not like the young lager lads whom were arrogant or even violent.

'You want to stay long time?'

Shaking her head, she said, 'not tonight I have to go to my daughter's birthday party.'

The Englishman introduced to her as Toby smiled and said, 'that's alright. Can I get your phone number? I'd like to see you again.'

'You can find me at the bar we not allowed to give out phone numbers. Against company policy I hope you understand.'

Looking crestfallen he said, 'that's alright, you're young you probably have a boyfriend.'

'No, I like you. No boyfriend OK?'

They both knew she was lying but polite fiction was the best way to save face. Over in his usual place in the corner Jimmy drowned a life of regret with multiple shots of rum. He shouted to no one in particular, 'I'll drink to that.' It took a lot to get Jimmy drunk. He wasn't there yet.

The couple parted with a kiss and she went back to the bar. Boss Fleur wanted her to work late so she used a better excuse than the last one about a funny tummy.

'My grandmother is very sick. I think she may die,' she said in Thai. With a mother with chronic sickness due to a lifetime of back breaking work in the rice fields that was a little true but still a lie.

'Yes, I was sorry to hear she went into the hospital. She is a fine lady.' Her boss looked cross but she relented with a curt nod.

She left with a mental note to visit her poor grandmother in hospital. A lie could only go so far and Fleur Trin had a kind of in-built detector for untruths.

After catching a taxi scooter home, she opened the door to her small apartment to see Sirawit waiting for her. Startled she spoke in a controlled voice to rein in her anger.

'I told you not to come here. The police are after you.'

He got up and gave her a kiss on the cheek. She flinched, in no mood for loving or excuses. The many men in her life and were greedy to want more than she could give.

'My daughter will have a mother in jail if this happen. Why don't you leave me alone?'

He grabbed a hank of her hair and said, 'it is too late for that. You are in this right with me.'

She let out a scream of terror, of sheer frustration and mindless panic.

CHAPTER 38

Sirawit walked along Soi 8 his movements casual his racing mind less so. It had been a good day, a *productive* day, as his American friends would say. He stopped at a food cart and bought some hot Thai green chicken. He sampled it then gave a thumb- up to signal approval to the smiling vendor with green tinted hair. He walked faster. A man was following him, Sirawit stopped and the stranger made a show of looking in a Pharmacy store window. Slowly Sirawit moved down the street now hyper-vigilant and suffering from high anxiety. A doctor had already told him he wasn't paranoid, that condition was fear of something that didn't exist.The good doctor was well aware of the sinister forces Sirawit was up against. Segments of two armies and the Metro Police wanted him dead, of this he was certain. Sirawit wasn't wanted by the police, at least not officially, but that didn't mean they weren't after him.

He ducked down an alleyway knowing he could lose the tail by going in and out of different shops. As the pace quickened he knocked over a stall and beads, bracelets and clothes splashed onto the pavement. Seeing the shocked look on the face of the vendor he pressed three thousand baht into his hand. Not doing so could attract the police. Would he live to spend the rest?

As he neared the end of the alley the man of about thirty rushed towards Sirawit. He saw the glint of a knife and dodged him with a deft side step. The man went sprawling onto the pavement hard enough to draw blood. Then just as Sirawit thought he had the man's measure another assailant appeared from behind. This one had a gun. Having to make the decision to fight or run he ran.

Sirawit almost got to the herbal shop his cousin Taj owned. Up the at the corner he could see two uniformed policemen trying to look the other way. Breathing heavily, he saw the trap. As he reached for the door handle the man hunting him fired his hot pistol, the bullet colliding with Sirawit's head and severing the spinal cord. As he lay frozen and dying he looked up at the last person he would ever see. As numbness and a freezing cold shot through his body he coughed.

'Why? he asked in a raspy voice as life drained out of his body up towards a glowing full moon. It hovered bright and huge as his soul and more melted into its embrace. His spirit lived on and like a ribbon twisting in the wind his nat moved in and around the living as a reminder his restless soul once lived on this Earth.

'Why not?' the hunter replied as he pumped another bullet into his victim. The 33-calibre shot blasted out the back of Sirawit's head and the soul dream vanished in a heartbeat. The body now lifeless was vacated by his spirit to join the spirit world of ghosts, of spooks. His would not be a needless death. His murder would be avenged by these apparitions of the night. Each evening after midnight they would come from the Dark Side to haunt the guilty and seek justice. Each and every night.

As the killers fled bystanders crowded around the corpse. Maybe the dead had something to tell about what had come to pass, what lay ahead. He seemed not quite dead. Perhaps this soul that travelled to the moon was now back or had never left. In the crowd, someone mentioned the word aura, another spoke of the word karma. It was uncanny. Even with a gunshot wound to the head his face was unmarked like a wide-eyed if seriously dead JFK on the autopsy slab back in the last Millennium.

As a stream of black blood stained the pavement the ambulance and the police arrived. Soon Chief Timon was there and he supervised preparation of the crime scene with police tape and chalk outline.

At the Bikini Beach Bar, the impact of the killing was seeping into an already desperate situation.

'We have a crisis on our hands,' Teerasak said in a tremulous voice. He fell silent then bowed his head in sorrow. Krit Maung did the same. Unable to converse past a few basic Thai words, his burning eyes spoke of sorrow and also signalled a fierce determination.

'Sirawit was like a son to me, I will never forget him.' At this his voice choked and tears flowed down his cheeks.

Seated nearby Chailai held her head in her hands weeping.

'He was my husband and I will never get over his loss.'

'We must do something to avenge his murder. We must do this before we are also liquidated.'

CHAPTER 39

'Do you love him Grace?' He stood with his arms folded across his still broad chest, body language less hostile than defensive.

'I love him as much as any man,' she replied to her father knowing this would sound ambiguous, fuzzy to a man who had always compartmentalised his emotions.

'That's not really an answer but I know it will have to do.'

'I'm glad it meets with your approval.' His hint of bitterness made her react with, 'Oh, dad do you have to be that way?'

Ralph Winters gave a wry smile and said, 'do you know how long it's been since you said something like that to me?' 'Too long dad, far too long. And you've been gone too long.'

'I'll do what I can for Brodie.' Ralph smiled with a certain warmth, the kind of warmth that didn't always come easy to a man who had been in Intelligence and used to masking his emotions most of his life.

'Dad you don't have to do this.'

Reaching for her hand he said, 'yes I do. Let me do this for you, for him.'

'You haven't asked me why I was away.'

'I didn't want to ask if you didn't want to tell.'

'I was in a very bad place honey a place you don't want to know about. I was knee deep in a South American operation not unlike the Contras if you remember them.' She shook her head to show she didn't and he went on. 'But it was never exposed thank God.'

'So how did that lead to your fake death?'

He sat down as if this unburdening, this confessional, was taking a physical toll.

'There were death threats.' He spoke with a pained smile, it wasn't enough for his sceptical daughter.

'But you've had those before father how was this different?'

'Our operating team was drawn into this swamp of attrition. There were atrocities on both sides. Some unspeakable things.'

She was about to say something then stopped. When someone in the CIA, a close relative or not, mentions shock and horror you didn't argue for the nitty gritty. All her life there was this don't ask don't tell thing going on. That was a given. It was clear to her real honesty as opposed to the fake kind was too much to expect from a master of deceit and chronic Company Man.

He was back alright and true, it was like he had never gone away, only she was left with the thought that it may have made no difference if had really been around all those years. He was a returned ghost like the ones Brodie spoke of more and more. He flitted in and out of existence yet wasn't really there. Who was her father today, what he said he as or was he crafting an image of someone she wanted him to be or someone he wanted her to believe in? The Spin Doctor of Spy Craft was a riddle he might not understand himself. It was too much.

'Goodbye father,' she said as she turned on her heel and walked out.

Ralph Winters poured himself another drink and contemplated the Bay of Pattaya from the Penthouse window. Winds were blowing up a light chop as Jet Skis duelled in the Gulf of Thailand, throwing up rooster tails of white water. Gathering clouds in the distance foretold a night thunderstorm. Ralph braced himself for that storm and all the storms to come.

CHAPTER 40

B rodie and Grace sat facing each other in the hotel lobby. If it was the last time it would be more dreadful than explosive. There were too many explosions.

'Finally, you're going home.'

'And you're not.' She said as she stirred her coffee.

'Not unless someone gives me my passport back. That's not going to happen until the hearing and maybe not even then. I'm in a pretty tight fix if you haven't noticed.'

'I see. So where does that place us?'

'I still love you so that is up to you Grace. You know we both got caught up in this little war going on here at least you have an exit strategy.'

'Well as it happens I have extended my stay here. I had no idea my father would turn up.'

'Nobody did, I mean didn't you think he was dead?'

She gave a pained look then said, 'yes for the last two years my mother and I have lived with the idea he was dead.'

'Pretty convincing too. I wonder how he pulled that off.'

'Brodie he's in the CIA haven't you heard they can do anything. Anything. Overturn elections and overthrow governments. I mean he was methodical alright, he even left an inheritance. The word we got was that he was killed in an accident and the plane was never recovered.'

'Yeah I guess that's kind of neat really.'

'Neat, are you serious?' she asked in an angry tone. She was jumpy and hypervigilant, not unlike her father.

'No, I'm sorry it must have been traumatic to hear of his death and it must have done your head in to find all that was made up.'

As tears came to her eyes she said, 'yes Brodie you have no idea. He did what he thought he had to do. He always was and still is a company man. Let's face it the only reason you're out is because of his connections.'

'And that was facilitated by one Major retired, now recalled to active duty,

Dane Van Dyke. Didn't he propose to you?' She gave him an indignant look.

'Well actually that's none of your business.' There was a long pause as the words were left hanging in the air. This wasn't going well. Communication wasn't going anywhere and he resisted the urge to leave.

Grace let out an audible sigh. 'Sure, yes he did propose although he assures me it has nothing to do with my father.'

'And you believed him Grace. Looks to me this world of Intelligence is sparing with the truth. Or do we call if a post-truth world filled up with alternative facts.'

'Sure, fancy words for lying but isn't that the stock and trade of Intelligence and I use the word Intelligence sparingly I guess the idea is that the truth needs to be protected by a bodyguard of lies.'

'So, who said that? Donald Trump or Saturday Night Live?'

'Winston Churchill as a matter of fact.'

CHAPTER 41

With Grace gone he sat alone in the hotel lobby to contemplate his future.

With only an older tourist couple, probably Russian, there he felt very *alone*. Prospects were bleak for getting out anytime soon. At least all this chop was kept out of the papers. He could see the headlines now, stock market analyst imprisoned for terrorist outrage. The iPhone rang. The ring tone was loud with a capital L.

He saw the call sign, Spike Cawley, someone he hadn't heard from since the disaster party many months ago. Or had he seen him before? He wasn't quite sure. Anyone for short term memory loss?

'Spike what's up?'

'I'm in Pattaya thought I'd drop by you know check out the action and all that.'

'Drop by, you mean catch a flight?'

'Bro I've already done that. I'm here in the Golden City of Pattaya. Didn't you hear me?'

He held the phone to his chest trying to think. He'd been warned by the Master of Deception himself Ralph winters, to lay low and tell no one about the deep shit he was in.

'Hey why not I'm here in Soi 7 in a little place called the Hotel Metro. You'll love it. I suppose Maggie is with you?'

'Nope you suppose wrong. I'll always love the lady. It turned out we were incompatible. My income didn't match her pat-ability.'

'Well you might have heard that Grace and I are over.'

There was a pause on the other end before he heard Spike say, 'I didn't but I don't know about Maggie. We've over too so there's not much communication between us in fact there's none. Visiting the kids is becoming a problem but never mind about that I'm here to get out of my head.'

'Alright you're here so come over let's meet at a bar on the corner of Beach road and Soi 7 called the Calypso Bar. It's got a great view and we can check things out pretty good there.'

He could hear laughing, then the words, 'yeah well I guess we don't want too much of a good thing but in the meantime, we won't let that get in the way of us having a good time just the same. I'm ready to rage, ready to party,' he said breaking the last word into two loud syllables. Par-ty.

Within half an hour they met at the bar called Fridays after a last-minute change of venue. Sunset was already upon them and they drank Margaritas as they did a bit of girl watching. Brodie looked around as night fell and saw that most of the clientele were doing the same.

''What do you think Spike kind of unreal isn't it?'

Smiling widely, he said, 'it's more than unreal its mind blowing.' He quickly turned his head as a beautiful statuesque woman in skyscraper heels floated past.

'Look at her. Pretty tall for a Thai don't you think?'

Shaking his head, he said, 'looks like you got caught out in one of the country's great insider jokes.'

Looking innocent of local street life his friend asked, 'what, what do you mean?'

Brodie clapped him on the back and said, 'I'm afraid that lady ain't a lady my friend.'

'Really Jesus she looks the part. Christ she's pretty.'

'Sounds like you want to take her home,' Brodie said with a cheeky smile.

They walked past the Cowboy Go-Go Bar where Thai women in mini-skirts lounged on bar stools with legs jacked up looking very available. He saw a woman as tall as a willow and was left wondering about her gender. She was lithe to the point of muscular and seemed very capable of kicking his ass. Thigh tendons flexed sending a ripple of muscle tone across impossibly long legs. The looker had a voice. It was borderline *she-male* and all the more forceful for that. As she spoke her Adam's apple bobbed like a cuckoo announcing her sex.

'Hey you want good time? You want to buy me drink?' she asked. Brodie and Spike exchanged looks. Brodie said, 'why not?'

They strolled up to the girls and ordered drinks.

After two drinks, he managed to lose her. There were more golden fish in this stream, this flow this traffic of people and people movers. The two friends watched for game, something would turn up.

While quaffing Tiger beer stubbies Brodie watched as Spike began to stroke the legs of a tallish woman clearly not a tranny. Aping him Spike put his arms around a woman who was short but made up for it with a winning, cheeky smile and live wire personality. She didn't look half bad either even with a blue wig.

'So, what is your name?' Brodie asked not sure if he would get an honest answer.

'My name is Pam,' she said as she extended a hand and they shook hands as he introduced himself in response. She reached for a cigarette and he hurried to light it for her. She winked her appreciation and moved closer to him.

'Brodie, Brodie, nice name I know Englishman name Brodie. He take me to Phuket and we stay at Pattong beach long time.'

He kissed her on the cheek and said, 'whoa hold up we just met I'm not ready to go to the other side of the country.'

Pam winked and said, 'so what you ready for. You ready for me?'

As he thought about the proposition of taking her upstairs he felt a playful punch on the arm.

'Come on no time like the present Brodie. What have you got to lose?'

Quite a lot actually, he said to himself although now was not the time to let Spike in on his situation. No point in spoiling the fun. Wasn't spike prone to panic attacks? Maybe it was a falling off to get back on aversion therapy kind of thing. He wasn't about to frighten a guy who was a little bit scared and a little bit scary. They would meet this challenge, pole vault over this Mexican Wall of the mind. He was tired of being afraid, tired tip toeing around levels and floors covered in broken glass.

Spike stood and holding his new squeeze close said, 'the young lady wants to show me her bedroom.' He kissed the girl who called herself Princess and said, 'I don't know about you but we are going to make tracks and get something happening.'

Both couples were guided upstairs past a huge man with folded arms who looked like a South-East Asian version of Mohammed Ali. Brodie looked him up and down then said to a grinning Spike, 'maybe he can be my bodyguard.'

'And I'll be your long-lost friend, right? Do you need one mate?' Spike asked only half serious.

'No comment. Come on we came here to have fun let's get to it. No going back. No second thoughts.'

The ladies giggled as the couples went into adjoining rooms.

CHAPTER 42

Later after midnight in walking street Spike strolled with his arm around his new partner Tan. This one with purple hair might stay a while, at least until the money ran out. With bar fines going up Brodie was happy to go freelance. Not that he really wanted another woman in his life. Finding someone he didn't have to pay for was the new challenge and in that way, he was in exactly the wrong place.

Walking street was packed and crowded with *farung* in bars advertised with too bright fluoro lights and spruikers on the street touting for business. 'Come and see the Bangkok Shock Boys fresh from their Honk Kong sell out concert.

Come and see beautiful Thai see beautiful Asia girl.'

As he spoke three women in panties and push up bras circled him like Champion fillies at the Derby. Gawking from the kerb Brodie liked what he saw.

Spike had his handbag with the blue hair and seemed happier than Brodie could remember. Was he leading him astray? Considering his drunken friend was pushing forty and was now very single the question was academic. As to whether Brodie was leading himself astray now that demanded a response. On a whim, he speed-dialled Grace.

'This number is out of service or disconnected,' came the canned response. It felt like a rebuke, an insult and it was all of that.

He looked at the iPhone with the photo of Grace then quickly replaced it with a wallpaper pic of a Phuket Island, the kind that shot straight out of the sea like snap frozen magma. Then he got an idea and announced to Spike and Pam, 'alright smile I want a photo of you two.' After snapping the mobile memory, he motioned for the two to follow him into a notorious place he'd been told about by a British bar fly with a tattoo covered body. Snakes wound around his arms and tunnelled crystal skulls.

They strolled past more body guard, spies, he was sure were sent by Ralph. He started to move towards a food cart selling sweet smelling fried chicken until Spike caught his arm and said pointing to a place across the road, 'how about the Russian bar over there?'

Brodie swivelled until he saw a huge bar attached to a hotel called St. Petersburg. It had a windmill like the famous clip joint in Paris only with a Slavic touch with kicking neon Cossack dancers going around in an endless circle. As it turned the pink and yellow lights flashed as if telegraphing some filthy secret. Neckless bouncers European in appearance possibly American but more likely Russian or English flanked the marble entrance. 'Come inside best girls in Pattaya' one of the security officers said in thickly accented English. The stone-faced greeters looked like they were straight out of the KGB or whatever they called themselves now. The two men looked at each other and laughed.

'Not a good idea Spike, not a good idea at all.'

Spike, looking confused said, 'why not. Might be something different you know.'

'I know but these guys are killers from what I've heard. Word on the street and I only know what people tell me, word on the street is that the Russians tried to take over and they lost.'

'What do you mean they lost?'

'I mean they lost big time. I know Thailand is the land of smiles but there's also this dark side. A side you don't want to know about. You could just as easily call it the Land of Lies.'

'Try me,' his plucky friend said warming to the intrigue.

'Ok when the Thai gangsters saw they were being bought out with laundered oligarchy money they began to react.'

'React?' Spike asked. Even over a few days he was beginning to know the Thailand they didn't mention in the travel brochures.

'Yeah react in the most real sense. One of the Russian working girls was shot in the head. Then the next day all the working girls in Pattaya were rounded up by their Russian minders then put on an Aeroflot jet back over Siberia and onto Moscow. End of story.'

'That's a great story how come I never heard it before?'

Brodie put a reassuring hand on his friend's shoulder then said, 'you know some of the best stories are kept out of the papers.'

'Sounds like you're speaking from experience.'

'Maybe I am but I can't talk about it.'

Spike gave his squeeze another kiss only more syrupy and languid. Before they drowned Brodie tapped his pal on the shoulder. Knowing what he knew he couldn't leave them.

Coming up for air Spike smiled and said, 'I'm done, I'm ready.'

'Glad to see you back. Now this will amaze you, old friend. It will simply amaze you.'

At that he beckoned the love birds to follow him inside. As they entered the darkened room with gyrating lights and girls dancing on tables, two of the house women could be seen throwing ice as they took off tiny bikinis to reveal rounded cheeks and perfect breasts. The room began swirling like some manic carousel until he passed out. Solution? Another vodka an orange. The he spray painted the table with vomit before passing out a second time.

CHAPTER 43

Nursing a coffee after the punishing night out Brodie checked his watch again. He didn't remember how he got home. Was he suffering some sort of PTSD or even brain damage. Sure, that would explain a lot. He held his head between his hands as if it were one of those old gumball machines that just needed a bit of a shake to get right. Then sketchy images of being helped into a pick- up truck taxi called a *sentego* came back to his awakening brain like some scratchy black and white movie. Nervous energy got him tapping on the imitation marble table. Spike and Pam were late although it was only 2 in the afternoon, a time when many hungover farung were usually sleeping.

Chailai shared a Diet coke with him and he stroked her arm as much to reassure himself as to calm this always hyper vigilant lady. She bowed towards the small shrine to Budda in a *wai* and Brodie did the same. She did the same with the *nat* shrine, as if to cover all the bases as Brodie followed suit. The *nat* or ghost seemed to be watching him beneath the headdress, surrounded by offerings of whiskey bottles. Both got the nod from this respectful farung. It wasn't as if he believed, more that he needed all the luck he could get. Chailai was the one and this was something that came from the centre of his heart. Adventures out on the town with Spike only convinced him even more that she was the only girl for him in the Land of Smiles. He lightly kissed her and she flinched. It was jarring, and he was quick to act. How could he be happy if she wasn't? The calculus of that was enough to drag in a fog of cognitive dissonance that would hang over him for years.

'You look worried. Is everything alright?'

She lowered her head looking sad. Not quite stricken, Chailai didn't do stricken. She had seen too much, lost too much to cry the tears of a heartsick girl. The world was tough but she always found a place of refuge, a place to curl up under, a space to survive. He knew her hard-scrabble background in dirt road village where she watched her father die, cut almost in half by an overturned tractor. People he knew back home would lay down and die or sign up to a lifetime of psychiatric counselling in the face of that kind of disaster.

She gave a weak smile and said, 'no it's nothing, nothing to worry about.'

Moving his head close to her he said, 'I always get worried when someone tells me there's nothing to worry about.'

Looking into her eyes he could see tears forming. Chailai cleared her throat and said in a tone he took as frightened, 'you must leave Thailand Brodie. You must go soon. Too many enemy they want to kill.'

He gave a quick laugh. She was right of course. He wanted to know more.

'Well you know I have to go through that court case. No getting around that they have my passport.'

Chailai's eyes flared as though she had received an electric shock from a cattle prod. No question it got her attention. Life altering reality checks were the coin of the realm around here.

'I want you to see someone.'

'Here you mean?'

Chailai shook her head and replied, 'no not here. Come with me, you have to meet someone.'

'Who would that be Chailai?'

Without speaking she motioned with her head and walked to her scooter. Handing him a motorcycle helmet he got on then held on as they navigated winding streets crowded with shoppers, drinkers, players. She steered and pitched past mobs of young and old until they arrived at a two-star hotel.

Stepping off the machine he noticed flaking paint and rusty downpipes. Not exactly five stars, but ideal for hiding out. They were journeying to the western suburbs of the City a place called the Dark Side. Here the neon and bright lights were scarcer, the girls fewer and older with moneyed punters back beachside.

They climbed rickety stairs to the second floor and then to room 101. Knocking lightly a beefy red-haired man with an American accent opened the door to say in a cheery, unreal voice, 'hi Chailai come in.'

They entered the room where three women in their late teens or early twenties were seated on a bed. The girls seemed new to the trade and he felt ashamed for them and of himself. Yes, this was no rendezvous for consensual sex. There had to be another purpose in mind.

Chailai turned to him and said, 'these women were some of those rescued by Sirawit before he was killed.'

Feeling her pain, he struggled to find the right words. 'His death was a terrible loss but at least he didn't die in vain.' 'No but there is more work to do.'

'Tell me what I can do. I'll try my best.'

Shaking her head slowly she said, 'you need to stay out of jail Brodie. You go inside again you not get out. Ever.'

'I want you to listen to these women and what they have to say. They speak Burmese and a little Thai but no English.'

Brodie nodded not quite sure why he was there. Struggling to be patient he kept quiet. Then a hunched lady Chailai said was Rohingya from Myanmar began speaking in halting Thai. He had heard of them and wanted to know more. He googled it to find they were supposed to be the world's most persecuted minority. She began talking as Chailai translated in passable English.

'I came from a village in south eastern Myanmar. My father and my brother were put in jail for protesting the government. We are punished for wanting a life we find enough to eat, where to have job and support family.'

As he listened he noticed that Chailai's English was much improved. He wondered if he could take credit for that and decided he could but wouldn't tell her that. A teacher is only as good as the student.

The woman who was lucky to be alive went on speaking then stopping to let Chailai to catch up with her.

'My mother Kiu and I were not allowed to visit brother or father. My younger sister was raped then shot by soldiers. Anyone who resisted was stabbed or shot, sometimes drowned or beaten to death.

There was no way out from the slave factories. Life inside was like death. When the men inside all Rohingya made riot against jail they were shot and killed. Nobody know this and nobody care. We knew we would be next so my mother and my young son escaped across the river into northern Thailand.'

There was a long pause before the woman known as Ruok began speaking again. Now she had tears in her eyes, her voice beginning to crack. 'Once inside Thailand my mother met a man who said he could help us.' Then more tears and quiet sobbing before she went on.

'We trusted him and gave him our money. He took me to a place and I have not seen my son or my mother since. I was kept in a room with 20 other women with nothing to eat. Then we were taken to Chiang Mai before going to Bangkok.'

'What did you do in Bangkok?' he asked. More tears.

She spoke then Chailai translated. Chailai asked a question as if to clarify the statement or rephrase it. Not a linguist or translator herself Chailai was doing exceptionally well.

'We worked in factory from sunrise to sunset. We make things very dangerous. Some get hurt some get injured. Then we were taken to boat off Pattaya. We work during day and locked up on boat at night.'

Ruok wiped away tears then went on as if telling the whole story was more important than the pain that came with it. Would pain like that ever go away? He doubted it and knew people back home who stayed hurt all their lives. He listened as the tsunami of tragedy began to embrace him and watery tentacles breached his heart.

'My mother died on a farm in northern Thailand.' Motioning with her hands to show eating and drinking she said, 'my mother died of hunger and she died of thirst. Her slavers were wild pigs, animals.'

Brodie intervened with another question. 'Who told you this?' Chailai duly translated both question and answer.

'One of the guards felt sorry for me. He say he love his mother and knew I loved my mother. He say she die in the fields in the heat. She was buried there.

No one knows where. Even as guard he was prisoner.'

Now there were wracking sobs and Brodie stood to say, 'tell her thank you for speaking with us and that we're sorry for her loss,' he paused before saying, 'and we feel her pain.'

CHAPTER 44

Chief Timon glared at him from across the large wooden table. 'Well I'm here Chief. I have to report every day so here I am.'

There was a moment of silence. The Chief cracked his knuckles with a sinister smile, his bald head gleaming under the light and looking like a demonic skull.

Was he fantasising about cracking Brodie's skull?

'Yes, you are here and if not, we would have a warrant for your arrest. You might be able to hide but you would never leave the country. If we find you after you evade law, you stay in jail until you die or get out as old man. I know any men like this think they above law and end up inside to contemplate their foolishness. '

Brodie visualised this very possible fate. Alone, yet in a cell with forty men and an over flowing toilet and a worse than bleak future. Brodie wasn't about to give this sadist the satisfaction of knowing the ongoing terrorising was having an effect that ghosted his every waking thought and fitful sleep punctuated by nightmares. He knew what it was like to be incarcerated forever because he was there every night. Brodie gave a smile and said, 'that's comforting to know.'

'Mr Jamieson, you do not seem to understand the trouble you are in. the people you have associated with are charged with terrorism against the state.

They are killers and will be punished. This is no, ah walk in park as you Americans say.'

'I'm not American,' he protested as the Chief gave a dismissive wave of the hand as if there were no difference between the two. Perhaps just as some Australians or Americans lumped all Asians together, or used to, it wasn't hard to imagine how this lawman could confuse the two.

You could end up in jail for 10 or twenty years like some of your countrymen who are locked up for drugs.'

With a nervy tone in his voice Brodie said, 'nobody said anything about drugs.'

The Chief clasped his hands together then said, 'no this is true. You have powerful friends Mr Jamieson. Things could be very different if they were not here.'

Brodie cleared his throat. He had no idea how much money Ralph had handed over but guess it was substantial. The conversation wasn't going in the direction he wanted. Fact was it was heading south. He preferred not to have any conversation with a Chief of Police whether it was deep in Thailand or in Australia. How did the line go, anything you say can and will be used against you and this guy didn't do small talk I gather? Feeling a throbbing in his head, coupled with a hot flush across his cheeks, Brodie made frantic moves to dissipate the negative energy that threatened to overwhelm. He looked at the white tiled wall then back to the Chief then back to the wall and the wall seemed much closer as if his world was imploding into some sinister singularity.

'Do I still have to report? Can't I go home and testify through Skype?'

Chief Timon let out a laugh revealing white teeth that looked as if had an excellent dentist. Of course, that was one of the attractions in being here. Come to Thailand and get new teeth, new and improved boobs. Yes, the Chief had a beautiful smile to go with his dark persona. Unlike other people he knew his age there was no sign of dentures.

'We are not in Las Vegas.'

'I'm Australian.'

'Yes, but you have American connections in high places. In fact, I know you are a dual Australian and American citizen.'

Brodie gave a pained smile that was something even Grace didn't know about but assumed Ralph did. Ralph was a Company Man. Ralph knew everything.

For a second, he thought of saying he'd only just become acquainted with Grace's well-connected father and thought better of it. This thing wasn't going away any time soon, so he had to play the long game. His legal representative Omar was giving him close instructions on how to respond and now he realised the importance of the right tactics. Keeping out of jail and getting back home were the main concerns.

'I believe you have information you can tell us about some dangerous operatives still at large. If you can help us with our investigation you could help your situation.

Feeling a tremor in his hands and legs as if the ground underneath was shaking with the force of a tectonic shift Brodie tried to hold it together before he cracked and folded or maybe confessing to something he didn't do just to make it stop. That was an old torturer's technique. Imploding or getting sucked into catatonia could lead to another round of interrogation and he could be trapped in that washing cycle forever. Suspicion alone was enough to get him incarcerated again with an even more uncertain future, an ant crawling up a hill only to fall back down then start over.

'Chief Timon I wish I could tell you. As I understand it Sirawit is dead and I only met him once or twice. We spoke maybe half a dozen words.'

'What words, what words did you exchange? There is much that can be said in even a yes or a no. So, tell me Mr Jamieson what words did he say to you and what words you say to him.'

Under the table the trembling dialled up. His bladder felt ready to burst like a water balloon. The thought of asking to go to the can was considered then rejected. Isn't that what drug smugglers asked for? A quick dash to the head so white stuff can be flushed down the toilet or a film style escape through the back window or scampering in ceiling air ducts, while the Chief looked at his watch and sipped his coffee, was a comforting fantasy.

'Well we said hello and goodbye of course. You know the usual pleasantries about the weather.'

The Chief pounded his fist on the table and shouted, 'I am not a fool Mr Brodie do not make the mistake of playing me for idiot. Many men, many women have tried this and lost their lives.'

With a dry mouth and a feeling, the room would explode into a thousand glassy splinters of broken dreams and lost opportunities he bounced his leg up and down to work off the nervous energy. The Chief was threatening execution, wasn't he? Could his life end in this room through the intrigues of one man? The answer had to be yes, yes and yes.

He squeezed his eyes tight as if to banish this hellish new normal. Opening his eyes with the realisation it wouldn't work he tried to get a grip. No way was this Digger going to get banged up abroad. No way.

With any trace of a smile gone and his voice at a level tone to fit in with the gravity of the situation he said, 'look I met them I had no idea what they were up to end of story. I wish I could tell you more I really do.'

The Chief gave a hollow laugh then slapped his palms on the table to make another loud bang. 'I want to believe you.' He paused to stare at him with bulging eyes, then said, 'but I don't if you want to tell me the truth then tell me it is very simple. You know more than you say. Share your information with us and you will be free to leave the country.'

'You mean after the trial.'

The Chief sighed as if this were obvious. 'Yes, we have legal system here just like they have Australia just like they have Washington DC. You think we no have. You wrong. A trial will not be necessary if you give right statement, yes?'

Playing along, Brodie nodded. Who was he to disagree with the Chief of Police?

The man who had killed so many paused then said in a softened tone, 'if you tell us the right information, the correct information then there may be no need for you to attend the trial.'

'You mean I could talk my way out of it?'

'If the talk is the truth then yes you would be free to go.'

As Brodie weighed up his options there was a soft knock on the door and a slight man entered. He walked to his Chief and whispered in his ear.

The Chief's eyes widened then he said, 'it seems you have a visitor. He paused th said, 'so I will detain you no longer.'

Brodie smiled and said, 'I didn't know I was being detained.'

This time there was no smile. 'You are to remain in Pattaya until the adjournment. All conversations are confidential of course.'

'But of course, they are.' Putting out his hand to shake he said with a mock American accent, 'it's been real nice talking to you Chief Timon.'

The Chief frowned without responding. To Brodie's mind he seemed to be signalling, *you'll keep.*

He walked outside and saw Ralph Winters waiting for him with a youngish Thai man. Although over 70 he seemed to have unlimited amounts of energy and stamina.

Shaking hands his *almost* father in-law pointed to the man standing next to him and said, 'glad to see you survived the latest third degree, I'd like you to meet Apasit Bundwit one of the best lawyers in Bangkok and Pattaya.'

'But I don't need a lawyer.'

Ralph gave him a look and said, 'son take it from me you need a lawyer and a good one at that. All that's taken care of.'

Ralph moved his arm forward showing them the way. They got into a limousine and drove in silence to the Hilton. After taking the lift to the Penthouse suite Ralph called in room service. It was going to be a long night.

CHAPTER 45

B rodie ran and tried not to look back. Inside his head he couldn't help but hear the ominously worded earworm 'Wanted' by Peter Tosh. He had always been a fan of this assassinated Rastafarian, a martyr to Reggae. Now the words spoke to him. *They're trying to find me. Wanted by the evil forces.*

As the reggae music did loops in his head and became background, ambient, he dodged motorcycle taxis and Tuk- Tuks as well as street vendors, one with dresses and hats piled high like a portable clothes boutique. Then veering close to the bars, he knocked over a table splashing beers and shattering glasses on the pavement. After rounding a corner, he crouched near a set of concrete steps and watched as two men raced by. Taking a chance, he ran down the street and before he got to the end noticed that the men had back tracked to find him. Brodie whistled and got on a motorcycle taxi.

Later he went to an address an anonymous person, he assumed was Chailai, sent him via Snapchat.

At a seedy hotel on the Dark Side he knocked on the door and was motioned into a cramped room with peeling, yellow paint and worn furniture, like the diseased guts of a dead animal. A meal of rice and vegetables was being cooked on the hotplate and the aroma helped to overcome the usual dodgy plumbing. He shook hands with a man about 60 whom he'd seen around the Cowboy Bar. The Chief had him high on the list of wanted men and Brodie knew just being in a room with him was more than dangerous. It was suicidal. No matter he was feeling a bit suicidal. Maybe he could make that work for him.

In heavily accented English the man said, 'my name is Teerasak, Krit and I have important information for you.'

Brodie had seen Teerasak around. He nodded and said, 'you might be a bit late I already have people chasing after me.'

'Do you know who they would be?'

'You mean aside from the police and the usual suspects? No, I don't.'

'Usual suspects, who are these usual suspects?'

'Sorry it's a figure of speech I don't know who they are. I can only guess they might be connected to the people that killed Sirawit Puna.'

'How do you know this?'

He shrugged and said, 'I don't know really but call it an educated guess. I mean I get hauled into the police station every week that's one of the bail conditions. I hear things you wouldn't get on the street. Usually I get the third degree which wasn't part of the deal as far as I'm concerned, but hey we're in Thailand.'

'Yes, I know our Chief Timon is hard man. A very cruel man who wants to destroy us.'

'Why does he want to destroy you, me?'

'He is nothing but puppet for powerful forces. This goes up to high level. He is part of this slavery.'

After gving a sceptical look Chalai said, 'he is paid to look other way. That is why many Maung are left to wander the streets. When no one knows who you belong to it is best to leave alone.'

'Yes corruption goes high.' Teerasak ground his teeth and facial muscles moved adding to the overall impressipn of strength.

'How high Teerasak?' Brodie had a vision of generals plotting his downfall, vultures on the make.

Looking unsure he said, 'that is not for me to say. We will never get to these people, so we cannot speak of this.'

Brodie pondered that and decided against pressing the matter. How did the saying go, what he didn't know wouldn't hurt him? No that wasn't right, it went the other way, *what he or she doesn't know won't hurt them.* In effect, a nicely put way of excusing lies white or otherwise.

'So where does that leave us?'

Teerasak cupped his hands under his chin in contemplation.

'The Chief will try to get you to make a deal that includes informing on me and my people.'

'But I don't know anything, how can I tell him anything?'
'You know me now that's enough. You will be asked or persuaded to inform on me and they will make up facts,'
'Alternative facts?'
'Yes, that is true, there are lies dressed up as the truth.'
'Yeah a lot of that getting around I guess.'
He will use Chailai as bait to get you too.'
'You mean as a dobber or blagger, a snitch?'
'Correct, or how your American friends say ah,'
'Snitch, it's called snitching.'

CHAPTER 46

In the back of a stretch limousine Brodie sat with his would-be father in law. The patrician former spy seemed like a father, perhaps an old-style TV father like Robert young or Fred McMurray or Danny Thomas, full of wisdom and sage advice. Someone both reassuring and vaguely intimidating. He was there to help but he could also take you to the wood shed.

Thinking he might start confessing with this father confessor Brodie spoke first, pre-emptive strike mode.

'You know Grace and I aren't really together anymore. She's only here now because of you.'

'Yes, I know and you probably also know there is a lot of baggage between us, between Grace and I.'

'I don't know much she never spoke about it before you arrived, got back into her life. Before the separation she told me you all lived in Mexico.'

Ralph winters cleared his throat and said, 'yes we did and they were glorious years. Some children take a break up worse than others and that was my second marriage,' he paused, then said, 'and not the last.'

Brodie wondered how many wives this guy had but thought better of asking.

As the chauffeured Mercedes Benz sped past run down residential blocks and tacky looking shops Brodie said, 'you don't have to say any more Mr Winters it's not really my business.'

Ralph looked at him with a stern face and said, 'I know that there are some things I want you to know. You're in a great deal of trouble and I mean get you out if not get you off.'

Brodie nodded, now was not the time to argue with his patron. It occurred to him their mutual separation from the tempestuous Grace was a kind of common ground that made them natural allies.

'I can speak of this now because I am officially retired.'

At this he gave a smile. Could it be that as with other secretive, nefarious organisations, including the mafia and outlaw motorcycle gangs, there really was no such thing as retirement short of the grave was there? Something along the lines of you can check out but you can never leave. Here he was at the Hotel California. The man with the inscrutable face and military posture was a lifer in for the duration, he'd be plugging away at the opposition, any opposition until the end.

Lounging on the beach in retirement hell wasn't who he was or what he wanted to be. The man was an education and Brodie was learning fast. Brodie gave him a wide-eyed attentive look so as to urge him on.

'It was a simpler time. Not so much in the states but in Mexico. This was well before the nation- wide drug war that is still tearing the country apart,' he stopped to look out the window as if recapturing that previous life-time then continued.

'The Cold War was officially over but of course it wasn't really and still isn't in many ways, really over. I was operations chief for Central and South America. Of course, Castro and his lot had our attention for the longest time. Forgive me but I have nothing to say about operational matters then or now. Now of course I'm out of the loop.' He gave a sly smile that seemed to undermine his words. Brodie assumed that spy craft habits were part of his DNA and he couldn't help being deceptive.

'Grace and her mother began to feel cut off in Mexico and worse. Her mother began questioning my career and its purpose as if this wasn't part of the arrangement when we married. She thought I would change or my career would change and that was an unfortunate assumption. Grace followed along with her mother and when the inevitable separation came they both left barely without notice.'

'You mean she didn't tell you she was leaving?'

'Not in so many words. It was abrupt. We had discussed it but as she later told me by phone in faraway Australia she didn't want to have a heated discussion or be persuaded to change her mind. I let it go. Yes every once in a while, I would jet Grace back to Laredo or more often Los Angeles. She was young somehow, she got used to it. Grace told me half her friends came from broken homes.' He sighed then followed this up with, 'I suppose that's a consolation of sorts.'

Not knowing what to say Brodie watched hick stands of banana trees and dense undergrowth zip by underneath as though they were on a Vietnam era search and destroy mission. Clearing his throat, he said, 'it must have been very painful. That would have been hard.'

For a moment Ralph's eyes became rheumy as if holding in tears. Of course, old CIA men never cry. His gaze took on a steelier quality, face muscles set and jaw jutting that to Brodie was typically American or a certain type of American warrior ready willing and able to take on several wars in several hemispheres simultaneously. The man was getting old, right? That didn't mean he was going soft and it didn't mean he couldn't express emotion. Needless, unendurable tragedy would see this elder company man camp alone with his grief and after that seek a response by any means necessary.

'Well it wasn't easy I can tell you that my friend. There were people who urged me to take her back one way or another. I don't think your homeland of meat pies and kangaroos is especially secure. Events have proved that.'

'I get it whatever it takes?'

Ralph didn't reply. The upshot was that he could make it happen.

At this Brodie had visions of masked company men using duct tape to take mother and daughter to some covert hanger where a CIA jet awaited. On return, both would be subjected to stupefying drugs to bring them around to his way of thinking. Would that even be possible? Brodie wanted to think it wasn't but when you considered the world's foremost intelligence agency, able to decapitate heads of state or start or stop revolutions then anything was possible.

'But you didn't do that.'

Ralph looked through the tinted car window again. Here was a man used to asking questions not answering them.

'No, I didn't, I couldn't live with myself if my wife and daughter lived under my roof as virtual captives like they were part of some intervention. People have the wrong idea about the company and company men. We aren't all monsters you know.'

Brodie nodded and said, 'if I didn't know it before I know it now.'

Then out of the jungle they stopped on a rise that overlooked a series of large buildings.

'Do you know where we are Brodie?'

Shaking his head, he said, 'no not really. Is that some kind of government facility?'

'Close but no cigar. In some sense this overgrown, overfed sweatshop is of by and for the government but it is a commercial place that manufactures phones.'

'What iPhones, Samsung, Pixel, Huawei?'

'All of the above and more Brodie. Some of the people you got entangled with run under the banner of liberating the work slaves here.'

'I didn't know,' he lied with the thought this could be some elaborate ruse to get him to confess complicity in state crimes.

There was a long silence between them until Ralph said, 'I know you might imagine that it is counter-intuitive for a so-called company man like me, active or inactive, would be interested in an issue some would describe as of commercial interest only.'

Brodie was indeed wondering why they were there. He dared not speak.

Without his patron, his lucky charm God knows where he would be.

'This is not about business it's a humanitarian issue. If there is large scale work slavery going on here and elsewhere throughout southeast Asia, that is a security problem not just a humanitarian problem.'

'I see, why are you telling me all this?'

'I wanted you I want you to know what stakes are involved here. Your life is in danger.'

CHAPTER 47

'So how can I help?' he asked Teerasak as the older man toyed with worry beads. They were the original angst spinners yet they hardly seemed to work for this troubled man with much on his mind. A fear of the raging spirits, the nats heightened the tension. Heavy beads of sweat gathered on his forehead and Brodie wondered if it was more than the sky-high heat and humidity.

'You can help by staying out of jail and maintaining the support you still have.'

'Which means exactly what? Do I testify against you or what?'

'Tell them what you really know. Which is nothing. There is only a family connection connecting me with Sirawit and nothing else.'

As they spoke the bank of CCTV monitors kept track of movement in the front, back, and sides of the hotel with aerial coverage provided by a mini-drone. Then three men came into view, each wearing tee shirts one with the sunrise symbol of Japan and the name *Tokyo*.

'They're coming we must leave.' Teerasak looking alarmed threw his disposable, self-destructing cell phone into a bin.

'Who are they?' Brodie asked only to be met by silence.

'Follow me,' Teerasak said as he raced to the back door. To their amazement there was no one there.

Breathing heavily Teerasak said, 'when we get down the stairs go to this bar and they will give you sanctuary.'

With no time to look at the note both ran down the stairs two steps at a time.

When they got to the bottom they split up like escaped prisoners. Brodie ran to the street filled with the usual food cart vendors and loudly dressed tourists then took a hard left. He ducked into a market place and quickly bought new clothes including an oversized hat trying to blend in like a tourist in the capital of planet sex tourist, Pattaya. Convincing no one he busied himself with his reflection in a mirror as what he assumed were police in civilian clothes raced past him. The man with the drawn Colt 45 revolver convinced him of that.

Dying in the gutter wasn't going to be his fate if he could help it. This was no time to make mistakes and he wouldn't.

He dialled Grace and she picked up immediately.

'And what do I owe the pleasure of your voice Brodie?' The tone was flat. He knew he had to think fast.

'Is your father there?'

'No, he's not and what if he is has all this attention from the police addled your mind Brodie?'

Sounding nervous he replied, 'No reason, so how would you feel about a visit today?'

There was silence except for the crackling of a bad line.

'Are you in some kind of trouble, Brodie?'

'Well nothing more than usual, you know me Grace,' he lied. There was a kind of pact with her father and he was in no position to break it now.

'Yes, I know you and I know when you're lying. I want you to be straight with me Okay?'

'I'll tell you everything when we meet up. I can't talk on the phone, you never know who might be listening.'

'Alright meet me in the lobby, no wait come up to the room. Brad isn't here.'

'Are you still with him Grace?'

'What's it to you Brodie? Who I see or don't see is none of your business. You know I never took you for a stalker. I'm trying to be nice. So, I ask again, what's it to you?'

'Nothing really, I just want you to be happy and I know how that sounds.'

'I'm still here because of you,' the phone went silent before she followed up with, 'and because my father is here.'

'Yeah well I think he's a real gentleman he cares for you Grace he really does.'

'I guess that's why he sent the word out that he was dead and then forgot to remember to tell us.'

'What can I say he's from that world. Strange things happen.'

He could sense rising anger on the other end of the line. Somehow, he'd become an apologist for one of the world's greatest spooks. It was a funny feeling, like being a double agent in a double cross and not knowing which side of history you were on, the right side or the wrong side. This wasn't going well.

The idea that things between them could be worse off after this call didn't bear thinking about. He'd lost a partner and gained a father in law.

'You're talking about my life you're talking about my family. This is not about shit happens or some other trite remark Brodie. There's nothing funny or humorous going on. Jesus you'll never change, will you? My father can be very persuasive he wouldn't be a company man if he wasn't.'

'I thought he was retired and kicking back in some beachside mansion.'

'Who's being naïve Brodie, these guys never retire it's not that kind of job. Fact is it's not a job it's a calling like the priesthood.'

'That sounds ominous anyway are we going to meet or not.'

There was a long pause before she said, 'alright you win we can meet up at the Beachcomber on Beach road. Look it up. It's nice, relaxing, something I can do with in these hectic times.'

On the patio of the Beachcomber Brodie sat drinking his Tiger beer. In the corner was a nat shrine, they were popping up everywhere. He looked at his phone watch again. She'd said she would be there in 15 minutes and that was 20 minutes ago. The thought she would stand him up was more than depressing. Then she walked off the street smiling and looking fabulous.

After ordering drinks and enjoying a meal of *Gaeng Daeng*, Red Curry and chicken, lightened with *Som Tum*, or spicy green papaya salad the couple sat in silence. It was the most peaceful moment between them in a hell of a long time. Then in unison they laughed.

This cleared the rest of the fractured ice that had separated the two for the longest time.

'God what a bizarre trip Brodie we've been on,' she declared in a tone of wonder. 'Did you ever think we would end up like this?'

'You mean with me in and out of jail and you nearly married to a handsome stranger who turned out to have connections with your long dead and now very much alive dear old dad?' Shaking his head and sounding bewildered, as if karma in the land of karma had lifted them into another plane of existence, he said in a tone meant to convey they were in this together, 'no, not in a million years honey. We couldn't make this stuff up. You'd have to be a Hollywood script writer on too many uppers to get through one too many all-nighters to think up that one.'

'Yeah sure I can buy that. Or you'd have to be some kind of weird clairvoyant with telepathic powers, something cosmic like that.' They laughed again it was good to laugh. Crazy and menacing the laugh could scare the local ghosts of the more virulent type away.

Silence came over them again as they took stock their hectic lives.

'So where to from here Brodie? We can't laugh or cry it away.'

'Well you know I can't leave the country until the court case is over.'

'You know my father Ralph could get you out. He has a private jet at his disposal.'

'And become a fugitive? Not on your life. Even a CIA man and a highly respected one as I understand he is wouldn't be able to finesse that.'

Grace gave an enigmatic smile and said, 'I wouldn't be so sure of that if I were you. He is a man of the world in the deepest sense and in a way neither one of us will ever fathom.'

He nodded and signalled for the waiter to bring more drinks.

'Alright but it still wouldn't pay to just abscond. I'd never be able come to Thailand or even to Asia or anywhere else for the rest of my life.'

She looked down on her drink with the cute parasol and said, 'what man can do can be undone.'

'Alright I'll take that on board although I'm not ready to quit Thailand just yet.

I have business to attend to.'

'You mean those guys at the bar where your girlfriend works.'

Shaking his head vigorously he said, 'I don't have a Thai girlfriend.

Grace made an audible sucking sound with her straw and said, 'Brodie it's me you're talking to.'

CHAPTER 48

Brodie and Dane walked down teeming Walking Street. It seemed like there was no in or out season with summer on somewhere in the world all year. It was after 2AM and there were armies of men, British, Australian, and Korean, all looking for women and a boozy, sexy time. Brad was one of the few Americans.

'How come there aren't many American around. I heard around the time of the Vietnam War the place was full of them, they owned the place.'

Dane placed a reassuring hand on Brodie's shoulder as if his protective, pedagogical instincts just kicked into gear.

'Well you're talking ancient history mate, I hope you don't mind me calling you mate.'

Brodie gave him a playful punch on the shoulder and said, 'not at all, I suppose you picked that up from Grace.' He didn't want to comment on the use of the word mate, untrusting of those who picked up his mannerisms or lingo to assume some kind of fealty or comradeship.

They stopped in front of the Alcatraz *A Go Go Bar* and accidental ally Brad said in a welcoming tone, 'nah I got that from you Brodie. You're my kind of people.'

Brodie looked at him for a long moment as girls in tight short skirts and very high heels glided past to the left and right of them and coming the other way.

He saw a bald-headed man with tattoos snaking from his forehead and neck down his arms and presumably over the rest of his body. He looked English but Brodie wasn't about to ask.

'In answer to your question Brodie the average American working Joe doesn't have the pay scale that you Aussies and the Limey guy looking very pleased with himself over there.

'So, what you looking at cobber?' the illustrated man said in a hard tone suggestive of physical violence.

'Sorry I was talking to my friend,' Dane said in an equally tough tone suggesting he could handle himself. The illustrated man, just one of thousands of men and women, mainly men, with serpentine graphics that snaked around and over arms and legs and slithered up necks and even across faces, stared then directed his attention back to his girl. Brodie could imagine Dane, ex-military man, taking out that English bastard and anyone who wanted to throw in with a kick to the diaphragm followed by a knew in the solar plexus leaving him to kiss the pavement wondering what the hell happened to him.

They moved on as 70s disco music and other period pieces blared out from an endless row of bars, each with women in bikinis or otherwise scantily clad calling out or preening for customers. Neon signs flashed and blinked, he fixated on one that showed a cowboy throwing a lasso over a rouged smiling woman, over and over again.

They walked past a bar with the usual line up of nearly naked women sitting on bar stools some looking excited, some with the glazed expressions of exhausted ladies who had given their favours to busloads and carloads of men from four continents.

'Hey you want to buy me drink? You want to buy me drink?'

'Not tonight sweetheart,' Brodie said in a light-hearted voice. He was begging to get outside his head and have a bit of fun.

'What about you Brad?' he asked knowing his rival and his former partner were finished as an item.

'Well I'm easy as you say.' The conversation paused again as raucous music blared, *heard it in the grapevine*, and the array of neon flashed to the beat of frenetic hard-sell. In the distance, he could hear in an aural volley of direct competition, Credence Clearwater Revival belt out '*I ain't no senator's son*'.

The song was a time capsule that took him back decades to when he lived in California. Took him back in fact to when he first met Grace. It was at a party and their shared experience living in the very guts of Uncle Sam so to speak made them fast friends and more after meeting at a party that was otherwise a bore.

'I know that which means that Grace is free now too.'

They high five then Brodie fist pumped. Sure, his unofficial bodyguard was free but was Brodie? Both knew that, and it wasn't worth talking about. Not yet anyhow. The hairy dog of jealousy was bound to re-emerge like some mutant swamp creature in a Drive- in Movie. Both were extinct only they didn't know it.

'Way to go so we're all free!' the two men looked at each other as if where to take it from there. Maybe it was more like freedom wasn't all it was cracked up to be to paraphrase Janis who was belting out those words in the third bar doing its own imitation of tacky retro-world.

'Look at all the tats these guys have,' Dane said with a sceptical look.

'Don't they have them where you come from?' Brodie asked knowing in Australia they were rife up and down the food chain. He had even spotted a female Deputy Principal with inked in pictures of her kids when they were babies.

'Not really sure, bikers and sailors and ex-cons with a few middle-class people thrown in but not like this. What about Australia? I notice you don't have one.

'Well just lucky I guess but sure we have it bad back in Oz. Housewives of the still married kind, accountants and cops you name it. More women with tramp stamps than you can poke a stick at. '

'Poke a stick at, what is that?' Brodie smiled, happy to see his mate still wasn't yet a master of Australian speaks. Come to think of it the man could no more imitate an Australian than a grizzly bear could impersonate a kangaroo. For Brodie things were different he had lived in Los Angeles and could make like an American.

'Oh, just something we say back home. But as far as tats go we got it bad.'

'And what's wrong with tattoos mate?' Brodie turned to face a heavily inked man with a London accent. Looking fierce with nose, ear and face rings the suggestion he and his decorations were out of order had him with his head leaning forward Liverpool kiss style, clenched fists ready to hammer out any supposed disrespect. Standing in front of his Thai doxy like a pirate about to do battle as he boarded a ship of prey, the threat of a bloody fight wafted in the air along with the aroma of fried chicken and curry from the food carts.

'Nothing and I wasn't talking to you.'

The man in the singlet and bald bullet head replied, 'well I'm talking to you so get used to it.'

'I don't want to be part of this conversation anymore.' He turned to leave and get away from the angry Englishman. Then he felt a heavy hand on his shoulder and the ominous words, 'not so fast. You're not getting away that easy boyo.'

Dane formed a wedge between the two and said, 'now let's be reasonable the man said he wasn't interested in an argument so why don't we call it quits.'

The stranger then put up his fists in a boxing stance and began to move around making feints like he was the Pac Man or Ali. Something about his body language suggested he knew his way around a boxing ring with a little street fighting eye gouging thrown in. Brodie felt a buzzing in his ears signally an internal warning bell had gone ballistic. The idea of being beaten senseless in a crowded street didn't appeal and could even see him wind up in jail again. He was about to suggest making a run for it until his American friend made a surprising move.

'There's no need for physical violence friend, no need at all.' Dane sounded calm.

'Then I suggest you hightail it out of here pal. Isn't that what you *yanks* say, hightail it?'

Bradley smiled and said in a sardonic tone, 'only if you like old cowboy movies which I don't.'

'Well I don't like you Brad Pitt. In fact, I dislike you so much I am going to beat the living hell out of you.' At this he began to move towards Brad, fists held high and a murderous gleam in his eye. The man really was a pirate, maybe cutting off ears or worse was on the cards

'I wouldn't recommend that old son.'

The man with no name said, 'you don't recommend it do you what a ponce.'

He turned to smirk at his bitch and she rewarded him with ab uncertain smile. Even if her lover killed the arrogant American there would be much explaining to do. He darting eyes told Brodie she was already inventing an exit strategy whoever was the last man standing.

The unhappy stranger took a haymaker swing and Brad neatly sidestepped it like a practised UFC fighter or Muay Thai man. The comic stripped bald geezer, his face contorted into a mask of lethal hatred as if he'd just emerged from hell to settle some scores, then tried to crash tackle the American only to be punched squarely in the side of the head. Looking bewildered he collected himself and took another swing, this one with much less heft or accuracy than the last. The fight was now in slow motion as the pirate's brain began to shut down in the face of concussion, his balance gone from a smack in the ear. He lunged forward punching the air with meaty fists, and again Brad expertly dodged a blow that could have inflicted a broken jaw or concussion. He might have been some kind of local boxing champ but he was no match for a former SEAL. Brodie watched as his friend then punched an already punch drunk and drunken brawler and there was a loud smacking sound as facial bones cracked. Still standing Brad punched him again. This hit connected with the bastard's nose and squashed it to the sound of crunching bones like an egg being crushed in your hand. This time the bastard didn't get up and lay groaning as blood trickled out of his mouth and left ear. His lady knelt beside him and Brodie wondered if she would leave him. If not, this was one he owed her and he had no doubts the bastard pirate would pay up.

They walked away with no sign of police. Maybe the police let the *Farung* duke it out and watched from a safe distance or more likely looked the other way. They were good at doing that weren't they? It was much easier that way letting these invaders beat each other's brains out or drank themselves to death with bar fines and tips in the bargain. Unless, of course someone got killed and that was always bad for business. They passed a bar called the Ice House.

'How hot do you think it is Dane?'

'Oh maybe 120 degrees.'

'Yes, or using Celsius, maybe 35 or 36 degrees humidity maybe 100 % so it feels much hotter.'

As he brushed some sweat from his forehead Brodie said, 'how about we go into the Ice House now that you mention it. Sounds like the place to be in the tropics. I'm up for it.'

Dane smiled widely and said, 'yeah well I'm up for it too. We're on the same bandwidth here.'

They moved inside and yes it was cold. So cold in fact, as advertised, the room was made of ice, floors, walls and ceiling. The bar girls had snow bunny outfits on with leg warmers that wouldn't stay on long he figured. Sure, it was cool and with a capital K. The chill and clouds of condensed air made it unusual, worth exploring. It had a tonic effect and in honour of that he ordered a, 'gin and tonic and one for my mate here.'

Dane gave a wide smile and the two men clinked glasses in a toast. As they sat he could see bar girls dancing on the counter. One girl barely out of her teens had goose bumps and shivered. To counter this, she kept her legs rigid and this had the effect of giving her movements of a puppet on a string.

Dane held up a clutch of high denomination baht notes, still no more than about $20 American. She exhaled as if relieved and hopped down from her high perch.

As she took up a stool next to her new patron he said, 'hello my name is Dane and this is my pal Brodie, what's your name sweetheart?'

She gave an anxious smile and said in a sharp high-pitched accent, 'I am May, you are American?'

He nodded and said, 'yes but don't hold that against me.'

She leaned closer to him and put her arm around his neck to signal she was willing to hold a lot more against him given half the chance.

'You sure don't waste time, do you?' She gave a wide smile that was almost authentic. The old Hollywood saying 'if you can fake honesty you've got it made' was made for the ladies and Lady Boys in this town.

'No waste time want good time.'

Brodie smiled in appreciation of her plucky sense of humour and said, 'yes we have a saying back home I'm here for a good time not a long time. I mean life is too short, right?'

She nodded with wide eyes and a fixed smile as if not quite understanding what they were saying. It didn't matter the expression on her face suggested she might be a card but at the end of the banger she wanted to get down to business.

'Yeah you want buy long time?' Brad leaned back to compare notes with Brodie.

'I guess you know what she means by long time?'

Brodie nodded rolling his eyes and said, 'anybody that doesn't after a few weeks in Pattaya has got their head in the sand.'

'Or up their ass,' Dane said to Brodie's surprise. He hadn't heard the upright American swear before. It was another side of a man he barely knew despite appearances.

'Mr Brodie, you want to see me and pay bar fine?'

'She sure knows how to get right down to business,' he said as he threw down 3000 baht.

She took the money then handed it to the lady who was clearly the mama-san. The older woman smiled with cold eyes and said, 'you have fun, you American you know how to work hard, play hard.'

'And you know how to make the right noises to make me feel welcome.'

Brodie leaned close to his fast friend in that he really felt the man was now his friend and said, 'are you going to take her to a room or something?'

His American pal gave a playful elbow in the ribs and said, 'or something like that.' He looked at the young lady with beautiful wide eyes and said, 'nah not me too much collateral damage. I may not be with Grace now and neither are you of course but her father is here and explaining this is too much like hard work.'

'But he's retired, right? What difference would it make? He's been out of her life for so long he doesn't really have a say, does he?"

'Ah Brodie, Brodie, Brodie you don't know the half of it. I don't need a blemish on my brilliant career now do I?'

'What as a businessman I don't see how,'

Dane put up a hand and said, 'it's complicated shall we say. You don't want to know.'

The girl with Bunny Ears got closer and began to whisper in his ear. Up close he could see she had delicious purple lipstick on and he fantasised licking it off. He could only imagine what she was saying and wasn't about to ask for the translation. Thai sometimes had a way of smiling as they called you names in Thai. More ribald fantasy crowded his thoughts. As the three of them dithered on the next move, men in heavy cold room coats, breathing thick clouds of condensed air, hauled in more shimmering ice, using ice picks. It was as if they were in some ancient Chicago packing shed a century ago. Brodie began to shiver like the bar girls and they were working in 15-minute shifts. The time for a coupling upstairs or back in the hotel room was fast approaching, otherwise all bets were off. Dane dived into his wallet again to pay her off when out of the corner of Brodie's eye he could see one of the ice men lunge at them. He pushed his drinking buddy out of the way and the ice pick buried into the bar stool.

Dane got his bearings and unleashed the girl who ran in the other direction as fast as her Mt. Olympus high heels would allow. As she disappeared the Ice man yanked out his weapon and tapped in on his gloved hand. He began to circle Brodie and Brad as if lining up a swing that would hit home. It was clear a blow to the head would be fatal and somehow the bandaged head of a mortally wounded Trotsky filtered in from his cobwebbed cognitive archive.

The bar was now cleared of customers and staff as they fled out the door towards safety or what would pass for safety at the minute. Terrorist attacks were often aimed at the runaways with a secondary explosion or sniper attack, so there was no immediate place of safety. They were on their own. A triple 0 call wouldn't do. Like before they'd have to make a run for it or fight it out and it was clear his American friend wasn't for running.

'Ok now surely we can work this out like grown men. Maybe a cup of tea and a sit down would be more constructive.'

As the assailant moved back then around to Dane's side Brodie noticed another man with a long-handled knife come from the staff room. Dane was a bull surrounded by armed bullfighters. Brodie didn't like the numbers. Dane said out of the side of his mouth, 'get outside Brodie this is going to get ugly.

You can't help me.'

'Nah mate we came together we can leave together. Want me to call the police?'

Dane shook his head and said, 'not yet we can do that later these guys want to dance we can dance. Get near the door and make sure no one comes inside unless it's the cops.'

Confused Brodie nodded he could only guess at what was really happening.

Was this a planned hit or something more random?

'Yeah ok I can do that, sure whatever you say.'

He knew that if his fellow clubber somehow got killed then he would have a lot of explaining to do. At the first sign of blood, theirs, he would make the call.

As he stood at the entrance like a desperate and freaked doorman at a killing party he waved away disappointed customers like a cop with the words, 'nothing to see, sorry come back later. We're going through renovations and the bar is closed for the night.'

Outside Brodie and curious onlookers could hear tables and chairs crashing. He gave a cheesy smile as if this were all part of the show.

The waiting was too much so he went back inside and locked the door. The ice man made another thrust with the evil looking ice pick, sharp and mean enough to tear our face off, and missed. Dane grabbed his arm and twisted it until the weapon clattered to the floor. He could see Brad give the ice man a sharp blow to the face, crushing the man's nose which then spurted thick jets of blood. Another hard punch to the head and he was unconscious. As he did the man with the cane cutter swung hard just missing Brad's neck. The nimble American crouched down to duck what could have been a fatal blow then rose to give a sharp kick to the back tendons of the wannabe killer's right leg. He shouted in pain and tried to regain his bearings, only it was too late for recovery. Brodie watched in awe as Dane gripped the man's arms then kneed him in the groin. He yelped like a whipped dog before Dane placed his hands around his neck and said, 'who sent you, who put you up to do this?'

'No English,' the man lied before Dane punched him square in the face. With it came the sound of breaking cheek bones and nose.

Dane repeated the words in Thai.

'Do you have a family? Do you want to see then again? I suggest you tell me what I want to hear. '

'I die, I tell you I die,' he said, his English amazingly improved.

Dane throttled him until his face began to turn blue. It looked like the usual from the Gitmo playbook Brad pulled out a wad of notes.

'This is a year's worth of pay you tell me and you can keep it and you can keep your life.'

'He is name 'Gam Peerapat. He kill me too.'

'If you're lying I will hunt you down and I will do that before he can.'

'I tell truth, I tell truth. You must believe me.'

Dane smiled, 'after trying to kill me how can I trust you.'

He threw down more bills as he stood. 'You better be telling the truth I will find out.'

Outside they could hear police whistles. Dane hissed, 'come on let's go.'

As Brodie made a move towards the front entrance his bodyguard said, 'no this way there's something I have to tidy up.'

They rushed to the bar back office and Dane went straight to the security recorders, took out the cassettes and pocketed them.

Outside he hailed a tuk-tuk and they got in.

'Take me to the Sheraton,' he said and they drove off. As they went down Beach Road Brad said, 'change of plan,' a he looked to the rear to see if they were being followed. Turning back to face the driver he finished the thought with, 'let us off in Soi 5.'

He threw some bills at the driver, more than he asked for.

They walked through streets with, at 3 am, now thinning crowds.

'What do we do now Dane? We've just left the scene of a crime.'

Dane stopped to light a smoke something Brodie hadn't seen him do before.

'I didn't know you smoked.'

'I don't usually let's say this is a different kind of night.'

'I'll say it is. Alright wise-guy what do we do now?'

'We sit tight, and I'll make inquiries about this Gam.'

'Will you really track down that bastard's ass if the lead doesn't pan out?'

'Of course, only I know that the lead will pan out.'

Brodie stopped walking and said, 'I don't understand.'

'This Gam Peerapat is a real person, I already know of him. He's on a UN watch list.'

'And what are you going to do about that, go to the police?'

Dane gave him a searching looking under the halo of street lights. 'Now you know better than that. There are a lot of excellent people in the police only our local police chief isn't one of them.'

'So how do we find him?' Brodie knew he was being annoying it was the anxiety that forced him to keep asking.

'Well let me ask are you sure you want a part of this Brodie you saw what happened in there, not very pretty and it could get a whole lot worse.'

'I might not be a hundred percent sure but I know I can't leave the country yet so we'll have to get him before he gets us.'

'Yes, well that won't be easy the guys have paid off a lot of important people and that will be hard to get around.' He paused then finished with, 'and that's a gross understatement.'

'Right, we'll build a bridge and get over it I guess.'

Dane laughed and said, 'sure we will I have a few resources at my disposal this Gam knows nothing about. I think he'll be in for a big surprise.'

'Should we tell Ralph? I mean what he doesn't know won't hurt him.'

The Major, named Brad, gave a knowing smile. The more Brodie knew the man the less he thought the breezy sounding name Brad seemed to fit. Dane was more like it so he was using it more often when addressing his unofficial body guard. 'Ralph already knows. You have to remember Ralph knows everything.'

'Are you sure about that Dane, Major Dane? So, all this just happened came out of nowhere like some subatomic particle popping up on the other side of the universe?'

'No, you don't understand. Believe me. He knows everything but keeps his own counsel. Some of this is classified. His style even in retirement is we used to call Spy-craft, but I didn't say that. No one ever prospered underestimating Ralph Winters. He might be retired officially but unofficially these guys never retire.'

'What do you mean these guys never retire? Sounds like he's in the mob, in a gang.'

'If he's in a gang then it's the biggest gang of its type in the world. He's CIA Brodie you already know that. I don't know why

I'm telling you this.' He stopped and looked up at the night sky as if for some absolution then went on. 'He was once in charge of whole continents. HUMIT and SIGNIT, that's human intelligence and signals intelligence so he might still be a consultant or have contacts. He knew everybody. Still does.'

'Why *are you* telling me this Dane? Someone like me has to be out of the loop.'

As they neared Brodie's hotel Dane stopped and said, 'I'm only telling you this because I know that Ralph has already briefed you otherwise I would have kept my mouth shut. I thought you would have figured out that he has taken a shine to you.'

'What, even though Grace and I have broken up?'

Dane gave a hollow laugh and said, 'maybe especially because you and Grace have broken up. Let's face it that what you two have in common. He can sense your pain, your sense of loss. I'm sure he sees you married to his daughter.'

'Yeah well I guess it makes some sort of crazy sense when you think about it.'

'So, what do we do now?' he asked again, heart beating erratically, his mind racing.

'We sit tight and keep this to ourselves and that means not saying a word of this to Grace.'

'Why would we keep Grace out of it? I mean if her father already knows why not her?'

'Let's say it's like the mafia. You keep family out of all the dirty business as a form of plausible deniability.'

'Yeah what they don't know won't hurt them right?'

'Yes, if you want to put it that way. Stay indoors if you can help it. Keep out of the bars don't go in the pool. Tomorrow we'll get you into a new hotel room.'

As light began to peep over the horizon he asked, 'who's we?'

'The Fairy Godmother. Look this is critical you're going to have to trust me or this won't work. We could get you out of the country now, and there's an excellent argument for that but unless you want to spend the rest of your days hunted by Interpol you'll just have to sit tight.'

'Here take this,' Dane said as he handed him a small cell phone.

'What's that?' he asked as he turned it over to see if there were any bells and whistles. There were.

'That my friend is an encrypted phone that will also self-destruct with the press of a button.'

'Are you sure all this is necessary?'

'Couldn't be surer of anything in the world.'

As night morphed into day revealing umber coloured clouds and a sparkling sea Brodie shook hands with Dane who walked at a quick pace and disappeared down a side street. Brodie made for the hotel lobby feeling energised by their talk and with no traces of a hangover. The evening had been life changing and he had racing mind from to the new and increasingly wild world he rocketed into.

Some tourists came to Thailand and never get out of jail. Brodie beat the odds with his release and it seemed he was now blessed or cursed with a kind of immunity. As he lay on his bed he thought of the insane turn his life had taken. He and Grace came out to Thailand to kiss and make up maybe even set it up so he could propose. More about that later. Now almost three weeks later they were over, and life was a raging typhoon. After two days in jail where he contemplated suicide as an antidote to staying inside forever he'd been released by a white knight that also doubled as his ex-girlfriend's new squeeze. Then Grace's dead father emerges and intercedes with the authorities to obtain his release. As if that weren't enough the white Knight named Brad is found to have a connection with Dad Lazarus and they are both associated with Spook Central, the CIA. Then when he thought things had settled down he and Brad are nearly killed. That nightmare finished at sunup although the memory this wouldn't go away. He couldn't leave if he wanted and there was a snaking suspicion dear old dad had something to do with that. Somehow, he drifted back to sleep concentrating on the women in his life. Chailai and Grace had starring roles in this movie.

CHAPTER 49

Next morning, he awoke latish, about 8AM. Some of the lads, like the superannuated Jimmy didn't get up until noon or later. Normally after a night out he would have slept in until noon like so many *farung* giving themselves a potted detox and storing up energy for the nightlife, it was only adrenaline kept him alert and ready for anything. 8The call came at 8:30.

It was the Major, retired.

'Your new hotel is on Soi 15 get a cab don't get let off at the hotel.'

'Really do I really have to do that?'

There was silence on the other end before Major Dane said, 'yes Brodie you really have to do that. This is mission critical, no mistakes, you can't afford them. Don't make my job any harder.'

When he hung up he packed and did as he was told.

He was there within 10 minutes after hailing a cab. The new digs weren't so bad if not exactly five stars but then there was no point in drawing attention to himself, no point at all.

For lunch, he had room service deliver something called Thai Butterfly Chicken Curry. He was getting a taste for Thai food although not the jail kind which smelt like puke. That scabrous taste would probably never leave him.

After showering he decided to look out at the beach and the Bay from a kind of communal balcony that was on his floor, the fourth. The railing was low, too for tall farung, and seemed a health and safety hazard. It was a beautiful day, the expansive view of the Bay of Pattaya and beach was liberating.

He called Grace who answered with the question, 'why won't your call sign come up Brodie?'

'I don't know maybe technical difficulties,' he lied. Truth was she often didn't pick up if he dialled it straight. They exchanged more pleasantries, neutral topics like the humid weather even if this kind of small talk was increasingly irrelevant in this dangerous world. Brad's sober warning *don't tell her anything echoed in his mind.*

'When aren't you getting back Grace, my ticket has already expired so has yours. Why stay?'

There was a pause then she said, 'you know why, my father is here. If I leave now who knows when I'll see him again. The idea of that is too painful.' 'Has he said he'll come out to Australia to see you and your mother?'

'He says a lot of things how much is true is anyone's guess. He never saw us in the past, not in Australia, we would hook up in New York or Paris, never Sydney much less where we are on the Gold Coast. I'm not sure Australia is on the agenda.'

'I assume while the going is good you're going to stick, around right?'

'Right, sure, something like that.'

'How does your father feel about this?'

'Oh, he wants me to leave yesterday. I protested but he bought me a ticket,

I'm taking off next Saturday.'

'Alright that should work out. I don't want you to tell my family about this when you get back.'

'Why not?'

'It's embarrassing, and I don't want them involved.'

'Come on Brodie this is getting weird. Something is going on and I don't know what. There seems to be this weird connection between you and Dane and my father.'

'I know looks like old man Winters has taken a shine to me.'

'Excuse me this is my father you're talking about.'

She stopped, and her nostrils flared, never a good sign. 'You're lying there's something you're not telling me. I know you I know how you think.'

'Well I've changed Grace.'

'In three weeks come on unless you've been Zapped by gamma rays.'

'Look its fine don't worry so much.'

'I work for a bank Brodie when someone tells me not to worry I get worried.'

'Look grace it's been nice talking to you.'

'Sure, next time come up with a few more answers, will you?'

'Oh, before I go how are things with Brad?'

'Not that's it's any of your business.'

He kept quiet thinking she would abruptly end the conversation.

'We had fun for a while and he wanted to take me back to the states, something I'm not prepared to do. I think he wants a step mother for his three kids and I don't do kids.' There was a long pause before she said, 'at least not yet.'

'Looks like the handsome stranger wasn't quite what you thought he'd be?' She gave him a look and he dropped it.

'Say how about we meet up for dinner say Wednesday night around 7?

'Sure, I'd like that.'

'Brilliant we have a date.'

'Only it's not a date get that straight buster.' She gave a smile him a *Yim soo smile*; the things are not so bad I better smile.

'Roger that and out.'

Then feeling optimistic elated, he went to the 10th floor pool. Such a move was against all advice yet in the face of all the risk he was empowered, it felt right and that had its own logic. After a quarter of an hour of watching some fetching western ladies swim and loll in the sun he made his way back downstairs. A voyeur was not what he wanted to be however ludicrous the notion in an open-air brothel that is Pattaya. As the elevator doors opened at his level he looked down the hall to see his room door open. Before that registered a man came out and firing. Brodie ducked and frantically pressed buttons until the elevator doors whispered closed. He began to sweat and shake at the idea he might well die today. As he got out, he heard more shots as his hunters raced down the stairs.

Running outside he darted through bars and pushed past seller's carts, knocking down one sending mangoes, fruit drinks and fried chicken onto the pavement. Another shot, and he turned to see a man in early middle age take aim and fire again. He missed. He wouldn't be so lucky next time. He picked up the running like some Usain Bolt act only here was a running man running for his life. Barging into a bald shaven tourist with a huge gut covered by a tee shirt emblazoned with the slogan *Washington State is Great!* both men fell to the pavement. As the overweight American began bleating in what could have passed for a southern accent anywhere from Texas to Virginia, 'why don't you watch where you're going?' Brodie scrambled to his feet and kept going. Weaving in and out of crowds of tourists that clogged streets and overflowed from bars everywhere, he looked back to see a man with a knife in his mouth gaining on him. Hands- free he tried

He turned a corner and tried to lose them in a large open market fronting Beach Road. Bright colours flapped in the wind as advertisements or clung to sweaty backs as cheap knock off tee shirts. Grabbing a tee shirt from a rack he threw down some money at a shouting vendor who wanted to sell him more stuff. As she protested in Thai he threw down more money and grabbed a pair of shorts and a hat. The woman of middle years smiled in delight at her success showing several gold teeth in the bargain. With his medium size, just about anything would fit except the fat boy clothes meant for the pale skin tourist whales who took up two seats on an airplane. Ducking in a change room he stripped off his clothes and put on the new ones before darting outside then veering off to a restaurant in the distance. The dumbstruck vendor behind the cash register gave the forced smiled called a *feun yim*. His daughter next to him said in Thai, 'another crazy farung. He has not long to live.'

Her father nodded and said under his breath, 'yes and when this *farung khi nok,* when this bird shit foreigner dies they will blame Thailand. Brodie gave a smile to show he understood Thai and the meaning of the insult. Having lost face, the two hurried away and melted into the crowd. His chaser was still there sensing he was.

Pretending to read a newspaper that he found on one of the tables he made like a loudly dressed tourist. After some moments, he couldn't help sneaking a peek and just managed to see the chasers race past. Keeping up the pretence he was rewarded when they came back and looked inside before taking off again. He was no running man and would have been caught up with and worse.

He called Dane, the only person outside the mysterious Ralph that could help him.

'They're after me Dane. It's a miracle I wasn't killed.'

'Where and when did this happen?' His voice revealed no surprise, maybe a hint of vindication.

'Just now in the hotel room and I had to run for my life. They'll be back. I don't know what to do.'

'Get out of there now and take a cab to this address. Do it.'

'I'm not sure I have all my stuff including my passport.'

'I'll send someone for that. If you want to keep alive you have to get out of there.'

CHAPTER 50

He tilted his head to eat his *siap kai jiew mop* or Thai omelette with fish sauce and beef. A Burmese romantic song with a catchy beat was playing and he could only understand the words *cherry pie* popping up in a sea of Burmese.

She gave him a yim soo smile, the smile you give when there's nothing better to do. It was a holding pattern smile.

He eyes widened in horror, 'I see a *phi tai hong*, a vengeful ghost.' He put his arm around her in a protective gesture and said, 'honey that's all superstition.' Looking unconvinced she said, 'alright let's go out. I'm tired of hiding like some lizard under a rock. To hell with them.'

Later as they drank into the night, he kissed her, something most of the bar girls avoided, and she smiled. It wasn't her usual smile it was what the Thai called *yim mee lessani* or wicked thoughts smile. Was she hiding something? Of course, she was, everyone in Thailand, including him, did that. Was hiding something a crime? Now that depended if Chailai herself was a mole and then they were cooked like staring fish on a food cart. Sure Thailand, the Land of Smiles, Thailand, the Land of Lies. He didn't want to think about that.

Like some time-traveller, like some wandering, restless *ghost*, he was airlifted by private jet to Chiang Mai within hours. He knew it was chartered by the Company like the infamous Air America on some deep cover mission which this was in fact, but he wasn't about to ask. He assumed the rest of the team including Braddock, Teerasat, Maung and the rest flew separately to avoid detection. All that was *need to know*. Taking a taxi, he arrived at the Lotus Hotel as planned. To blend he ordered a meal and a drink from a fetching waitress who seemed uncommonly interested in him.

Waving away her questions like she was some kind of blood sucker he sent her away with a 500-baht tip when she came back with some side dishes and roast duck in black bean sauce.

He chomped loudly on *som tan*, green papaya salad. He was so starved he inhaled the meal with loud chomping sounds that began to draw attention.

He ducked into a 7/11 and bought three large containers of bottled water. It was going to be an ordeal and just buying the stuff felt like good preparation. Fancy food or even fare from the food cart would be off the menu for the next few days. That was alright it suited his urge to economise.

He lifted his drink into the air to give a *kambei* or toast.

He walked to the edge of the ancient moat and wall, snaking off into the distance was the Mai Ping River. He was here for two days maybe three. It was a role he was made for. Braddock and his men were never going to allow him to go. So, Brodie would be the fifth column, the organic surveillance camera. He hadn't wanted to be enlisted in this nasty little war it just came out that way.

He took another slug of sangha beer. It tasted bitter on this hot day. Bitter and just how he liked it. Somehow his tastebuds were different as though he'd gone through some kind of genetic mutation.

'You understand that all comments on the King or the government or the coup or the generals all strictly forbidden. We stop twice a day to play the national anthem.

He saw three kathoeys or Lady Boys closing in on him. One had a prize fighter's build with the hard-faced look of someone not used to the word no. One smaller man had a matt of hair over his forehead and eyes that acted as a mask. His muscled body had the tautness of an athlete running on high octane fuel. 'Do they let Katoeys complete in the Olympics,' he asked as someone threw a coaster at him.

'Shut up, why don't you?' came an American voice. Resisting the temptation to take him on Brodie moved on.

At Chiang Rai the situation wasn't much different as he did a bit of remote viewing of his own through surveillance cameras he assumed were company assets. From afar like an Oracle of Delphi, could see a United Nations of foreigners in and around town. Off in the distance he could see an unseasonable storm cloud rolling in. His hands began to shake and he realised he was shivering with cold as if hed been parachuted into the Siberia rather than souteast Asia.

'Its cold,' he said to a waiter orbiting his table.

The young man with slick back hair smiled and said,' yes we are in northern Thailand not tropical Thailand like Phuket.'

The smiled widely showing brilliant white teeth. As he did another gust of frigid air shot through the room and the wiater's smioe disappeared.

'I would like to order some *glooai tawt* please,' he said to the waiter who then hurried from the room. He sensed a change in the man just as the atmosphere in the room had shifted.

Putting it from his mind he dipped into *guey teow* noodles. There wdere more pressing issues that had to be faced.

Outside he could hear the pop, pop sound of an AK-47 from a street gunfight.

Dodge City Asian style.

Meanwhile the team flew into Chiang Mai Airport. Braddock and the men collected their baggage and walked to the prearranged taxis.

Knowing the ETA and unable to resist the urge, Brodie made an encrypted facetime call. 'Aren't you afraid we'll get searched?' Brodie asked only to be met with a withering look.

'Get off the line now, 'he said in a heated voice. 'I can't talk but that's taken care of. I shouldn't tell you any of this except you are part of the mission. I didn't want you coming here. That was Ralph's idea.'

Brodie went quiet. So, yes of course he was there on sufferance. As someone designated as in need of care and attention he imagined the logic went it was better he was within reach even if that risked unintended consequences.

The team arrived at the hotel by cab, again so as not to arouse suspicion. A fully remilitarised and weaponised Braddock gave another of his briefings.

'Gentlemen we are not here to fuck around. We are in a special place, a sacred site if you will. Right here in Chiang Mai is the ancient capital of Thailand. It was once the most fortified city in the kingdom with a moat and a wall. Look hard enough and you'll see ruins that were part of that defensive fortification.'

Teerasak watched the learners, the soldiers. One man named Po had a slack mouthed expression that seemed to say why are we talking about this?

Teerasak gave him a sharp look and his expression and body language changed at once.'

'We have a few advantages here but overall it only amounts to a slight edge. Don't throw away that advantage your life could depend on it,' he said then repeated it in Thai before Teerasak completed the triple translation by speaking in Burmese.

They then booked out of the hotel and were driven by someone Brodie didn't recognise but guessed was Burmese going by appearance and accent.

Once there they put personal belongings in cargo containers that doubled as sleeping quarter's trailer park style.

'We can't all be holed up in a downtown Motel, now can we?' There was no response to the rhetorical question. The men nodded to each to each other. All their lives were in the hands of this crazy American and none of them would be anywhere else. There was a small if important piece of land here that could well determine the rest of their lives.

They went through the inventory just like before. Automatic and semiautomatic rifles and Smith & Wesson, Walther, Glock and Colt handguns were unpacked and packed in each soldier's kits according to the allocation. Flares, grenades, smoke bombs and various incendiary devices including what they called a plasma bomb that could reach 3000 degrees and illuminate a 10kilometre area were put through the audit and check-listed on an iPad.

Brodie went back to another hotel near the town centre. He had a minder with him a genial Thai named Pirapat who would apparently stay with him for the duration.

The next morning, he got the signal on his iPhone that the company of commandos was on its way. Brodie did what he was supposed to do and watched. After the meeting the night before Braddock moved close to Brodie almost shoving him against the wall. 'Fuck this up and I will come after you. {ut the lives of my men in danger and you will lose your own or it won't be worth living.'

Without speaking he nodded.

'Terrific,' Braddock said with a welcome smile now do the job you're supposed to. On that note come on I'll buy you a drink.'

They walked down the stairs like gunfighters who could drink and play cards then settle the argument with a .45.

For security reasons, all the spying and moderate drinking was to be done inhouse so to speak in the tiger Lilly Hotel. Staying in one place had its advantages.

That night there was a massive thunder storm. He peered up into the night sky and watched spidery trails of lightning linking earth to sky.

It felt like a portent, like one of those ghosts Chailai obsessed about.

CHAPTER 51

As the Chinook got closer to the ground, the twin rotors slowed to make a hefty whoosh, whoosh sound, flattening the grass covering the slight incline.

'This is no stop off men once you disembark I take off. That's the way we have to play it,' the pilot said beneath aviators and a peaked cap. Braddock knew him from the service even if there was a no ask no tell policy. No sharing of old war stories from another lifetime, no free exchange of sentiment. INTEL, any INTEL, it was on a need to know basis and he wasn't about to alter that handy regulation any time soon.

As the men jumped off he waited until he was the last man on board. He gave a thumb's up to Red and he jumped the metre and a bit. As he landed standing on the ground the helo rose vertically into the air. He watched it disappear behind a bank of low lying clouds.

After a once over to check everything was in order, knives and guns sheathed and holstered, he checked his GPS and took point to lead in a north westerly direction.

There was still adequate light although in late afternoon that would flick to darkness quicker than most *farung* expected.

Special Ops veteran Jerome Blake slipped on the wet undergrowth and fell back only to stop when he twisted his body 180 degrees. The rest of his men, behind him including Commanding Officer Van Dyke, stopped until he repositioned himself by standing, then resumed the trek up the rain soaked incline. Teerasak called up to him as if to urge him on, 'at the crest of this hill we should have a view of the camp.'

'Yes, and not a moment too soon. I can take the slog to get here, I just don't like being out in the open, 'Brad said between grunts. He was combat ready even if the mountain climbing was more than he remembered. The fact the two camps of the Great Se Wa were hundreds of miles apart and in completely different terrain had something to do with that.

At the top Teerasak was proved right when they made a base that neatly overlooked the target. Through the night vision scope that served as binoculars Braddock could see guards and detainees milling in the yard behand the razor wire walls. Even a drone wouldn't give a better view than this. He unpacked and assembled the Noreen 338LM Lapua sniper rifle accurate to 1500 metres and in the hands of a marksman like Braddock could hit a target at 2500 metres well within the range on their bunker hill.

The last light faded with the massive burning sun sinking beneath the ranges.

The sounds of darkness in the wild slowly filtered in as insects and short horned deer and small mammals began to chirp and squeal. Strange lights danced close to ground then shot off into the sky. Teerasak knew this could be explained away as the grinding of rock to create Earth Lights even if he knew the truth. The noises and the visions were the restless souls of those who had suffered a raw death. The howling were the cries of those buried alive, burned alive or put to death in some other outrage. These restless spouls wouldn't be restless for long. Salvation was on its way. The green hills would change colour to white, to red and the rivers would change course as the undead found peace and lay to rest.

He checked his GPS then sent it to the Chiang Rai base. As an afterthought, he also sent it to the Chiang Mai and Bangkok base. Something told things were going to get a little hairy before the night was done.

Looking through the night vision scope he could see men and women struggling against uniformed guards. It looked like Se Saw's army had gone through a refit with new uniforms and equipment. In the greenish glow of shapes and people he spotted what he had come for. The self-styled general strutted around as if playacting the role of the warlord that he was. In the magnified, enhanced light Braddock witnessed this man who would be God take a struggling woman by the hair and pull her down to her knees.

'Ok baby come to papa,' Braddock said under his breath. The cross hairs were gently nudged over the target. He began to put pressure on the trigger only to stop when the plastic general suddenly stopped to his haunches and lit a cigarette. Braddock, the best sniper in Burma, squeezed the trigger and the top of Se Saw's head blew off in a splash of brain, blood and fragmented bone.

Burma's King of enslavement fell back and his lifeless body came to rest with one leg pulled towards his right arm as if imploring the gods for another chance. If they were there, the gods or the ghosts of these lost souls weren't listening. As their leader lay dead his soldiers scattered, some firing wildly unsure of the direction. The blackness of night only added to the panic.

Search lights were played over scrub from the bottom of the ravine through to the top just missing their encampment. Quickly assembling the rifle and packing his kit away as his men did the same the men moving back in the other direction down the hill.

When they got to the bottom an RPG grenade exploded and split a tree sending earth and splinters showering over them. Aside from a bit of grazing and a few flesh wounds including a bleeding arm belonging to Teerasak, they were OK.

Major Braddock said under his breath, 'two can play that game soldier.'

Ohm fired a mortar and it hit the top of the hill. A secondary explosion told them it had found soldiers and ammunition.

Then the sharp crack and thud of gun fire followed by the steady syncopation of automatic fire got the men prone on the ground. They exchanged more fire. Braddock knew they had the advantage of night vision and he signalled his men to spread out in a flanking move. He motioned for Teerasak to take the left or western flank while he and his men would take the right. With Ghillie suits and black face he had to use his slim advantage.

After a hundred metres of slow, cautious movement forward the men crouched into firing position as four soldiers from the Burmese Liberation Army were caught by mortar fire and body parts were sent flying through the air.

The gunfire and explosions didn't stop for what seemed hours but what timers recorded as 47 minutes.

CHAPTER 52

As the Chinook got closer to the ground, the twin rotors slowed making a whoosh, whoosh sound and flattening the grass covering the slight incline.

'This is no stop off men once you disembark I take off. That's the way we have to play it,' the pilot said beneath aviators and a peaked cap. Braddock knew him from the service even if there was a no ask no tell policy. No sharing of old war stories from another lifetime, no free exchange of sentiment. INTEL, any INTEL, it was on a need to know basis and he wasn't about to alter that handy regulation any time soon.

As the men jumped off he waited until he was the last man on board. He gave a thumb's up to Red and he jumped the metre and a bit. As he landed standing on the ground the helo rose vertically into the air. He watched it disappear behind a bank of low lying clouds.

After a once over to check everything was in order, knives and guns sheathed and holstered, he checked his GPS and took point to lead in a north westerly direction.

There was still adequate light although in late afternoon that would flick to darkness quicker than most *farung* expected.

Teerasak motioned with his hand and the men peered through a raggedy curtain of rust stained palm fronds. Pointing to a bamboo structure at the bottom of a valley he said in a thick Myanmar accent, 'this where they are we must move at night.'

In a muffled tone, so as to not alert their target, Brad said, 'remember this is not a firefight. We come in search of Intel.'

'Our friends may not want to get interrogated.'

'Well we'll cross that bridge when we come to it. Only shoot if fired upon.'

The small company of men nodded their understanding. The situation would be unforgiving of mistakes.

They moved down through the dense scrub under a moonless night Major Braddock taking point. Night vision goggles enhanced with infra-red gave a slight advantage, assuming of course the enemy didn't have the same kit. The recalled Major didn't make assumptions. There was no reason to assume the target was any less equipped. Millions in black money could buy whatever you wanted. The advantage was surprise.

Teerasat made the first contact knowing he risked his life. With so many work slave, captives already dead that was an acceptable risk. Dying to save others was his mission statement. They waited in the dark then unexpected relief. The *exchange* was not the firefight they eared. With a choice, irresistible bribe of bundles of well used American dollars, they gained entry without a single shot being fired. Soldiers, and Major Dane didn't see these pirates as soldiers, were paid little or nothing and easily bought. Money ran the state and the underworld since the era when the place had been a Chinese satrap. Dane knew the area had changed little, there were still Warlords and slaves, gods and Demons. Did they have the Karma or fate to survive this?

The reactivated Major stood outside the towering bamboo great house then moved towards the Big Man. The seated man surrounded by what looked like kimono wearing concubines had the taut expressionless face of power. He was clearly the leader although no one said as much. He barked out orders in Burmese which Teerasak translated to Thai and English. Krit ground his teeth at the spectacle, the look on his face one of controlled rage.

'He says you have no business here but for a fee of 100,000 Baht he will tolerate your presence without protest.'

Major Dane reached into his sack and pulled out a wad of American dollar bills then counted out the money. The greenback was connective tissue for players on either side of the law or working both ends against the middle. If there was one thing the company was capable of it was supplying cold, hard cash and endless amounts of it.

'There is an extra ten thousand US as a thank you for having us.'

The rouge chief looked at the mountain of cash and seeming satisfied nodded and motioned with his head for them to follow as h got up. As they moved around the cavernous structure he looked up to see dangling human skulls strung up on wire. All clenched teeth and empty eye sockets the skulls seemed to mock them as if to say *you will soon be with us.*

Dane gave a wry smile and said sotto voiced to Teerasak, 'looks like the last guests didn't pay up.'

Teerasak nodded without smiling. They both knew this was only the beginning and anything could explode with unforeseen consequences.

The sound and smell of Hurricane lamps and an open fire gave the sense of an indigenous camp or an army cook out. A tepee or a mud hut with all the props of a local tribe of hunters and collectors came to mind. Guns and knives were on everyone and even up on the walls. Brad made a mental note for an exit strategy should the hosts or guests become disenchanted with each other. The wrong word or inflection of a word could trigger that. If it came to that, if it blew, he wanted his men to be outside not caught like rats in a trap. Heavy body armour would provide a margin of seconds to bring that off.

The Chief thrust out his hand in an awkward movement suggesting he was new to this western custom. Twisting his face into a sinister smile the overall effect was surly with an underlay of violence. The man was a tiger who could snap from approachable, tolerable, to murderous like a tropical storm that could tear into one side of a hill and spare the other.

'My name is Om', he said in a sharp tone in Burmese that was quickly translated into English.

Dane shook the extended hand followed by Teerasak. Krit stepped backwards clearly not wanting to touch someone responsible for so many deaths in his country. Gam appeared not to notice. After introducing themselves they sat down on surprisingly comfortable cushions. The man known as Om stared at them with an intense gaze that seemed to ask, *what do you want?*

Dane spoke first, translator at the ready. Translation could be tricky exact meaning rubbery. They would get to the meaning of all that was said and done by the end of the evening, at least he hoped so. A firefight would destroy all that delicate furniture in a heartbeat. Bonding over bottles of scotch and Vietnamese vodka was a start.

He opened a bottle of Dewar's Blended Scotch Whiskey and filled shot glasses his host generously provided on a tray held by an attractive woman. They exchanged smiles. Was she being held against her will? Probably even if she may have been persuaded with fists and whips to forget this.

As the naked light flickered and wafted oil fumes through the dark chamber the men bargained. It was clear, if unstated, that human lives depended on the outcome of these talks, it was that simple.

On the fire, a boar was being roasted and the aroma met with the guests' approval if smiles and feasting eyes were anything to go by. A feast was better than a firefight.

After eating and wiping their hands on the backs of some young girls, a disgusting local custom he was told, the Chief took them outside where a rising sun exposed he sight of groups of men and women, mostly women, tied together and huddled in bamboo cages.

'Have you captured these people? Are they prisoners of war?' Brad asked and when translated the answer came with much excited talk and the shaking of heads.

As the Chief rattled on Teerasak said, 'he says he liberate these poor villagers that he wants freedom for them. He saves us from death, from terrorists and Burma Army.'

Dane gave a sceptical look, he'd heard that excuse before and it was almost never true. The host was lying. This sized operation couldn't survive without the Tamadow, the true power behind the Burmese military. Still he would play along.

'I want to take them back to Thailand and I shall arrange safe passage.'

When the translation came through there was a howl of laughter with the leader revealing missing or gold-plated teeth.

As the laughter, subsided Dane came with an alternative offer.

'Your opium production has drawn a great deal of attention.'

When Teerasak looked uncomprehending his grasp of English reaching its limits Brad tried again.

'This place could be shut down and your business would be destroyed.' He paused as the message filtered through.

The rooster, the man who called the shots snarled, his lip curling in a clear signal of distain, spoke sharply and it looked like there could be a battle after all. The outcome of that would be uncertain at the very least. Better to go for the Quarantine than going ballistic. Better yet it was smarter to press the recall button than take the risk.

Major Van Dyke pressed the button on his phone which called in the chinook in Chiang Rai waiting on standby. There was a closing window of time and if it slammed shut it would be a miracle if anyone got out alive.

'He says you Americans are in his country and he will fight for his country to the death.'

Dane nodded this was not going to plan. He had a sense he was waiting for the last flight out of Jonestown. On impulse, he threw a new thick wad of American dollars on the table. The three men looked at each other as the gang leader's men drew closer. If the Yankee was put to the sword then all this would be academic and it would all be over.

Then without warning the leader smiled and signalled for the uninvited tourists to follow.

Walking through muddied grounds the dozen men or so including the leader's soldiers Dane could see a triple storied wood and bamboo barn or what passed for a barn in Burma.

Pointing upwards they could see dozens of men and women crammed in locked rooms, some called out in weak voices while others stayed mute as if waiting to be inspected like so many cattle.

The leader barked orders and his men began to open the bamboo cells. Some cowered in the corner as if delaying their death and had to be coaxed out. Dane helped one young woman out of her pen, disbelieving eyes signalled the shock to her system.

'I have a helicopter coming soon and I want them all to have some food and water. We don't want anyone dying on their first day of freedom now do we?' The leader with uncounted thousands of dollars but shy of a million smiled again although now it was less a sneer than a triumphalist sneer of victory. Even a warlord understood that killing American operatives could lead to bad karma of the worst sort.

The next few hours were restorative as bedraggled men and women drank deeply from coconut vessels and then inhaled pieces of bread dipped in some sort of local stew until the sound of the Chinook reverberated overhead.

As the men, women and some children were shepherded into the yawning mouths of two huge unmarked Chinooks, Major Van Dyke looked at his watch. By some miracle the whole operation had only taken three hours without bloodshed. A veteran of three theatres of war he sensed they had been too lucky. Running out of luck and you could end up with a bullet in the brain or burnt alive. One last tour of duty could be the last anything like Rock on his fourth in Iraq, blasted all to hell before seeing his new born son. He didn't want to be that guy. So, this was it. As the last of the freed captives disappeared into the noisy helos, he and Teerasak walked backwards M17s at the ready. He didn't wave goodbye to the bandit king and his band of killers he knew they would meet again.

Flying over thick stands of brush and jungle they were back in a Bangkok Military airbase, which doubled for Company Covert Ops by early morning. Not wanting to stay in the capital after dropping off many of the rescued into the hands of several NGOs including UNHR officers, and aftoer refuelling they were airlifted to an airbase outside Pattaya.

CHAPTER 53

In the Hilton Chailai and Brodie went to the marble topped counter where she produced her ID papers. It was a detail not always copied by lower stream hotels and provided an extra cushion of protection on top of the onion layers of security already there.

Once given the nod of approval by a wary manager they got into the elevator crowded with well-heeled tourists one with a Vuitton bag and diamond encrusted watch. Chailai kept fixated on the Vuitton bag of an older lady who looked like she'd enjoyed the attentions of a cosmetic surgeon. You could buy such bags and accessories in Pattaya but they were usually fake.

Once on the penthouse floor they walked down a long corridor to a couple of official looking Thais Brodie knew to be part of Ralph's security detail.

As the two showed their ID one of the security men spoke into to ear piece. With a nod, the door clicked open and they were ushered inside. The place had large mirrors and vintage Italianate furniture.

Ralph stood with his back turned to him as he typed something into his Smart Pad.

Without turning to face them he said, 'so good of you to come I hope it wasn't too much of an inconvenience.'

Brodie suppressed a smile. The statement was a polite fiction. They would have come whether they wanted to or not.

'What can we do for you Ralph?'

'Come, come Brodie where are your manners? You haven't introduced your lady friend to me yet.'

Another fiction. They all lived in a world of face, of appearance, staged exteriors, contrived personalities, where nothing was quite what it seemed to be. Of course, the man knew everything there was to know about Chailai, probably even more than the lady knew about herself.

'Oh, sorry this is Ralph. We've spoken about her.'

He turned and said, 'yes and I've taken an interest in your case. Before we discuss that I want to show you something and tell you something.'

He reached for a remote and a massive TV emerged from the wall. Craning his neck slightly to the side Brodie could see that it was no thicker than a nickel coin.

The screen came to life with grainy film Brodie recognised.

As helicopters flew over low rises and then descended to pick up impossibly long lines of awaiting evacuees Ralph ran a monologue.

'This footage has been around a long time, so you might not remember it. I was there in Saigon in 1975 and before that when the war going in full flight.

When Congress pulled the plug on finances there wasn't much time to get out.

Nixon was finished politically before he was gone.'

There was a long pause as if speaking about these past events encased in aspic had transported him back in time.

'I had the opportunity to leave well before that and my mission there even now is classified. I'm telling you all this because its mission critical. There were people still there, my people, and I couldn't with good conscience leave without them. Believe me it was a hard sell, we had superiors in Washington that would have been happy to deep six our operatives.'

'Operatives you mean spies?' Brodie asked only to be met with a frown.

'Not all operatives are spies Brodie, this is not 007 or Get Smart. Operatives come in all shapes and sizes I can assure you. Someone who is nondescript like a repair man can blend into a space like a jungle cat and do important work. Anyone can play a part. I'm talking about the clerical staff, the typists, the cooks, the drivers and yes, the soldiers that had fought shoulder to shoulder with us for the better part of 60 years. You see once we left we knew there would be a purge. Maybe not a purge along the lines of Khmer Rouge and the Killing Fields, but life would have been difficult to say the least.'

Ralph walked to the sliding doors and looked out as if looking back towards old Saigon. Saigon before it became Ho Chi Minh City. Saigon when it was a military base for the most powerful country in the world. His Saigon.

'We had some very sensitive projects that had to stay covert and ditching our friends was no way to do that so I stayed to the last minute until that could be expedited in real time. Time, time, we had so little time it's a wonder any of them or me survived it.'

'But you did survive Ralph. Do you think maybe it doesn't help to relive it?'

Ralph faced him and said, 'I'm not telling you any of this to take a waltz down memory lane my young friend. I can do without the emotional memory thank you very much.'

'So why you tell us Mr Ralph? Do the ghosts haunt you at night?' Chailai asked with a fearless expression. Her body language, her tone, screamed she wanted out. Would the old man trick her into being enslaved like her sisters over the border were tricked, killed? Why was this old man torturing her? Why didn't he and all the *farung* including Brodie leave her alone?

'I like your spirit young lady. You remind me of some of the people I worked with all those years ago. As for the ghosts, you're right they do come at night. There are so many I have to corral them outside the room.' She gave him a sad smile, knowing about his suffering made him more human.

'I'm sorry. I am you. They come to me, it is where I live.'

He frowned as if sensing he was out of time and all his old stories, including ghost stories, had a use by date. There was more silence then he started again.

'Let us bury the dead Chailai. Your only chance of survival is to take a plane, one of my planes, and go with Brodie to Australia or if you want we can get you to the states.'

With a distraught face she said, 'what about my daughter, my mother, my family?'

Ralph walled to a drinks cabinet and asked, 'what's your pleasure? A coke, a scotch or one of my favourites coconut water?'

Brodie said, 'a gin and tonic for me a coke for Chailai?' Putting his hand lightly on her shoulder he asked, 'coke is that alright?'

She looked down on the enveloping hand then nodded as if choice of drink was the furthest thing on her mind.

'I have helped you Brodie because I wanted to help you. The mess you got yourself into involves issues my company has been watching for a long time.'

Brodie started to speak only to be met with a restraining hand for silence held out by his host. 'Please bear me out this is far too important for us to get bogged down or side-tracked.'

Chailai gave Brodie a wild-eyed look as if to say what have you got me into?

He clicked the remote and the old footage dissolved to be replaced by a map of Southeast Asia.

Moving his hand, he was able to draw a line between Burma and Thailand then over to Cambodia.

'The working slave trade is vast. Hundreds of millions of people in fact. That includes indentured servitude or wage slavery. At a basic hourly rate below $10. Some even say the majority of employees in the US are working poor and virtual indentured slaves.' Ralph coughed into his fist giving Brodie the sense this man of many faces didn't want to criticise his home country, as if it were a violation of some basic human instinct.

'Be that as it may that is another point although one that grieves me. Now that you and your associates have exposed these networks of modern slavery and have finessed the escape of many including those I assisted with in Burma some of players are getting antsy to say the least.'

'So, what are you saying Ralph? We can't change history it happened. If you'd asked me that I would be involved in cracking a people trafficking scheme I would have called you crazy. Truth is I still can't get my head around it. I can't believe it happened.'

'Well you better believe it because it did happen.' Ralph gave a stern look. Furrowed brows with a helping of passive aggressive. The master game player wasn't playing games.

'Mr Ralph so we die, yes?'

'No, you don't die if you follow my advice. You must get out. Yes, you can take your daughter as far as your mother goes that might take longer or we might be able to get her to another destination offshore. Maybe Canada or New Zealand if not Australia or America. I can find a place for you and only ask for your full cooperation.'

'Are you sure about this Ralph you know Thailand can be a great place to live especially if you are from here in the first place.'

'I'm as sure as the nose in the middle of my face. As sure as night follows day. I know about these things Brodie trust me I have your best interests at heart.'

'And what about Grace? How does she play out in all this?'

'I already told you this has been taken care of. She's coming back with me to New York we have some business to attend to.'

'You mean like a will or something?'

'I'm afraid that's none of your business but I can assure you that it's important.'

Brodie turned to Chailai and put his hands on her shoulder to say, 'how do you feel about all this? Are you willing to do this, leave the country?'

Averting her gaze as if not to be drawn into his orbit she said, 'only if mother come. If not, I stay.'

The old company man slapped his hands together and exclaimed, 'well that's it we have a deal and not a minute too soon.'

'How do we go when do we go?'

'Go about your business in Chailai's case that means staying on at the bar in the meantime as if nothing has happened. As for your Brodie, I'll assume you'll continue your young man about town tendencies with your drinking buddy.' For the first time since during this shock meeting he smiled.

'Yes, even if Spike takes off in two days and even if I'd rather spend that time with Chailai,' he said as he placed an arm around her waist.

'One more question Ralph do you believe in ghosts?'

Ralph looked down and shook his drink the ice tinkling in the glass.

'Aside from the fallen comrades who come to me at night no.' There was a silence between them.

'You know ghosts usually take two forms. They can be the spirits of those who have departed, like restless souls.' He paused then said, 'or ghosts can be seen as nothing more than the diluded visions of someone suffering from a melancholy disposition.'

Brodie felt satisfied, this explanation from an experienced man was what he wanted to hear. In recent weeks the ghosts, the nats, came around every night.

'Shakespeare put boths kinds in Hamlet and McBeth.'

'That's pretty much what I think.'

Ralph gave a knowing grin and said, 'you know they call intelligence agents, spies, spooks.'

'I guess I'm getting a bit superstitious. Must be in the air.'

Ralph frowned slightly then said, 'yes old son I think you might be right.'

On the other side of the double-glazed widow a massive storm was brewing as if in some stratospheric cauldron.

'We sure have had a stormy few weeks,' Ralph said before laughing. The couple joined in. It was true, there was nothing to worry about.

CHAPTER 54

S he leaned over and whispered into the customer's ear, 'you like that girl? You want her sit with you?'

She gave a thumbs' up sign to show he was in business. A loud crack followed and then smoke of a flash bang grenade. Chailai grew frantic as she was grabbed around the legs and lifted up. Then a whirl of movement, noise and smoke rocketed her into a world of trouble. Kicking her legs and twisting her body Chailai tried to see her kidnapper's face but couldn't. Within a minute she was bundled into the back of a minivan and they drove off. Two streets away she was lifted out of the vehicle and placed in the back of a cab with heavily tinted windows.

A man spoke in Chinese accented Thai then placed a cloth to her nostrils.

What seemed like a thousand years later she awoke, the only noise being the lapping of light chop against a boat hull. Around her ladies sat or lay with tie cuffs. The blurry voices and slack faced expressions gave away the fact all were heavily sedated and in a tight fix.

She whispered to a woman who looked like she was new to Thailand, 'we are getting out of here.'

Looking confused the young woman nodded and said in Burmese, 'yes thank you.'

In her best Burmese, which wasn't much, Chailai said, 'stay close to me and do what I say.'

The woman nodded her understanding, her eyes now alert with the super charge of adrenaline that came with renewed hope.

Over in Soi 7 Brodie and Spike were cruising the bars. It was a normal night in Pattaya Wednesday 9:45 PM. They got a *Songthaew* to Walking Street and on to the rocking Siam Bar.

Inside they saw the usual layout of middle aged or older men seated on bar stools while topless women danced to a pounding rock beat. He heard a song he hadn't heard in years Eddy Money's 'Take me Home Tonight'.

This was the Lounge Lizard's desperado swan song and it took him back. A classic pick up song in the aftermath of Disco. Then more muzak from before his time. You wanted a girl you had to get a girl even if it took all night like the jive song went. With Chailai about to become something like a de facto wife he felt he'd earned the right to play up one last time for old time's sake. He tried calling her again and it rang out.

Spike nudged him in the ribs and pointed out a woman with tremendous breasts. Her hooters seemed to defy the laws of Physics.

'I wonder if they're real Brodie.'

He shrugged and said, 'who cares they do it for me that's all I can say.'

As if knowing they were talking about her, the lady knelt down and cupped her tits to say, 'you like, you like bar fine tonight?'

The two exchanged looks and Spike said, 'you said it mate this is your last taste of freedom so go for it.'

Looking flustered, feeling awkward, Brodie said, 'are you sure, I mean you might get lonely and all that.'

Spike made a show of scanning all the heavenly bodies and said, 'are you kidding? How could you get lonely in a place like this? Come on after all you've been through go for it mate.'

'No thanks I might sit this one out.' Cheating on Grace was one thing, cheating on Grace and Chailai was too much.

'Don't worry about me Spike knock yourself out.' They smiled at each other, the outcome a foregone conclusion. Brodie urged his friend along with a motion of the hands as if waving away a domesticated pet. It worked.

The *Playboy Philosopher* looked smug, pleased with himself. Like some white slaver he took the lady by the hand and threw four thousand baht on the counter. She was his for now. While some of her sisters did various things with ping pong balls he made his escape with the prettiest girl in the bar.

They walked up rickety stairs and went to a room with the bar girl taking the lead. He felt like saying something cheesy along the lines of *I guess you've done this before* but thought better of it. *Like a lot of the bar girls he met they might laugh along with farung jokes at the end of the day there really wasn't anything funny to laugh about.*

Once inside she made a lunge for his cock. He said, 'hey why don't we get to know each other first?'

Looking confused as if not quite sure why he was there, Brodie embraced her and said, 'sorry that was a joke but you aren't.' As if she required more assurance he kissed her with passion. Her mouth tasted of honey and he worked his way down to kiss breasts as she undid her red bra.

As she began taking off her clothes he began to cheer as though she were still at the bar. It was an act to get around the strange concept of love for money.

She gave a little smile and they made love.

He walked back down the spiral stairs and cheers erupted. Spike had backup with a crew of lager lads that had to be English. They laughed and raised glasses as if Brodie was free of his virginity. He gave a winning smile knowing that his days in Thailand were numbered and life as he knew it was over.

They idled away for more hours after midnight until both were royally drunk and were beginning to sound like Peter Cook and Dudley Moore also before his time yet still famous as the last of the great booze comedians.

'Now if you were a plastic surgeon specialising in tit jobs then this would be the place to be.'

Brodie drained his bottle of beer and said, 'sure and if you were a gynaecologist you could experiment with a third orifice.'

Putting up a correcting finger Spike countered, 'well we or rather women already have a third orifice.'

It got worse and it didn't matter they were on vacation right whatever happens in Thailand,

They drank until closing time 4 am. Walking out, each propping up the other in agonising slow motion they could see the dawn light and it was beautiful.

Sitting in the gutter hi phone told him it was 4:22 am. Neither wanted to go back to the hotel room, neither wanted the night to end.

Placing an arm around Brodie's shoulders Spike said, 'it's been great Brodie.

This trip has, 'As his voice trailed off Brodie finished the sentence for him, 'yeah I know this trip is a trip. What can I say? I bet you never thought you'd stay in a jungle retreat with someone like Ralph Winters.'

'Are you kidding not in my wildest billion years I wouldn't. Are you jiving me?' Brodie put his arm around his friend and the connect was complete.

CHAPTER 55

S tanding together with Grace in the private hanger Brodie felt a wave of sadness come over him. With a much greater sense of his own mortality small acts of kindness were more important than ever.

'When will I hear from you Grace?'

She gave a tight smile as if trying to contain her emotions.

'I'll be touch Brodie although I can't say it's not like I'm going to the other side of the world because of course I am. '

Standing off at a respectable distance Ralph gave him a sympathetic look as if he also felt her loss and of course he did. How could he stay away from her for so long? Sure, he did it for her, for his family.

As they spoke her father then walked to the other side of the Beechcraft jet to speak to the pilots. Was he issuing a new, covert flight plan? You never knew with the old spook, this Crypto-Guardian Angel from a parallel Universe.

'Is he going with you?' She turned to see her protective father look over his shoulder, then said, 'no he tells me he has business to attend to. That wouldn't have anything to do with you now would it Brodie?'

He made a face just this side of sheepish and replied, 'I don't know I hope not but with everything going on it might be a good bet to say it's a definite possibility.'

'I know things happen and you have to make the right choices. I get it.' 'I don't,' he said as he placed his arms around her waist.

They kissed and then after a bit of stilted body language and hanging back, Ralph joined them. The man had a granite faced expression as if he were just holding back emotions that hadn't been called on in living memory. Brodie figured some form of emotional insensitivity was a kind of occupational hazard for men in the murky world of intelligence. It was one of the prices demanded of anyone in the life, the company life.

They kissed again and then she boarded the business jet with no markings. He watched it take off into a balmy Thai evening. With no idea where she was going, the stated destination was more than likely a cover story, he wondered when or even if he would ever see her again.

Feeling sorry for himself he made for the drinking houses.

At the *Sunny Boys Bar,* he drank while Chailai served drinks. Did she mind his presence? If so she never said. Bar girls normally spoke painful truths when the money or the relationship or both ran out of gas. He waved to her and she gave a curt nod. He understood this was her place of work. As he waited for her to clock off he joined a toast with the much older and very drunk Londoner, his old friend Jimmy.

The man extended his hand and said, 'my name is Jimmy my friends call me Jim or Jimmy.'

'I'm Brodie pleased to meet you, we've already met Jimmy great to see you holding up the fort,' he said not sure where the conversation was going.

'I've been living here on and off for ten years,' he said his thick East Enders accent that made him sound like some charming villain. Of course, like many dedicated drinkers young or old he was all that. Brodie also numbered in their ranks.

'You must like the place.'

Jimmy made a scowl and said in a dark voice, 'truth is I hate the place can't stand it.'

Brodie kept silent. There wasn't much to say. Jimmy lost a few brain cells along the way and had emerged as a bar fly amnesiac. Maybe each day was ground hog day the past and future gone only the resent left in an eternal drunken twilight. Was he some A grade lush contrarian? Or was he a *Farung khi nok*, a bird shit foreigner?

With a wave of the hand, as if to banish any such notion, his new old best friend called out, 'another round of scotch on the rocks for me,' then turning to Brodie asked, 'what about you mate what's your poison?'

Brodie suddenly felt like taking a walk. Getting plastered with a dipsomaniac wasn't his idea of a productive morning.

'Look I was just about to go I'm taking off in a few days.'

'I thought I heard you say to that lovely lady over there that you can't leave for a few weeks.' There was a gap before the Londoner said,' I'm sorry I didn't mean to pry, just a habit I guess. I can't help it I'm curious by nature. Over the years it's got me in lots of trouble that's for sure. Anyway, if shouldn't matter if you're going tonight or next year we are on Thailand time.'

It was a conversation they had weeks ago. Resigned Brodie said, 'why not I'm ready for a bit of the old amber fluid. Make mine a Singha Beer.'

They drank. They talked. Well into the night. The man had some interesting stories, most of which he'd heard before but now slightly altered. He was in the Navy not the army, he'd served in Malaysia but was far too young to have fought in Burma in War 2, something he was keen to hear about even if Jimmy was making it up with a little help from Google. Jimmy had it bad even if there were Jimmies in every bar in town. Every man he'd met here had a story whether it was true or not, an open question.

As he stirred his scotch with his finger the East Ender said, 'I grew up tough. You had to be tough. My grandfather worked for the Krays, ever heard of them?'

Brodie scratched the day-old beard growth that was starting to change his appearance. In the cracked bar mirror, he looked some indeterminate age between thirty-five, and forty-five, give or take. The added touch of whiskers gave him the appearance of some wild, misunderstood renegade like Che or Fidel, out for what he could get including a Revolution.

'Didn't they make a movie about these guys sort of England's answer to Al Capone.'

Jimmy stubbed out his cigarette and signalled for another round. 'Yeah you could say that although not that big on the old violin cases with machine guns and all that Untouchables stuff. Us Brit villains had a different style we did, not so much genteel as wary and not so in your face. Anyway, me pop was in the bar when Mick the hat was killed, that was in the movies too.' Brodie drained his glass and was rewarded with a new one. He took a sip of the dark coloured spirit drink and knew it was Jack Daniels, probably a triple, but wasn't going to ask.

'So why was he killed? A bar is a pretty public place to kill someone even Big Al usually got someone to do his dirty work for him.' There was a pause and then he said, 'oh I forgot in the Kevin Costner film Robert de Niro, I mean Al Capone, killed those two guys who had other ideas about running the outfit, killed them with a,'

Jimmy interrupted to complete the sentence, 'smashed their heads in with a baseball bat.

CHAPTER 56

In the hotel room, a group of half a dozen men sat around a large table playing cards. Brodie entered the room not knowing exactly why he was there.

Major Dane Van Dyke, retired, looked up from a large map, a general planning for war.

'Glad you could make it Brodie I want your input on this.'

'What are we talking about exactly men?'

He recognised Teerasak, but the rest besides the reactivated and reenergised Major Braddock were strangers. There were no introductions here it wasn't that kind of meeting. Ralph and co always prized their plausible deniability and things weren't going to change any time soon.

'Come over here Brodie.' The reformed military man American style waved him over and Brodie followed. Yes, he finally had a seat at the table.

'Here we have a local map of Pattaya and surrounds and another one of Thailand and Burma or Myanmar whatever you like, and Cambodia. This is where the operation will take place.'

'Operation? Are we talking about a raid?'

The men exchanged looks then burst out laughing. Feeling naïve he said, 'Alright I get the picture carry on don't let me hold you up. You know if there is anything I can do to help then don't hesitate to ask.'

Major Dane gave a sardonic smile then said with a commanding tone, 'that's why you're here pal in fact that input could be vital.'

As they pored over the maps images were thrown up on the wall from a laptop not quite a PowerPoint but close.

'Here is a picture of Pranit, Gam's proxy in Thailand. This is just after the little scare we gave him inside his supposedly impregnable lair just over the border.'

The looming, larger than life image showed an unsmiling man with a scar down his cheek suggestive of a sinister past. Then an image of an erect General in medal covered uniform, came on screen.

'This is General Natchapon Anuratis, he is on the take and is vulnerable on several levels. Even if he has something like consent from the ruling Junta exposure will destroy him. You know the worst crime is getting caught. Some of the Thai and Burmese Generals have a very lucrative operation going and I'm sure some of his colleagues either want a cut or are happy to see him knocked off. As with a lot of things the worst crime is getting caught. He is here to expedite the sale of slaves working or not and he has the assets to do it. Word on the street is he wants out although we are,' looking away from the screen and back to the group he finished with, 'not going to allow him this luxury. The man, according to confidential sources is responsible for the deaths of seven people that we know of a most likely many more besides.'

'What's he doing in Pattaya?' Brodie asked wanting to have answer on everything whether it was at hand or not.

'My guess is he has been called or recalled here. This thing is blowing up and someone will have to pay of course. Doesn't look good if you have too many slaves near the tourists, I can tell you that.'

'How long have there been slaves in Thailand?'

Dane stifled a chuckle. 'You mean not counting the wages slaves in the bars trying to feed a family?'

Brodie felt the heat rise in his cheeks. Had he exploited the girls here too? Of course, he did. With all the bragging rights, back home and the scoring of young women that wouldn't give him the time of day back home this was the dirty little secret that no one wanted to talk about.

Oh, about as long as Thailand has been around, although this is another level entirely.

'How are the authorities going to take this?' Brodie asked incredulous that they could bring this off.

'Not well, how would you like it if someone in the know told the world your wonderful tourist destination is a holding pen for thousands of work slaves?'

Brodie rubbed his jaw which unshaven this morning was beginning to feel like sandpaper.

As if all the talk was wearying the Major pulled out a flask and said, 'some scotch?' Brodie shook his head, at 4 pm the time was fine it was just that he felt an over powering need to stay straight. Jimmy's example was a cautionary tale.

As he drank the scotch neat from the flask he gave a satisfied grunt then shook his head Brodie took to be a coping mechanism.

'The reason it happens here is that it's barely noticeable. Plus, if it's married with an anti-drugs and military security campaign then you have a full house. A lot of the funding comes from drugs although its useful to remember this is not a drug raid. Let the DEA guys deal with that and they will.

The local overlord Pranit ticks all the boxes so even if he used to deal in large quantities of drugs in the Golden Triangle he now says he's drug free.'

'Where does the security come in?'

As Brad proceeded to dumbbell combinations with hand weights, he looked at Brodie with one eye in the mirror. His musculature was ripped, six packed and incredibly fit. So, the man was a gym junkie. Brodie wondered if he had ever used steroids and one look at the sculpted arms and legs crammed with muscle tone told him it was a definite possibility. He knew to keep quiet. About all that.

'Our Pranit was a leading figure in the Tamadaw military that ruled Burma for decades. They're still around only hidden. He has the connections even if no one trusts him. On our side, here in Thailand is another General in the Thai Army right now his identity is unknown but won't be for long.'

'So, he's untouchable, is that it?'

Dane waved a scolding finger across his nose and said, 'I said connected not untouchable. No one is untouchable out here except someone I won't talk about. Maybe. Very few people are untouchable not even Ralph is in that category even if he's close.'

'I want to come along and see what I can see. You know scope things out.'

'Hey kid this is not the latest stop off in a theme park some of these guys shoot real bullets.'

'I can do it I've even been going to weapons practice out on the shooting range near Dow Mueang Airport.'

Major Dane, recalled to active duty, held out a revolver Brodie recognised as a Smith & Wesson Chiefs Special Air Weight revolver .38 calibre bullets. His knowledge of firearms had increased out of sight during his stay here. It was a coping strategy linked to his survival instinct. 'Sure, you can handle one of these my old Australian friend?'

Brodie reached for the gun and Brad pulled it away as if teasing.

'I won't give you a gun but I will give you an important task.

CHAPTER 57

Myint pulled on the nets as Yei joined him. The skipper shook his head at the poor catch.

Moving his arm through struggling fish including undersized bass and salmon he said in Thai, 'this is not enough for the quota. We can't go back to port with this. He called out to his offsider who was at the wheel.

'We have to go out further the satellite shows big schools near the Vietnam coast.'

As the skipper spoke Yei lost his footing on the slimy deck and fell backwards.

He shouted in pain then reached for his back.

Myint rushed to his side and tried to massage the hurt only generating more hurt. 'He needs a doctor,' Myint said in passable Thai. His language had improved as a matter of survival.

'We are not going back, we cannot go back.'

The trawler chugged ahead further out than ever. It would take even longer to see a doctor, long enough for the casualty to die. Over the next half hour Yei's pain got worse if his groaning was anything to go by. The Cambodian Captain shouted with a furrowed brow.

'I don't want to hear this, shut up.'

The skipper went below deck and emerged with a bottle of Vietnamese Whiskey. Myint smiled at this. Perhaps it wasn't as bad as he thought. Holding the half full bottle close to the patient's lips he gave a slimy smile.

'Drink this the last time I gave an onboard amputation it worked. I told him to keep drinking as I cut off his leg.'

'What happened to him?' Yei asked as he grimaced in pain.

By late afternoon there was another catch, this one better than the first.

By 9 PM they were asleep except the lead deck hand keeping watch.

As Yei slept he was dragged to the back of the boat. Waking he shouted, 'what are you doing, what are you doing?'

The Captain produced a long- bladed knife and said, 'I told you to shup up.'

As Yei tried to call for help the blade was held against his throat. 'I told you to shut up now you will shut up once and for all.'

As Yei gurgled a scream the knife sliced through his throat and his oesophagus until Yei's head dangled like a broken doll.

Alerted by the commotion Myint rushed towards the nearly headless Yei only to be stopped by the deckhand holding a revolver pointed straight towards him.

As the captain and another deckhand weighed down Yei's body with lead sinkers Myint watched them roll him into the sea. It was a torture to watch his friend become food for the fish and the roles of fish, fishermen and food were reversed, as if the world had been turned upside down through some kind of black magic.

As he heard the slash Myint saw something lift from the water. More light than substance, the apparition, rose into the sky making sounds Myint took for ghostly screams. With such a raw killing, Myint recognises this nat, this ghost, for what it was. There was a reckoning to be had.

CHAPTER 58

He took another swig of the six- pack-sized bottle of tiger Beer. It was his third and he didn't feel a thing. PTSS had a way of doing that. The fear built up a solid wall to empathy high enough so a pole vault would hardly get you over. 'So why did you come back to Thailand, Spike?'

Hr paused and took another swig before going on. 'I mean I've been a captive in my own right but you are free to come and go. That's something I really appreciate now. Freedom. Freedom and all the freedoms that come with it.

Freedom of speech, freedom of movement.'

Spike shrugged his shoulders and said,' I don't know what do you want me to say? I guess it seemed like a good idea at the time.'

Turning back to the entertainment, Spike gave a wink and jerked his thumb at the topless girls dancing on the bar. Contrary to all advice he was back in Walking Street. Even Spike was back on walking street and Brodie thought he wouldn't be seeing him for a long time, maybe never. His life was being pulled out to sea in a high tide misfortune. Right so what was the name of that Bond movie *Never say Never Again* and you didn't need to go over to James Bond Island to pick that up.

'Ok it's more than the girls, more than the booze. I even went to Hawaii and it wasn't the same it was ordinary.'

Brodie toasted by clinking his beer against Spike's and said, 'you and me both.

Thanks for coming back, it shows a lot of guts realty it does.'

'Thanks so do you want to blow this bar it's starting to get old mate.'

They strolled past packs of men on the hunt and some Russian couples.

'I'm feeling a bit hungry,' he said as he craned his neck looking for the right restaurant. He saw people eating and talking at a place on the second floor of a place fronted by a massage joint and more bars.

Once inside they ordered the main idea was to get drunk.

'You know I feel like I've lived here for years. Years and years and years.'

'The more you do, the more complete the experience. You have done more in ten weeks than some do after living here for twenty years. They just repeat the same year over and over again.'

'So that's why you came back. You thought maybe you could do the same thing. Live five, ten years in a few weeks and months.'

Spike guzzled his drink then said, 'if you put it that way I guess you're right.'

Brodie picked up his fork and began eating the duck breast. It tasted fresh, succulent and totally different from the overcooked stuff from the hot food stalls.

As he scooped rice with a spoon he saw an arm cross his field of vision before a hand seized his wrist.

As he looked up the stranger put a cloth to his face and he blacked out.

Completely comatose he had no sense of the chaos all around. Spike was also knocked out but not before he punched one thin man of middle years. The last vision he had was of the bastard wiping blood from his lip.

Brodie was hustled from one vehicle to another so as to lose any tail. It worked. With the police taking ten minutes to arrive at the scene of the crime there wasn't much risk. For now.

In a whirlpool of dreams Brodie saw a grinning man fingering a long-bladed knife shouting something in Thai or was it Burmese? He got up and ran from the room only to find that outside the door full of bullet holes there was a fivestory drop. He twisted and turned in space knowing that when he hit the pavement he would bust open like a ripe watermelon and die. Then like in some bent Warner Brothers cartoon he bounced off the busy street, just missing a kissing Thai couple clearly in love and oblivious to everything.

There came a change of lighting as the daytime vision of the street went black. It stayed black or rather various hues of black, like some moody monochromatic painting. Then more changes, he could see Grace and her father Ralph waving from the deck of some impossibly large ocean liner. Was that the Titanic or the Lusitania or maybe some other doomed ship passing over to the other side?

He called out, yet they didn't seem to notice. Then came faint words from his father in law drifting back from a listing deck towards him, drifting from another lifetime. 'Brodie, I tried to warn you. We all tried to warn you.'

By his side his dutiful daughter nodded her agreement and smiled. It looked like Grace but Grace if she had a lobotomy or shot through with some weird hypnagogic drug. Convincing yet unreal, it was a Carny vision from the other side, the side where *Ghosts of Burma* dwelled.

He called out as the voices faded almost to nothing. 'Can I come on board? It looks nice up there surely there's room for one more.'

In unison, they shook their heads as if wired together and operated from afar.

'No, it's too late for that I'm afraid far too late. I'm sorry I can't help you.'

Ralph looked at his watch and said in a suddenly jaunty voice,' oh I almost forgot I'm late for a game of bridge. I'm up against a man who has won any tournaments you want to name.'

'Wait, wait please, I'm a hostage please help me get of here.' His voice Beginning to crack, Brodie felt hot tears course down his cheeks.

As father and daughter disappeared so too did the ocean liner. The great boat began to fade like an old photo left out in the sun. It grew sketchy, a pencil drawing being slowly erased, rubbed out to nothingness. Here reality was on the other side only he couldn't get back to it just yet. The mission wasn't over until it was.

Stricken Brodie began to writhe about as pain shot though his churning skull, leeching into desiccated bones.

Then he felt his face being slapped and heard words in broken English, 'you wake up we got business to settle.'

Coming to, Brodie thrashed his arms about in a defensive reflex like a disturbed patient in a Psyche ward. Trying to speak words spilled from his mouth in an incomprehensible babble.

Then he felt a fist collide with his face. He stopped the flailing about and feeling something loose in his mouth pulled out a bloody tooth. Then a sharp reality check and he knew where he was.

'You talk to me you live. No talk you die, you understand American?'

Before he could take exception to being called an American he was slapped again.'

In a voice now choked with rage, with shame he could be in this desperate place where hope had to be checked in at the door, he said, 'if you keep doing that I won't talk to you at all.'

His interrogator moved his head and another man, clearly much younger, drew a huge hunting knife and made a surface cut along his chest that drew beads of blood. Brodie looked down at blood and knew he was about to die. Then as if he needed further convincing the chief tormenter took out what looked like a US army service revolver and placed the barrel against his head.

'You talk,' he said as he cocked the pistol,' then finished with, 'or you die. You know this do not throw your life away. Your American daddy gone he cannot help you. The police will not help you.'

The Chief fired into the ceiling then cocked the gun again and placed it against his ear.

'I shoot you not even hear bang you fall over dead before you hit ground.'

At this the man gave a smile to reveal a mouthful of rotten teeth and gold fillings.

'Alright so what is it you want to know?'

'You know what I want to know.'

Stringing it out he said in a calm voice, 'no I'm afraid I don't know.'

'Workers from Burma you say you want to free but you keep for you. You have Thai girlfriend you buy and treat like sex slave.'

Shaking his head in fury he protested, 'and that's a lie, a filthy lie.'

His torment's smile widened to reveal gold ca;ped teeth, and he said, 'no lie this is true. You know this you and all the degenerates that pollute our country.'

'I was trying to help them,' he insisted knowing how it sounded. Knowing his interrogator was gaining traction and enjoying Brodie tried to spit only to release a spray of blood and the remains of another tooth.

'This true you know this. You no better than me Mr Brodie. Send them to Apple factory and work to death. World all has Smart phone but people die making this.'

Not wanting to accede to his rhetoric but wanting to keep the conversation going as a preliminary to negotiation Brodie said in a crafted grudging voice, 'well yes that happens, no one can argue with that and as I understand it the big players are trying to fix that.'

The stranger stared at him with bulging eyes like some clever spider monkey and said, 'just like they pay tax. They exploit working slaves. We give them job.'

His voice trailed off as a realisation came they were both working both sides of the street.

'Alright, alright, the Americans, the Australians have a lot to answer for. It's not pretty. Capturing and killing people because they are in demand as employees who are forced to work for nothing.'

As his captor Popeye licked the edge of the blade then stuck out his tongue to reveal blood he said, 'life in Asia, southeast Asia is hard. You don't work the government give you money yes?'

Brodie bowed his head and said, 'that's true not even the Americans have that.

What am I saying the Americans especially don't have that kind of safety net?'

'No safety net here you fall off high wire in Thailand, in Burma in Cambodia you land on concrete and you die.' He clapped his hands together hard so it made a sharp sound like the crack of a rifle shot.

The man who seemed to have long experience in extracting information by any means necessary, smiled and said, 'this still joke to you. I cut off fingers, I curt off hand and you not think this funny. You go back home cripple no one look at you.' He gave a wide smile and finished with a perverse thought. 'You end up gimp as Americans say. Cripple, invalid shut-in. You ashamed you self, never come out no want people see cripple old man.'

With no wish to hear more detail about the hellish outcome his tormenter had in store for him Brodie tried stalling.

'Look all I know about Burma is that it has some great Buddhist temples although not nearly a wonderful as the temples in your country here.' The man spat a red gruel coloured by blood and betel nut juice.

He motioned with his head again and his young assistant in the black arts held his hands against the top of the kitchen table.

As Brodie vainly tried to twist his way out of position he watched as the older man held the knife high to get enough momentum for a decent amputation.

Then a loud bang and the room filled with smoke and flashing lights. He could see men in uniform police or army rappel through the skylight.

The man with no name made a lunge for his gun and was shot in the face. He shrieked and tried to touch his nose, only his nose and his face had disappeared under a mask of blood and pulp. Looking at his bloody hand, he fell to the floor.

CHAPTER 59

B rodie left the way he came. He couldn't see because he had a blindfold on and it occurred to him the rescue could be anything but. He knew he was in a mini-van due to the sound of the roller doors before they were slammed shut.

He could hear Thais speaking. No English. Was this just an elaborate ruse while he was spirited across the border where the real fun and games were? Was he instore for the best the Burma Army could offer or would any of these bad actors be doing him a favour by handing him a pistol and leaving him in a locked room?

Then a shaft of light and the cloth blind was lifted off his battered face.

The light was so bright, so sharp he shielded his eyes with his forearm.

Sergeant Detective Timon Kittikachorn stood over him and gave what passed for a smile.

'You had many people, many important people worried you not make it this time.'

Rolling his head and neck as if to squeeze out the grogginess and get his bearings he said, 'you mean Ralph Winters?'

Without answering the question directly Chief Timon said, 'you lucky you not in jail. Our jails are different than yours.'

With slow, drugged diction he said, 'yes, I know I've read the book, seen the movie.'

'What movie?' the lawman said in a sharp tone as if on guard and out of his depth. Was this westerner, this decadent westerner playing tricks. One of the westerners that despoiled his country as they satisfied their base instincts every day? Of course, the town itself was a prize example of by and for the decadent west. No getting around that one really if you uncovered the filthy little secret that has hardly a secret like calling a working girl a loving partner when she wasn't. That kind of polite fiction allowed superannuated men to playact love while engaging in wild sex. One thing he had learnt was you can't win an argument with a cop while you're in custody. They hold all the cards and can turn your life to shit. Brodie scrambled for an example.

'Bangkok Hilton if you really want to know. It's about a guy.'

'I know this movie and what it about. It show what happen when you break law and become criminal in my country. Sometime you die.'

As he spoke Brodie again slipped into hallucination. Madness pulled him under again, a king tide of desperation and galloping paranoia, maybe the gremlins wouldn't let go this time and he'd be lost in the vortex to spin and spin for all eternity. Reality was locked in a cell with 50 angry men meant for half a dozen. The one toilet was a stinking hole in the floor where the occasional sewer rat emerged to bite squatting bums and psychologically scare you for life. A place where the guards took pleasure in pitting one inmate against another in Thai kick boxing fights that could and did end in death. Where the food tasted like human waste and infection could lead to amputation. One year of that was enough to finish you off with an average sentence of ten years. Would he kill himself in those conditions? The wars showed people could put up with anything. Would he take his own life when that life became hell? Probably not only he'd never be the same and already he'd changed out of sight.

'Are you going to give me a lecture or are you done?'

The Chief raised his hand as if to strike then slammed it hard on the table.

'You still laughing boy. You lucky you have important friend or how you say influential?' Timon drew out the last word so every syllable was clearly articulated as if this term was new to him which it most likely was.

'We punish in Thailand for real mate,' he said pronouncing the last word with a passable mock Aussie accent, 'and without your bodyguard you would die or be locked away forever.'

Brodie forced a smile and said, 'well that's a comforting thought. Glad to see you still putting on the charm. It's always nice to see you Chief. Now are you done? May I go or I under arrest?'

He got up to leave in a sudden move meant to decide the matter once and for all. Listening to a self-important police officer with anger issues was as torturous as what he had just supposedly escaped or rather been rescued from.

'You may go and my advice,' he paused as if to keep Brodie in check for just a few more minutes or seconds.

Trying not to look jaded or insolent he closed his eyes as though to better protect himself from the inevitable shit storm.

As he caressed the gun in his holster in a gesture that was almost obscene he said, 'if you know what is good for you then you will leave on the next available flight. Stay here and you will run out of luck.'

'I will run out of luck? Not perhaps, not might but will. That sounds like a threat.'

Taking his hand off his firearm Timon the Wild East sheriff with attitude said, 'no threat only warning. I know you no believe I want save your life.' He walked around the table as if burning off nervous energy. 'You make many enemies Aussie man you leave this town you leave Thailand or bad Karma come your way.'

'Karma I have a hippy Aunt who is always talking about Karma. My mother always told me her sister took something and was never the same. Knowing her kooky sister like we did, that wasn't hard to believe. I know it's Buddhist the concept of Karma, do you believe in it Chief Timon?

Moving his face close to Brodie, uncomfortably close, the Chief spoke between clenched teeth as if it were a terrible strain to keep from tearing him up into dog food. 'yes, I believe. I live it.'

Then as if to appease even a pacifist deity like Buddha he faced the little shrine near the corner, and with clasped hands did a bow and *wai'd*. Like some sufferer of OC, he had to do this to keep his world from imploding into some catastrophic shift of folding, intersecting tectonic plates. He breathed in the freedom of clear air, a deep-sea diver just cracking the surface after fathoms, endless fathoms of ocean.

Suddenly shamed Brodie had the urge to call a taxi then catch a flight south of the equator.

'I'm sorry for all the trouble I've caused, and I think you're right. My luck is running out,' he said as he rapped the table with his knuckles to knock wood.

He didn't have a religion yet that one was right up there with broken mirrors and black cats.

CHAPTER 60

'Get ready men or I should say team with Mon,' he said with a nod to the best female shootist he'd seen, 'coming along. One thing I need to say,'

As wind blew in from the Indian Ocean Operations Commander Braddock lifted a lite beer to his lips then finished his sentence. Deep azure waters were edged with white sugary sand. It was the glamourous Thailand with perfect beaches and enchanting isands ot shoot straight up from the depths as if pushed by the unseen hands of tectonic plates. Not that this was a sightseeing tour. As vacationers sailed and suntanned, the team was in conference.

'This will be a different operation and I don't expect the kind of luck we had last time. Along with Mon we have Krit whom you all know as well as his fellow Maung Yin Wai.'

Yin stood as if to take a bow. 'Thank you,' he said in broken English.

'What village are you from?' Jerome asked. Looking confused Krit hurried with a translation for his fellow Maung in exile.

'He is from Homein and he knows border lands we going to very well.'

'Maybe you press your luck too much. You don't have to come with us. If we are captured, we will be killed. You might survive maybe not.'

Dane didn't react to what he thought was provocation. It didn't pay to have too many doubts before you commit even if it was always case by case. As he said every operation was different.

'Let's have another drink no time for that where we're going and if there is I don't want to know about it.'

As the bar girl, dispensed drinks from a tray her shapely proportions proved to be a distraction. He stood and wai'd a bow, 'that will be all thank you.'

He blew a kiss and said, 'isn't she wonderful?'

There were grins and more mouthfuls before he thought they were settled enough go on. Brodie kicked away an empty bottle of Jim Beam that rolled onto his foot. He watched Teerasak drain a bottle of vodka then throw it on the floor in a histriponic move like some cossak drinking shot glasses then smashing empties into the fireplace.

'We take off from the airstrip in the morning at 6 am in Pai and get taken close to the border.'

'Why not over the border?' Jerome Blake a former reservist but skilled and with the right mental and physical stamina to take this thing to the end paused before answering his own question. 'If anyone's forgotten, unregistered crossings are expressly forbidden. We get caught somehow a certain interested partner, and I'm not saying who, anyway they will disown us and they'd be right. So that means we have certain advantages and we have certain disadvantages. Truth is if I didn't think this mission would make it I wouldn't have signed on or put my men in danger.' There were cheers until he put up a quieting hand before going on.

'This is something I believe in and that I care about. It's about freedom and I know these are just words. You men are on the right side of a dirty war and if someone doesn't help out then who will?'

There were more cheers and the bar girl reappeared. Brad had hired out the place for the night he had bar staff waving any uninvited guests away.

'Now I know some of you guys,' he nodded to Teerasak who was quietly translating. He did this expertly and the men listened then nodded their understanding. The harsh demands of the dangerous cross border work perfected his communication skills as a matter of existential survival.

'I know some of you guys, hell, probably most of you guys don't really care about diplomatic violations and the rest of that. That really the least of you worries. That's the problem with all you freedom fighters is you'll do whatever it takes. I used to be like that maybe I still am.'

As Jerome fell silent the group erupted into cheers. Brad made of motion with his beer bottle then joined in a group high five.

Next morning, they flew to Chiang Mai and stopped for the night. For security reasons, they waited several hours then took a transport helo to Pai.

The men wanted to wait out the last night with poker and hard liquor. Brad shook his head and the men took it knowing it was right. There were things waiting for them. Glorious things like salvation and redemption but also the prospect of failure ending in death. That death could be quick like a bullet through the spine and it could be a slow torturous end while in captivity. Teerasak and he had talked about it more than once only usually in indirect terms like, 'I may not come back from that last hill.'

Then one night just after the first and only mission so far.

Teerasak spoke of the family he hadn't seen in three summers. He was in pain and yet said he 'didn't want to see them until the war was over'.

Close to tears and with the booze talking too he said, 'my son and his two daughters don't deserve to become a target when they coame looking for me.' With the support of all there he went on about his fears as if speaking about his pain was a pathway to channelling it, using it to stay strong. Teerasak spoke of family. They were in Thailand or at least most of the family. His wife refused to leave because her mother wouldn't leave. His daughters would visit her and there they were most vulnerable. Someday he would get her out whether she wanted to or not. He could not let this woman he no longer lover put the family in danger.

Teerasak said, 'I want them to shoot me get it over with. A man under torture is a man stripped of dignity.'

'Only if you let it Teerasak,' Dane said both of them knowing he the person who had never been tortured, boring lectures of all sorts no exception.

Later Braddock and Brodie talked alone in another room.

'I'm flattered that you want me in on this, but wouldn't it be safe for me to stay in Pattaya.'

Dane grinned. 'Not unless you want to get interrogated again by the police Chief. In understand its become a bit of a habit for him to haul you in.'

Resting his hands on his chin Brodie said, 'sure but that begs the question of why I'm in the loop.'

'Ralph believes in you. Do you believe in yourself Brodie?'

He nooded, the meeting was over. He was in. There was no going back.

CHAPTER 61

'This is where we go,' Teerasak said with an expressionless face. Often smiling and laughing even in crisis, today at the closest large city near the Burma border, Chiang Mai, it was strictly business.

Dane Van Dyke rolled his shoulders to ease the back pain. R&R could come later if it came at all. His idea of celebration was drinking alone in a hotel far from here and offshore.

Getting to the remote hamlet in a country and region often at war with the world was mission critical.

'What's the best way to get there?'

'We must have money to pay off any military or soldiers we come across. A firefight with them would destroy the mission.' There was a pause as he stood staring at his ally and benefactor.

'Yeah, I know, and we'd probably get killed in the bargain. And it would be embarrassing for the United States government.'

'Now I know why I'm not coming,' Brodie said as he wondered if he still had a chance of hitching a ride into the Apocalypse like Errol Flynn's son Sean back in 70. And look what happened to him!

'Well we, that is, the people I work with, have a few remedies. I'm connected with a company that has nothing to do with the USG.'

'Like plausible deniability Dane?'

'Yes', he said as he looked off into the distance. 'There's that and the fact this is off the books. I have a task for you here although you might be better off going back to Pattaya. The choice is yours you are under no obligation to come.'

Everyone says I'd be better off going back to Australia. Trouble is I can't leave, at least not yet.'

'Why don't you it's save me having to reply to your stupid questions.' He gave a wide smile.

'Yeah I know Braddock you don't like me but you don't mind having me around.'

The smile widened, and he said, 'sounds like my second wife we never did get on much but God did we have a great time of it.'

The next morning, they were gone, and Brodie had his job to do. As said by the Major recalled to active duty, Brodie would be gathering information not spying although the distinction escaped him.

As he casually picked up his glass and sipped watered down Saki Brodie looked through the photos and the secure phone Brad gave him. He remembered the instructions of the mission leader on the last night together.

'This is a security phone Brodie.' Holding out the cell he moved his finger to a circular app and said, 'it will self-destruct if you press this flashing cog.'

You must keep updating it every two hours and I'm going to change that setting to 40 minutes. So, unless you keep keying the security code the device will commit Hari Kiri.'

Brodie held the compact Smart phone in the palm of his hand and as if speaking to it said, 'sorry pal you don't want to live forever. Think of it as a valuable public service.'

'You see any of these guys you send a signal to is not a text and not a call it disappears. All communication is deleted once it's heard or read like Snapchat on steroids. When that task is completed then you get the next flight to Bangkok and high tail it out of here understand?'

Brodie, now looking serious, said, 'yes I can do that.'

When Dane left some time after midnight Brodie wondered if he would ever see him again just as he had with Grace.

Now sitting drinking, he was doing a pretty good impression of a *Farung* drunk.

'You like buy me drink', a lady who could have been Lao or Cambodian but probably not Thai said as she floated, like some ephemeral geisha, in his direction.

He gave his sweetest smile and replied as he showed the wedding ring on his finger from another lifetime. 'Sorry my wife and I are just here to see the temples.'

'Sorry *mai pen rai*.'

As this delectable butterfly glided off to another potential customer he rubbed the ring for good luck. Somehow it kept the bad spirits at bay. He remembered Ralph's caution, 'thinking it makes it real. You have to get out of your head if you want to get through this.'

That was fine, yet still he had to keep the ghouls at bay. The came to him last night when Sirawit came to his room and sat on his bed.

'Promise that you will not let me die in vain,' he said with wide staring eyes in a translucent head he could see through.

'I promise, I promise yu this.' At this Sirawit's ghost melted into the walls and he was left alone with his promise knowing it could not be unkept. He had promises to keep and miles of jungle to go before he slept.

Then as if to touch all bases he gave a *wai* to the Buddha shrine near the corner of the room. Staring at the ring he knew it had special powers like a genie, maybe even the power to stop bullets. Eyes closed he placed the gold band against his head as if to invoke this power. He'd picked it up in a pawn shop in Hong Kong the gold alone worth the price unless it wasn't. He was still alive, wasn't he? That was enough. That was enough to keep him believing.

Then came the long game. He sat through the day and into the night watching for signs or tells from people coming and going. Then just after noon he got an encrypted message to catch a flight back to Bangkok. As he boarded a taxi he could see military vehicles moving down the main street. Getting locked up in a Thai jail again was a horror he couldn't face.

In the rainforest, Major Van Dyke, recalled to active duty, hacked away at thick vines and brush with a machete. Under dun coloured clouds there was just enough light to bring a glint from the sharp blade. It was tough but nothing he wasn't used to. The undergrowth wasn't as bad as say Cambodia not that this meant there were no leeches or clinging stinging vines. Or thorns with venom that could lead to toxic shock inside five minutes.

They moved into a partially cleared area with various crops including rice and poppies for opium. So far, the mission was incident free even if there was movement that could prove critical.

In full camouflage and low to the ground the uniformed men that appeared over the rise didn't see them. Camouflage and Ghillie suits made the men all but invisible to the uniformed men standing around a tin shed or carrying loads inside. Were they guarding black market opium trade or was it a military action or maybe all three? He checked the satellite imagery and confirmed military manoeuvres and he had a number.

In a voice, just short of a whisper but clear enough the men and single woman in his unit, he said, 'we wait until they're gone, all night if we have to.'

Teerasak pointed to the GPS on his phone and said, 'we are close could be those trees over there,' as he pointed a dense thicket of trees that stood out from the cleared fields. The Major was tempted to act although this wasn't the right light for that.

They waited until nightfall then well into the night because of the half moon. It wasn't until after 10PM that these enemy soldiers, regular or irregular, left their detail voices loud, shot through with mocking laughter, before fading into distant echoes as they went over the rise and vanished.

Major Dane wondered what they were laughing about and dismissed the thought as not mission critical. No ear worms here. It was fine trying to divine what the enemy thought. Trouble was that only went so far before it interfered with situational awareness.

When the voices disappeared into the inky night Teerasak volunteered to reconnoitre. Along the way he found a booby trap. A covered pit that a special Lidar app revealed as hiding sharpened sticks covered in dung and some type of poison, possibly cyanide.

Once he got to the thicket of Ironwood trees he couldn't detect any dwellings or structures save for a moss stained Satellite dish dating from the last century.

He gave a signal and the rest of the group came to him.

He spoke to Mon in his serviceable Burmese, 'I have a plan. Could you go up that hill and see if you can find the place you were taken to.'

She shook her head and said as tears brimmed in her eyes, 'too long a time. I don't know if I can remember.'

Teerasak hugged her as Brad said, 'tell her she doesn't have to go. She's fluent and we're not. Tell her this will help all the sisters who are still there. We don't know when we can get back to this place. Maybe never, otherwise this could end up as a search and destroy. No one wants that.'

As Teerasak spoke to her gently, as though to the younger person who is badly frightened was.

'We may all die but if we don't get in there they are all going to die.'

She stared at him mute with wide terrified eyes. All around was the landscape of her old life and living nightmares. In the distance, she saw plumes of smoke coming from burning villages. The sounds and the sights dragged her back to the past. She reached out into empty space as she saw her five-year-old son taken from her arms. Auk was there she could feel his presence, his spirit. In this waking dream, she knew he was dead even if his soul would haunt these lands until all the captives were freed. Overhead helicopters thundered and dropped fire-starters or bombs as they swooped low she could hear the *whoop whoop* sound that brought destruction, and deaths of many. In her village, soldiers locked her mother and daughter in their home and set it on fire. When they were gone only the white skulls and bones dead were left. With no time to grieve, Mon took her older daughter and ran for miles until she reached a Bama village where her married sister lived. Rae, married to a Bama giving her protection, took Sre into her home with the knowledge certain awaited mother and daughter if she hadn't.

Then the rolling thunderstorm passed. Mon was back. The dream, the nightmare was over, and she came back to reality. Aom's lost son, the ghost of her lost son whispered to her words of comfort, of encouragement. Mon knew he would guide her and as if to confirm this a final display of lightening and explosive thunder jolted her upright. His ghost, his nat and the fine grace of Buddha would guide their small company of free warriors. Blinking away the fog of dreams the sky, now free of black clouds turned a dark electric blue. It was another sign. She was back and all the wrongs would be righted and the lost returned.

'Alright we pack up and get out of here. Maybe the United Nations will do something. Let's see it only took Aung San Suu Kyi 20 years to be released, who know we might have better luck.'

As he began to set a new destination for a return back over the border Mon put her hand on Brad's forearm and said in English, 'yes, I do it, I go.'

Mon promised to come back and she would make good on that promise.

She wandered up the hill as though lost calling out the Burmese word for help.

The sun was yet to appear as the men loaded up in the two Chinooks. Dressed as national park employees, which gave them the look of fire jumpers, the men checked their gear and firearms.

As this was done each boarded the already revving Chinooks. Going through the rear it gave the now routine feeling of being swallowed whole.

As they flew over the ever-steep ravines and mountains Brad gave the signal to set their GPS. This should already have been done but Brad's ex-army insistence on double checking in unison ensured no one would be left out or left behind.

As the sun came up they could see the sharply etched topography.

They were going to a different camp to the previous. Like all warlords the Colonel liked to move around. Intel filled in the rest and that included pillow talk and bar talk filtered in from the Agency. It was enough to keep them alive but only just that. The operation was Major Dane's baby and he had the tacit approval of men close to the president. His president, the only one like him to ever come along and that would happen again. There were only so many shots you got in this life and Brad knew that he ever wanted to make a difference, that is really make a difference then he would have to act now. No, he didn't want to die, and no he didn't want to live forever either. The trafficking in human flesh was disgusting to him even if so many subtle and not so subtle variations of it existed as close as Phuket and Pattaya. No this wasn't that kind of slave labour; this was the kind of slaving that happened off the west coast of Africa centuries ago. This was the kind of slavery that kept small children hostage while their mothers fell dead of heat stroke on the factory floor or were beaten to death by armed guards using rifle butts and boots. That wasn't the kind of factory with gleaming surfaces and shiny new equipment the government usually liked to tout. You know the kind of place with enthusiastic bright uniformed employees, smiling, happy at their work, eager to please and grateful to serve such a generous employer.

No even the good ole USA could really bring that off outside the blessed confines of Silicon Valley and he wasn't convinced it worked that that there either.

Ten kilometres inside the border they were disgorged. No one landed in Myanmar if they could help it so this was a good as it gets.

As waved off the helos he wondered if they would come back. The plan was to execute the mission and then get out. He wasn't going to leave anyone behind. Not unless any of the Myanmar men wanted to stay in their homeland and fight it out. That was a fanciful idea. When the Bay of Pigs unravelled there was talk in Washington of the American backed invaders taking to the hills to inspire an uprising. Only 2 years after the revolution of 59 and with Castro himself leading the counterattack there was simply no way this was going to happen. Things were even more gnarly and less clear cut than that famous fiasco. There was the Golden Triangle and the Drug Lords that cultivated the poppies right down to the final product. Gang warfare wasn't a bullet fuelled street war like in East LA. This was a real war with regular and irregular soldiers. There were territorial disputes among the assorted mafia gangs and then there were the more traditional territorial disputes between nation states that involved borders made by the King of Siam. Colonial boundaries didn't respect ethnic or religious boundaries, and each were so distracted about their own needs than worrying about the welfare of the enemy. There were times when Washington seemed to be like that.

CHAPTER 62

Under a camouflaged biodegradable tent near a thick stand of eucalyptus tree

Broaddock projected an image from his smart phone.

'First, we check out gear,' he said as he unharnessed his pact. Leading by example the gear: a handheld GPS locater, maps, first aid kit, M17, Heckler & Koch M23 .45 handgun, a Gemtech suppressor/silencer, a Russian made Spetsnaz Ballistic knife and several grenades. He didn't intend to use the grenades, but you never know.

Holding up a mean looking automatic sniper rifle he said, 'now this one is state of the art people.' As he spoke Mon and Teerasak translated into Burmese and Thai.

Putting the stock to his shoulder he assumed firing position. 'This is a TrackingPoint firearm which can shoot accuately up to 1500 yards. It has a networked tracking scope that can correct for target distance, wind speed and direction, gravity and even the rotation of the Earth. It does more than you need to know. We can even tranmit live footage of the shot.'

'Are you going to do that?' Jerome n ot sure if streaming was the way to go.

'No way, this is covert, and it stays covdert.'

With the weapons all accounted for after he visually checked for any defects.

He picked up an M11 automatic rifle then slapped on a 500 round magazine. Putting that down he checked the look and feel nthe laser sight and magazine on the Heckler and Koch G 3.

'We have three automatic weapons and they will be used by me, Teerasak and Jerome. Any questions?'

'Okay team our mission is in effect from now,' he raised his smart watch and said, 'at 21 hundred hours.'

Major Braddock gave the signal to pack up the kit. Then they donned the night vision goggles and his irregular army or Platoon really moved into green glowing darkness. It was a moonless night and night vision would give an advantage over the enemy.

They moved in single file, not even 20 men but with enough firepower to take on a modest army along the lines of the killers they were in search of.

They moved for about half an hour and his GPS told him they were close. As they passed a lush stand of Banyon trees a flock of giant bats exploded from the cover streamed out into the night sky. These creatures were known to attack or even kill and Teerasak clutched his amulet, a gift from his daughter Pika to ensure good karma.

Teerasak kissed the charm, sensing the enemy was close. So close he could hear breathing.

In his old age, the General was getting careless. Once content to direct his operations at command post deep in the interior the man was bold enough to move operation closer and closer to the border to where they were now 50 km from Thailand and 200 km plus to the nearest medium village of Homein. The alliances the Colonel had formed with the army were as fragile as a crystal glass. They would go along with whoever had the upper hand going on the theory that losers were unlucky partner. Implied spectral support of the USG was basically bluff. If they, any of them, Myanmar, Thai or American, were to be killed or captured officers on both sides of the Potamic would scramble to denounce these unauthorised renegades or more likely nothing would be at all. He stowed the thought now was not the time to speculate they had a mission.

With the night scope on his Lapua sniper rifle, capable of making a kill shot at 1500 metres he looked to the far side of the ravine. In greenish light, he got a bead on the camp. The Colonel had gone up in the world with satellite dishes with reinforced temporary housing and bubble top dwellings that could have come straight from Antarctica or dome misguided experiment in extraterrestrial habitation.

He moved the sight across groups of uniformed men. The irregular soldiers were looking more regular by the minute. They looked like Burmese army, but he knew they weren't. not even close. Then darted past a group of laughing soldiers playing cards he caught sight of his prey. The phoney General and much besides, Sao Ne Saw, sat watching his men play and punctuated with swigs from a bottle of Johnny Walker whiskey. He slapped his knee as though impressed with a hand. If he'd wanted to could have seen that too but this was not a game of reality poker. Now he had a bead on the main actor he used the scope to find the prisoners and was soon rewarded when he saw a tent large enough for dozens of captives. The heat seeing device showed him many warm bodies huddled in the tent. Don't worry he said to himself. *We're going to get you out of here.*

He signalled for his men to make a flanking move up the sides of a steep ravine.

With the element of surprise, he divided the group into three for the north, south and west facing wall made of bamboo.

Once they were in he sent in Teerasak to negotiate. Instinct alone told him Sao Ne Saw wouldn't buy if and the advantage of surprise would be lost.

Getting down to business without having to listen to this demented maniac had its charms and he realised his situational awareness was being submerged by his desire for revenge. That wouldn't do. Revenge could get you killed. Emotion, love for a hostage or hate for a killer that needed killing could make you sloppy. It could get you killed faster than an electronic bullet.

Teerasak came back with a dour expression.

'He says to come in. His words mean we have much to talk about come on in.'

'What do you think?'

Teerasak gave a pained expression and said, 'it could be a trap, but we said that last time and we got what he wanted.'

'A firefight could end in collateral damage, like the murder of the hostages.'

Brad gave his own pained expression and said, 'yeah and we would have a lot of explaining to do with the blowback from that I can tell you.

Keep some of the men near the confinement area. If this explodes we must release them and get them out. I'll talk to the General who is really a colonel.'

Moving closer to the wood and plastic headquarters he took off his night vision goggles then his helmet. He was greeted at the entrance by the emperor of enslavement Sae We Saw himself.

With a toothy gold studded grin that seemed to have had work since their last meeting the two leaders of men shook hands. In the background could be heard a faint buzzing sound.

'Is has been some time since we last met,' Saw said before his words were translated by the ever handy Teerasak.

'Yes, we have to stop meeting like this.'

Saw stared uncomprehending of this phrase.

'I suppose you know why we are here, why I am here.'

His enemy laughed out loud and near to the edge of derisory.

'Is it to sample our wonderful pork stew. You know people marvel over Thai food, Vietnamese food but they must come to Myanmar or the country called Burma when you and I were both young.'

Brad stood impassive. He was in no mood for this.

'You know why we are here. You must release the prisoners and this is no request.'

Saw laughed again leaving a sneer. 'This reminds me of an ancient villager who fought against an invading Chinese army. He was the last man left. The General leading the Chinese told this lone survivor he could submit and save his life or die needlessly like the rest of his village.'

'And hat did he do surrender of die?'

Putting a brooding finger to his lips he said, 'neither is the truth. He obeyed the command and was spared. He even worked for a time with the invaders. One day while working as a house servant for this same general he saw an opportunity and thrust a dagger straight through the heart of a man who was responsible for the deaths of his parents and his wife and daughter.'

'I see so you are willing to relent and save the battle for another day?'

'Perhaps I think so. Do you play cards Mr Van Dyke?'

Seeing the look of surprise on his face in realising the bastard had done a background check on him he replied, 'well normally I wouldn't but seeing how you've asked me so nicely I don't see why not.'

They played into the night. In the beginning, he begged of all offers of drink only to relent sometime after midnight. The buzzing had morphed into a faint shrill like the cries for help from little people in the forest and beyond the hills. Braddock dismissed all such noise as mind mischief. Whatever the bumps in the night they weren't mission critical. There weren't rats big enough in the basement to scare him. He had to be the captain with a steady grip as they navigated through these treacherous waters.

'That is full house so I take this,' he said as he pulled the kitty of thousands of American dollars to his side of the table like some overconfident riverboat gambler.

'I like to play with men who know how to play and know how to drink. I am getting close to the end of my American dollars. We could trade with the lives I hold close to my heart here in my home.'

'That sounds more like it Saw. How about each prisoner, let's call them customers or clients shall we it's so much more civilised, let's say that each client is worth one hundred dollars, alright?'

Grinning widely Saw said waving away the translation, 'Yes I like this game. I like you value my clients very much and I think they are worth far more than

100 dollars apiece. I think fair price is $1000 per client.'

Still playing poker Brad said, 'I get your point but I wouldn't go any lower than $500.'

'No more like $200 you ask me to give away my treasure.'

'And I said no lower than $500 or we'll have to make other arrangements.'

The smiled ceased and he lowered his hand to reveal a full straight. He clawed back the modest sum of $600 and said, 'Yes I agree to this. Drink?' he asked as he held up a new bottle of Johnny Walker.

Brad shook his head knowing he'd had his fill. Yes, the drink could have been doctored and the fact he'd taken his host at his word allowed for the kind of bonding that could be crucial whatever the outcome.

They played into the night and as day broke Major Braddock had $ 50,000.

'So how many clients are we talking about Saw?'

Saw nodded to Teerasak to revert to translation as if when it came to money he didn't want to reply on his own linguistic skills.

'Three hundred here,' he said putting a finger to his temple as if this might be a memory aid, then said, 'yeah, and another two or three hundred in camps not far away.'

'Tell me, Gringo as my South Americano friends call you Americanos, you only have $60,000 you need another $100,000 to buy the freedom of my workers.'

Brad smiled and said, 'yes well I think I can arrange that.'

'When do you want to make the swap?'

Brad smiled again as the winning feel began to seep in. Now was not the time to get overconfident. He could do that when they were able to sit back in Phuket.

'No time like the present. I can have my men here at first light tomorrow. With one proviso.'

Saw's haughty triumphant look was instantly replaced with one of concern.

'What conditions you did not mention these conditions. Do you want to purchase their freedom or is this some trick, some game you are playing?'

Shaking his head Dane said, 'no this isn't poker even if you can play a great game yourself.'

Saw's eyes narrowed as though sensing the very trickery he'd mentioned.

'No tell me straight Yank what is it you want?'

'I want everyone to get out safe. That is your men and my men and the hostages. You really couldn't think you could hole yourself out here forever did you Saw?'

'You forget American you are in my home not yours. You must show the gratitude of a deserving guest.'

'With your men, out of here there will be no danger of a fire fight. I swear some of our guys still think they're in Iraq. You know trigger happy.'

'Are you trying to scare me American?'

'No but I know I'm scared. Scared that someone could miscalculate, react in the wrong way and a lot of people get hurt. I don't want that, you don't want that, we don't want that.'

Saw narrowed his eyes. Still drinking he was halfway through his third bottle. Dane had retired from the field. There was a far more important battle to fight without getting plastered.

'I will think about this.' He fell silent to ponder then within less than a minute he said, 'alright, I do not trust you, but I do trust Americans with money. For short time. Americans know about money, so we do business, 'he said as he thrust a hand forward.

CHAPTER 63

Holding onto the upright pole on the city Harvester bus, a relic of past wars, Mon told the driver to slow down. The factory was on the edge of a disused quarry and had been built in a day only weeks before. She knew of this place and who was here.

With the company uniform and clip board Mon walked into reception.

In Thai, then in Myanmar she said, 'I am here on orders from Central Office.

We have orders to move the workers to Bangkok.'

The manager squinted in incomprehension.

'Show me the papers I do not know this order. We have a factory run that has to be completed.'

'How long will that take?' she asked trying to sound as officious as possible.

'The girls clock off at 5Pm before the other shift takes over.'

Looking at her smart phone watch she said, 'yes alright we can do that. It is now 4:45. Direct anyone who has already clocked off to board the bus.'

Nodding his head, the manager tried to place a call. Mon upholstered her pistol then spoke with a smile.

'This directive comes from the top, our esteemed Commander Ne so asking too many stupid questions will only hold things up. I have heard goods things about you Nuttawat and I think you will go far in the company.'

The balding man smiled then said as if seeking further approval, 'did you really hear. I always try my best and want to do what's best for the company.'

'Well help me help you get the women organised. The sooner the better the next shift can finish this run. They are needed immediately at another factory that was offline. It will save the company millions of dollars. You will have a bonus so consider this a down payment,' she said as she slipped a thick wad of 800,000 baht.

Looking down at the bundle as if this were the greatest sum he'd seen in his life or at least the greatest sum he had laid his hands on in his life.

'Where do you want me to start?' he asked. She pointed in the direction of the factory floor and they went through an entranceway. The rattle and click of precision machinery was loud enough for some of the workers to take solace in ear plugs.

Picking up a loud hailer she saw on a table Mon motioned for the manager to stop the assembly line.

In a tinny amplified voice, she said, 'good evening honourable workers. This is a company emergency we are relocating, we are evacuating to another site on orders from central office in Bangkok. Shut down your work station. Take nothing with you but personal belongings and move in an orderly fashion to vacate the campus.'

There was a hub- hub of chatter as the ladies on the factory floor expressed their alarm and sense of confusion.

She motioned for the Managers to assist and soon the minders and security men were helping the workers to unwitting freedom.

On the bus Mon nervously counted the numbers then called in another bus, this one a retired Bangkok municipal people mover.

'Let's go she said to the driver who was unaware of just what was happening.

She slipped him three thousand baht then said in Thai, 'this is helping the team. Thanks for cooperating.'

He smiled and pocketed the money. Everyone would get their cut today. She would make sure of this.

In 20 minutes, the first bus left then another until Mon's bus pulled out of the side road onto the highway.

As they drove on the highway a convertible 60s model Ford Impala edged in parallel. Seeing something was amiss she got a handgun out of her bag. It was a petite sized Walther. She never went anywhere without it.

A longhaired man in an elegant silk shirt held up a semiautomatic assault rifle. The bullets raked the side of the people mover with one woman on the bus crying out in pain. She fell into the aisle bleeding heavily.

Mon took aim and fired once. The man with the semiautomatic dropped his gun then bent over clutching a stomach ripped open like a can of fish and red sauce. He tumbled backwards into the road and was hit by a truck following close behind. She then shot at the driver who tried to swerve to avoid the line of fire only to be clipped by the shoulder guard then flip into space and land on its back wheels spinning.

Not letting down her guard Mon only allowed herself to breathe when they took an off ramp and drove a few more streets until they were at a car wreckers yard.

Back at the Camp of the Great Khan shots rang out as the mission team walked through the gates.

Jerome took a firing position as the others took cover.

He motioned with his hand for Teerasak and Braddock to take a flanking position.

Major Van Dyke was behind a truck and Jerome called out. 'We've been double-crossed. Try to,' His speech abruptly ceased, and Dane could see him topple over. Then Yin ran to his side and shook his comrade in arms. Lifeless eyes stared upwards. Jerome moved his lips in an effort to speak. Transfixed Yin hugged him close only to be shot through the neck, severing his spine.

Dane grabbed Teerasak's sleeve as he tried to join them.

'Forget it they're gone.'

Firing off an M11 automatic assault rifle four of the counterfeit general's men were hit.

Some how they made it to the woods with the bodies of Yin and Jerome. Major Dane resisted the urge to call in an air strike. No, it wasn't that kind of war.

As night fell Dane announced we are going to take our dead back over the border.'

'Yin came here to be with his people and with his motherland. He must be buried here.'

In no mood to argue Dane said,' fine I understand. That's how it should be.'

Under a half moon Krit said some words of respect in Burmese. He lit some incense then in front of a small statue of Buddha he wai'd then wept.

Before dawn the men were chopperred out.

'Where will Jerome be buried?' Teerasak asked in a voice numb with shock.

'He'll be flown back stateside. I'll have to make some calls when we get back to base.'

Teerasak then spoke in a soft voice as the new normal set in.

'He died a hero. He died doing what he love.'

'Yes, I guess he thought he had more time. All the time in the world before he slept.

CHAPTER 64

Overhead ceiling fans made a whirring sound that seemed to skip a beat like an arrhythmic heart.

Seeing his visitor craning his neck as though to find the source, a doctor listening for an irregular heartbeat in an office setting, the General smiled and said, 'I hope it doesn't bother you I was offered a new Panasonic inverter air conditioner'. He paused then said, 'but I declined.' Ralph put on an expression saying why?

'It's simple the old fans remind me of the past when my father was the commissioner for this whole area. He was a British government officer when Burma was a British colony. He was always proud of how far he had come from a poor village. It is my fond hope that I honour his spirit and think of him always.'

There was a pause until the General said, 'did you know my father? He was very important.'

Ralph gave a smile meant to convey understanding, 'no I'm sorry I didn't he would have been a very interesting person to know.'

The General took a cigar out of a metal container and said in a voice radiating self-satisfaction, 'these are the best cigars from Havana. I buy them when I go to Ho Chi Minh City. You remember it as Saigon of course.'

'Yes, I was there once or twice during the Vietnam war. I did two tours. So long ago now. I was only a junior officer barely out of Officers Candidate School in Virginia when I was *in country*, as we used to say.'

The General took a deep puff of his cigar and blew it just over Ralph's head. The disrespect was clear and intended. Annoyed but not about to show it he said, 'let's get down to business, shall we?'

The General nodded before inhaling again. Sensing something was wrong and anticipating the worst, his face was ashen, ghostly. He knew he would cross the river and join his ancestors soon.

'You are in charge of two refugee camps correct?'

The General nodded then said, 'yes I am in charge unless I am away on important business and then my second in command Chironn Tuwit takes over in my absence.' He paused then said with a smarmy smile, 'he is an excellent officer and a credit to Thailand.'

Ralph smiled again the man had just created his first alibi. He loved it when they got creative. He wondered how many more lies were to come.

'What is your point Mr Winters?' The man's English was excellent it was his attitude Ralph had trouble with.

The Inquisitor kept his smile intact and said, 'my point is that there have been irregular transfers of refugees and refugees themselves have disappeared presumed dead. Millions of dollars have been siphoned off some of it relief aid.'

The General slammed his fist down on the table and said, face red with outrage, 'this is damned lie. You are not here on official business and I want you to leave my office immediately.'

The General stood as though to reinforce that thought, as if standing would make it all go away. It didn't.

Company Man Ralph looked him up and down as if taking in an errant subordinate.

'Sit down General we are just getting started.'

Taking out a thick folder of original documents he began placing items including several indictments for upcoming trials. The General looked ghostlier than ever his distant gaze and slack expression a reaction to life changing experience. His face a mask of fear, the General really was dead, only the man didn't know it yet.

Later in the day Major Braddock paid the good general a visit.

'So, what do I owe the pleasure Mr Van Dyke or should I call you Major?' General Natchapon Anurat said as he toyed with his shrimp cocktail.

Major Dane gave a taut smile.

'Well I am retired,' he lied. 'So, mister is fine.' He cleared his throat then went on. There are a few recent events I think you should be aware of General.' The General began to sweat despite the frigid air conditioning.

'I would like to freshen up it has been a long day,' the sweating man said.

The recalled to active duty Major nodded his consent. As he heard the toilet door close he took in the view of a sprawling Bangkok. Then came a shot and he ran to the prone Genera, his head half missing the rest leaking blood and brains. Outside he could hear A Myanmar love song, a duet that sounded incredibly sad. Did the military man take the honourable way out? With no honour in his deeds leading up to this Dane saw it more as a coward's escape from justice. Mon was right the General's spirit would be terrorised by the ghosts of the murdered. Outside an unseasonable cold wind gusted through an umbrella trees, its branches lifting as though in a *wai* to the fallen. As if to keep his Karma up he wai'd if not to the ghosts then to the memory of the martyred. Then, as if to touch all bases he prayed for the passed after crossing himself. It was a ritual he hadn't done in years. Anything to keep the bad spirits, the bad luck at bay.

After hearing about the suicide of the General, dead after a shot to the head Brodie hurried to make his appointment with Braddock at the Hilton. Clicking his iPhone alive he realised he was 5 minutes late for his 9 am meeting. By the time he got to the 12th floor he was almost ten minutes late. Entering the room, he was greeted by Braddock with a steely handshake. 'Glad you could make it Brodie we have to talk.'

Confused he asked, 'sure, what about exactly?'

The recalled to active duty Major gave a wry smile. 'There are a few things you need to be aware of. That discount you got on the package deal to Pattaya was pretty damn good, excellent in fact.' Brodie frowned not sure where this was going.

'Maybe it was too good to be true.' Brodie fell silent as the meaning of what his fellow American was saying sunk in.

'Someone would have had to have remote access to offer a phoney deal.' Braddock smiled again, he seemed to be enjoying this.

'Strictly speaking the deal wasn't phoney like an Internet scam. The accommodation was real only it came from an interested party. It was all arranged, expedited under the radar if you will.'

'Arranged by who? You, mean the company? Was it you and Ralph who contrived all this?'

Major Dane looked away in an evasive move suggesting the answer to the question was in the affirmative. Brodie felt transported to a world, a universe that was a hologram, where everything was fake with nothing or next to nothing was genuine, authentic.

With a frown and a touch of anger in his voice he said, 'tell me I have to know. You and I, Ralph too, have been through a lot, too much to snow me after all that. It's incredible I don't believe it.'

'Yes, I realise that, and I understand you're upset. You need to believe it Brodie, because it happened just as surely as the sun came up over the Gulf of Thailand this morning.'

Brodie wanted to tell him he was more than upset only to realise he still needed these practised spooks to get out of the country.

'I can neither confirm nor deny operational matters. Sorry that's company policy going back to every president since War 2.'

Brodie threw his hands up in despair, 'well we wouldn't want him off-side, now would we?'

Dane gave a tight smile. Maybe the enjoyment factor was fading in view of the fact most of what Brodie had been told was a lie. Yes of course, his friend was a master of deceit and could even be lying now. That's what chronic spies did, alleged retirement made no difference. He was being played and he felt foolish, naïve.

He felt a hammering in his head that promised to hang on like mustard gas, a noxious cloud that would spread through his internal organs before the inevitable. The stress also attacked the visual cortex as he hallucinated walls expanding and contracting, a living creature struggling to breathe and wired into his central nervous system.

In shock, Brodie gripped the sides of his chair as blood drained from his face. He felt he was at sea under water in a typhoon, knocked sideways and vertically by raging currents that could drown in seconds or dash brains against a rocky foreshore. Was all this their invention, a made-up legend crafted for ulterior purposes? If so, neither were about to tell the truth outside cryptic riddles that could also be fabricated. Maybe the universe really was a hologram reserved for those pretending to be something, someone they were not.

Dane now spoke in a tone that was less than convincing. 'Relax, Brodie you don't have anything to worry about.'

Brodie felt his head swim in that washing machine of oceanic turbulence. 'You know whenever someone says that to me I start to worry.'

Before I go I have to ask does Grace know about all this?'

The military man nodded. 'She knows. Her father told her by phone and that's all the intel I am privy to on that score my friend.'

Staring at this bearer of bad news, terrible news retrofitted onto the new reality and new normal, Brodie left quickly in a huff without saying anything further, speechless, catatonic, and yes at sea, that terrible churning sea of lies and half-truths.

CHAPTER 65

He went to the Cowgirl Bar and said goodbye to Chailai. It was the decent thing to do after all they'd been through and he wasn't sure she'd care.

'When are you coming back,' she said in better English he'd heard from her.

As he sipped his beer- his last? - he said, 'that's hard to say not any time soon. Someday I promise Chailai.'

'I miss you already,' she said, a phrase he figured she must have got from Facebook. Social media the great leveller.

'And me-too Brodie,' someone said from behind. He turned to see it was Mon.

She gave a winning smile. With her were two women he recognised as fellow- Burmese. They bowed with clasped hands in a gesture that oddly mimicked the Chief. To up his luck, his shaky Karma, Brodie did the same. It had been a long week, along month. After 37 days in country, much of it held against his will, he knew he was different that things could never be the same. Not after so many ructions, so much death. The alignment of the stars was altered maybe the Earth was even off its axis enough to change everything. After everything he half expected another tsunami dwarfing the big one all those years ago.

'Mon when I get back I'm erecting a *Nat* shrine in honour of you and the Kachin and the Ron and the Shan.'

'You are forgetting.' Mon looked at him with a slight frown.

Wanting to get it right he activated the search browser in his mind. The URL was there all along.

'I know,' he said slapping his hand on his knee. 'The Rohingya, how could I forget?'

They laughed together even if it wasn't very funny.

'I will miss you Brodie.'

Touched, Brodie moved close to Mon and kissed her on the cheek. Struggling to keep from crying he said, 'and I will miss you too Mon.' As Chailai bent her head he hurried to her side.

'Chailai, I will never forget you.'

'And I will always love you.' As she spoke a vase fell from a shelf. It didn't break. Knowing this was a good omen and the *nats* were with them, they all laughed again.

CHAPTER 66

'Tell me, do you have an irresistible urge to go overseas again?'
Spike sipped his coffee with a thoughtful expression. The two agreed that a non-alcoholic outing was called for. Besides Singha beer just didn't taste the same on the Gold Coast.

'Not on your life. I want to get back my goodness keep my Karma.'

'You've gone oriental on us Brodie. Have you taken up Buddhism or Muay Thai again?'

Leaning back on his chair to better take in the pedestrian traffic he said with a languid air, 'well the Muay Thai was a life saver as you know. Could be I want to give something back.'

'Give something back, come on it's me you're talking to I think you might be getting a bit carried away.'

Taking another sip to drain his cup of expresso he said, 'look you know and I know that I should be in some disgusting prison losing teeth and hair and my sanity as the years slide by. After a couple of years not even the current affairs reporters want to know about you. You're a non-person you don't exist. Nobody cares about you except your mother and she dies on you while you're still inside. All the guilt and shame washes over you every night, every day. It's in the air and part of the furniture and no it never goes away. Its hell and you wish you were dead and there are plenty of villains inside who are happy to accommodate you on that.'

'Yes, I could have washed up there as well. I must admit I still get nightmares over it.'

'You too Spike?

His friend nodded and replied, 'yeah me too. I still feel it, I can still feel it, taste it and I can't help but think that in an alternate lifetime on the far side of the universe and we are feeding the worms in some Burmese killing field or dying slowly in some crazy house or bent Big House run by professional sadists.'

As Brodie pondered how to respond he heard a terrific bang that had him diving for the pavement. Pulling the wrought iron table on its side to serve as a kind of shield he shouted, 'did you hear that Spike?'

'Of course, I heard it do you think I'm deaf?'

There was another bang this one not nearly as ear shattering and they saw the vintage Mustang the backfire had come from.

'God that was close, real close.'

'The sound came from a car muffler not a gun. But yeah it was close enough to sound like the real thing.'

As they drank the diamond light of summer midday faded into night. There was a long silence.

'All that is still in my head Spike. When do you think it will go away?'

'I don't think it will ever go away short of electro-shock therapy and I might be crazy but I'm not signing on for that.'

CHAPTER 67

'You have nice day ok?'

Pey looked at Mon for approval and got a smile just short of that. As Pey began to frown Mon washed away her worry with a wide smile. They began to laugh and Swe Ying joined in. Of the three Mon would have the best chance of being understood by tourists, even ignorant Americans.

'We will do more,' Mon said in Burmese then finished with, 'when they build the casino there will be much work. I have to be ready. We all have to be ready. I am happy my son's soul is at rest.' She bowed her head, 'Auk is Aom's son and he is my son too. We have all been through so much together.'

The girls nodded their understanding. The women embraced. After working almost two weeks in a department store called Gem each deserved a break. No time for break, no time for family, no time for life. Each second precious, a sliver of peace in a world darkened by the storm clouds of evil. Now there was light and there was breath.

'Let us eat I know the place.' Taking her friends by the hand she steered them towards an alley off Soi 8. Stopping outside a restaurant named the Irrawaddy Moon she said, 'the owner came from my village but long ago. Everyone he knew is dead except for my grandmother Lin.'

She led the way as they stepped inside the darkly lit space with a few dozen tables.

They bowed in greeting to the beaming host who introduced himself as Maung Sein. Then as if by instinct they paid respect to the small statue of Buddha by bowing with clasped hands then did the to the makeshift Nat shrine reining above them. Mon lingered a moment under the *Nat oun* hanging on a pole draped with a red and orange headdress tied with offerings of bananas and coconut. 'I will never forget you son you have saved so many including your mother.' She wai'd again then turned from the keeper of her soul to face her friends with her bravest smile. She wanted to cry for her son, for her daughter. Yet understood they would not want that. Now the dead were buried, their raging spirits avenged and able to rest, she too would return to the land of the living.

Pulling out a bottle of French wine from her capacious bag she said, 'who wants a glass of Chardonnay?'

Pouring glasses on the table reserved the night before they laughed and toasted the good fortune finally come their way.

Pey said, 'may the ghosts of Burma find the rest they desire.'

After three more toasts they sat and ordered meals of beef or chicken with rice. Then within only 15 minutes steaming dishes of Myanmar fare came to the table one after another.

Mon ate slowly. Lately she had been gaining weight and while blade thin by western standards she was beginning to dread seeing herself in the mirror.

Getting fat made you old and stupid like the Generals with no feeling. Doomed.

Sher took another morsel of rice cake then gave a *wai* that was like a punctuation note to the conversation. Karma had kept her alive, she could hardly take leave from her belief system after all. Her Ghosts of Burma would ensure this.

Then a bang and a vase shattered. The bullet ricocheted hitting Sre Ying in the leg and this drew screams. Mon knew gunfire when she heard it most villagers from Karen or Rankine had. After two undeclared civil wars, she had emerged unscathed. Now in Thailand the *Land of Smiles* she gets shot. Like a fighting General getting killed in peacetime to die like this would be strange and her soul would morph into a ghost, forever haunting the streets of her adopted home country. Mon would do all she could to avoid this horrible fate. She rushed to Sre whose leg was gushing rivulets of bright red blood. Tearing off a section of skirt Mon applied a tourniquet. Sre drifted in and out of consciousness and her friends gathered around while a crowd drifted in from the street to see what the commotion was about. People had witnessed so much death would one more make a difference? She wanted to scream at them to get out although with her alien status this was forbidden as were so many things. One day this would all change.

As Mon dialled the police she saw one of the invaders take aim with his gun. Then the *nat* shrine exploded in a shower of plaster and glass. The ghosts were angry and even these killers looked afraid. Her silent, invisible helpers were doing their work. Scanning his face, listening for clues she took him as Thai although she wasn't about to ask. With both hands gripping the revolver, arms straight out Mon recognised him as a professional. In a quick move, she got out knife with a serrated blade and threw it without hesitation. It found its target in the man's chest. Seeming to buckle at the knees like a chimney stack crashing to Earth the youngish man staggered out the door and was helped into a car Mon guessed was stolen. They didn't get far. After driving off in clouds of burnt rubber the car collided with a bus and burst into flames.

She turned back to face his confederate who had his own gun. Unlike his lost partner in crime this one was clearly an amateur Mon figured going by the trembling hands. She circled him and he let off a shot that bounced around the ceiling and exited through a window. Moving around the table to find the best position in a bad situation she felt like a matador stalking horned prey.

With darting eyes, he seemed desperate for an escape strategy. As the confusion grew she took her chance and leapt into the air just as her Thai martial arts master taught her.

The kick connected with his head and his face contorted into a rubbery mask. The crunch and click told her his nose was shattered and his jaw broken. She punched him again with even more force. All the frustration, all the resentment poured out in these acts of physical violence. She punched him again. Then again and again. Crimson blood flowed like spilt wine. She kept doing that until her fist was grabbed by a hand much larger than hers and one belonging to a police officer. Now after being forced to stop she saw what she had done. His face was unrecognisable and he was barely breathing. Feeling waves of shock, she realised she would have killed him without the police intervention. As paramedics swarmed around the patient the policeman laughed.

'It is alright you do not need to hurry. In the Philippines, he would be left to die.'

'But we are not in the Philippines. We are in Thailand the Land of Smiles.'

This only made him laugh harder. Brodie looked down on the crumpled man who, for all he knew, was forced into crime to feed his family. The desperation the poverty didn't make you better it made you bitter. He wanted to work on that. Waiting in Sydney Grace would help him through it as they faced a life together.

CHAPTER 68

'Do you mind telling me what is all this about?'

'I'm not sure what you mean.'

'How did all of this come about the way it did. Me getting sucked into the ongoing civil war and then my partner meeting by you her long lost father by coincidence here in Thailand.'

Ralph clasped then unclasped his hands before saying, 'there are no coincidences.'

'Yeah like meeting up with Grace, no running into Grace while you are busy setting me free from a fate I don't even want to contemplate, just happened by chance which I'm pretty sure is wild coincidence, right?'

'I think you're tougher than that. You've already proved that Brodie no question about that no question at all.'

'You haven't answered my question. Yu must have wanted to see Grace your only daughter and I suppose the best way was through me.'

Ralph chuckled then said, 'I'm afraid you give yourself too much credit son. Over the years I could have seen Grace by forcing the issue but I knew she wouldn't want that or rather her mother Esther didn't want that or anything to do with me. That's why she exiled herself in y9ur beautiful country of Australia.

It sure has a lot of great beaches.'

Listening for any condescension he detected none.

'So out of the goodness of your heart you rescue a lost Australian only guilty of having one too many and more than his share of Dutch courage. Then this recovering drunk is released through your brilliant efforts and your ability to communicate with bureaucrats because you used to be one.'

Ralph laughed with a light tone indicating he took no offense. It occurred to Brodie the man didn't care and was only toying with him. It didn't matter if he was in or out with Grace her father couldn't be sure she'd run off down under never to appear again. Better to humour him, humour her and achieve the desired target. It was all about targets and goals wasn't it. Every mission had to have a success strategy and an exit strategy if things didn't work out. Ralph was a great survivor and there weren't many like him left.

Leaning back on his chair in the walled beer garden that still gave a tremendous view of Beach road he said, 'I know you think I'm strange.

Someone from another planet or another era, they're really one in the same.

You think you know my world but you don't you can't.'

'I've learned a lot since I've been here,' he said defensively.

Ralph gave an indulgent laugh and said, 'I'm sure you have even if there is a long way to go. I'm still learning, this situation baffles me as much as it does you I can assure you,' he lied.

Brodie narrowed his eyes. Was his prospective father in law trying to recruit him for the company or was there some other more devious plan in store for him.'

'there has to be a way to get a handle on this Ralph. I'm sorry I can't figure it out.'

Ralph laughed again and said, 'how can anyone figure out how things work out here. It's like trying to gauge the mood of a chronic schizophrenic. Even his doting Doctor with his patient records can't divine when a lunatic will reach out and cut your throat a piece of folder binding.

'I don't see how that relates to the country we're in. A place, I'll never forget, that nearly swallowed me whole and spat me out.'

This place has been in chaos since 1945. There have been coups going on since then with the military, more often than not, calling the shots. It's the reds versus the yellows and the poor against the rich even if some of the super- rich aspire to lead the poor. It's the story of two dozen families give or take who own everything you can see hear or eat and everything in between.

I just work here. Correction, I used to work here only work here. I don't profess to know how this place ticks how the gears of the machine mesh or how the circuits message and process at the atomic level.'

'Think you'll ever get there Ralph?'

The man was lying even if he had saved his life and could do that again.

'No only it beats being back in civilisation pardon that antiquated expression. The west is led by a savage and that has put all the despots in perspective. Doesn't excuse it mind, just puts it in perspective when you consider the fact the man has created a great propaganda tool for the enemy.'

'The enemy, excuse me? We aren't supposed to have enemies.'

Ralph grinned, 'is that what they teach in grade school these days.'

Brodie shook his head. This was beyond a patronizing generational talk outlining what it was all about.

'Ralph do you believe in ghosts?'

Ralph stirred his drink with his finger.

'You mean like tormented spirits?'

'I mean like Asian ghosts, Ghosts of Burma, ghosts of Thailand. The *nats* or ghosts in Burma are supposed to be the spirits of people who have met violent deaths. Mon told me the nat of her son helped guide her through the forest and even watched over them on the missions across the border into Burma.' Ralph looked out across Pattaya Bay as though in deep thought.

'Yes, I know of these ghost spirits. It's still a part of modern Japan and China.

It's still a part of everyday life here in Thailand and in Burma right across Burma.'

He fell silent for a moment as if concentrating on how best to express his opinion without disrespect.

'The ghosts in my life if you can call it that are the memories of the lost, the needlessly lost in war, through some criminal outrage. People fear the dead, speak to the dead at least in the imagination. Some of my ghosts come out at night but they don't tell me what stock to buy or which direction to go when I get to a five ways intersection.'

'I thought I felt it the other night. I could have sworn I heard Krit calling out to me during that white squall that hit the bay a few weeks back.'

'Yes, you though the imagination can be a powerful thing. Funny thing is we investigated all this in Langley. The Company was interested in it because the Soviets were researching apparitions, the supernatural. Couldn't afford to let them get a head start on that extra-dimensional, extra-sensory box of tricks. I'm sure you've seen those reality shows, if I can call it that, you know where they try and make a recording of apareons, of ghosts,'

'So, what was the upshot of that. Did you break on through to the other side?'

Ralph gave an indulgent chuckle and said, 'nothing as dramatic as that. You have to remember that the equipment used cameras, microphones, night vision can be used to capture the supernatural can also create it. You talk about voices and visions and all that can be conjured out of nothing.'

'How is that done?'

'Now you don't want me to give away all the trade secrets? Besides you might try it yourself and you're in enough trouble as it is.'

Seeing the disappointment on Brodie's face Ralph added with a more upbeat tone, 'we did have some success in remote viewing, one or two that could read minds or rather take note of tells and psycho-social indicators so as to get inside the head of suspects under interrogation. The interrogations were usually outsourced overseas but this stuff was classified. The outcome didn't justify the lavish budget, so the program was cancelled. Now it's all Cyber encryption and all up on the cloud.'

'Sometimes I still feel it.'

'If you want to feel it, if you are predisposed to feel it you will. Don't worry about it too much Brodie you'll get over it I'm sure.'

'Look, are you going to get Grace and I out of here?'

'Sure, you can leave now if you want.'

His pale blue eyes stared at him as though daring Brodie to doubt his insincerity.

"Sure, I'm ready for that. Grace I'm sure would be glad to leave she never really did like the place.'

'Well remember Grace left and came back again, against my recommendation I might add.'

'Mine too, she never did like being told what to do.'

'Which explains her resentment against authority and the abandonment issues.'

He shook his head slowly as if realises this was his daughter he was tailing about.

'I want to make that up to her. If you do marry her Brodie neither of you will ever want for anything.'

Brodie gave a tight smile. 'That's very nice of you but I always pay my own way.'

The two men smiled at each other knowing the statement wasn't true.

'I can get all the paperwork and the arrangements for the company jet by tomorrow morning.'

CHAPTER 69

'So, tell me what's happening Jimmy?' Brodie asked as he pulled up a bar stool. He was ready for a drink. Jimmy was from the old school. Like Errol Flynn, another lost Australian, he would drink himself into the grave and have a hell of a time doing it.

''I'm ready for a drink old son it's been a hell of a week.'

Jimmy looked at him one eyed and said, 'hell of a week, matey every week is a hell of a week for me.'

Brodie tapped his drink against Jimmy's bottle of San Miguel.

'That's a different brand most people around here drink Singha or Tiger even Budweiser.'

Jimmy narrowed his eyes as if he could just make out the shape and form of his newest drinking buddy.

'Well I ain't most people. I picked up a taste for the stuff when I used to hang out in Angeles.

'Angeles where's that in Mexico or someplace?'

Jimmy, rousing from his alcoholic haze gave him a mock startled look and said,

'Mexico now that's a hoot. What would I be doing in Mexico?'

Brodie gave him a playful punch on the shoulder. 'Now what are you doing here?' he said with an exaggerated arched eyebrow.

Jimmy put his hands over his head as if deep in thought.' You it's funny you asked that question because I've been pondering it myself and I haven't yet come up with an answer.'

Brodie signalled for a drink and took out a wad of baht and said, 'what are you having mate, drinks are on me.'

Jimmy the boozer gave a broad smile and said, 'well thank you my Aussie friend that's might generous of you it really is. If you're paying, how about a double, Mai Tai cocktail?'

'A double Beach cocktail never heard of it. Anyway, like I said I'm happy to pay.'

Jimmy gave a maniacal laugh and said, 'nah just joshing you. I don't sip those fancy drinks they don't agree with the old constitution.' To underline the point, he began to rub his sizeable beer belly.'

They laughed and drank then laughed and drank some more.

'What time did you get in today Jimmy?'

He made a face of concentration, all frowns topped off with a faint tapping on his forehead as though coaxing out the information.

'Well let me see the answer is quite simple my young friend, 'I got in the time I always get in which is opening time about 9:30, ten.'

'You must be the first one here.'

Jimmy kept his frown and said, 'yeah something like that what's it to you?'

'I was wondering if you have seen this bloke in your travels,' he said as he scrolled through his photo gallery until he found the image of his stalker.'

'Why what's it to you friend? What are you some kind of cop?'

'No but I'm sure you're heard the cops have been on my case ever since I've been here.'

'Now why would that be Brodie, you getting on the wrong side of the law?'

'I guess you could say that Jimmy I guess you could say that. There are a lot of things going on that most of the happy or not so happy tourists wouldn't have a clue about.'

Jimmy gave him a limp pat on the shoulder and said, 'welcome to Thailand pal.

Things are not always as they appear.'

Brodie concentrated on his beer not wanting to lead the discussion. Let this river take him where it flowed.

There was a long silence that Brodie was not about to break. He waited and the n it came.

'You know Brodie I didn't always look like this. I was like you a player.'

Brodie shook his head as if to take exception. 'No, it's alright you don't have to explain I've seen you around you are a player whether you like it or not. You have all the tells of a player. The clothes the beautiful women, I could go on.'

'Please go on it's kind of flattering. Anyway, I had a bar once in Phuket. I was fresh from retirement, that's early retirement from a senior level public servant job in Sydney. Almost a million in Super, a lot of money back then, hell it's a lot of money now. Yeah, I pensioned off the wife too. She was happy playing bride and we'd been together to jut to put up appearances. When that was over and the most boring job in the world was no more I felt free, as free as when I was 17 only you knew it was going to last.'

'Let me guess you came out here and the rest is history, right?'

He punched him again only now with more force. 'Look who's telling this story?'

'OK Jimmy I'm listening.'

'Listening? You better be your life could depend on it.'

'Oh, mate you don't know the half of it you don't. '

'Alright, alright, first my story then you can spill your guts.'

'You have to understand, there I was cashed up with a bar I paid too much for and women hanging off both arms. It was heaven you know the honeymoon phase. And yes, I know all about the ghosts you speak of. They come to me after midnight.'

Off on the far horizon a bolt of lightning flashed over the night sky.

CHAPTER 70

Downing a lager Brodie watched as Mon stood on the table. 'Listen everyone, listen, there is a gathering on Beach road at midnight. Many of our friends will be there' she said in a reedy voice no used to addressing more than a few people.

'Our friends will be there, and we must show we are one.' Raising a fist in the air he saw Mon in a different frame, a new frame. The former slave, virtual or not, was showing an ability to connect outside what was a tightly restricted space into an expanding universe.

Mon got cheers and confirmation.

She got down from her concrete table dais and walked to Chailai and Brodie.

'Are you coming tonight Chailai?' Mon asked in a bright tone.

Shaking her head Chailai put her arm on her friend's shoulder. 'I'm sorry I have to work here,' she lied. The two ladies knew it was a lie although neither was about to lose face by saying so.

Mon looked at Brodie and asked the predictable question, 'are you coming Brodie?'

He turned to Chailai as though seeking permission and she nodded with a smile. He didn't quite understand if she really wanted him to go even if as a *farung* he had the perfect excuse for being ignorant.

As Mon spoke Thai in an excited voice to a small group including Min Zaw Aung, Brodie ordered another round, Wild turkey for him and fruit juice for Chailai.

'Why don't you want to go?' he asked not quite sure but suspecting the real reason.

Chailai looked away and Brodie was starting to get the sense he was intruding.

'I have things to do. My mother is in Pattaya,' she lied.

He sipped his stronger than he would have liked drink then shrugged his shoulders.

'Are you sure you don't mind if I go?' he asked feeling juvenile for having to ask.

'I don't mind you remember what Mr Bradley said don't get in trouble so don't go.' With a cross look on her face he was left wondering what to do.

'Alright I'll be careful. I get the idea something big is about to happen.'

In a hissing voice so she couldn't be over heard she said, 'yes something big maybe something gets you back in jail.'

'Alright I'm not going,' he lied then took refuge in the booze.

The dinks didn't stop although as a concession to the warning he went back to the beers. Now was not a time to start a fight with someone who was part of his support system.

At just after midnight he followed the crowd that flowed onto Beach Rd. Traffic was almost stopped even if that never really occurred on Beach Rd. or any well- travelled Thai roadway, it just slowed down like a snake basking in the sun.

He said to one man who could have been Thai but he guessed not. 'Is this where the celebration is?'

The man smiled and said something he knew wasn't Thai and guessed was Burmese.

He turned to another man an asked are you Thai?' The slender man smiled showing teeth in need of work. 'I am Myanmar, from Burma,' he said as if not knowing which name to use.

'Thank you is this where the celebration is Mon told me.'

The man smiled and nodded vigorously. 'Yes, you friend of Mon? She is over there,' he said pointing in the direction of the stone edifice that was a popular meeting place for Thai and *farung* alike, a list that now including Burmese and probably Laotian and Cambodian. Who said *Pattaya* belonged to the farung? Of course, the farung only rented the place until they became *farung khi nok, or* bird shit foreigner then they were thrown. Underlining that very point he watched a drunken man from England going by the large Union Jack tattooed on his chest being taken away by tourist police. Not going quietly, he began singing as other Brits clapped and cheered. He was doing what they wanted to do minus the arrest.

'No surrender, no surrender to the IRA,' he sang in a hoarse voice that might have been going all day and night.

As the police van moved past the mass of party goers Brodie made towards Mon then stopped. Another police van pulled up from the river of traffic flow and he decided to watch.

He put down his bottle, now was not the time to get ticketed for public drunkenness. As dour faced police officers, all Thai went through her papers he wondered about an exit strategy. Then while he looked at the legs of a magnificent lady that might have been a wealthy trophy wife or a high-class hooker he noticed the cops taking off. Was Chief Trion orchestrating all this? 'The people deserve better. There are many refugees from my country of Myanmar, many refugees without food or shelter. Unless this government does something, someone should petition the United Nations,'

Mon spoke in Burmese then Thai. With a bullhorn, he waited for translations. A middle-aged lady was dog sign language on the steps as if nothing was going to stop the word getting out. With drinking, not an option for someone who couldn't afford any kind of ticket he walked towards a food cart. He ordered *Khao kha moo* or rice with stewed pork shanks and sat on the concrete steps facing the ocean. As he savoured the succulent pork he could hear Mon's voice drift in and out of consciousness. Something was being lost in translation here.

'We must stand up for our rights,' she said to wild cheers. Moving about slowly he heard Burmese, or at least what he thought was Burmese, being spoken. He wondered if this was the greatest congregation of Burmese ever and decided it was. As the crowd mushroomed he saw that it stretched right down to the pier at the end of Beach Rd where it hits walking Street.

'We now have some wonderful singers and dancers to entertain you,' she said after at least two languages delivered the message first.

A group of female dancers and singers were joined by a male lead singer who looked late middle aged.

A Mon watched she was approached by a woman with a microphone.

'My name is Angelina Suarez. Plaase may I speak with you?' Mon, always wary of strangers nodded.

'You have achieved great success Mon Thaik. The Maung used to be here on suffrance now Pattaya is a kind of sanctuary city.'

'Yes, we have come far. There is a long way to go.'

'Which brings to my next question, do you think the borderlands Shan and Karen and even far from the border in Kachin, do you think this should be an idependent state?'

Frowning at the provocative question she said, 'land locked states have trouble surviving with poor trade and surrounded by enemies.'

'What about a free state and autonomous state?'

Looking confused reporter Suarez clicked on her Smart Phone tranlater and the words came out in Burmese.

'That would be nice. Burma has called itself a democracy for years yet it is a dangerous prison for many. Maybe someday.'

CHAPTER 71

The Jet Ski roared under the moonlight one moving ahead of the other like both were high on Meth. The commotion drew attention as the teak decks of the large pleasure boats filled with onlookers.

Meanwhile Brad and Teersak along with Kit and Por cruised towards the largest boat of all. Brad knew from unofficial Intel that Pranit was on board. He had heard talk he was leaving Thailand and setting up somewhere else in the Asia Pacific region maybe beyond that.

'You men know what the plan of action is.

Krit spoke first in halting English. 'We find and capture Pranit and neutralise his soldiers while you find slaves.'

As he maneuverer at what seemed a leisurely pace even if their discovery would lead to certain death. They could be shot on sight as possible spies although no excuse would be necessary under the circumstances. Even if somehow Brad talked his way out he'd never be safe in Asia again. Game over.

He shook his head and silently laughed at the though. He wasn't safe now.

Would he ever be safe? The answer was simple.

As he swung the submersible to the underneath of the powered boat with its own helipad, he put on his disposable breathing gear. It gave five minutes, no more.

With black face and waterproof containers for the Uzi machine gun and three locked and loaded Glocks they exited the sub.

He motioned for his crew to spread to either side of 30-metre-long boat. The boarded the vessel at various points, one man climbed the fore and cut a guard's throat before lowering him silently into the water. It was a promising start.

As he hugged the hull he could hear men and women on deck. The conversation was casual with no indication they were aware they were under siege.

He waited until he could hear the cabin crew grew bored of the view or the long gone jet skis.

Then giving a silent message that came through as a vibration on their encrypted, self-destructing phones they all climbed on board.

CHAPTER 72

Brodie looked up at the vast metallic ceiling then down to take in the business jet.

'I feel like I've been through this movie before.'

Ralph gave a smile, the kind of smile that comes so easily to Americans.

Was smiling and saying *have a nice day* mandatory for Yanks. Maybe not he'd been running into a lot of unhappy Americans lately not including our Grace or her protective father.

'Very funny Grace always said you have a great sense of humour.' 'Is that all she said?' he asked and was rewarded with a frown.

'At the risk of sounding like some kind of interfering busy body, or,'

'Like an overprotective father?'

Ralph held out his hands in a concessionary gesture, a confessor pleading for absolution.

'What can I say Brodie she's my daughter and I'll do anything to look after her and make sure she's happy.'

There was now silence between them. It was shared knowledge her happiness was erratic and linked to abandonment issues. Tears appeared in her eyes, the first he'd seen since she was little.

'I don't know what to say.'

Ralph put a hand on his shoulder and said, 'you don't have to say anything Brodie. Truth is, and please don't tell this to my daughter, the truth is that I think you were good for her.'

'Thanks Ralph I appreciate that. I had no idea.'

As the plane began to rev Ralph said,' well that must be my lift. I really must be going. I'd say drop in some time but I never know where I'll be or what I'll be doing.'

'Burt you're on vacation Mr Winters you don't have to do anything or go anywhere.'

Both men were silent the only sound being the whining Rolls Royce engines then both laughed out loud.

CHAPTER 73

'So, what will you do now that the revolution is over?' Mon smiled at the question from Lun Min Aung, some of the words in Burmese some in Thai. Their friends Yei Swe and Khin Myint laughed then they all laughed. It was good to laugh after so much disaster, so much conflict.

'The revolution as you say will be over when we can live, work, eat in freedom.'

'At least we are not chained up to a cruel master.'

The group went quiet it was too early to celebrate anything except the fact they could meet and drink in peace.

'There might be a chance to study and work in Australia maybe even Australia.' Yei tapped her on the shoulder as if to admonish her audacity.

'How did you get this did you bribe someone?'

Mon gave an indulgent smile. 'No, it is not like here. You cannot bribe the American or Australian embassy.'

The girls exchanged looks then burst out laughing.

Yei gave her a searching look then said, 'if you didn't pay for this how did you get this miracle?'

Mon lowered her eyes then said, 'I'm told that I am quite well known from YouTube and Twitter.'

Now Mon shared their laughter. Of course, it was absurd you couldn't bribe an American or an Australian. Bribery was a part of life in their part of Asia. It glistened like dew on a Lilly pad at dawn, it laid on the streets a lizard waiting for prey. In was in the greedy faces of tourists and the even more greedy petty officials. They knew many American and Australians who paid bribes for special treatment or even just to stay out of jail. Especially, to stay out of jail. Chailai's lover Brodie and his influential minders escaped the law with money and more than money.

They drank more iced tea. It was a habit she'd picked up from her American friends, the cultivated kind that didn't guzzle beer. As Mon poured herself a glass she heard a loud bang, and in an instant, found herself on the ground with the other girls. Of course, a loud bang had to mean a bomb. Didn't it always mean a bomb?

As they waited cowering for the second explosion a farung peered below the concrete table and said in a boisterous voice, 'just gammon you ladies, just having a bit of fun with the old fireworks.'

To prove his point, he held out a string of firecrackers then lit one before throwing it onto the street. As it went off with a deafening bang exactly like a gunshot or battlefield explosion Mon began to weep.

She was back on that long-tailed boat as mortars hit the Irrawaddy River throwing up huge columns of water that left her soaking. Zaw her friend from the village and the man who vowed to save her steered the boat through the river detonations each one of which could have killed her and the other four ladies on board. Mon knew she would die. There was only one chance. She began to plead with the river Ghosts and asked them to tame this angry river and the men who made it angry. The praying made for concentration as people and things were blown to nothing.

She watched as another boat was caught in fire from the Burma side of the river. An older woman Mon knew to be a grandmother was stitched with gunfire that opened her stomach like a gutted fish. She stared in horror as her entrails and intestines spewed out onto the floor of the boat. Mouth open as if screaming no sound came forth. A bullet to the head mercifully put her out of her pain.

The boat slowly pulled away to safety but only after long minutes that stretched to eternity. Perhaps today they would all join the ghosts, find refuge in death. With the constant RPG fire, she had a life expectancy of minutes or seconds. Another bang, this one imaginary as her imagination took over, made her scream. She would not die today she said to herself before the muffled sound of words from someone vaguely familiar drifted through the fog of war. 'Mon, Mon, are you alright?'

She peered up from the racing carnival inside her head and said, 'who is that, is that you Yei?'

Yei reached to a pale Mon and they both stood up from the temporary shelter.

'It's alright Mon I'm here.' She gave her a searching look and said,' you were back there, weren't you Mon? Back where your mother and daughter died on that terrible day?'

Mon nodded not ready to speak yet coming back into the world. Maybe it would easier. She knew she would never get over the loss of her son, her husband and mother. Never. Outside a wind began to pick up and the roof was pelted with rain. Mon stepped outside and looked up. Thick black clouds shot through with lightning were spinning and stretched to forever in all directions. She heard that keening sound and knew it was the undead. A shape moved far up into the skin then zoomed down to head height. She saw a woman's head trailing veins and guts and she knew it was Lun's lost soul.

'The battle is not over Mon. We shall free the rest.'

Mon looking heavenward she repeated, 'yes we shall free them all, free them all.'

The force 5 wind blew off a tin roof and it skittered into the night sky.

CHAPTER 74

7 0 miles away in the Gulf of Thailand, factory ship *Golden Dragon* pitched up and down like a cork in a tub as rough weather closed in. The Sonar and satellite showed a massive typhoon coming with orders to fix all unsecured cargo and close all hatches.

'There are two hurricanes converging Captain, ship's mate Kwai said moving his arms in a circular direction then slamming his hands together to make his point with a loud smacking sound. A heavily sedated Captain Pan Thi looked at him with bloodshot eyes and murmured, 'the seas are too high to make it to port.'

Kwai, his face red and in shock bowed in frustration as if to a cruel Buddha.

'We are already taking on water. We could send out a mayday call for help.'

The Captain frowned at this scenario. 'And ask to be arrested and have the ship impounded. Do you really want to take the blame for all of this?'

Below decks 40 men squatted or stood as the ship pitched vertically and horizontally. One had an open would on the back of his shaved head. Without medical attention it was hard to see how he would make it. The blood loss had the unintended consequence of making the deck slippery with one man already losing his footing and slamming his face into a bulkhead. The red smear the collision left on the wall added to the scene of blood and gore all over the hold.

On deck their environment was more treacherous by the minute. Kwai felt the wind ratchet up like a great doomsday clock just before midnight. He shivered under the cutting rain. It was colder than he ever felt in the gulf, much colder as if hurricane force winds were blowing down from Siberia. He craned his head upwards and watched as boiling storm clouds spun slowly like a massive whirlpool. Lightning flashed through the clouds as cracking thunder claps made his ears hurt. He signalled for the remaining deckhands to go below. Anyone not tied with a safety harness could be blown off in seconds. He gripped the railing to keep that from happening to him. The wind howled, the noise drifting to speech.

'Kwai why did you kill me? Why did you leave my children orphans?'

He spun around to the left then to the right in an effort to find the disembodied voice.

'Who is that?' he shouted in Burmese. Then as the keening wind warped and bent like molten metal in a blast furnace it took on the sounds of mocking laughter.

'You knew you could not escape me. You and the captain and the enslaved men you force to kill and torture slaves even lower than them shall pay for your crimes.'

Putting on a defiant face he shouted at this demon.

'You are only a ghost you cannot hurt me. You are the smoke that blows away and disappears. You are not real.'

A loud thunderbolt split his ear drums like a smashed mango and he put his hands up to his ears in a feeble protective move. As he did a bolt of lightning struck the ship's radar mast and it exploded. All around the once darkened sea was illuminated as if from below by a subterranean city or some unknown force of nature.

Within minutes the storm cleared and he was about to shout in joy only to stop short. All around the factory ship were other ships, white coloured vessels belonging to the Thai Navy. A cannon shot was fired across the bow.

An officer with a bullhorn called out,' lay down on the deck with your hand over your head. We are boarding the ship any resistance will be met with lethal force.'

Knowing what was in store for him Captain Pan Thi opened a drawer near the wheel and took out a Smith & Wesson revolver. The intercom system was playing a wistful Burmese pop song that seemed to speak to the unfolding disaster. Walking onto the deck with the gun against his head as the lachrymose tune played out he leaned against the railing and shot himself then pitched into the sea. Within minutes he was dragged out of the water bleeding but still alive. Realising he had failed Captain Pan Thi shut his eyes tightly as if this would make it go away. As he was taken to the infirmary he caught a glimpse of sailors pouring over the deck of his ship like so many ants on a succulent find.

CHAPTER 75

In the streets of Pattaya a few blocks away from Chailai's bar in Second Road, police sirens and tinny messages broadcast from an armoured vehicle could be heard. The music drifted in and out adding to the strange atmosphere. Beyond that could be seen the turret of a tank as if the revolution was here. The cable news from New York and London was that there was a Revolution going on. He couldn't see only one tank even if he half expected more to be there. He moved back indoors having no wish to be collateral damage. Meanwhile it was all up there on the TV screen until with a flick of the remote it switched off.

Who was it that said the Revolution would be televised?

'Stay inside this is a direct order from the Central government' came the mechanical voice in English after the Thai orders. The sharp, mechanical tones echoed off buildings to create an eerie effect like some new world order was being announced before mass detention in remote re-education camps somewhere off in the jungle. Was this the ghost of Pol Pot?

'Sounds like chaos out there Ralph,' Brodie said.

'Nothing out of the ordinary, This is Thailand after all. I think I told you there has been an ongoing civil war since War 2. Thailand wasn't in that war and has never been defeated or invaded. Quite a record for a nation bordering Vietnam and Cambodia.

'Except you could say the place was invaded by American soldiers on R&R.'

Ralph raised his ever-present glass and said, 'yes and that's another story mind you. That's what made Pattaya what it is for better or worse. What used to be called Cocao-Colonisation when self-flaggellation became a western addiction.

Nows its back to being all about money. If you don't have it you want it and will do almost anything to get it. The jails are full of men and women who tried to cut in on a long line. Its still like it was when I was starting out, back when President Kennedy was still alive. Yeah money is a bitch and you don't have to listen to Pink Floyd to know that little truth. Those that have it prey on the poor resulting in the kind of slave factories we helped put an end to. For now. The agitation is a rash that gets angrier the more you scratch it. The invaders, the tourists don't see or look away. Can you have happy tourism under an authoritarian regime? Of course, you can if you play your part according to the script or better yet go to sleep and pretend it's not real. You can drink yourself to death just don't mention the leader or anyone close to him.'

He paused and turned to take in the magnificent view just outside the bullet proof windows. When he spoke again the tone shifted and became more careful as if hedging. This was Asia it paid to hedge your bets.

'Even so I love the place. It's not Angeles in Luzon where people are gunned down in the street like Billy the Kid. Unrest is part of the environment here, like the wind and the rain it is what it is. Most tourists don't even notice it or pretend not to notice it. You can see that in the Philippines where tens of thousands are shot in the street and not a single foreigner.'

'Makes you wonder. As long as foreigners turn a blind eye people can playact the terror doesn't exist.'

'That's about right although there are some advantages in my line of business.'

'I thought you said you were retired.'

Ralph smiled and said, 'Sure, I am retired Brodie. My business is business,' he lied.

'In fact, politics is business if you take a global view, something I have to do by necessity. Not that I want to play word games I'll leave that to the real politicians.'

He stopped for a moment as if reviewing an internal transcript then completed the thought left hanging in the air like secret wind chimes.

'Of course, real is a rubbery concept where we are pal. Appearances and attitudes have a way of altering according to the climate, the culture. Now that the idea of ghosts has taken hold, even among the farung, the situation is fluid. It's a big ball of clay you can mould it into any form you want, which is why outside parties including my country and over the horizon, China, see an opportuhity to influence events. This has already happened with the two rescue missions.'

'It's a wonder the higher ups here and in Burma didn't protest the penetration.

Hell, some could see it as invasion.'

'You make it sound like rape.' He shrugged his shoulders as if this were an accurate comparison then went on. 'Fact is leaders in Burma and Thailand were and are in on this.'

Brodie opened his mouth wide as if to better take in this new shock.'

'You mean you were given official permission?'

'Not quite. I've seen this kind of thing before like when we tried to topple Sukarno in Indonesia. Bombing raids were effective until we blew up a church. It took a little longer to bring about his ouster. Back here in Burma, Myanmar, if you will, If the raids had screwed up, failed, things would have been different. They, the government, the Army, didn't intervene because it was a matter of survival. They couldn't afford to oppose this so the next best thing was to sacrifice the rogue Generals on both sides of the border, sacrifice them and anyone in their thrall. So, I press,' he held out his forefinger and made a show of pressing a phantom button, 'delete and they vanish.'

'As simple as that?'

'Yes, bearing in mind that most governments around here are military dictaroships. Eliminate one or a dozen and there are always the ones coming up who can slot into position. Look at Burma, Cambodia, the Phillippines. Happens all the time ghosts or no ghosts. That's just a superstition, these ghosts, these *nats*, that regimes use for their own ends. Happens all the time.'

'I didn't know it was that sweeping. You don't need magic or ghosts in a that scenario.'

Ralph gave an indulgent smile for his naive young friend.

'Just like a Manhattan crime case run by the NYPD, offenders were offered leniency for immunity or reduced sentences.'

Ralph gazed out the window again. 'Remember Brodie, everything is political nowadays, they even have *political economics* going by he not exactly original idea people are motivated by either greed or fear. That one is as old as the scriptures and has been around since Adam was a boy.' He shook his drink making the ice bang against the glass.

'Anyway, all that is academic. It doesn't pay to meddle in politics here and I never do.'

Brodie focused on Ralph's face looking for tells as to the truthfulness or not of what he was saying. The tells weren't there even if Ralph's alibi didn't wash.

He had some type transnational authority, not exactly a licence to kill but close.

Later they heard Ralph had been shot. As a matter of fact, he died.

With Grace back in American and not picking up it was left to Brodie and Braddock to pay their respects and show up for the cremation.

They watched in silence as the cask moved on runners until it was tipped into furnace. As licking flames consumed the last remains of Ralph the doors closed and he was no more.

Over drinks with Jimmy he said, 'Jesus after all he's been through to get gunned down in the street is incredible.'

Staring into his drink before lifting his head to speak Jimmy himself looked close to death.

'Well you have to remember where we are old boy. Expect the unexpected. He got it, but I think its more he didn't want to let go of the life.'

Draqining his beer Brodie asked, 'the life you make it sound like he's in the mob.'

'Only the biggest mob in the world! That is in terms of clout. Enough power to topple nation states and change the course of rivers or hold back the sea.'

'Do you think he'll come back as a ghost?'

There was no sign of usual habit of debunking of cynical ridicule.

'God, I hope not. Can you imagine what kind of supernatural force that would be. My theory is he hung on too late, clung to the power like some leech on living flesh. He couldn't help it. He didn't know what else to do.'

'Yeah I guess his time was up. He had a charmed life until he ran out of luck. He was Ali going back for the last fight. His last fight robbed him of his spirit, his soul until he just up and died all those years later.'

'So, he didn't know when to quit.'

'Yeah he left it too late. The world changed only he couldn't. That's what killed him son.'

Brodie's ears started to ring and he felt a tingling on his forearms. A sign?

He poured himself another two shots in case the Spook named Ralph showed.

CHAPTER 76

'Thai Airways Flight 309 to Los Angeles now Boarding at Gate 45. Repeat Thai Airways boarding now at Gate 45.

'You'd better go now,' Yin Maung said in Burmese as she kissed Mon on the cheek.

Brimming with tears she said in halting English, 'I will miss you all. When I finish my study and my job I come back.'

Yei, fresh off the prison boats and just getting used to new found freedom, embraced her and said, 'you are so fortunate to go to America. This is an honour and you have earned this. You are alive we are all alive so let us give thanks to those of us not here. There was a group hug and urged on by airport staff Mon ran towards the Gateway.

As they waved Yei said with a fatalistic tone in Thai, 'we may never meet again. I will never forget you Mon, never.' She turned to her friends and said, 'I hope she will be happy.'

The Hustle Bar was heaving to Thai pop music. The rhythm was trance inducing and had a wild mercurial feel that promised to become an ear worm if he listening long enough. Once dug in, it could be heard all over even at rowdy soccer matches played to a raucous Bhangras beat. Someone threw a cloud of pink and yellow dye that coloured everything and everyone in its path. With bright primary colours, all over his tee shirt Brodie felt like he was at a kid's birthday party.

'We are law abiding and happy to be in the free land of Thailand,' Mon said through the loud hailer. It was he kind of thing the trigger-happy junta liked to hear. A player all her life, she knew how to play the survival game for real.

As she spoke the citadel was surrounded by police and military vehicles.

'Let us show our appreciation or our brave men in blue and green,' she said in Thai then English somehow forgetting to use Burmese. After securing funding in the mythic US Mon was back.

Some of the women in the celebration demonstration ran up to soldiers and police to give them garlands of flowers like they were in Honolulu.

One soldier gave a wide smile then returned a kiss from a Rohingya woman in her early twenties maybe younger.

As he stood he could feel someone close to him. He turned to see Chailai.

She kissed him on the cheek and said, 'I thought maybe trouble, big trouble. Now I see everyone happy.' As if to give proof to the statement she gave a beatific smile. He took her in his arms and said, 'I'm glad you could make it, glad you can see all of this.'

'Yes wonderful, 'she said beaming. The old girl was more relaxed and happy than he could recall. This time Brodie felt she really meant it. 'I didn't want to see you in trouble Brodie, enough trouble for you without more police.' He pulled her closer to him and kissed her on the cheek.

'It's great to see my friends, your friends, have a future.'

Chailai grew serious, the smile disappearing like sun obscured by clouds.

'And us Brodie what about us? Do we have a future?'

He fell silent not wanting to tell her any more lies. He was done with dishonesty, with spin, with flat out lying.

'I wish I could tell you the answer to that question. Grace wants to get back with me and her father has indicated that's the way he is leaning.'

She frowned and her voice took on an edge. 'He not your father, Grace not your wife. You tell me you leave her that we get marry, have children. You promise me,' she said as she punched him on the shoulder without bothering to smile.

'I sorry Chailai I don't blame you for being angry. I have certain obligations.'

She pouted and said, 'yes sure old man American save your skinny ass, now he owns you. You like bar girl sell highest price.'

Not wanting to point out she was the actual bar girl, not a pretend one, he said, 'I want to tell you the truth and not bullshit you sweetheart. There has been too much of that going on.' They kissed. They were over.

At 5pm he got a text from the other side.

'I checked out the afterlife and its not for me.'

He texted, 'I thought you were dead, gone.'

'You thought wrong.'

'You've come back. '

'I never left. As far as the other side goes its not all its cracked up to be. I much prefer being among the living. Of course, for operational reasons we might keep this our little secret. Before you ask Grace already knows. I made sure of that before she got wind of my untimely demise.'

'It's a wonder you didn't turn into a nat.'

'I did for the amusement of my enemies. They wanted me dead so I gave then what they wanted.'

'No ghosts?'

Now on Facetime he could see Ralph make a face of mock disappointment.

'No ghosts, no nats, no super nature. This is it kid,' he said as he spread his arms wide as though to take in the whole world.

'So that's all there is, this reality?'

'I'm afraid so if you want to get out of this world you can use alcohol or something else like you'd find back in the Golden Triangle.'

'No, I'm good,' he said as the conversation came to an end and he and his future father in law were over and out.

About to board her flight from Kuala Lumpur Airport to San Francisco Mon made a quick trip to the restroom. As she applied powder to her face a woman came up behind her and stuck in a needle. As the agent coursed through her bloodstream she lunged forward and scratched the woman who looked more Cambodian than Thai or Burmese on the face drawing blood. As her killer fled she looked upwards at the fluorescent ceiling lights.

Speaking in an inaudible whisper she said, 'I'm coming to join you Yin, I will follow you Auk and Seerasat. I'm coming I won't be long.'

The lights began to flicker then went on and off like a strobe. She could see her life in those flicker, raising a family in a remote village, becoming a champion for her people, escaping death so many times she'd felt invincible. Her vision blurred, and she felt tired. She felt like resting for as long as the rivers flowed.

'I'm coming home my friends, I won't be long. Make a place for me, I will be there soon.'

A western woman of middle years walked in and began to scream. The screaming didn't stop until airport security arrived. No longer breathing and withut a pulse Mon was stretchered off with a sheet over her face. Then born of raw death a miracle. Mon transformed into a ghost, a nat as her spirit left the body and shot through the roof into the starry night sky.

CHAPTER 77

On a beautiful New York Spring day at an haute cuisine restaurant over-looking the Hudson, Brodie felt more content than ever since the Thai adventure.

Mon's murder was a blow that left him for days until he vowed to live for her. Her killers were connected to the Burmese army and fled Singapore on a flight to Beijing then Yangon according to investigative reporter Angelina Suarez. The story was picked up by the news channels and she became an international celebrity in death, something she nearly achieved when alive. Mon lived every second on this Earth, every bit of strength devoted to her family, to her village, to her country. She would not be forgotten. Was this fearless soul also now a ghost?

He had come to terms with it, fabrications and all. After all that's what spies did right? Isn't that what his future father-in law talked him into? Maybe even Grace had been in on it all along although he doubted that. She told him she accepted what her father had *'said and done, despite or even because of our close connection.'* If his reattached partner could accept the unacceptable so could he. Reaching for Grace's hand he said in an emotive voice, 'thank God you came Grace.'

Raising her eye brows, she said in a joking tone, 'so you didn't think I would turn up is that it?'

Shaking his head, he said, 'no that's not it. After all we've been through I guess I'm always waiting for the next thing to happen. That's all.'

She squeezed his hand and gave a sympathetic smile. 'I know we'll probably be wrestling for that forever.'

A sound like fingernails scraping a blackboard came from nowhere.

'What was that?' a startled Grace asked.

Before he could answer the table began to rock up and down and sideways.

'I don't know,' he said as other diners stopped eating, drinking and talking to see what the commotion was.

'Maybe its one of your ghosts Bodie.' The couple smiled at each other. There was no laughter the ghosts were too close to laugh at. Far too close. Whatever it was went away as fast as it had arrived.

Taking her by the hand he said, 'come on let me buy you a New York pretzl.'

She smiled, the storm over. 'Sure, I'm up for that. It's fascinating to watch the Americanisation of Brodie.'

He smiled back. She finished the thought. 'Sorry, I forgot you're one of us. You were born here, you're eligible to run for President.'

He murmered as if to himself. 'Yes, one of us. Its nice to belong.'

Then as if shrugging it off he gave a laugh. 'Let's start with Senator. Maybe CEO of my own company.'

'You mean our own company?'

He laughed again. 'I guess that means we really are getting married.'